In His Eyes

Other Books by Stephenia H. McGee

Ironwood Plantation
The Whistle Walk
Heir of Hope
Missing Mercy
*Ironwood Series Set
*Get the entire series at a discounted price

The Accidental Spy Series
*Previously published as The Liberator Series
An Accidental Spy
A Dangerous Performance
A Daring Pursuit
*Accidental Spy Series Set
*Get the entire series at a discounted price

Stand Alone Titles
In His Eyes
Eternity Between Us

Time Travel
Her Place in Time
(Stand alone, but ties to Rosswood from The Accidental Spy Series)
The Hope of Christmas Past
(Stand alone, but ties to Belmont from In His Eyes)

Novellas
The Heart of Home
The Hope of Christmas Past

www.StepheniaMcGee.com
Sign up for my newsletter to be the first to see new cover reveals and
be notified of release dates
New newsletter subscribers receive a free book!
Get yours here
bookhip.com/QCZVKZ

In His Eyes

Stephenia H. McGee

By The
Vine Press

Cover Design: Ravven
Cover Model: Taylor Bobo
Featured House: Belmont Plantation, Greenville, Mississippi

Library Cataloging Data
Names: McGee, Stephenia H. (Stephenia H. McGee) 1983 –
Title: In His Eyes/ Stephenia H. McGee
350 p. 5.5 in. × 8.5 in. (13.97 cm × 21.59 cm)
Description: By The Vine Press digital eBook edition | By The Vine Press Trade paperback edition | Mississippi: By The Vine Press, 2017,
Summary: Ella masquerades as a Yankee officer's widow in order to care for a rescued child, until Westley returns after the Civil War
Identifiers: LLCN: 2017904786 | ISBN-13: 978-1-63564-009-0 (trade) | 978-1-63564-008-3 (POD) 978-1-63564-010-6 (ebk.)
1. Civil War fiction 2. Christian historical 3. Christian Romance 4. Clean Read Historical 5. Historical Romance 6. 1800s Historical Fiction 7. God's healing love

Chapter One

Ella Whitaker braced herself for another of the woman's screams. Swallowing her fear lest it show in her eyes, she bathed Cynthia's sweat-soaked brow. "There, now. That one is passing." Cynthia panted and turned her head to the side, letting out a soft moan. Grasping for any measure of comfort to offer the woman, Ella forced a cheerful smile. "The midwife will be here soon, and she will be able to help ease the pain."

Cynthia let out another wail as the next contraction gripped her. Ella couldn't be sure, but she thought the pains were getting closer together. She dipped the cloth again and moved to wipe Cynthia's rouge-smeared face once more, but the woman seized her wrist.

"Ain't no midwife coming for me, girl." She closed her eyes and sucked air through her stained lips. "Not a one wants to be known for helping the likes of me."

Ella shook her head and crossed the bare floor. She had to take only two steps to cover the cramped quarters before grasping the welcoming cool of the knob. "I'll go down and check. If she cannot come, then surely one of the wives down below can help. I really shouldn't be here for a birthing, being unwed and all."

Cynthia's next scream sent a shiver down Ella's spine. "Get it out!"

Her heart beating furiously, Ella snatched open the door

and scrambled down the Buckhorn Inn's creaking stairs. Below, the stale air thick with the smells of travelers—horses, dirt, and unwashed bodies—made her cough. Several coaches had arrived this morning, dumping out scores of volunteer troops for a respite before continuing their journeys to their homes. Men huddled in groups and gathered at the long tables gulping their ale and laughing over cards like they hadn't just lost a war. It wasn't even high noon, yet already some of them laughed too loudly and stumbled when they stood. Two weeks now she'd had to work here, but she didn't think she'd ever grow used to this dank environment.

Ella scrunched her nose. Whether she liked it or not, she *must* grow accustomed to her new home, for it seemed this was her only future now that she had to face the world alone. Smoothing her frown and resisting the urge to cover her nose, Ella burst into the kitchen. At least it smelled like overcooked meat and burned grease in here.

"Mrs. Hatch, I need your—"

The older woman spun away from the crowded prep space with a loaded tray in her hands and a scowl on her wrinkled face. "There you are! I told you not to disappear on me again. We need more girls servin' the men. You're out of the kitchen today. We have a score more of them than we did yesterday."

A new pang of fear gripped her. Ella bunched her stained apron in her fists. The innkeeper's wife shoved the tray into her stomach, forcing the air to flee Ella's lungs.

"No arguing from you, girl," she said before scooping up a pitcher and scurrying for the door. "Get going."

Ella found her breath. "Wait!"

Mrs. Hatch turned back to look at her before pushing the kitchen door open. "What? I got men out there that needs more drink to soothe their wounds."

"This is more important."

The woman hesitated and Ella seized her chance. "The woman upstairs is in the throes of childbirth and needs help."

The other woman's face contorted.

"There's no midwife but…but… you've birthed children," Ella blurted before Mrs. Hatch could respond.

Mrs. Hatch's thin upper lip twitched. "I ain't going up there with that trollop. She's got the French Disease. It's enough I even let her in."

Ella's jaw tightened. Mrs. Hatch had only let the woman in yesterday because Cynthia had paid twice the normal amount for a few nights of lodging. That… and she had Federal currency.

"She's diseased." Mrs. Hatch softened slightly. "Don't you see? It's best you stay away from her, lest you get it too and ruin any chance you got of snagging a man."

Whether or not the sickness could be passed along to another person during childbirth, Ella had no idea. She'd heard that it could only be passed by way of the secret things that happened between men and women, but who was she to say? Ella hesitated. Mrs. Hatch could be right, but even so, Ella would still help Cynthia. She opened her mouth to say so, but the other woman spoke first.

"Besides, she deserves her lot." Mrs. Hatch wagged her finger. "You have duties here."

Ella lowered her eyes, speaking softly. "But…I think something is wrong. Someone must help her."

"Look here. There's plenty of waifs on the streets looking for work. You ain't the only scullery maid to be had."

Fear bubbled in her empty stomach, and Ella lifted her eyes back to Mrs. Hatch's scowling face. True, she needed her work. How else would she keep a roof overhead and at least something once a day to fill her belly?

Mrs. Hatch lifted her bushy eyebrows. "So, then, either you get that food to the patrons or you get out of my inn."

Ella gulped and opened her mouth to reply, but the other woman had already pushed through the door and disappeared. Wavering slightly, Ella numbly followed her employer out the door, mumbling to herself about her cowardice.

If she must serve or leave, then she would serve quickly and be done with it. She couldn't go back out there alone again…unprotected. She shoved the memories aside.

Ella dropped plates of boiled ham and lumpy potatoes down in front of men still dressed in an array of grays and butternut that had passed for the ragged uniforms of the Confederacy and tried to finish the task as soon as possible. After placing the final chipped plate from the tray, Ella hurried away before any of the men could grab her as they had done the last time Mrs. Hatch made her come to the dining room.

She breathed a sigh of relief at not being manhandled just as a scream cut through the rafters and pierced through the clangor of the dining area. The room fell into a lull, and Ella held her breath.

Mrs. Hatch cut a glance to Ella then back over the frowns of those gathered for their meal and a glint came into her muddy brown eyes. "Looks like one of the gents done found him a strumpet from Miss Lissy's."

A wave of raucous laughter rolled over Ella, filling her with indignation. She thrust her chin out at Mrs. Hatch and whirled around, hurrying for the kitchen. No one should be left alone in such agony, most especially with the heartless laughter of careless fools behind their back.

Ella tossed the serving tray on the brick floor and gathered a pot of water and two drying cloths. Then she straightened her spine and headed for the stairs.

As she opened the door to Cynthia's quarters, Ella feared for both the mother and babe. No matter the woman's reputation or sins, someone must help her. Gathering her strength, Ella stepped into the room and set the pot of water and the cloths on the small table beside the bed, removing the nearly dry basin. Taking up the washing cloth again and securing a smile on her face, Ella turned back to the struggling woman.

"You...came back," Cynthia said, gasping.

"Of course I did."

Cynthia mustered a weak smile before succumbing to another moan. "Not many would. Do you know what to do?"

Ella shook her head. "I'm sorry. None of the married women could get away and...."

"No need to lie. I know the truth of it." Another pain wracked her body, and she bit down on a wad of the bedding to contain her scream. When it passed, her shoulders slumped. "Ain't going to make it."

Ella bathed the woman's head with the tepid water. "Hush, now. You'll be fine. And the babe, too." Before the woman could protest, Ella bowed her head. "Lord, we ask that you would spare this mother and her child. Let the birthing come easier...and, please, help me know what to do."

When she opened her eyes Cynthia was staring at her. "Nobody ever prays for me." Tears fell from her faded blue eyes and made tracks down her reddened cheeks. "Not since that Remington woman took pity on my sister and me last year. Good folks, them."

Suddenly she clutched Ella's hand. "The baby is coming." Her face contorted. "Quick now, you'll have... to catch him."

Ella hesitated for only an instant before throwing back the bedclothes and revealing the woman's legs. Sending up another request for strength, Ella prepared to grow up beyond her maiden years. As soon as she glimpsed the messy truth of the miracle of birth, Ella knew why such things were shielded from girls. But she was twenty-two now, and hardly a girl. Already an old maid. What could it matter now?

Cynthia leaned forward on her elbows and began to push. Ella grabbed the clean cloths she'd brought upstairs with her, and after a moment of Cynthia's grunts, a sodden mop of dark hair appeared on a tiny head.

Another push and cry of agony and the head came free. Ella frowned. She'd never seen a child fresh from the womb, but she didn't think they were supposed to be that color. The babe looked nearly purple, and it didn't move. Panic clawed at Ella's gut, and she glanced up at Cynthia just as the woman's eyes rolled back into her head and she collapsed onto the pillow.

"Cynthia! The child is almost here. Come now, bring it on!"

Please, Lord, we need you!

The words, or perhaps the prayer, roused the exhausted woman a moment later and she positioned herself to push again. The head came fully free, followed partial by its shoulders. Ella prepared to catch the child, but then it seemed to catch. Peering closer at the discolored flesh, Ella notice that something had entangled the infant's neck. "Cynthia! Something seems to have wrapped around the baby's throat."

The woman groaned. "It's...the...cord. You'll have to cut it free."

Ella's eyes widened. "Surely that cannot be good!"

"You must! You must or...or... it will die!"

Startled, Ella thrust her bloodied hands into her pocket and pulled free the tiny knife she'd stolen from her father one night when he'd been too inebriated to notice. She flipped the blade free and then stood motionless. She couldn't possibly cut flesh, could she?

Cynthia's next scream of agony startled Ella's mind out of her shock. She would do what she must. Working carefully to lift the band of flesh from the baby's neck, Ella sawed through the bloody mess with tears blurring her vision. Just as she thought she could no longer stand the feel of the flesh in her hands, the cord came free and she unwound if from the baby's throat.

Relieved, she slipped her fingers under the tiny head and gently pulled, but the child would not slip free. Ella looked up at Cynthia, who panted heavily. "You must push again."

She shook her head. "It's dead."

"Now!" Ella snapped.

Cynthia pushed back to her elbows and gave one final heave, and the wee one came free into Ella's arms. "A son, Cynthia!"

The woman turned her head away. Ella looked back down at the still form, and her elation slipped away. He didn't move. Didn't cry. And his skin looked so waxy and blue...

Oh, Father, save this little one.

Not knowing what else to do, Ella turned the wee boy over and began rubbing on his back, patting gently. Just as she'd nearly released all hope, a sudden tremor came through the infant, and then a strangled cry. Ella kept patting and began to jiggle him just a bit until the cry strengthened.

Thrilled, she turned back to Cynthia. "He lives!"

Cynthia gave only a slight nod. Ella wrapped the child in the clean cloths. "Here, now." She stretched him toward his mother. "See your son."

"It is not my son."

The soft words hung on the air, and Ella frowned. "Of course, he is. Here, look at him. A fine child to be sure."

The woman sobbed but still kept her head turned. Ella pulled the child back against her. The baby squirmed, then opened two little eyes. Dark pools of wonder stared up at her, and something within Ella lurched. "Cynthia," Ella said, her voice barely a whisper. "Look at this beautiful child."

The woman refused to turn her head, and so Ella placed him on his mother's chest. "He must eat, Cynthia. That much I know. Won't you at least let him eat?"

As though to confirm Ella's request, the child's face scrunched and a wail filled the room. "See now, he's hungry."

Cynthia looked at Ella, and finally relented. Pulling aside her ragged gown, she wrapped her arm around the baby and lifted him. In a few moments, he began to suckle. Relieved, Ella collapsed on the side of the bed. "There, see? Our prayers have been answered."

Cynthia didn't respond. She closed her eyes and let her head fall back against the pillow.

Poor woman must be exhausted. Ella came to her feet. She'd want a new gown, and some clean linens for certain. Ella could probably take the ones from the pallet she had in the storeroom. As long as she could slip them past Mrs. Hatch without the woman taking notice of her. Best to busy her hands and be sure the new family had what they needed.

Ella glanced down at the bed to see how to best remove the bedclothes and halted her thoughts. A crimson stain spread across the bottom of Cynthia's gown and onto the sheets. "Cynthia! Is the bleeding normal?"

She looked up to find the other woman gazing down at her child. "No. I will not make it."

The words held more strength than she expected. Ella drew a sharp breath. "Don't say such things. I will go and fetch a doctor." She clenched her fists. "Whatever it takes, I will see that someone comes to help."

Cynthia gently laughed as she drew the baby closer. "You are a good girl. So kind to care for one like me." She looked up at Ella with something sparking in her eyes. "Promise me something."

Ella dropped back down on the bed, but said nothing.

"Promise me you will find him a good home when I am gone."

Ella struggled to withhold tears. "Don't say that. You'll be fine."

"No, dear girl. I feel the life slipping from me." She patted Ella's hand. "Tell me, do you think…do you think the God you prayed to would have me, even as I am?"

Ella bobbed her head and clutched the woman's hand. "I am sure of it. You need only ask." At least, that is what her mother had always taught her.

Cynthia gave a small smile. "I did, a bit ago whilst you were turning pale looking at the bed."

Ella's brows rose.

"Don't fret. I am…thankful that my torment has at long last come to an end. Perhaps the next place will be clean and beautiful." A smile played on her lips, contrasting with the pain in her eyes. "Maybe then…maybe I can be clean and beautiful again too."

A tear slid down Ella's cheek, and she swiped it away. "Yes, it will be very beautiful there."

Cynthia gazed down at the child, then looked up at Ella with concern. "Please." Her face puckered. "I've not much time…."

"Yes. Yes, I will find him a home." *Somehow….*

"Take him to the Remington place. They are good, God-fearing people there. Took care of me once. They had a wet nurse. Take him there. Mrs. Remington will find him a home."

Ella choked down a sob. "I will. I promise."

Cynthia placed a gentle kiss on the baby's brow. "Goodbye, little one." She settled back against the pillow. Then, before Ella could react, the light left her eyes.

Choking on sobs, Ella picked up the child from his dead mother's arms and snuggled him against her chest. "There now, wee one. Don't you worry. We will have you a home by morning's light."

Then she kissed his downy hair and prayed she hadn't just spoken a lie.

Chapter Two

Major Westley Remington III heard voices somewhere in the distance. They danced about somewhere just out of his ability to decipher them, tempting him to break free of the cloak of indistinct shadows that hung over him. He attempted to rouse himself but found the task nigh impossible. Caught between the lands of dream and reality, he drifted about like a man caught in a current without a raft.

Forcing himself to focus, Westley attempted to open his eyes, but they remained firmly closed despite his best efforts. He gave a grunt, but somehow could not find the energy to move his limbs. The mere effort seemed to steal something from him, and he began to sink back into a slumber. But not allowing himself to do so, Westley focused on the world outside the inky recesses of his mind. Noises flittered to him, but he could not find their meaning. Content to lie still lest he slumber once more, he listened purposefully.

Light shifted across his eyelids, making them little red veils over his world. He found a measure of comfort in that. It meant he wasn't blind. Merely…immobile. The second thought undid the peace of the first. What if he were somewhere on the field of battle, his body frozen and unable to shield itself from trampling hooves and the enemy's sabers?

Fear began to worm into his belly and he stiffened. No. The ground beneath him felt much too soft and the din of voices could not be the fearsome sounds of armies clashing. He listened closer. Unable to stand the unknown, he mustered his strength and pried open his crusted eyes, blinking against the sudden light.

"Oh! Captain!" A female voice pierced through the swarming pain gathering in his head, and Westley turned his face toward it.

"Here, take a drink, sir." Cool hands slipped under and lifted his head and then metal pressed against his lips. He tried to get them to function, but they felt cracked and stiff. Half of what he attempted to consume dribbled down into his beard. He coughed and, though still thirsty, fell back with exhaustion.

"Well, it seems that he lived after all. Looks like I owe Major Carlson dinner."

Westley tilted his head and blinked his eyes into focus. Before him stood a squat man in a dark blue uniform who peered down at him with bespectacled eyes. "Where...?" he croaked.

The man rocked back on his heels. "You're at the Hillsman Farm, fellow. Been here since Sayler's Creek."

Westley tried to clear his throat but succeeded in little more than a weak cough. "How...?"

"How did you end up here, or how did the battle go?"

Westley nodded.

"We got them right good. Cavalry set up blockades against Anderson's advance and cut through Ewell and Anderson's lines. We hedged those Rebs in with nowhere to go. Got three corps of Lee's army that day. Yes, sir. And three days later he had no option but to surrender."

"Lee surrendered?" Westley croaked. Blast his voice. Why couldn't he speak?

The man scratched his russet beard, and Westley couldn't be sure if the man had understood him or not. "You've been racked with the fever for a long time. At one point one of the orderlies almost sent you out with the dead until one of the nurses realized you were still breathing—nearly too shallow to see, mind you—and she had you brought back in."

He opened his mouth to inquire how long ago that might have been, but darkness edged in on his vision and his mind began to cloud. The last thing he heard before slipping into the darkness once more was the voice of the man standing over him. "Perhaps I conceded to Major Carlson's victory a mite too soon."

The next time Westley awoke, he had a clear head and a gnawing sense of unease. He blinked away the discomfort of bright daylight until his eyes adjusted enough for him to see clearly. Frowning, he managed to get himself up on his elbows.

He glanced down, unnerved to discover he wore nothing but a linen shirt as he sat on a sturdy bed. A patched quilt covered his bare legs and rested against his waist. Westley lifted his eyes to survey the room in which he found himself. Hewn plank walls and a squat structure indicated an old, common home of some kind. A farmhouse, perhaps? But whose?

Thrusting back the cover, Westley struggled to sit up and swing his legs over the side of the bed. The sudden movement caused a surge of pain, his head to swim, and an unwelcome revolt in his stomach. He had to close his eyes a moment, lest he tumble off the bed, or worse, retch.

"Oh, no, you don't! You get yourself right back in that bed, young man."

Westley's eyes snapped open. A portly woman in a starched white cap stood in the doorway, one hand on her rounded waist and the other holding a bowl. The smell of something hearty drifted to him and his stomach rumbled. They stared at one another for an instant. Then, remembering that his legs were exposed, Westley looked down at his feet and tried to shift the quilt to cover his embarrassment.

"You're right blessed those toes of yours aren't green." She huffed. "Or there at all, for that matter."

Westley looked up at the woman in confusion, and her face softened. She crossed the plank floor in a swish of yellow gingham skirts and placed the steaming bowl on the rustic table beside the bed. Westley's eyes followed the food before returning to the woman's ruddy face.

"That doctor wanted to take your leg, you know. He was downright determined that you were getting the gangrene and that amputation was the only way to stop it."

Fear constricted in Westley's chest, but he wouldn't let it show. If he had lost a limb...he didn't even want to think it. He wiggled his toes just for the comfort of knowing he still had them. He regretted the move, as searing pain shot up his left leg. He flinched, instinctively reaching down to massage his thigh.

"You broke that one right good. They set it, and we all thought you'd wake up fine, but then the fever came."

His manners came back to him in a flood—a torrent bursting through a dam of forgetfulness—and he suddenly loathed his indecency. What kind of gentleman sat about in nightclothes with his extremities exposed? His mother would have been aghast. Westley shifted his weight despite the pain and put his legs back under the bedclothes, cutting his eyes to the woman, who didn't even possess the wherewithal to avert her steady gaze.

The woman chuckled. "Boy, there's no need for modesty around me. I've cared for seven boys of my own, not to mention all those who came through my house." She turned serious. "That battle was a bad one, that's for sure. But it finally brought this terror to an end."

She drew a breath and plastered on a smile as she scooped up the bowl. "Here. I brought you some broth." She tugged a straight-backed chair with a cloth-woven seat over to the bed and settled herself on it.

Westley could only focus on her previous words. "The war…" His raspy voice sounded strange to his ears, and he tried to clear his throat.

"Hush. Take a few sips of this to ease your throat. Then you can talk."

Westley gave a brief nod and let the woman feed him like an infant. He suspected that if he dared to try the task himself, this stern nurse would only put up a fight. It was not a battle he cared to engage in at the moment. Besides, the liquid tasted too good for him to argue. He hadn't had chicken broth this good since Sibby's back home. The thought of home sent a pang through his chest, and he pushed the sentiment away.

"Besides," the woman continued as she spooned liquid between his unkempt whiskers, "I'm sure I already know the things you are likely going to ask."

He grunted his reply.

The woman smirked as she lifted the spoon to his mouth again. "The battle went well, and the Federal Army gained the victory."

Westley smiled. Good news, indeed.

"We don't know what happened to you, but we guess that you took some kind of tumble because you snapped your leg just above the knee."

Murky memories of his horse rearing clouded his mind. There had been blood. So much blood. Then the horse fell over on him….

His countenance must have darkened, because the woman shifted the subject. "I'm Mrs. Preston, by the way. We've been a mite curious over who you are."

Westley swallowed three more spoons of the warm broth before attempting a reply. "You mean you don't know?" As promised, the warm liquid did wonders for his throat. His voice was still raspy, but functioning.

She handed him the bowl and spoon, and along with them a measure of his dignity. "We saw a scrap of paper pinned inside your jacket, but the words were smeared. Federal Major, by what was left of your uniform was the best we could tell."

Westley took the bowl from her and lifted the spoon for another sip. "Major Westley Remington, ma'am, of the Third West Virginia Cavalry Regiment, Third Brigade, Army of the Shenandoah."

"Good then." She patted his hand as though he were a child who had correctly recited his lesson. "Well, Major Remington, I am pleased to make your acquaintance."

"Likewise, ma'am." Though Westley had to wonder if the term *acquaintance* applied to someone who had likely already known him in intimate ways brought about by caring for one out of his wits.

She folded her hands in her lap. "Do you have any idea how long you have been here?"

Apprehension buzzed within him. "No, ma'am."

"It's May the second, Major."

Westley paused with the spoon almost to his mouth. *That would make...* He frowned. When was that battle? His frown deepened. Why couldn't he remember?

"You came here with the other wounded after the battle at Sayler's Creek..."

Ah, yes. He vaguely remembered a doctor. Bristly fellow. He'd said the same.

"That was on the sixth of April."

Westley swallowed, allowing himself a moment. "I've been here for a month?"

"Yes, sir. In and out of consciousness so much that I had a hard time keeping enough food and water in you to keep you alive. Didn't think you'd make it. They even started hedging bets. Never seen a man so eat up with the fever hang on the way you did. As the weeks passed, we started to think you would sleep for all eternity."

"Where are my men?" Westley resumed eating again, scraping his spoon against the side of the chipped porcelain so as not to miss a drop.

The woman shrugged. "They mustered out, I suppose, now that the war's over."

Westley nearly choked. "Over, you say?"

"You missed much." She turned to look out the window, but Westley kept his focus on the sadness that filled her eyes.

His chest constricted. Such a reaction could mean only one thing. "We...lost?"

She snapped her honey-brown eyes back to him. "Oh, no. The United States obtained victory and succeeded in restoring our country. Three days after you fell, Lee surrendered at the McLean family house out in Appomattox." She cocked her head, her cap sitting precariously on the mound of gray curls. "Don't you remember the doctor telling you?"

Westley shook his head.

"Ah, well. You were a bit feverish." She offered him a smile. "Well, Lee surrendered, but then Lincoln was shot—"

Westley dropped his spoon. "What!"

She fanned her face with her hand. "That scoundrel J. Wilkes Booth shot him in Ford's Theatre. Took them what seemed forever to find the cur."

"And justice?" The words came out as nearly a growl.

"He was killed when they attempted to capture him, and a trial was held for the conspirators. Hung four of them, sent the others to jail."

Westley let this information settle. "Johnson is president then?"

"Yes. And emancipation is being enforced. The South has been taken back into the Union."

Relief washed over him. These years of horror, blood, death, and the loss of his family and dearest friends had at long last come to an end. "That's good."

Mrs. Preston slapped her knee. "Good, indeed! I thought this bloody mess would never end."

Westley had to agree. He'd felt the same. A military man from a line of military men, he'd thought himself prepared for war. Welcomed it, even, in the naïve way of a young man yearning to earn his glory on the battlefield. Turned out he had no idea how much it would truly steal from him.

Mrs. Preston rose and reached for the now empty bowl in his hands. "Now, best you get some rest. You're still a long way from being ready to leave."

Westley surrendered the bowl. "I thank you for your kindness."

"You are very welcome. It is my duty to care for you poor boys as best as I can." Her eyes misted, and she gave him a nod as she slipped out of the door.

Westley wondered how many of her sons had survived these tumultuous years. He didn't have long to contemplate it, though, because as soon as he settled back down in the warm blankets, exhaustion once more overtook him, and he drifted back into the quiet peace of sleep.

Chapter Three

Ella pulled the babe closer and tried to ready herself for the task before her. Night would be falling soon enough, and if she didn't hurry, she'd be caught out in the unrelenting shadows. Breathing a request for forgiveness, she plucked Cynthia's cloak and shawl from atop the valise on the floor, then glanced back at the body in the bed. She'd covered the woman's form but had not been able to clean her up.

Forgive me.

She grabbed the valise as well and headed for the door. Surely the woman wouldn't need these things and wouldn't begrudge Ella taking them. She would need something in the days ahead as she tried to secure the child's future.

That's what she told herself, but the guilt niggled anyway. The babe squirmed, drawing her attention back down to him. How long would it be before he would want another meal? She didn't know much about children, but she did know that newborns ate every few hours. She wouldn't be able to wait until morning to find the place Cynthia had told her about. It had to be midway through the afternoon by now, and she must hurry. Hopefully, the Remington home would be nearby.

Ella still hesitated in the room. She hated to leave Cynthia like this. All alone with no one to care for her body properly. Where would they bury her? Would any marker be left to indicate who she'd been?

Ella nuzzled her nose into the baby's hair. Would that be what happened to her? With no family and no security, would she also wind up dead and alone somewhere with nary a soul to mourn her? Tears threatened, but she forced them back. No time to have pity on herself. This sweet babe needed her, and she would not leave him to starve. She tried to position him in her arm and put on the cloak but found the task difficult. And how would she carry the valise in one hand and the babe in the other without growing too weary?

The shawl. She dropped the cloak and spread the shawl on the floor, positioning the child in the middle. Then she scooped both up and settled the babe against her small bosom, wrapped the two ends around herself and then back to the front, and knotted the ends behind the baby's back. Ella slowly removed her hands. The baby remained comfortably positioned against her, and she had the use of both hands.

Thrilled with her accomplishment, Ella swung the cloak over her shoulders and fastened the clasp at her neck, then picked up the valise. She cast one final glance at the child's mother, then set her jaw and descended the steps.

Mrs. Hatch stood at the bottom of the stairs, a scowl etched in her angular face. "You defied me, girl."

Had the woman been waiting on her? "You were wrong. Someone had to help or they both would have died."

The woman's eyes flitted to the baby hanging at Ella's chest and took a step back. "What are you doing?"

"Cynthia is dead. I must take the babe to a wet nurse."

Mrs. Hatch fingered the cloth at her neck and eyed the child as though it were some kind of wild animal Ella clutched. "A dead trollop? In my inn?"

"Yes. And a baby who needs to be cared for."

Mrs. Hatch's eyes darted to the stairs and back to Ella. "That child is diseased, girl. Best you leave it up there with her." She lowered her voice to a whisper. "I'll have some of the boys dispose of them."

Outrage swelled in Ella, and she grasped the baby tighter. "You'll do no such thing!"

Mrs. Hatch's eyes hardened. "It's what's best."

"I think not. I am going to find him a home."

"Do what you like, girl. But all you'll do is prolong the inevitable and make that child suffer. Ain't no one going to want him, and even if they did, not many are left in these parts that could feed another mouth."

Ella pressed her lips into a line. Was the woman right? She glanced down at the boy. Even so, she could not live with herself if she didn't at least try. "I must take him."

Mrs. Hatch pointed a bony finger at her. "Then you best gather what belongs to you and be out. And don't even think of coming back. Not only are you too daft to listen to reason, you likely contracted what she had."

Ella wrinkled her nose. "I wouldn't dream of it." Yet, even as the angry words spurted from her lips, regret clawed at her. Where else would she go? She'd had just enough funds to take a train from Woodville after her home had burned and Papa died. She'd ridden the train as far north as she could go, then took work here in the lackluster town of Parsonville, situated just north of the ravished town of Greenville. She'd hoped to catch a boat up the river, but as Greenville had been left in ruins by a Yankee gunboat and she had no funds to carry her anywhere else, here is where her foolish hope had abandoned her. She'd scrubbed the kitchen at the Buckhorn Inn for meals and lodging alone.

Mrs. Hatch's beady eyes landed on the valise and Ella clutched it tighter. "Stealing from the tart, eh?"

Ella set her shoulders. "I don't think she would mind me having this."

Her employer opened her thin lips, and Ella could guess the greedy words that would come next. She held out the valise.

"But you can take it. I'm certain the disease won't carry to clothing...right?"

The older woman stepped back, and fear sprang into her eyes just as Ella expected. She waved her hand. "No, no. You go on and take it. Lord knows you have little enough in this world."

Ella smiled at the false kindness and gave a nod before passing the woman and heading for the kitchen. In the storeroom she shoved her only other dress and a few under-clothes into the valise on top of whatever else was in there. She would have to look through it all later, lest Mrs. Hatch change her mind and come for it before Ella could make it out of the inn. Not giving the place one final glance, Ella exited the kitchen, passed the defeated soldiers, and stepped out into a warm May afternoon. Now, how to find where she needed to go?

She looked down the street. Just past the general store stood her best hope—the livery. Lifting her work dress, lest she fray the hem any more, Ella stepped out into the street and walked as briskly as she could without drawing attention. Thankfully, the baby seemed to be content, and if she drew the cloak close, his tiny form was nearly hidden. It was a bit warm for such a wrap during the day, but wearing it seemed preferable to carrying it.

In the livery she found an elderly man mucking stalls for three scraggly-looking horses. Not many decent animals had survived the war and the army's commandeering. They'd lost all of their good stock back home. That's what had set Papa's drinking aflame, even worse than when he'd first begun after Mama died.

Ella lifted a hand. "Sir? Excuse me, sir?"

The man turned. "Eh?" He straightened. "Oh, sorry, miss. Didn't hear you come in."

"That's quite all right. I wondered if I might ask you a question."

He leaned against the shovel. "Certainly. Could use a rest for my back anyhow."

Ella couldn't help but smile at the man's good humor. Solid for a man of his years, Ella guessed he had once been quite a bull of a man. Wispy white hair sprouted from around his large ears but left the top of his head untouched. He smiled at her, and Ella was surprised to see he still had all of his teeth.

"I am looking for the Remington house. Might you know where that is?"

His gaze dropped down to the baby tied to the front of her dress and something lit in his eyes. "Belmont. Ah, yes...um, well, I hate to be the one to tell you, miss, but Mr. and Mrs. Remington both died this past winter. No one is left there to take in the..." He rubbed the back of his neck and averted his eyes. "The, uh, unfortunate girls anymore."

She blinked in surprise before she gathered his meaning. He thought her one like Cynthia. She could feel her cheeks redden. "Oh! No, sir. I am not looking for that kind of help."

The man's eyes widened. "My sincerest apologies. I just haven't seen you before and, well..." He looked down at the baby.

Ella stood taller. "The child is in need of a wet nurse. And soon. I was told one resided at the Remington place...?"

The man brightened. "Certainly." He scratched the back of his balding head. "I could give you a ride. Make up for the embarrassing misunderstanding."

Ella hesitated only for an instant. "I would be most grateful, sir. Thank you."

A quarter of an hour later, Ella sat on a bench seat of a buckboard next to the old man as they jostled their way out of Parsonville. Ella held the baby as best she could, lest he bounce too hard. Amazing that he could sleep like that. Perhaps he would be an easy babe. Or perhaps he was still too weak after having nearly suffocated.

Such a sweet thing. His little dark lashes splayed across rounded cheeks. A pang constricted her chest. She would hate to give him up. Oh, it was what he needed, of course, but... Looking down at that angelic little face clenched her heart. Perhaps there would be work for her at—what had the livery master called it? Belmont?—and she wouldn't really have to be separated from him just yet.

She buried the hope down in her heart and tried not to let it sprout too quickly. There were far more people around these days who needed work than places that provided it. But Ella was willing to work for nothing more than a roof and a bit to eat. Perchance that would be enough.

As the sun began to drift closer to the tops of the trees, they rolled into the crumbling ruins of Greenville. Another town of burned homes and ruined lives. Just like back home. Had the Remington home even survived?

She turned to look at the man beside her. He had spoken nary a word since they'd left from Parsonville, and Ella had been content to be left to her own thoughts, but now something bothered her. "Sir?"

He didn't respond. Ella raised her voice and leaned a bit nearer. "Sir?"

He startled and turned to look at her. "Oh. Yes?"

She jutted her chin at the scorched ruins they passed. "Are you certain the home still stands?"

The man looked back at her. "I reckon so. No Yanks have been burning through here in some time."

He turned his focus ahead again, as though he were none too interested in conversations. She likely wouldn't get anything more. He hadn't even given her his name. Not that she had told him hers either. Perhaps it was better that way. She merely needed the ride. Nothing more.

They rode about a quarter hour more out past the southern outskirts of Greenville before the livery master pulled up on the reins and brought his two gaunt mules to a halt. He indicated a stretch of water just up ahead. "Follow the river road there a bit more. You'll pass by Willoughby by the river, then see another road on your left. Follow that 'un for a bit and you'll see Belmont. Big brick house. You won't miss it."

Ella shifted uncomfortably. "You'll not take me on to the house?"

He refused to look at her. "Bit rough on the wagon, see."

Ella looked at the dry road without any patches of mud and wondered what he could possibly mean. He shifted in his seat. "I best be getting on back now."

Understanding dawned. Of course. He didn't wish for anyone to see him delivering a girl to the Remington house, a place that obviously had a reputation for seeing to fallen women. Ella mustered her best smile. "Thank you, sir, for your great kindness. I would have had a time toting this babe on my own."

He returned her smile and then climbed down from the wagon and rounded to the other side to assist her. Valise in hand and the baby secured, Ella lifted a hand to wave goodbye, but the fellow kept his head down and didn't send a glance back over his shoulder.

Ella squared her shoulders and marched forward, grateful she didn't have to make the entire walk. Why, it would probably have been well past nightfall by the time she'd made it on foot.

She followed the road that snaked along the Mississippi as instructed, and after she rounded the bend she saw a long drive lined with fields. Through a handful of large magnolias stood a massive brick house. Her breath caught. A mansion for certain! Why, the people there would surely have the ability to care for one small child. Relief washed over her, and she clutched the little one close.

"Here, now, sweet one. See? I promised you would have a good home. And, my, I don't suppose there is any finer than this one."

The baby squirmed and let out a bit of a cry, and Ella paused to rock him a moment. He opened his eyes and watched her as she smiled and cooed at him, and then his lids drifted closed once more. She continued toward the house. He would want to be fed soon. That was the first time he had opened his eyes since right before Cynthia had nursed him. He squirmed once more, and she quickened her pace.

As Ella neared the house, she noticed four fine horses held by a young man in a dark blue uniform. Without thinking, she ducked behind the large flat leaves of one of the magnolias, dropping her valise to the soft earth with a muffled *plop*. Her heart thudded. Had he seen her?

She peeked out, but the Yank kept his focus on the house. Ella shifted to see past him. Belmont stood proud, boasting fine red brick and a sprawling porch not only for the bottom floor but for the top one as well. Ella counted eight windows across the front that looked like they might be taller than she, and no fewer than six chimneys. But she didn't have much time to admire the babe's new home, as the three Blue Bellies standing at the front door drew her attention.

The one with a sash about his waist and a saber hanging from his side pounded on the door. They waited, and Ella held her position. After a few moments, the man pounded once more. If there was anyone inside, they must have heard it. Her chest constricted. Had the home been abandoned?

She was about to decide that was, indeed, the case when the large front door swung open. She couldn't quite see who stood on the other side, since the soldiers blocked her view. The man with the sash, who apparently led this group, spoke loudly enough that Ella had no trouble hearing him.

"We are here to speak to Mr. Remington about the compliance of these lands with the Freedmen's Bureau."

The men shifted enough for Ella to see a dark-skinned woman at the door. She stood about middle height, with a trim figure and a straight spine. The woman exited the house and closed the door behind her, regarding the men with concern etched on her features. Ella placed her fingers to her lips. Could she be the wet nurse? Ella eased up to a nearer magnolia, this one just out from the porch. No one seemed to notice.

"I's sorry, suh, but the elder Mr. Remington died this past winter. Him and the missus both."

"Then who controls these lands?"

Her gaze darted back to the house. "There ain't no slaves here, mister."

Ella couldn't see the man well enough to be sure, but she guessed he wasn't convinced. Many slaves would have been told to lie about such things. Ella wondered about the truth of the words herself.

"All the same, we will speak to someone in charge here to be certain United States laws are being carried out."

The woman began to wring her hands and a sinking feeling gathered in Ella's stomach. If the owners were dead and no one else had claim to the house, then the Yanks would surely seize it and claim some kind of outstanding taxes or make up a violation to one of their ordinances. She'd heard the like plenty of times before. Her jaw tightened. Then what would happen to the people living there? Would they be dispersed? What would that mean for her babe?

Her mind froze. *The* babe. Not hers. No. He wasn't, couldn't be, hers. She clutched him tighter all the same. She had made a promise.

"Mister Remington the elder has gone, but these lands were

given to his son." She bobbed her head, sending tight, dark curls shaking. "He was in the Federal cavalry. Yes, suh. Went all the way to that military school, just like his papa and grandpapa did."

The men seemed interested in this. The leader stroked the blond hair on his chin. "West Point, you mean?"

She bobbed her head again. "Yes, suh. That's the one."

The man glanced at the men around him. "Well, that is good to know. We would like to speak to him."

The woman shifted her weight. "Well, he ain't here…"

"Then when shall he return?"

Ella watched the scene before her and a wild, maddening plan began to form. She had to be out of her head even to think such things, but intuition told her that if she did not do something, then all hope for the boy would be lost. She straightened her shoulders and did her best to put on a confident air.

Still, she hesitated.

"Well, we don't rightly know. They sent a fella sayin' he was missing…" The man stiffened and the woman hurried on. "But we don't know anything for sure. He could be back any moment and…"

Her words trailed off as all of a sudden the child at Ella's chest let out a shrill wail. Ella startled. Knowing she had but one opportunity, she stepped from behind the tree and did her best to look as though she were just walking up the drive and had not been hiding.

She caught the look of surprise on all the faces on the porch before looking down at the babe and cooing to him, partly to calm him and partly to simply avoid the stares of those at the house.

Calm. Be calm. Oh, Lord, help me. I've lost my mind.

Ella lifted her gaze and planted confusion on her face, her

eyes sliding over the men and landing on the woman on the porch. She glanced down at the child, who continued to whimper, and let as much pleading as she dared show in her eyes. The other woman's brow puckered, and her gaze darted between Ella and the child.

If this doesn't work…

She ground the thought beneath sheer determination and put on her best haughty look. "Cindy, what is going on? Do we have guests?"

The other woman's mouth worked as Ella ascended the steps and tried to position herself so that only the woman could see her face.

Please, she mouthed.

The woman's surprise disappeared beneath controlled features. She indicated to the three Federal men by the door. "These here soldiers done come to be sure Belmont is doing right with the freeman stuff…" Her voice trailed off.

Ella gave her best reassuring look before turning to face the men. The baby squirmed and let out a piercing wail again. She looked back at the woman she'd called Cindy after the child's mother and smiled sweetly. "It seems I took too long in my walk, and he is dreadfully hungry. Perhaps you could feed him…?"

Something sparked in the woman's eyes and they flew wide, revealing the whites around her black pupils. "Oh, yes, ma'am. I reckon he sure is! I's going to take him inside to nurse."

Relief washed over Ella so strongly that her knees nearly buckled. She untied the shawl, keeping her back to the soldiers and wrapped the ends around the screaming child. She passed him to the other woman's waiting arms. "Thank you."

The woman seemed to catch the sincerity in Ella's words and offered a tight smile. "Of course, ma'am. We be in the nursery when you finish talkin' with these here soldiers."

Ella watched the woman disappear inside, trying to ignore the ache that settled on her as soon as the little bundle slipped from sight. She forced herself to remain composed and turned to the men staring at her, pulling the fine cloak around her to hide the scullery maid's clothing beneath. Thank goodness she'd worn it.

"May I help you, gentlemen?"

"Your maid said that all of the Remingtons are dead?"

Ella's heart pounded, but she simply arched a brow. "Did she? My husband's parents have passed on, but I am certain my husband will return soon." She wrapped her arms around herself. "He promised me he would return to see our child."

The officer glanced at the others at his side and they shifted their weight, clearly uncomfortable. "Do you speak for these holdings in your husband's absence then?"

"I do."

"And you understand freedmen's laws?"

Ella tilted her head. "If you are referring to the abolition of slavery, I certainly do. We have never owned another person here, sir. To do so is against our faith in the Lord, who loves all men as he created them." At least that part wasn't a lie. Papa had been too poor to own a slave, and Ella didn't think it was right. Besides, the wet nurse had said there were no slaves here, and Cynthia had claimed that the Remingtons were Christian folks. It seemed to be near enough to the truth.

"Very well," the officer replied after an extended pause that had sent Ella's stomach to fluttering.

She almost opened her mouth to wish them good day and hurry inside to check on the baby when his next words stalled her.

"And I presume you know that they must be paid a wage, not just given the same amenities they have always been afforded. Such things do not make life any different."

Ella blinked. "Of course."

"So your people are paid?"

Ella fidgeted, searching her mind for any bit of information she had picked up that could help her. She seized on something that might avert this man's scrutiny. "The house servants are paid from my husband's earnings, of course. We have plans of letting out the land for planting and will share the crops with the workers."

The man seemed appeased, and Ella hoped she had stumbled on the right thing to make him go away. Then he frowned again. "And how many people do you have to work these lands?"

Ella's heart thudded so loudly in her chest she felt certain the men could hear it. She drew herself to her full height and did her best to emulate the fine ladies she had sold lace to back home. "Sir, as you obviously noticed, I have just had a child and my husband has not yet returned to me. We plan on letting out the land, and as spring is upon us, those plans will be carried out soon. Now, if you will excuse me, my son needs me."

The man had the good graces to look apologetic. "Certainly, ma'am. We won't take up any more of your time."

A genuine smile spread over her face. She dipped her chin. "Good day to you, gentlemen."

The man tipped his head and donned his blue kepi, then lifted his hand to gesture the other two men off the porch. Ella turned and reached for the doorknob when his voice stopped her once more.

"You won't mind if we return in a few weeks to check on the progress you've made with the planting, will you?"

Oh, dear. Well, at least that gave these people a little time to figure out what they would do. She clasped her hands at her waist and faced him once more. "Of course not."

"We may even have more to send you, should you require

extra hands."

Ella cocked her head. Odd. "I'm not sure if that will be necessary, but I will let you know once we see how to settle our own people." She had no idea how many called Belmont lands home.

Seeming satisfied, the soldier gave a small bow and then spun away. Ella watched them mount their horses just to be sure they were leaving, then grasped the doorknob and hurried into the house to find the babe.

Chapter Four

Ella leaned against the heavy door for just a moment to regain her composure. What had she been thinking? Had she made things worse for these people? What would they do when the soldiers returned? Pushing the worry away for another time, she stepped forward into the wide entry and put a hand to her throat. Thickly woven carpet cushioned her feet, and she lifted them to be sure she didn't trail in any dirt. Overhead, a chandelier sparkled, and she imagined it would send shimmering light across the blue walls and decorative plasterwork come evening. Everything about the place, from the wide doors cased in carved frames to the shining wood floors and grand staircase, spoke of wealth and luxury.

Even amid the destruction of war, this house seemed barely touched. Perhaps because the Remington man had been in the Federal Army. Ella took a step forward. Now, where to find the woman who had taken the child? The house stood quiet, the only sound Ella's own erratic breathing.

"Hello?" she called tentatively.

A second later a young girl Ella guess to be around twelve darted from the doorway on her right. She skidded to a stop and smiled up at Ella, her teeth looking all the whiter against her ebony skin. "I'm Basil." She reached out and grabbed Ella's hand. "Sibby done said to bring you once you came in da house."

Ella allowed the girl to guide her to the stairs, then she dropped Ella's hand and bounded up the staircase. "I saw what you did with them soldiers," she said, grinning over her shoulder at Ella.

Ella smiled, not knowing what to say. The girl didn't seem to expect an answer, though, and made the turn on the stairs to go up another flight. "She's up here in the nursery with that little one you brought. He yours?"

Ella pressed her lips together. Did she lie and say he was? Her heart yearned to do so. Surely they would let her work here if the baby was hers, right? Ella let out a sigh. "No. His mother died having him."

The little girl giggled. "Didn't think so. You don't look like you just had no baby."

Had the soldiers thought the same? Ella declined to answer as they reached the second floor, and Basil led her through the first door on the left. The room featured a large canopied bed with mosquito netting hanging against its rose-colored quilt, and beautifully carved furniture sat against the high walls of the same hue.

As though sensing her thoughts, Basil waved her hand at the room as she walked to a door on the left-hand wall. "This here was the mistress's room. It connects to the master's room on the other side," she said, pulling the huge door open, "and to the nursery on this 'un."

Basil flung the door wide and motioned for Ella to enter. "I see you downstairs later." Her narrow face scrunched. "Sibby said I can't be botherin' you until she's had her time for talkin'."

Without waiting for Ella's response, the girl spun around and scuttled away. Ella drew a breath and stepped into the room. Every bit as elegant as downstairs, the room featured a crib with netting, a rocking chair, a thick rug, and a washing tub. Such luxury! The little one would be cared for, sure enough.

Her gaze landed on the woman who rocked the babe in the chair. Up close, she looked younger than Ella had thought. Trim and strong-looking, she had short, tight black curls, a nose that flared at the tip, and dark eyes that studied Ella as boldly as Ella studied her.

Ella looked down at the little one, her hand fluttering to her chest as though it already missed his presence. "How is he?"

"He be just fine, now that his belly's full."

Ella let out her breath. "Oh, thank goodness. Cynthia said I could find a wet nurse here."

The woman, whom the little girl had called Sibby, rocked slowly, snuggling the child with experienced arms. "And here I was almost out of milk. Been 'bout a week now since I helped with one of my people's babies, but now she done started weaning, and she was the last of 'em. We ain't got no other babies about what needs me."

Ella clasped her hands. "Will you be able to care for him?"

The woman's deep brown eyes studied her. "Who is you anyway?"

Seizing an opportunity to appear more than a farm girl with no prospects and no security, she straightened her spine and decided to take on her full name, a name that had passed no one's lips since her mother had died. "I'm Miss Eleanor Whitaker. I was present during the birth of the child." Her eyes dropped down from Sibby's knowing gaze for fear that the woman already saw through her sham. "His mother did not survive the birthing."

Sibby stared at her for so long Ella began to fear the nurse would cast her out of Belmont. Then finally she gestured toward the single person bed. "Sit, and tell me what done happened."

Ella sat, glad for a place to rest her weak legs. She released her story in a gush, as though the words burned within her, keeping her eyes on the patterned rug underneath the nurse's scuffed boots. She didn't look up until she had finished the tale.

When she did, the other woman, whom Ella guessed to be

about her own age or perhaps only a bit older, offered her an encouraging smile. "Yeah, I remember them two. I nursed Cynthia's sister's baby until the missus found him a place at the orphanage."

"Cynthia said that the Remingtons were known for helping girls like that."

Sibby's features softened, and compassion shone in her eyes. "You one of those girls?"

Ella wrapped her arms around herself. How close had she been to becoming one? That night came back to her, but she forcefully shoved it aside. "No."

"Didn't think so."

What use was it to try to appear anything more than she truly was? Naught but a farm girl turned scullery maid. "I earned my keep in the kitchen."

"I figured somethin' like that."

Ella found that to be something of a comfort, and the breath left her.

"I'm Sibby, but Basil done told you that."

Ella smiled. "Sweet girl."

"Where is you from?"

"Woodville. Southern part of Mississippi, getting close to Louisiana."

"Confederate?"

The question surprised her, though Ella didn't know why. Of course, this woman would want to know who she sided with. Hadn't everyone? Ella shrugged. "In some ways, yes. Not in others."

Sibby frowned, so Ella hurried with an explanation. "Papa never did care who bought our horses as long as they had money. Once we even had a colored man in a fine suit from up north buy six of our colts. And we never had any slaves, just a few poor farm boys who worked the horses and kept the stalls.

We did everything else on our own." She looked at Sibby earnestly. "I never did think one person ought to own another, though."

"Hmm." Sibby regarded her for several moments. "But still Confederate?"

Ella stiffened, but saw no reason not to tell the truth. "If I had to say one way or the other, then yes."

"Why?"

Ella tilted her head. This woman seemed nothing like what Papa said slaves were—skittish as an unhandled colt and as bright as a barn cat. And she was certainly quite bold. Ella liked that about her. "Well, I felt in my own heart that the country should stay together, even though the entire thing was really about money and the fact that the North needed the raw supplies from the South to support their factories—couldn't go adding foreign taxes and the like. Then the slavery aspect became part of it, and I figured that was a good thing, too. The South wouldn't have let go of their workers without some persuasion."

Sibby grunted. "Sounds loyalist to me."

"But then they invaded our lands, burned our crops, and pillaged our homes. They stole our horses, our livestock, and even our furniture. A confiscation act, they called it. I called it robbery. It became not a war between armies, but an assault that settled not on soldiers, but on women and children. They attacked those most vulnerable, leaving regular people destitute, starving, and desperate." Ella shook her head firmly. "No. I could not side with people like that."

Silence settled and they sat beneath its weight for some time. Ella felt certain the woman wanted to ask her to leave, and Ella couldn't bring herself to offer to go, as would be proper, so they continued a stalemate that she knew she would eventually crumble beneath. She simply couldn't deny the ache in her chest that begged her once more to hold the boy. No matter her dignity, she would not give up hope of finding employ here, where perhaps she would not suffer men's attentions and the baby could remain near. She would beg to stay if that's what it took.

"So," Sibby finally said, "what did you tell them soldiers to get them to leave the porch?"

Relief surged in her only to quickly be replaced by heat rising in her neck. She dug her fingers into her skirt, lamenting the foolish words desperation had flung from her lips. "I said I was Mr. Remington's wife."

To her surprise, Sibby let out a hearty laugh, startling the baby and making him squirm. She bounced him a bit, and then he drifted back to sleep. "Did you now? Well, I reckon that gave them what they was lookin' for."

Ella allowed herself a tentative smile. She'd tell Sibby later that the men would be returning. That would be something to disclose once she'd secured their future. She looked at the child. "May I hold him?"

Sibby seemed taken aback by her sudden request, but she rose from the chair and handed the child to Ella. She smiled up at the taller woman and accepted him gently, enjoying the feel of him back against her.

"What's his name?" Sibby asked as she settled back into the rocking chair.

Ella shook her head. "I don't know. His mother didn't give him one."

"Then I reckon you best do it. Child needs a name."

Ella frowned. She'd never considered what to name a child. Such a thing was of great importance. "I'll have to think on it."

The chair creaked as Sibby began to rock. "Well, there ain't no more orphanages in these parts that will take a baby." Her voice hitched. "Them poor children is scavenging in the streets like dogs, from what I hear tell. No one's got nothing to give them."

Ella's pulse quickened, and the words left her mouth in a gush. "Then could we stay here instead? I will work hard—I promise—to earn our keep. I will do whatever you need me to do."

Sibby's eyebrows rose. "You want to work here?"

Ella pulled the baby closer. "Please. I don't know where else we can go. I'll scrub floors and whatever else you ask of me so long as he is cared for and I have a roof and something to eat."

Sibby continued to stare at her, and Ella felt her chance slipping away. "I can sleep on the floor in the kitchen. It won't bother me a bit, and I…"

The nurse held up her hand. "You that desperate?"

Ella swallowed hard, then nodded.

Compassion swam in the other woman's eyes. "I ain't never seen no white woman offer to be sleepin' on the kitchen floor." Then her gaze narrowed. "You related to this child?"

"No." She smoothed the fuzzy hair on the top of the baby's head. "But I have seen enough suffering these last years. This child was born from unfortunate parents in a war-torn land. It's silly of me, I know, but…" Tears gathered and threatened to spill. "But I thought that maybe if this little one could get a chance in this world, then perhaps not all hope would be lost."

Sibby laced her fingers and placed them over her crisp white apron. "You is willing to work for that?"

Ella nodded again.

"And you would see that this here babe is cared for and loved?"

The tears escaped their confines and left two trails down her cheeks that she could not hide. "I ask only to be given a chance to earn a place to work and provide for the two of us, and I would love him like my own."

A smile played about the woman's lips. "Then I gots an idea."

Chapter Five

"What did you say?" Ella blinked back her surprise, certain she had heard Sibby incorrectly.

Sibby laid the boy in the crib and gently tucked a crocheted blanket around him before turning back to Ella. "It makes sense, you being white and all." She ushered Ella toward the door.

Ella hesitated a moment, glancing once more at the child. "I hardly think that has anything to do with—"

"It's what you told them soldiers." Sibby pointed at the door, her expression clear that they would have to have this discussion elsewhere.

Ella pulled her arms around her waist as she stepped into the next room. The opportunity to tell the whole of the mess she made presented itself. "Well, yes, but…"

"See? And they believed you is the lady here. So will any others that come sniffin' around." Sibby eyed her. "So long as you sound like a lady and not a maid."

Ella lowered her gaze. "I didn't tell you *all* of what went on."

Sibby looked over her shoulder from where she'd nearly made it out of the room that had once belonged to the real Mrs. Remington. "What you mean?"

"Well…they kept asking questions and prodding, and I was trying to get them to leave." She dropped her arms to her sides and attempted to stand up taller.

Sibby waited.

Nothing for it but to just blurt it out. "They plan to keep a check on Belmont to see that the freedman laws are followed."

The other woman's lips curved. "So next time they is gonna find you here as a Yankee wife and still no slaves. Then they'll go away and leave us all alone." She stepped out into the upper hall. "Basil! You keep watch on the little 'un and come get me if he wakes up."

The girl slipped into the room and gave Ella a wide smile. "I knew she'd let him stay," she whispered as she passed.

Too flustered to respond, Ella hurried out after Sibby, shaking her head. A pin loosened, painfully tugging at a lock of her hair. She pushed it back into place. "It's more than that. They want to see that the people are not *effectively* still slaves."

Sibby huffed. "We ain't been slaves since I was a girl. Nothing's changed."

Exasperated, Ella struggled for the right words to make herself understood. "They think we are going to pay people to work the fields and then share the crops."

Sibby stared at her. "Why'd you tell them that?"

Her shoulders slumped. "I said the only thing that came to mind. I'd heard men discussing such at the inn where I worked. I thought it would satisfy them and they would be on their way."

"But?"

Ella inwardly groaned. "But they said they would be coming back to check and make *sure* we were doing that." Sibby blew out a breath, but Ella forged ahead. "And…they also said they would send us more helpers if we needed them to continue the work."

Sibby's wide brow furrowed. "We don't want no strangers here."

Ella sucked a breath. Like her? They stood there for a moment, each considering the other until finally Sibby bobbed her head and started down the stairs. She made it to the first landing before Ella gathered herself enough to follow. "Does this mean I am to leave?"

Sibby paused and looked over her shoulder, giving Ella a sour look. "Course not. I can't let that baby starve."

Knowing she could still insist Ella leave without the child, she said carefully, "Thank you."

Sibby shrugged. "Sides, I got somethin' to show you."

Ella followed her down to the entryway, then turned right into the music room. Sibby opened the top to a small pump organ and shoved her hand inside. Curious, Ella stepped closer.

After a bit of searching, Sibby plucked a folded paper from within and held it out to Ella. "What I told them soldiers wasn't all truth either."

Ella unfolded the letter and scanned the brief words. "You already knew he wouldn't return?"

"I was afraid if I said all of them was dead—" Her voice wavered, and she averted her gaze to the window.

"If you had told them the truth, and said that Major Remington is assumed dead, you would have been in danger of them taking your home." She bit her lip. "I understand."

Sibby cast her a grateful look that revealed the shimmer of tears in her deep brown eyes.

"Someone must stand to inherit these lands." Ella tapped the paper. "Perhaps I can pretend only until one of the family arrives." Yes. That seemed like a good plan. It could be months before anyone came, and that would give her some time to figure out what to do next. Perhaps they would even allow her employment, and she wouldn't have to leave the babe.

Sibby tugged on her apron. "Ain't no family coming for this place. Either we keep it or the army takes it."

Ella's face puckered. "How can that be?"

Sibby looked out the window once more, and her voice took on a distant sound. "Mr. Remington was certain that as soon as the war ended, his son would wed the girl from Willoughby, combine these lands with theirs, and keep everything going."

Ella didn't want to argue, but that seemed entirely too impractical. "You said the son went to the military academy?"

"He did. What's that matter?" Sibby scrunched her face.

She shifted her eyes from Sibby's form at the window to the fabric covering the walls and then down to the pianoforte. While trying to decide how best to say what she thought without causing offense, Ella trailed her fingers over the polished wood of the instrument and wondered what life would have been like to spend one's days sitting about making music rather than hauling buckets of water to horses. "Well, I'd think a military man with a military son would consider that his son's life would perpetually be in danger, therefore would have had an alternate plan, if necessary."

Sibby lifted her hands. "If he did, I don't know nothin' about it."

Ella tapped her chin. "Then it *is* possible someone else could come and lay claim."

"That ain't going to happen. No one is coming to take Belmont from us."

Ella held her tongue against the foolishness of the statement. No point in arguing with the woman. She lifted the letter. "So if we know that the younger Remington man is dead as well…"

"They *think*. They don't know," Sibby retorted.

Noting that the letter had been dated weeks prior, Ella reasoned that if the man truly lived, he would have turned up by now. "Very well. But let's say it is true."

"Then you be his widow, same as you told them soldiers."

Ella looked down at her stained dress and laughed. "I do not pass for the wife of a plantation man!"

Sibby crossed her arms. "They believed you."

A miracle. "They did not look closely upon me, and I had to pretend only a few moments."

Sibby let her gaze roam down Ella's form, then lifted a shoulder. "I can work on you."

"Really, that's not necessary." She ignored Sibby's dubious expression. "I'll just work in the kitchen and help with the housework. I can work in a garden, too, and help plant crops. Then…"

Sibby laughed. "Ain't no white woman going to work in no field."

Ella cocked her head. "I have done so many times. Cared for livestock as well."

Sibby regarded her with disbelief.

"Not all women of my color are wealthy, Sibby." Ella bent her lips. "Some of us have to work."

"No." Sibby shook her head. "That won't do."

Ella pinched the bridge of her nose, then steered the topic. There would be time to convince the woman later. "What about planting and sharing the crops?"

"We can do that." Sibby brightened, becoming excited. "It could be a good idea." She leveled a steady gaze on Ella, her eyes brimming with meaning. "They will plant the fields as long as you promise them they'll see something for they work."

"Me? What does my word matter?"

Sibby regarded her as though she were daft. "Who else is gonna promise them?"

Ella opened her mouth to respond, but Sibby waved her hand. "Look here. We is able to keep our home cared for on our own. We don't need no masters tellin' us what to do. But Yankee or not, white folks don't think so. They see a bunch of us here with no white masters—or even employers—and they will take everything from us." Her hand fidgeted in her skirt.

"Most of us don't have no other place to go."

Ella could not deny that truth, so she said nothing. It seemed unfair, but then such was the case with everything in life.

"Now, ways I see it, you and me can make a deal." Sibby's hands flew about, punctuating each word. "You need a place to stay and help with that baby. We need someone with white skin to speak for us."

Ella considered the claim, which had merit. "So, I pretend to be the widow if any soldiers come by and the rest of the time I work here with you." She brightened. "That will be good. You do what you need to with your people and the lands, and if…"

Her words dissolved under Sibby's chuckle. Ella cocked her head. "What?"

"You still ain't understandin' what I sayin'."

Ella stared at her.

Sibby looked up at the ceiling and then back at Ella. "It's got to be more than just when them soldiers come by. If anyone even starts thinkin' that you ain't really Mr. Westley's wife, then them tongues will get to waggin' and we'll be had."

A good point, one which she could not counter. "Well, I suppose."

Sibby strode past Ella and to the doorway. "No. This here town is going to have to believe you *is* his wife and that child *is* Mr. Westley's son. There ain't no other way."

Ella followed her to the foyer but found no words to refute her. Temptation stole away every sound reason she should speak. How nice would it be…? She could pretend the baby belonged to her and have a place to live that was far and away better than that rancid inn. As though sensing Ella stood on the brink of decision, Sibby gave her a moment to consider. The deception seemed wrong, but…would she find any better options? And she had arrived at this place at just the right time.

What would one small lie hurt?

As soon as Ella gave a nod, Sibby gestured toward the stairs. "Then that little fellow has his name."

"Oh?"

"Yes, 'um." A sly smile slid onto her full lips. "He ain't no other than Westley Archibald Remington the Fourth, Master of Belmont Plantation."

Chapter Six

Sibby seemed rather pleased with herself. "Now, since we got that decided, let's get you settled." She eyed Ella. "Is you got any belongings?"

"Oh!" She'd forgotten all about the valise. "Yes. I dropped my things by that magnolia out in the yard."

Sibby strode to a door at the rear of the foyer just as grand as the one on the front and poked her head outside. "Nat! You out here?"

A moment later a big youth nearing on manhood came through the door, his smile wavering as his ebony eyes landed on Ella. "Who's that?"

Sibby smacked his thick bicep. "Boy! Where your manners?"

He rubbed his arm but didn't hide his scrutiny of the intruder. "What? I ain't got to cower for no strange white lady. What's she doing here?"

Sibby pinched his ear and he let out a yelp. "Uh-huh. You keep right on spoutin' that mouth, boy. I'm the one you's disrespecting."

This time the youth she'd called Nat looked apologetic, but Ella couldn't be sure if remorse or the painful grip Sibby had on his ear caused his broad lips to turn down. "Ouch! I's sorry, Sibby. I's sorry."

Satisfied, Sibby released him. "Now. This here is Eleanor…Remington. She's the new mistress here."

Nat's mouth fell open and he cut his sharp gaze from Ella

to Sibby. The look she gave him in return made Ella cringe, and he snapped his jaw closed.

Sibby straightened her apron and stood taller, her eyes daring anyone to disagree with her. "Least, that's what everyone is going to say. You got it?"

Nat looked none too pleased but nodded all the same.

"Good." Sibby patted his arm. "Now, she done left her bag out by one of the magnolias. Go and fetch it for me, and then gather the...house folks up."

He scowled at Ella as he passed, and the smile she tried to offer faltered on her lips. He let the front door slam, causing the chandelier overhead to quiver.

"Sibby, this might not be a good idea." Ella arched her eyebrows. "What if your people refuse to accept it?"

She snorted. "They'll do as I tell 'em."

The youth being evidence of the likelihood of such a statement, Ella was inclined to believe it. A small cry pierced the silence that hung over them, and both women took the opportunity to escape the tension in the foyer. They found Basil in the nursery, lifting the babe from the crib.

"He's a right fine boy, miss." She beamed at Ella. "Plump and pretty. What happened to his parents?"

Ella reached for him and snuggled him close. "His mama died in the birth."

"What 'bout his daddy?"

Sibby waved her hand. "You hush now. You got too many questions than what's good for you. Some things we just don't ask."

Glad she didn't have to attempt to explain despondent circumstances to such a cheery girl, Ella smiled. "Sibby is right."

Basil poked out her lip. "Nobody thinks I'm big enough for nothin'."

Ella gazed down at the perfect little face in her arms while

Sibby gently lectured the girl on proper behavior and how some things only came with age. *Such a beautiful child.* No doubt one day there would be young ladies fanning themselves over those expressive eyes and dark hair... Ella frowned.

"What?"

Ella glanced up to see that Sibby watched her closely, as though she doubted Ella knew what to do with a child. She didn't really, but it offended all the same.

"He has such dark hair."

Sibby glanced at him. "Yeah, he do. So?"

"Well, if you haven't noticed," Ella said with a turn of her lips, "it looks nothing like my own."

"Hmm." Sibby inspected her as though she hadn't yet realized Ella's features. "You do got some red hair."

Ella laughed. "You just noticed?"

Sibby shrugged. "That don't matter. You white folks have all kinds of colored hair."

"Usually features do run in a family, Sibby. Surely you know that."

She squinted at Ella, then looked down at the baby. "Well, you got that bright hair and them green eyes, but baby Archibald has dark hair and eyes like Mr. Westley. Should be all right."

Ella made a face. "Archibald?"

"Course."

She knew she must bestow the family's name on the child, but still... "Why not Westley instead?"

Sibby shook her head, tight curls trembling. "That's Mr. Westley's name."

Incredulous, Ella opened her mouth to retort, but Sibby continued as though her logic followed reason.

"That's not the way it goes. The first Westley Archibald Remington went by Westley. Then his son was Archibald, then Westley again. See? Keeps it clear that way." She gave a smug smile, as though she had just explained something extraordinary to a dullard.

Ella arched her eyebrows. "Well, as there are no others here to cause confusion, then I don't see why Westley is a problem." She lifted her chin. "I don't care for Archibald."

Sibby clicked her tongue. "That ain't how it's done."

"Sibby," Ella said with a snort. "Do you really think 'how it's done' applies? *How it's done* would have been with a proper wedding and a child born to the father he's named for."

Sibby glared at her. "You want this to work or not?"

The baby started to make little noises Ella guessed would portend hungry wails. "What if this is an utter disaster? Then what? When I leave here, I don't want to call my boy Archibald for the rest of his life."

"Humph. It's a right respectable name."

He loosed a fist from the blanket and flailed it about. Ella stroked his tiny hand, and he grasped her finger with surprising strength. Bright eyes stared up at her, and her heart lurched. Yes, no matter what happened here, she would not give up this child.

Nor would she call him Archibald.

Sibby groaned. "Fine. We don't have to call him Archibald. How 'bout Archie?"

"No." She liked that even less. "Perhaps we can call him something else entirely. He can keep the official name for documents and such, but we call him something more fetching."

"No, ma'am. We ain't doing that. You ain't going to convince the people around here that child belongs to the Remingtons if he is called by a different name."

Ella sighed. "Very well. Then Westley it is, so called for how much I dearly miss my husband now lost to me."

Sibby's mouth fell open, and Ella offered a sweet smile. "A good compromise, yes?"

"Oh, Lord." Sibby groaned. "What kind of mess have I done gotten us into?"

Baby Westley began to wail, and Ella bounced him. "There, my little Lee. Are you hungry?"

"Lee?"

Ella smiled and handed over the child so Sibby could nurse him. "Just as I am Eleanor called Ella, so he will be Westley called Lee. Surely you do not begrudge me giving something of myself to the boy who will be my son?"

Sibby took the baby and settled into the rocker, flicking an annoyed gaze at his mother.

Mother.

Ella let the word flutter through her, taking root deep into her heart in such a way that she could not fathom being anything different. Though not of her womb, this boy was nevertheless the child of her heart. A sense of rightness engulfed her, and she knew that it could be none other than the will of God. Someone to love.

Thank you, Lord, that I no longer have to face this world alone. Here can be someone who will love me. I promise I will be a most devoted mother.

She slipped from the room before Sibby could see the tears brimming in her eyes and decided to wait in the wide upper hall. She'd no sooner stepped from the room than Basil scurried over to her.

"What's going on?"

Voices bounced up the stairs and washed over them. "I think Sibby wanted a gathering."

Basil chewed on her lip. "Really? Somethin' wrong?"

Fear leached into her veins, causing them to form icy rivers along her arms. She clutched them to herself in an effort to ward away a chill that could not be cured with warmth. "Well, nothing, really. I don't think." She glanced at the stairs. "At least, I hope not." Would the people revolt against Sibby's will?

Demand she and Lee be tossed out?

Basil crossed her arms. "See? Nobody wants to tell me nothin'."

Despite herself, Ella chuckled. "There now. Don't get yourself in a dither." She patted the girl's thin shoulder. "Sibby will be down soon enough and tell it all."

Basil eyed her. "Got something to do with you, don't it?"

"It does."

"You's right pretty, you know that?"

Startled, Ella looked back at the girl. What an odd thing to say. She didn't have opportunity to refute the flattery, however, because Nat made the turn on the landing and headed right for them. He scowled at Ella and then turned his eyes to Basil. "You better get on down them stairs."

"But I was talkin'—"

"I said go!"

Basil shot Ella an apologetic look. "Just 'cause you is my brother don't mean…"

Ella missed the remainder of the words Basil grumbled as she descended the stairs. Feeling Nat's eyes boring into her, she tried to offer a friendly smile.

"Here's yo stuff." He tossed the bag to her, and it landed on her foot.

Determined not to wince, she kept her features even. "I thank you."

His eyes drifted down her form. "I don't like this."

Ella remained still, unsure how to respond.

"We all respect Sibby, as is her due. If she says you is going to stay, then that's what it'll be." He took a step closer, the combination of his large form and her short one caused Ella to have to tilt her head back to keep her eyes on his face.

She wondered about the woman who seemed to be in control here. She was much too young. But then, perhaps Ella was just more of a girl and less of a woman than she should be.

"If you go and give her any grief…"

"Nat!"

Ella jumped. Sibby stood in the doorway, a thin blanket draped over her shoulders and hiding the front of her dress, likely concealing the baby who still suckled.

"You make me get up from feeding this here child to come out here to scold you? A boy so close to being a man that he should know better?"

Nat cringed. "Sorry, Sibby. I didn't mean to bother you."

"Humph. You leave her alone."

He cast Ella one more scathing look and hurried down the stairs before Sibby could scold him further. Sibby rolled her eyes. "That boy means well. He's only lookin' out for me."

Ella offered a faltering smile. "That's good he cares for you." She was tempted to ask more into their relationship but decided against it. It was none of her business. She would not look into matters that did not directly affect the care of her child.

Sibby looked at her strangely a moment, then gestured at the bag at Ella's feet. "You got something else in there to wear?"

She scooped up the bag. "Yes."

"Then you come on in here. Mrs. Remington's room will be yours now. You go on and get changed. When I finish with the boy, I's going down to talk to my people."

Ella opened her mouth to ask if Sibby would be passing through the room while she changed, but she answered the question before Ella had the chance to speak it.

"And don't worry 'bout you being seen. There's a door that leads out of the nursery to the back porch. I'll go round that way."

Ella released a breath and followed Sibby back into the rose room, closing the door to the nursery after she passed through with Lee. Clutching the valise tightly, Ella stared at the room through the tears that pricked her eyes. Such finery. How had she gone from sleeping on the storeroom floor to an entire room of her own? Even at home, she'd slept in the open loft over the common room, the house's only private bedroom having been reserved for her parents.

Shaking away her disbelief, Ella tossed the valise onto the tall bed and opened it. She plucked out her spare dress, a faded yellow frock that carried the stains of too much kitchen grease. She'd tried washing it until the fabric had begun to thin, but still the stains remained.

She dug deeper, feeling a bit of smooth material underneath her fingers. She smiled. Perhaps she would find something fine enough for a lady to wear. Well, at least for a *pretend* lady.

She grasped the material and lifted it free. Silk the deep red color of wine shimmered in the waning sunlight filtering through the window. It might clash with the color of her hair, but that didn't matter.

She stripped down to her chemise, pulled a fresh set of stays around her, and then slipped the gown over her head. It fit almost perfectly. The tasseled hem pooled a bit around her feet, but if she managed to find some crinoline or a decent petticoat, then it should just brush the floor. She ran her hand up the smooth material of the bodice and paused.

A mirror. She needed a mirror. Near the window sat a dressing table, and atop it, a silvery looking glass. Ella hurried to it, her skirt making an odd swishing sound.

The reflection that met her eyes caused her cheeks to warm. Well, what did she expect to find in Cynthia's valise? Ella placed her hand at the base of her throat. An entire hand's width and still skin to spare before the top of the bodice.

The gown scooped low, so far down that her rounded bits of femininity were poking over the edge. Not to mention the exposure of her shoulders and the top part of her arms. Ella groaned. The rest of the bodice fit fine, though she suspected it had hugged to Cynthia tighter than it did her.

Ella clicked her tongue. Why did Cynthia have this dress with her anyway? Did she expect to get back into it after having the child? Pushing those thoughts aside, Ella examined the rest of the gown, trying to decide if the trollop's dress or the scullery maid's frock would cause her more harm.

Finally, she wrinkled her nose and reached behind her and started fumbling with buttons. As pretty as the silk was, it would not do. Better a maid than a tart. If they hadn't stopped midway up her back, she wouldn't have been able to get to them. Ella made a face. She must have been too enamored with the fabric to notice that part of the dress was missing.

A knock at the door stilled her trembling fingers.

"You done yet? We is waiting on you."

How much time had passed? "I…um…well…"

The door swung open, and Sibby's pointing finger dropped to her side. "Oh!"

The heat climbed from Ella's exposed throat all the way to her ears. She crossed her arms over her chest.

Sibby narrowed her gaze. "I thought you wasn't that type."

Ella looked at the gathered folds of the shimmering skirt. "I'm not. This belonged to Lee's mother. I didn't know…"

Sibby sighed loudly enough to pull Ella's gaze back to her creased face. "Now, look here. I might can get that dress turned into something respectable, but I ain't got the time now." She crossed over to the bed and began plucking through Ella's things with no regard for privacy. "What else you got?"

Tamping down her frustration and embarrassment, Ella joined her and lifted the yellow dress. "Just this and what I came in."

Sibby wrinkled her nose and dug into the bag, pulling out a

deep-blue gown. She'd barely lifted it before dropping it back to the coverlet. "This 'un is worse than what you got on."

Ella pressed her lips into a line.

Sibby bustled to the wardrobe. "No matter. The missus was bigger than you, but I bet she's got somethin'..." Her voice trailed off. "Here!"

She pulled out a black paletot and held it up.

"A winter coat? But it's far too warm."

Sibby leveled a sour gaze at her. "Then you sweat. If this is gonna work, then you can't go looking like some wench...or a trollop."

Ella accepted the woolen coat that buttoned all the way to her neck. She was covered, but her attire seemed odd, and, therefore, suspicious.

"Now. Let's get moving."

She nearly refused, but what was a little embarrassment in order to secure a home for her little Lee? It wasn't the first time people of any class or color had looked down upon her, and she doubted it would be the last. Let them think what they would. Lee would ever be worth the scorn heaped upon her. Drawing a breath to bolster her confidence, Ella embraced her new life as a deceiver.

Chapter Seven

$\mathcal{W}$estley ground his teeth against the pain and attempted once again to stand. Mrs. Preston clicked her tongue at him, but he ignored her just the same as he had the two days past when she had tried to gainsay him. The week he'd spent awake had brought him strength—and restlessness. He ached to be free of the bed. And the leg would hold him, if for no other reason than his relentless determination.

"You have to give it time to heal, Major." Her voice carried equal notes of pleading and chiding.

This he knew, and yet he grew ever agitated by the time it took to do so. Weeks had passed since the battle, weeks his leg should have healed more than it had. No, what caused this weakness was naught more than continued laziness. To gain strength, he would have to demand it of himself and force his body to cooperate with his wishes.

"You will gain your feet once more, but you must give it time."

Westley grunted a reply as he feared opening his mouth for a proper response would release a dishonorable yowl instead. Perhaps if he put only a portion of his weight…

The swish of her skirts across the floor signaled that Mrs. Preston had moved from her place at the hearth to come near, even though she had promised him space mere moments earlier. She would give him no peace about it.

An idea struck him, and Westley drew a breath before tugging up the corners of his lips. "I thought perhaps the bedding could be cleaned…?"

Mrs. Preston came around the bed and scratched at the white cap holding down her gray curls. "Well, now, I suppose that could be a good thing."

Feeling triumph rise, Westley once again shifted weight toward the farthest edge of the bed. The straw mattress could use a good fluffing, and the ropes underneath had begun to sag. He placed his feet flat upon a woven rug. Positioning himself so that the bulk of his weight went to the right leg, he managed to rise and straighten his back.

To be free of that accursed bed! Even if he gained freedom for only a moment, he would count it a victory won. Westley began to smile in earnest, until he felt himself start to sway.

Mrs. Preston yelped, and in an instant her stocky frame took up residence under his right arm. "Whoa there." I think you press the matter too hard, Major. The bedding can wait."

Westley groaned. "It could use fluffing and tightening, too."

His nurse stiffened. "Well, I've hardly had the opportunity to…" She pointed her finger at him. "Oh, no you don't. I won't be goaded by you, boy."

Boy? A career soldier and at the age of twenty and six years, Westley could hardly be called a boy. But he did not refute her and would allow her to mother him…to a point. He shifted tactics. "Please, might I at least find my rest in a chair? If I do not get out of that bed soon, it will not only be my leg that ails me."

His chest tightened and he tried to bury the fear that surged. Each day he had noticed that small things escaped him. Words he could not find upon his tongue, names and places he should know but did not. Perhaps it was superstition alone, but he couldn't help but feel the longer he wallowed upon the bed, the more his mind slipped away from him.

Mrs. Preston clicked her tongue at him again, but then her shoulders slumped. "The doctor says we cannot know if you sustained any injury to your head, even though we found no evidence of such. And, too, it could come from the fever or the lack of sustenance. But worry not, that too shall heal given the proper time."

Annoyed at being so easily read, Westley tried to turn the conversation back to whence it had strayed. "The chair?"

Mrs. Preston waved her hand. "Very well. If it will ease this tension about you, then I will fetch the armchair and put it at the hearth." She tilted her head to eye him from where she remained underneath his arm like a crutch. "But you will wait in the bed until I return with it, and you will allow me to assist you to the chair. If I find you have attempted to cross this room in my absence…"

Westley nearly chuckled. "I shall not test your patience, ma'am."

She slipped from beneath him and gripped his arm as he lowered himself to the bed, pretending that even so short a stand had not nearly exhausted him. Curse this weakness.

Mrs. Preston evaluated him with keen eyes, then gave a curt nod. "You will wait."

Westley stared at her.

She arched her eyebrows. "I'll hear you say it."

He unlocked his jaw enough to allow, "I'll wait."

Satisfied, she swept from the room in an abundance of plaid skirts. Alone, his shoulders sagged. To be reduced to such a state soured him—wasting away here as the lone patient when the rest of the men had returned to their units. He should be mounted on…

His thoughts stumbled. What was that horse's name? Panic began to flutter in his chest, but he squelched it as he had been trained to do. West Point taught him that fear only caused a man to be blind.

He focused his thoughts on the horse once more. All he must do is concentrate. A prized stallion of good Kentucky stock. Yes, he remembered that. Black as coal with not the first speck of white to mar him. A beautiful creature he had called...what?

A scraping sound drew him from his thoughts and turned his attention to the door. More scraping. Then a grunt. What in the heavens...?

Westley pushed his toes to the floor and almost attempted to gain his feet when he remembered his invalidity. "Mrs. Preston? Are you in need of assistance?"

Some muttering, and then she poked her head through the door. "You, sir, can offer none, and as there are no others about, the task falls to me."

Westley frowned. "Forgive me. I did not think through the predicament I asked of you." He indicated the slatted chair near the bed where she had oft sat to feed him or watch him eat. "This one will suffice."

A smile bunched her rounded cheeks. "Nonsense. Besides, I've already made it this far. It is closer to the hearth here than back to the living quarters."

Finding no choice but to remain seated while the woman struggled to shove a worn leather armchair through the door, Westley battled with his loathing for his condition. But there was naught to be done for it than to rest and to ask of his body only what it was yet willing to give.

Finally, the struggle ceased with the proper positioning of his new place of confinement, and Mrs. Preston ran a hand over her brow with satisfaction. "There. Now you can rest here by the hearth, and I will fetch you something to read. That will lift your spirits, yes?"

So much hope laced her words that Westley couldn't help

but smile. Where would he be without this woman's kindness? He owed her more than his bitterness. "Indeed, that would lift them considerably."

She brushed off her apron. "Good, then." She eyed him. "Well, let us see how well we can manage you on one leg."

The task proved more strenuous than he cared to admit, and the amount of weight he was forced to lean upon the woman frustrated him further, but at long last they had scooted, hobbled, and hopped their way across the floor and eased him into the welcoming embrace of the well-used chair.

Mrs. Preston blew air up her face, stirring a lock of hair that had come free. "Good thing I'm no flimsy girl, else I never would have gotten the bulk of you more than a step or two."

Westley cocked his head. "Pardon?"

A sad smile bowed her lips. "When I was young, I lamented that I was stockier than the other girls. Where they were fine-boned and small, I had no trouble besting my brothers at wrestling."

Surprised by the thought of Mrs. Preston tumbling about in the dirt, Westley felt himself grin enough to use muscles that had not been stretched in some time. "Truly?"

"Most certainly." She bobbed her head. "But my pa always said my build was a good thing. Said that a farm woman should be of hearty stock, not some wispy thing that couldn't help pull a calf or hoe a garden."

Westley had never given much thought to such things. His family owned two thousand acres of farmland on the banks of the Mississippi, but his mother had been a well-bred lady who never would have put her fingers in the dirt, let alone assist in the birthing of livestock.

"Still, I wished for a more feminine form."

Westley thought that her late husband must have found her pleasing enough to wed, but thankfully arrested the thought err it could leave his mouth. The high society types were not the only ones to wed out of benefit rather than affection. Had that been the case for her, he would not add to her pain by making her voice such aloud.

"Oh, don't look so pitying on me, boy!"

Once more alarmed that his features were easily read, Westley frowned, which gained nothing more than a chuckle from Mrs. Preston.

"In time I learned God always knows what is best. My Henry was a bear of a man, all brawn and muscle." She pointed a finger at him. "Bigger even than you."

She pushed the stray lock of hair back under her cap and fetched a blanket to spread over Westley's legs, though he wasn't cold. "If I had been one of those willowy girls," she continued, "I would not have been able to birth him seven hearty sons." A twinkle made her eyes sparkle as she stepped back from him. "Nor carry heavy furniture for an arrestingly handsome man who has taken up residence in my home."

Westley gaped, which only caused her to bark out a hearty laugh. "Come now. I cannot be the first to make mention of your looks. The girls must ache to touch that dark hair of yours or run a hand over such a stony jaw."

As his discomfort grew, Mrs. Preston seemed to enjoy herself even more. "One such as you must have a lady pining for you at home, no?"

Her question sucked away all the mirth that had risen within him. He turned his gaze to the ashes in the hearth. "No one waits for me, nor should they."

His words were gruffer than he intended, and she fell silent for a moment. "Forgive me, I spoke without thought."

Feeling like a rapscallion, he released the air from his lungs. "Nothing to forgive. You have shown me nothing but kindness." Westley shoved aside the darkness that threatened to claw its way within and forced a smile. "You mentioned something to read…?"

She offered up an apologetic smile and left him alone once more. Westley ran a hand over his face. He would not allow himself to succumb to pity—be it from himself or another. He must formulate a tactic to bend his body to his will and regain his place in the world. He needed to be ready to ride again soon.

If I ever ride again.

Westley set his jaw against the loathsome thought. He would heal. He *must* heal. Resigned that he must ask no more of his body than it could bear, he determined to work toward his strength but not undo his healing in the process. With Mrs. Preston's good care, he would be on his feet soon enough.

But what then? With the war all but over and him injured, would the army release him? If it did, where would he go? He'd spoken true words to Mrs. Preston—No one waited for him back home in lands that knew him as a traitor. It would do him no good to return there. He should simply leave it and start life anew. In the West, perhaps? The army could surely spare him there.

Westley nearly groaned. He should not abdicate his family lands. Father would have been disappointed that even now Westley was a traitor who sought to shirk his responsibilities to his family and his plantation.

But his parents were dead. He could no longer disappoint them. He alone would have to live with the decision to abandon the estate.

Perhaps he could petition the army to send him to join Federal forces near Belmont. They would surely take up residence in the South for a time to ensure the Southerners did not attempt further rebellion. It might afford him the option to hold his property and serve simultaneously. But would he want to? He didn't know if he could face friends and neighbors who had fought on the other side of the war and every day bear their hatred of him—he who had been born a Southerner yet had served in the Federal Army. Even the men in his ranks had shown distrust of him—for no other reason than the accent that marked him as Southern. For that, Westley set himself to removing the traces of it from his speech. Within the first year of the war, no one guessed he hailed from south of the line, and by the second, those who had known it seemed to have forgotten.

The muscle in his jaw ticked, and Westley rested his head against the back of the chair. As his father and grandfather before him, he wanted to make a name for himself in the military. Soon he would be able to leave here, and when he did, he would rid himself of the lands that no longer held anything for him.

Satisfied that it would be a good plan, Westley allowed himself to relax and think through his course of action. Moments later, footsteps at the door alerted him to Mrs. Preston's return, but he kept his eyes on the rafters above.

"Here," she said, thrusting a thick volume at him. "I believe you were right. Reading is just exactly what you need."

Westley accepted the book without glancing at it. "I thank you."

"I've marked a place for you." Without awaiting his response, she patted his shoulder and scurried from the room, no doubt heading to bake something or other.

When she had closed the door on his solitude, Westley looked down at the book in his lap and groaned. Then he tossed the Bible on the floor and stared at the hearth's ashes once more.

Chapter Eight

Ella pulled the curtain aside and watched horses plod toward the house, the carriage behind them ambling slowly. Each pounding of the hooves, though barely heard, sent shudders through her heart. One week. Not nearly enough time to learn all that she must know in order to be a lady. Sibby had altered the two dresses from Cynthia's valise, and the woman had worked a miracle to fashion an appropriate dress out of the blue gown.

Ella glanced down at the smooth sapphire silk with bits of white lace donning her tea bodice. She looked a bit more respectable, but still...

"Get away from that window. You want them to see you watchin' for 'em?"

Ella's breath caught and she dropped the lace curtain, returning it to its place to keep the insects from freely flitting through the open window. "Is that bad?"

Sibby groaned. "I's never gonna make a lady out of you."

Ella ignored the comment and took Lee, smiling as he made little cooing sounds. "I don't see why you let them come anyway." And without her consent, no less. "You know I'm not ready."

"Too much talk." Sibby straightened the starched apron around her waist. "We can't keep nosey neighbors away for too long without them gettin' suspicious."

"I've just had a baby. Certainly that warrants more than a week's reprieve?"

"Hmm." Sibby scrunched her nose. "You's right about that."

Ella's heart quickened, and a smile of triumph nearly bowed her lips.

"We'll have to say he's about three weeks, then."

Ella's hope shriveled.

"That gives you the time." Sibby gave a matter of fact nod that Ella had come to recognize meant the woman had said her piece and expected no arguments. "See? I done thought of everythin'."

Ella bit back her retort. In the one week she had made this her home, there had been several rules pressed upon her. Primarily that Sibby was in charge. Like nothing more than a convenient marionette, Ella did as instructed while Sibby pulled the strings. She tried not to let resentment take hold. Had she not been under the same control at the Buckhorn Inn? At least here she got to wear nice things and sleep in a comfortable bed.

"I fed him and then he had his nap, so he should be content," Sibby said, pulling Ella from her thoughts. "Nat brought down the rocking cradle, so you can lay him down and rock it with your foot. If he gets fussy, I'll take him."

Ella bobbed her head to each instruction, focusing on the little face that depended on her to pretend to be what she was not. A life as a marionette would be worth it if he could grow up secure.

"Now, you remember the story you's supposed to tell?"

A knock pounded on the door, startling them both. Had anyone on the porch caught their words through the open window? "Yes," she whispered, moving toward the entry. Sibby would open the door, but she would be there to greet the guests, just as instructed.

Sibby offered what Ella assumed to be a reassuring smile and went to answer the door. Ella positioned herself in the doorway to the ladies' parlor, bouncing Lee and hoping that these neighbors would neither stay long nor ask too many questions.

"Good afternoon, Mrs. Martin, Miss Martin. Right good to see both you ladies back out at Belmont."

The two women fluttered in like a flock of plumed birds, neither of them acknowledging Sibby. The older of the two, a tall, gaunt woman wearing a dress so deep navy it bordered on black, plucked gloves from her long fingers and thrust them at Sibby, oblivious to Sibby's glower.

The younger of the two turned light brown eyes on Ella, the look on her face indicating she expected something. Ella smothered her fear and focused on her role. Stepping forward, she plastered a friendly smile on lips that preferred to stay closed and spoke words she'd practiced earlier this morning.

"Hello, ladies. I am Mrs. Westley Remington, and this is my son, young Master Westley the fourth."

The younger woman glided across the floor in that practiced gait ladies had and peered down at Lee. "Oh, what a sweet little thing! Isn't he just precious, Mama?"

The other woman sniffed, and the younger one's eyes widened. She took a small step back. "Pardon me, Mrs. Remington. I forgot myself." Her fingers pressed into her yellow dress as though she consciously restrained them from reaching for the baby.

The other moved closer. "Yes, do forgive my daughter's manners. I am Mrs. Ida Martin of Riverbend. May I present my daughter, Miss Opal Martin."

Miss Martin inclined her head.

"I am pleased to make your acquaintance, ladies." Ella spoke the rehearsed line expected of her...merely stiff words for stiff people. "If you will join me in the parlor, tea will be served soon."

The women sashayed forward, and Ella looked for approval from Sibby, but the woman had slipped away. They took places in the parlor, and Ella settled on the settee with Lee crooked in her arm.

"My, but you sure did make it out of the war unscathed." Mrs. Martin's clipped words startled Ella and caused her composure to falter.

Unscathed? Something fierce shuttered in Ella's chest. *Hardly!* She'd lost her home, her possessions, and her dignity. She'd been reduced to… The thoughts tumbled to a halt. No. *Ella* had lost those things. Mrs. Remington had not. Hoping the heat she felt in her chest had not manifested itself on her face, Ella forced her voice to remain pleasant. "I do not think, Mrs. Martin, that any person in this nation escaped such a horrible war unscathed."

Miss Martin's gaze traveled over the fine rugs, polished furniture, and paintings hanging on the fabric-lined walls, and confusion puckered her smooth brow. Understanding bloomed and Ella hurried on. "But if you are referring to the furnishings, then, yes, we were quite blessed."

Mrs. Martin tipped up her chin. "I doubt that is the proper term for it."

Unsure how to respond, Ella looked to the younger woman, who appeared to be of a more pleasant disposition. Miss Martin smiled. "I'm sure my mother is merely wondering how you managed to retain all of your belongings when the rest of us were relieved of all of our things, leaving our homes nearly bare."

Mrs. Martin scoffed. "I do not wonder, dear. Such a thing is quite obvious."

Ella's pulse quickened. She'd been prepared to act as a Yankee, but now with such distrust and scorn laid bare before her, she wondered if she were truly up to the task. "I am quite sorry for your loss, ladies."

"As well you should be." Mrs. Martin tilted her chin even higher. So much so, in fact, that she began to look down her nose. "The things you Blue Bellies did were deplorable."

"I couldn't agree more." The words slipped from Ella's lips, embers of truth flung free of the fire hidden within.

Both women's mouths gaped, and Ella momentarily felt a surge of satisfaction. It was squelched, however, by Miss Martin's wide-eyed question.

"Are you not a Yankee like your husband?"

In a momentary decision, Ella reasoned the fewer lies she needed to tell, the easier it would be to keep her tales straight. Sibby would have to understand. "Not as you might think."

Intrigued, both women leaned forward. Miss Martin's pink lips turned up into a smile while her mother's drifted toward a frown.

At that moment Sibby bustled into the room carrying a tea tray and refreshments. She placed the set on the table and stood, eyeing the three women. Had she heard Ella's comment?

"Thank you, Sibby." Ella waved her hand. "That will be all. I will serve my guests."

Anger contorted the freedwoman's face, and Ella knew she would hear plenty about the flippant dismissal later. But if Sibby wanted her to act like a lady in front of neighbors, then that's what she would do.

Mrs. Martin nodded her approval, and Ella decided her action had been prudent. She'd been the object of such arrogant disregard often enough to know that any true lady would behave such.

Sibby stalked from the room, making her displeasure known to all, and then pulled the door closed with a resounding click.

The other two women averted their gaze from Ella, certainly to give her a moment to compose herself after such blatant disrespect from a servant. Ella didn't know whether to be angry or amused.

Since the sooner she served the tea the sooner she could see the guests to the door, Ella placed the sleeping baby into the rocking cradle and began pouring tea for the other women. Once they had full cups and their choice of sugar and cream, Ella served herself.

"Well, I must say, it is good to see that you have control of the slaves." Mrs. Martin's reedy voice distracted Ella from her recollection of how to hold the tiny cup properly. "The elder Mrs. Remington was far too lax with them."

"We have no slaves here." Ella balanced the delicate cup on her saucer. "All of the servants are free, as is the law."

A sly smile curved Mrs. Martin's thin lips. "Certainly. As is the case at Riverbend."

Ella suspected she missed something pertinent in the words but let them slide.

"What were you saying about loyalties, Mrs. Remington?" Miss Martin asked as she tucked a warm brown lock into her chignon.

Not certain if the turn of subject back to their earlier curiosity over her allegiances was more or less dangerous than the talk of slaves, Ella picked her words carefully. "When the war began, it is true that I agreed with keeping the country intact."

Mrs. Martin turned up her nose, indicating she had thought as much.

Ella tamped down her frustration. "However, as the war progressed, I became increasingly displeased with the Federal tactics used against our lands."

Silence settled as the neighbors studied her, but Ella forced herself to remain confident under their scrutiny. Just when she began to fear they would call her out as a liar, both women gave a solemn nod.

"Atrocities," Miss Martin whispered.

"Yes," Ella agreed. Nothing more needed to be stated, as everyone knew the terror slathered upon the South, and such things need not be named in good company.

After several moments of strained silence, Mrs. Martin finally spoke. "So you then changed your loyalties?" She took a sip from her cup, and the neighborly charade continued.

"In a manner of speaking," Ella hedged.

"You certainly must have enamored Mr. Remington," Miss Martin quipped as she plucked a small tart from the tray. "I cannot imagine he married anyone with Southern sympathies, as devout as he was to the Northern invasion."

Mrs. Martin bobbed her head. "Indeed."

Sensing her mistake, Ella gave herself a moment to think under the guise of taking a small bite from a tiny shortbread.

As though remembering something important, Miss Martin glanced up sharply. "We are, of course, quite sorry for your loss."

"I thank you."

Her pink lips turned up, giving light to a pretty, refined face. "You must have loved him quite dearly to overcome such differences."

Having been provided a way out of her misstep, Ella tried her hand at a mournful smile. "You are quite right. We married in a flurry of emotions, such as can happen when one wonders if they will have many more days upon the earth."

Mrs. Martin narrowed her eyes, and once more Ella realized she had opened a door that would require further explanation, so she hurried on. "However, if you do not find it too terribly ill-mannered of me, such wounds are a bit too fresh to discuss at the moment."

Miss Martin's eyes swam with compassion, and Ella

couldn't help but like her. "You are right, of course." She offered an apologetic smile. "We shouldn't allow our curiosity to infringe upon your mourning."

"Though without you donning widow's blacks, we can understandably be forgiven." Mrs. Martin glanced down Ella's dress with disapproval.

Having been prepared for this particular question, Ella waved her hand airily. "Of course. I do hope you will forgive me, but I have just now allowed my maid to begin fashioning a widow's dress. What with the baby and all, I wanted to wait for proper measurements."

Mrs. Martin opened her mouth to reply, but Ella silenced her with soft-spoken words. "And, I too long held out hope he would return." She put a hitch in her voice. "Although it has now become painfully clear such hopes are not to be realized."

The older woman, having enough manners to withdraw her criticism, gave a small sigh. "Oh, of course, my dear Mrs. Remington. We are quite sorry for your pain. It is a bitter taste all of us have been forced to partake of late."

Lee squirmed in the cradle, his soft coos drawing their attention. Grateful for a distraction as much as the comfort of him, Ella scooped him up and positioned him in the crook of her arm.

Miss Martin leaned a bit closer, her desire to see the child evident. Ella smiled. "Would you care to hold him, Miss Martin?"

"Please, you must call me Opal." She reached for Lee. "We are neighbors, after all, and I am sure we will be the best of friends."

Something fluttered inside Ella at the thought of someone wishing to be her friend, but she pushed it aside. The woman, who looked to be merely a few years shy of her own age, surely only spoke the words out of good manners. Experience had taught Ella that fine ladies often said things in the name of propriety they didn't truly mean. For some reason, none of them thought to name such things *lying*.

"Of course, Opal." Ella handed over her child. "And please do call me Eleanor, as I do so look forward to our getting to know one another better."

Eleanor, not Ella. She still regretted letting Sibby in on her shortened name. Though she'd never been ashamed of it before, in this peculiar circumstance it somehow made her feel less like she belonged than did *Eleanor*.

"A fine child, Mrs. Remington." Opal stroked his tiny hand. "How old is he?"

"He is just over three weeks old," Ella said, remembering Sibby's instructions.

"That old already?" Mrs. Martin scoffed. "Why, he hardly looks it."

Ella lifted her shoulders, not sure what explanation she could give. The woman couldn't possibly be able to tell the child's age with such precision, could she? Ella didn't know, so she thought it best to keep quiet.

"And, my, I would have thought we would have seen you arrive some time ago." Mrs. Martin tapped her chin as though she'd just thought of it, but Ella suspected she'd been waiting for the opportunity to voice such things. "Surely you did not travel during the final months of your expectancy…?"

Ella's heart began to hammer. "Well, I…"

Just then the door swung open, pulling everyone's attention to Sibby, whom Ella assumed had been listening from the entry. "Excuse me, ladies," Sibby said. "But I has got to speak to the missus."

Mrs. Martin sniffed. "As you can see, she is indisposed."

Ella pressed her lips into a line. Did she agree with her guest or with Sibby? Thankfully, Lee chose that moment to let out a high-pitched wail.

"Oh!" Opal said, stretching the child out to Ella. "I am afraid he has become unsettled."

"I shall take him." Ella scooped up the boy and stood. "Ladies, I must beg your forgiveness." Lee began to cry in earnest and she started to bounce him, raising her voice to be heard. "But I must tend to him, and I find I am quite tired. Please, may we schedule another visit when perhaps I am more recovered?"

Mrs. Martin slowly gained her feet, every movement about her refined and polished. Lee increased his volume, his sweet little face turning an angry red. Ella bit her lower lip. Goodness he had grown upset quickly! Ella glanced at Sibby, who gave a slight shake of her head. Ella should not relinquish him so he might eat? Ah, no, then she would be free to visit.

"Shush, my darling. Just a moment," Ella said, stepping toward the door. "Ladies, I have so enjoyed the visit, but fear my son will no longer wait."

"Oh, we do understand." Opal stood beside her mother. "Don't we, Mama?"

The other woman nodded, though she didn't look convinced.

Lee's cries grew fierce, so Ella hurried to the door, calling over her shoulder, "Sibby will see you out. Another time, ladies. Thank you again for calling."

The two stared after her as she scurried from the room in a gait that neither glided nor seemed lady-like, but that all the faster saw Ella away from their stares. As she found the solitude of her chamber above, a breath of relief went from her. "There now, Lee. That wasn't so bad, now was it?"

The poor child gulped air, his cries having been ignored long enough that he punctuated them with hiccupping sounds. "Oh, darling. I'm so sorry." Had he been born of her own body, she would be equipped to care for him without depending on another.

She rocked him in her arms as best she could as he continued to cry, her heart pierced by her inability to soothe him. Finally, footsteps sounded on the stairs and Sibby appeared, scooping the child away without a word and disappearing into the nursery. After a moment, Lee's screams quieted. Ella wrapped her arms around herself, wishing that she were the one he depended on.

Sibby had the milk he needed, and he would likely attach to her even more than he did to Ella. She tried not to entertain thoughts that roused irrational jealousy and strove to bury them under logic. If Sibby did not have milk for him, he could have starved. How selfish of her to wish she didn't need Sibby's help.

A new thought surfaced, and Ella wondered what had happened to Sibby's own child. She must have had one, otherwise she would not have milk to offer other children.

But she would have to ponder that another time. For now, the strain of strangers, falsehoods, and Lee's cries had wearied her in a way that concerned soul rather than body.

She paced the room, but that only furthered the unease building in her chest until it bloomed into a need to escape…to find freedom outside of the confinement of the house.

Deciding she could use time to herself, and needing to put off Sibby's scolding for later when she might be better prepared to take it, Ella slipped quietly from the room. Her feet felt heavy upon the stairs. She trudged down to the first floor then pulled open the rear door, allowing fresh air to stir the hair about her face. Ella drew a deep breath and exited the house, stepping onto the long porch that stretched across both wings of Belmont.

A few moments only, she told herself as she rounded the cistern. *Yes, surely a few moments would be fine*, she reasoned as she passed the smokehouse. Then her fingers lifted the edges of her skirt and she began to venture out past the edges of the yard.

Chapter Nine

"I grow weary of soup, woman," Westley said, the growl in his voice matching the one roused by his appetite. He'd eaten two bowls today already, and still they did not satisfy his stomach.

"Hmm." Mrs. Preston bobbed her head, once again not taking offense to Westley's mood. "I suppose your body is sucking it up too fast. I'll cook up one of the chickens for dinner and get some more meat in you."

His stomach rumbled again. "And until then?"

She laughed. "Men sure grow ornery when they're hungry."

Westley gave her a flat stare.

"Fine, fine. I've some bread fresh from the oven." She straightened the coverlet over him. "You stay here, and I will fetch it with a bit of cheese."

Westley narrowed his eyes. "And if I would rise?"

Mrs. Preston made a show of an exaggerated sigh. "Then I suppose your refreshment would have to wait while I made sure you could make it across the room."

Beaten, Westley leaned back against the pillows. "Very well. After, then."

Mrs. Preston crossed her arms. "You are a stubborn fellow, you know it?"

Amusement lifted his lips. "I've been informed of it a time or two."

"Humph."

She left him in peace, and as soon as her ample form no

longer warmed the room, he fell back into that worrisome place of self-loathing. Try as he might to shake the feeling, it ever more pressed upon him.

What has happened to me? Is there no way to be rid of these dark thoughts?

His gaze drifted to the book on the small table next to the chair at the hearth, and he heard his mother's voice as clearly as if she stood in the room with him. *The word of the Lord offers both instruction and comfort, my son.*

Westley turned his face aside. No. He would not entertain voices that did not emanate from living people. First the misplaced memories, then names and faces he could not recall, and now this? If he allowed such, he would most surely descend into madness. Mrs. Preston had said she'd seen men who'd suffered the fever show mental slowness, but none that lingered this long.

She'd assured him this too would pass, but he'd seen the concern in her eyes. The infection had raged within him, and he had spent three weeks hardly waking enough for her to get enough broth into him for survival. Who knew what damages he had sustained from that? What's more, they had no way of knowing if he had hit his head hard enough to cause lasting damage when he fell from his horse.

A few moments later Mrs. Preston returned with the promised plate of bread and cheese in her hands and a placating smile upon her lips. Telling himself she meant only the best, he brought his emotions to heel and offered her his best attempt at affability. "Ah, my dear nurse returns."

Her smile widened and she handed him the food.

"Where would I be without you?"

Her smile faltered and he cringed. He'd not meant the question in earnest, but rather as a form of affectionate gratitude for her care. She patted his arm, both of them knowing the real answer, yet neither wanting to upset the other by speaking it.

Westley shoved a slice of bread into his mouth and spoke around it. "When will the corporal arrive?"

"*Tsk tsk.*" She shook her head. "Have you abandoned your manners, Major?"

Westley grimaced, swallowed, and spoke again. "Forgive me. May I inquire as to when the corporal is expected?"

Mrs. Preston smirked and set about dusting the room. "They said soon. That is all I know."

"And you are sure they knew my name and rank?" Westley popped a piece of cheese into his mouth and consciously slowed chewing lest he reveal his ravenous hunger.

"I am." She lifted the Bible Westley hadn't touched since he'd tossed it to the floor and wiped it off.

"And they know I have been injured and am neither a deserter nor dead?"

She didn't pause her cleaning. "Yes, Major. The boy there told me word was already sent to family and to the necessary officials."

Westley snorted. "There is no family."

Mrs. Preston didn't respond, though she paused.

Feeling her heavy gaze upon him as he stabbed at a bit of cheese, Westley mumbled, "At best, they are sending a note to an abandoned house."

Mrs. Preston's brow creased. "You expect your home to be abandoned?"

Forgetting that he had not told her he hailed from the South, he shrugged. "Both my parents died this past winter, and I am their only child. It stands to reason."

Something close to pity entered her eyes, and he looked away before the weight of it could settle on him.

"It would be best to know for sure, though."

Westley considered it. If the army did send word to Belmont, only Sibby would be able to read it. Did she worry over him? He tossed aside the foolish thought. Once news of Jefferson Davis's recent surrender reached them, surely the Negroes that had called Belmont home would seek a new life in the North rather than face the scorn of defeated Southerners. Assuming they hadn't all left already since no one remained to care for them.

If he did return to his home, it would be only to see that any stragglers left. There might yet be a few, Sibby among them, who would hesitate to leave the only home they had ever known and attempt to eke out a living from the land.

That was something they would not be able to do for long, and an attempt that could prove dangerous. Freed or not, Westley wasn't fool enough to think they would be able to live at Belmont alone. If fortune seekers didn't run them out, then soon enough the Federal Army would commandeer the home to settle debts his father most surely owed. He'd been meaning to settle his father's accounts, but he'd been a mite too busy trying not to get shot.

"Some heavy thoughts pucker that handsome brow of yours."

Westley blinked and looked up at Mrs. Preston, whom he had forgotten stood in the room with him. "Just thinking about what I will need to do once I am strong enough to leave and deciding which responsibilities will require my immediate attention."

Sadness tightened her features for just an instant, then she brightened them with a smile. "That's good then. Making plans for the future will help you work toward healing." She crossed to the bed and plopped down beside him. "Tell me."

Westley withheld his lament at being drawn into yet another personal conversation. The woman had a way of working information from him, especially since he had no means of escape. But he owed her much and would not be rude to her. At least, as much as he could help it. "I think I may volunteer to go into the western territories."

Mrs. Preston's mouth turned down. "Oh, I had hoped you would have tired of the army."

"I am a career military man, ma'am."

Her eyes darted away, but not before he caught something in them. Instinct warned she hid something. "Mrs. Preston?"

She fiddled with her cap. "Of course, but—"

"What are you not saying?"

She stared at him a moment, then he felt her will give way to his own. "Well…" She fidgeted with her skirts, trying his patience. "I'd hoped you would be inclined to return to your home and be full up of this war. And then…"

"Then what?"

She drew her lip through her teeth. An oddly feminine motion, Westley decided, for one who often acted more akin to a man. "Then perhaps you would not be so bothered by your condition."

Westley straightened, fear he could not acknowledge stiffening his spine. "What say you?"

She fingered the frayed hem of her apron. "Well, nothing for certain, I think, but it's just that with your leg—"

"Which will heal."

She glanced away. "Not as well as we'd hoped."

His jaw tightened and he had to force his teeth to unclench to push out a nervous laugh. Surely she only worried for him. "Do not fret. I will see to it that I am well on my feet once more."

Mrs. Preston rose from the bed and twisted her hands. "I did not want to tell you just yet."

Westley growled. "Speak!"

She flinched, and he might have felt poorly for it if not that she withheld information from him.

She pinned him with a steady gaze. "The doctor thinks you will forever more walk with a limp."

Westley let the matter-of-fact words settle on him. Given without an ounce of pity, he deemed them truthful. He cleared his throat. "And when did you learn this?"

"Upon his visit two days past."

Westley exuded an outward calm that did not match the turmoil within. "He did not speak of it to me."

"He feared your emotional state."

Emotional! Westley snapped his jaws tight before words best not said escaped him. When he composed himself, he tried once more. "If you don't mind, Mrs. Preston, could you perhaps be a bit more specific?"

Understanding, then compassion, lit her warm eyes, and when she next spoke, her words were gentle. "What he referred to has nothing to do with your memory lapses, Major."

A comfort of sorts at least. "That is good." He'd thought the doctor meant to declare him unfit for duty and pronounce him soft in the head.

"But the doctor and I have both seen what injuries can do not only to the body but to the soul as well."

Not liking the turn of the conversation, Westley chose silence and stifled his impatience over the woman taking too long in coming around to the point.

"I've seen it time and again. Men who have lost their limbs enter into a place of sorrow they cannot easily be roused from. They become disinterested in their meals, they lose hope for the future, and soon they let themselves become hollow." She drew a long breath. "The doctor did not wish for any such despondent thoughts to affect your healing."

The doctor? More likely Mrs. Preston spoke her own concerns. Army doctors were nothing if not completely unconcerned with men's *feelings*.

She straightened her cap. "Therefore, we thought it best to wait to say anything about your leg until you had more time to heal."

Westley pressed the heels of his hands into his eyes. "There is still yet hope I shall fully recover," he said, more for his own benefit than to convince her.

"It pains me to tell you so, but the bone does not seem to have set straight."

Her meaning slithered to him, but he refused to let it sink its fangs just yet. "But I have both legs. I can still sit a horse."

She shook her head, becoming nearly as exasperated as he. "You will be whole, but for the rest of your days you will require a cane to walk." She stood firm before him, the compassion in her eyes warring with the harsh words that came from her tongue. "Therefore, I don't think it wise for you try to go to the western territories."

Westley forced strained words from his lips. "Leave me." He closed his eyes, hoping that sleep might overtake him and deliver him a momentary reprieve from this sentence of uselessness.

Instead of doing as he instructed, Mrs. Preston whispered something he couldn't decipher and then crossed to the hearth. A moment later a weight settled upon his lap. "Hope, dear boy." She squeezed his shoulder. "You will find it in there."

Westley cracked an eye only enough to peer at the heavy book in his lap. How he longed to throw it across the room. But knowing that she would persist unless he offered pretense of acquiescence, he fabricated a smile instead. "Very well, I shall try."

Mrs. Preston patted his arm. "There now, that's better."

When he didn't respond or make a move to open the book, she gave him a small squeeze and left him to his shadowed thoughts once more.

Chapter Ten

As Ella ventured farther from the house, a breeze picked up and ruffled strands of her hair that had escaped their pins. Sibby had tried to form some kind of fancy design of it, pinning some pieces and leaving others in little ringlets about her head. She'd found herself to be pleasantly presentable, if not even passably pretty. But now she wished she could let her hair down, constrained only in a long red plait that fell down her back.

She stepped over dried bits of cotton stalks, wondering why the land had not been furrowed and prepared for the planting. Already they were behind. These fields should have been put to seed. No wonder the Yanks had not believed her claims about working the land. No evidence gave validity to her words.

Ahead, a line of scraggly oaks broke the flat lines of the field, and Ella made her way there. She would like to see what lay beyond and perhaps get a better feel for this land she now called home. If she were to stay, she would need to figure something out soon. Sibby had resisted her requests to discuss planting the crops, though Ella couldn't fathom why. If the crops were planted and Sibby's people earned a share of it, that would satisfy the army and cover their needs. What could possibly cause the woman's hesitation?

She glanced back at the house. Sibby would be finished nursing Lee anytime now and would start to look for her. Always keeping her close. If not for the comfortable residence and care for Lee, Ella might have resented being watched so closely.

She slipped into the line of trees. A crack in the ground allowed for the passage of a small stream, and the struggling trees not plowed under for fields clung to the narrow banks. Ella studied the gap. It wasn't so wide that she couldn't jump it if she weren't wearing two petticoats and a hoop. Besides, if she were to tear the gown...

She glanced over her shoulder. Perhaps this would have to wait for another time. She doubted anything of interest stood beyond the abandoned fields anyway.

She'd just turned to make her way back when a noise arrested her attention. She stopped, straining to hear a soulful sound that drifted on the late afternoon breeze. A song she had never heard before slipped through the trees, its melody caressing each thing it passed. Mesmerized, Ella stood still and listened.

The sound grew nearer until its source became apparent. Ella drew a sharp breath and the singing abruptly stopped, replaced by a yelp.

"What you doin' in them woods?"

Embarrassed at having been caught in such an odd place, Ella forced a laugh. "Basil, you have such a beautiful voice. Why, you sing better than anyone I've ever heard."

The little girl's face brightened, but then she cast a worried glance over her shoulder. "You ain't supposed to be out here, Miss Ella."

"Why not?"

Basil glanced behind her again, confusion clouding her face. "Well, Nat said..."

"I don't intend any trouble, Basil. I'm merely curious about the land."

"Oh!" She smiled. "Well, I reckon that might be all right."

Ella looked past Basil. "Why are you out here in the field by yourself?"

She giggled. "Why, I ain't just wanderin' around in the field, Miss Ella. What sense do that make?"

Ella shrugged. She'd wondered the same.

"We live in them cabins back there."

Ella looked over the girl's head but could not see much. She squinted. "I see nothing out there other than some more fields...and then some more trees."

"Yes 'um. We lives behind that second row of trees." Basil bobbed her head, little braids bouncing.

"Really? Would you show me?"

Basil's brow furrowed. "What for?"

Ella glanced around and then leaned closer, feigning a conspirator's whisper—though she could be easily heard across the divide. "I'm afraid it is because I am incurably curious."

Basil laughed, the sound further lightening Ella's mood. Such a sweet girl. What must it be like to be so open and joyful?

"You sure is funny, Miss Ella."

"You'll show me then?"

Basil's smile fell. "No, ma'am. Can't do that. Nat done made me promise."

"But why?"

The girl drew her lips into a tight line.

Ella tried once more. "If I am going to stay here for a time, I only wanted to get to know the land and the people here. I don't mean any harm to anyone."

Basil shook her head. "Ain't that. You just don't belong there."

Well, no arguing that. Ella turned back to the house.

Leaves rustled behind her. "Sibby say you could come back here?" Basil called.

Ella's spine stiffened in defiance. "I do not need permission," she spat, a bit more harshly than intended. She looked over her shoulder to apologize and saw the girl take a mighty leap over the creek.

Basil landed on the other side, brushed her skirt off and straightened. If she'd taken offense of Ella's harsh words, she didn't show any indication.

"Do you always leap over the creek?"

Basil tilted her head. "How else is I supposed to get over it?"

Ella regarded her for a moment and then turned back toward the house once more. "How many people have to jump like that, Basil?"

The rustle of grass evidenced the girl followed closely behind. "Only those of us needin' to come on up to the big house."

Ella rolled her eyes. No information to be gained there. Ella had often wondered if the few people Sibby had gathered to see Ella on that first day were all the people who lived on Belmont lands. Judging from Basil's evasiveness, more probably resided here than she thought. However, there seemed nothing more she would learn from the child, and telling herself her curiosity remained pointless, Ella looked up at the porch.

Sibby stood with her arms crossed, staring.

Ella did not bother to quicken her strides. When she passed the cistern and stepped onto the porch, she eyed the other woman. "Where is Lee?"

"Sleeping."

"And who watches him?" Ella frowned, already stepping around Sibby to reach the door.

"I left the doors open. I can hear him if he cries."

Ella ignored her and started inside the house.

"Now, you look here. We got stuff we needs to talk about."

Ella set her jaw. "I do not feel like it now."

"You don't…" Sibby let the words trail off and followed her up the stairs. "What done got into you?"

Ella didn't know. All she knew is that she felt tired, alone, and flustered. She was frustrated with having to lie to women who looked down on her even though she wore fancy clothes and tried her best to fit in. Papa had been right. Never would she be good enough for the likes of them.

Ella slipped into her room and through to the nursery and spied Lee sleeping peacefully. Her heart lurched. She must remember to keep these emotions under control. Ever they sought to undo her, no matter how diligently she sought to control them with logic.

She turned to find Sibby staring at her from the doorway. "You all right?"

"I'm fine." She moved to slip past Sibby. "Now, if you don't mind, I should get out of this dress and get to work dusting the library."

"Humph. Done told you there ain't no need for you to be doin' all that."

Ella set her teeth but refused the temptation to send cutting words to Sibby. Heavens, what *had* gotten into her?

Sibby's voice softened. "I know them women can be tough."

Ella stilled. Feeling some of the fire go out of her, she dropped her chin. "You listened at the door."

"Yep." Sibby came around to stand in front of her. "Good thing, too, else you might've gotten you self into more of a mess."

Logic warned the words were true, even if her emotions demanded she defend herself. "I decided it best to have to lie as little as possible."

Sibby seemed to consider Ella's words, but then shook her head. "They was too suspicious."

"So?" Ella dug through the wardrobe for her work dress. "What does it matter? They can dislike me all they wish."

Sibby grunted. "And if they start talkin' to other folks, saying they don't believe you is Mr. Westley's wife?"

"Then they can talk."

Sibby groaned. "Give them soldiers *one* reason to make us get out and they is goin' to take it."

"On the gossiping words of women?" Ella flung the dress on the bed. "Pish."

"They take any excuse they get to take stuff from folks. Done seen it."

"Oh?" She lifted her eyebrows. "Is that so?"

"You think I's lyin'?"

"Well, one thing their suspicions are right about. This house didn't get razed. Why?"

Sibby threw a glance at the high ceiling. "They flew the United States flag and Mr. Westley was a Federal major."

"Hump." Ella crossed her arms. "Then they would have been looted by desperate Confederates."

"Flew Confederate, too."

Ella gaped at her. Impossible.

"Sure 'nough did." Sibby bobbed her head, once more speaking to Ella as though she were a child. "And folks round here knew why. They all respected Mr. Remington."

"Who would have been a traitor to *both* sides?"

"Who done loved his South *and* his son." She looked over Ella. "But if you asks me, I say it was all them prayers Mrs. Remington sent up. If ever a woman had hold of God's ear, was her."

Ella pondered the words and could find nothing to refute them. That both armies had left not only the house but all the contents alone was evidence enough that Sibby's words held true.

"Now. We need to talk about what you done said to them…"

Sibby's words trailed off with a loud knock to the door. Both women froze and stared at one another. The heavy knock sounded again, stirring them to action.

By the time they reached the front door, a third round of knocks made Ella's blood pound. Who could be so insistent at the door?

Sibby threw the door open. On the other side, a young man of no more years than Nat stood with his fist raised to pound once more. He lowered his arm to the side of his Yank uniform, then straightened himself.

"Good afternoon." His eyes darted past Sibby and landed on Ella, who was glad she still wore a lady's gown.

Ella tried to hold back her frustration. She'd *told* Sibby they needed a plan for the fields! And here the Yanks had come already, and she had nothing. She scrambled for any lie she could find as she stepped closer to the door but lost all her thoughts at the man's next words.

"I have come bearing a message that these lands are to be forfeited unless the taxes are paid in full."

Chapter Eleven

Westley stood by the hearth, dressed in a pair of faded trousers and a linen shirt provided to him by Mrs. Preston. Where she'd come by them, he didn't know, nor did he ask. Had he a cravat and vest, he might almost feel properly dressed. As it was, he would have to receive his company in naught but his shirtsleeves. But then, at least he wasn't in a nightshirt, still abed. His walking had improved to the point she allowed him to dress and move around the chamber.

A tap came at the door, and Westley gripped the top of his cane a bit tighter. "Enter!"

The doctor strode in, and on his heels followed a short, spindly man with an oversized mustache. The doctor, whom he had learned was a captain by the name of Albright, stroked his beard as he studied Westley.

"Well, I see you have gained your feet, Major Remington."

"Indeed, I have, Doctor." And soon he would be free of this cane as well.

"That is good." The look in his blue eyes stated he distrusted Westley's ability to move about on his own. He motioned to the man who came to stand at his side. "This is Corporal Nelson."

Westley shifted his gaze to the other man, who came to attention. "Good day, Corporal. Take your ease. As you can both see, I am on my feet and will soon be ready to return to duty."

The men exchanged a glance that soured Westley's stomach.

Nelson stepped forward. "Sir, I have come bearing a message from General Sheridan."

His pulse quickened, but Westley kept his face passive. "Speak, then."

The smaller man shifted his weight from one scuffed boot to the other. "His orders are that you are to take an extended leave of absence until you are fully recovered."

Westley started to growl, and the doctor held up his hand. "I'd say, Major, that these are most prudent orders. Force the leg too quickly and it may hinder your stride all the more."

Westley bit back disagreeable words. "I understand."

"Very good, sir."

"The usual ninety-day furlough is the extension then?"

The small man attempted to make himself seem taller, but he still only reached Westley's chin. "He said that by way of your great service, he has decided to grant you a more extended leave, should you wish it."

Westley's face must have revealed more of his thoughts than he wished, because Corporal Nelson lifted his eyebrows.

"He seemed to imply the furlough was a well-deserved reward, sir."

Westley ground his teeth. Curse it! How to insist he return without spurning the general's offer?

Another thought occurred to him, and he narrowed his gaze at Captain Albright. Did the doctor tell the general about Westley's memory lapses? Did that, more so than the leg, make the army feel it was prudent to give him extended recovery time?

His jaw began to ache, and he had to force muscles to relax ere he broke a tooth.

"You will, of course, continue to earn a wage," the corporal stated, as though money made up for Westley's humiliation.

Westley shifted his weight off his bad leg, a motion that did not slip past the doctor's notice.

"Giving you trouble?"

"No." It took every ounce of his patience to remain affable, yet he sensed he failed in his attempt.

Corporal Nelson glanced between the men but said nothing.

Westley cleared his throat. "Please send word to the general that I am honored by his generosity, but I shall report back for duty no later than one month's time." Better he set things on his own time schedule.

"But, sir..." The man twitched his thick mustache, his beady eyes darting nervously to the doctor.

"I have been healing for several weeks already, Corporal," he stated, his tone leaving no room for argument. "That shall be plenty of time for me to have healed sufficiently to return to duty. Already in the days since I regained consistent wakefulness, I have improved dramatically." He swung his gaze to the doctor. "Isn't that correct, Captain?"

A smile twisted the corner of the man's mouth. "It is, Major."

A small tap at the door drew their attention to Mrs. Preston. "Gentlemen, dinner is ready."

The doctor eyed Westley. "Are you fit to eat at the dining table?"

Given that he didn't fall over on the way there, he would make it so. "Indeed, Doctor. As I said, I am much improved." He flicked a glance at Mrs. Preston, expecting her to protest, but she gave him an encouraging smile that bolstered his confidence.

He was slow—humiliatingly so—but he made it to the dining room without the pain undoing him. Six weeks now since the injury, and his leg would finally hold his weight. At least, as long as he leaned heavily upon the cane.

Easing into a chair at the well-used table, Westley took in the dining space of Mrs. Preston's home. Like everything he had learned to be true of the woman herself, the space was simple, warm, and inviting. The beams overhead were sturdy, as were the humble walls free of elaborate paintings. The window on one wall stood open, letting the afternoon breeze ruffle the linens placed over the dishes to keep the bugs at bay until they began to eat.

"So, Mrs. Preston, I find I am a bit curious," Corporal Nelson said as he settled in his chair. "I am told this is the Hillsman farm."

She lifted the covering from a platter of roasted venison. "Yes, sir."

The smell scurried to Westley, and his mouth began to water. When had his nurse been able to get a deer? They'd had naught but chicken and mutton previously.

The corporal shifted in his chair to allow her to pass the vittles to him. "Forgive me, but I am confused."

"Preston is her married name," Westley supplied, stabbing three pieces of meat. "This farm belonged to her father, Mr. Hillsman."

"Ah, of course." The man reached for a bowl of potatoes. "How dense of me."

After they had served themselves and Mrs. Preston took it upon herself to ask a blessing over the meal, they ate in earnest.

"So, Doctor," Mrs. Preston said, "as you can see, my patient has fared quite well."

The doctor wiped his mouth. "So I see. In fact, I suspect he shall very soon be leaving you."

Her face tightened, but she smiled anyway. "I do believe you are right."

Westley reached for another helping of beans. "It is only by her good care I am alive." Never mind the doctor who had tried to take his leg and then let orderlies proclaim him dead. "Ever will I be thankful for her, and she shall always hold a place of high regard with me."

Her cheeks dimpled. "Oh, but I surely will miss having him about, even if he is an ornery one." She laughed. "Though I dare say he may have redeemed himself with such flattery."

The men laughed at Westley's expense, but he did not begrudge her teasing. Indeed, it felt good to be treated normally, and not as one who required tender care. "Ah, and I shall surely miss her unbridled honesty."

When the laughter died down, the corporal leaned forward. "Where shall you go during your furlough now that you are able to walk?"

Westley tapped a finger on the table, indecision once more nagging at him. Mrs. Preston gave him a small nod of encouragement. She'd made her thoughts on the matter abundantly clear, and Westley finally conceded she was right. "As I have come by the extra time, I shall return to my home to settle matters there."

"Very good, sir," Nelson said, as though Westley had answered a test question correctly. The man twitched his mustache. "And where do you hail from?"

"Mississippi."

As expected, the doctor's features showed surprise. Unexpectedly, the corporal's did not.

Dismissing the oddity as merely the man's ability to control his features, Westley leaned back in his chair. "As you can imagine, my father's lands will need to be seen to. I intend to take care of any expenses he may have left upon his death, then likely sell off the lands I have no intention of keeping."

"A difficult task, I'm sure," the doctor said.

"But a necessary one."

Mrs. Preston rose from the table and began taking up the dishes. "I'll leave you gentlemen to talk for a moment, and I will be back with some pie."

Westley watched her leave, then turned his attention back to the men. Corporal Nelson twirled the waxed end of his mustache. "I, too, have family from the South. They live in Alabama."

"Oh?"

"A most unfortunate splitting of allegiances, as I am sure you can understand."

Westley could. Though his parents had not begrudged his determination to stay loyal to the oaths he had taken upon graduating West Point, and he did not blame them for their desire to hold to the position of their home state, such was not usually the case for divided families. Often, such understandings did not exist between torn families that straddled allegiance lines. "This war has placed many a family against one another."

"You are quite right, Major Remington," the doctor said, patting his pockets as though hankering for his pipe. "I am glad to see it come to an end."

"I thought to take a furlough to my grandfather's home to see how they fared," Corporal Nelson continued as though the doctor had not interjected himself into the conversation. "Perhaps we might travel south together?"

Westley considered the proposal. Did the man offer because he thought Westley incapable of traveling alone? He pushed such rancorous thoughts aside. "I would be pleased for like-minded company, Corporal."

"Very good, sir. Would you be opposed to my making the travel arrangements?"

"Not at all." Westley rubbed the top of his leg under the table. He knew the rail systems were in poor condition the farther south one traveled, so they would need to cover at least part of the distance by carriage. Surely, though, the man would know as much. "I will need to get to the Mississippi River, in Washington County."

"Yes, sir." Nelson smiled. "I will see it done."

Wondering if he had just walked himself into some kind of preconceived plan, Westley considered the man's too-ready words. He didn't have an opportunity to voice his thoughts, however, because Mrs. Preston arrived with thick slices of apple pie. The scent of cinnamon and spice absconded with his concerns, and he turned his attention to the food and his thoughts to his home.

Another few days, perhaps, and then he would have to face Belmont once more. What would he find there? Charred ruins? His home ransacked? The servants gone?

It mattered not. Whatever state he found Belmont in, it would not deter his course. With his parents gone and himself unwelcome in Greenville, it would be best that he remembered good times from his childhood rather than what the place would be with his parents dead. The house and lands would be sold and his father's affairs settled. Then he would gain his place in the army once more and start a new life out west.

Chapter Twelve

Westley tried not to massage the leg that had begun to ache. He had thus mostly ignored the tingles and occasional sharp pains on this trip that had oft left him exhausted come the day's end. He hated to admit it, but Mrs. Preston had been right in her misty-eyed farewell. It was a blessing that he was not yet required to return to the army where long days in the saddle would surely test his leg more than these days spent cramped in a carriage.

Corporal Nelson had seen him to the northern borders of Mississippi, then taken his turn into Alabama. Seemed Westley had been wrong about that, too. The man didn't attempt to hover over him or worry about his mental condition. He merely provided companionship for the majority of the journey.

Westley took a deep breath of the humid air as the carriage drew nearer to Greenville. It had been four years since he'd visited—not since the war began. He'd exchanged letters with his parents, and had once seen his father in Washington, but he had not known that the day he'd bid his mother farewell at Belmont four years ago would be the last he ever saw of her. Regret gripped him, and though he tried to push it away as he did other emotions, it refused to budge.

Trees passed slowly with the sway of the carriage and Westley was once more glad no others shared the hired coach with him. He could bear the weight of his guilt in peace. Memories of his youth swept over him. They had come to this swampland in 1845 when he was but a boy of eight. His father and his uncles had bought up vast areas of land and started growing cotton in the fertile ground. Indian squaws had been hired to harvest it back then, before they built Belmont in 1857 and acquired 200 slaves. Then his mother said Jesus didn't want her owning another person and insisted that all the house slaves be freed. His father had consented but held his ownership of the field hands until the war. Then, in '64, when Father suspected that the South could not win, he granted freedom to those who had not run off, and the lands had lain fallow.

How he wished his parents had made it through the winter. Westley shook his head. Rather than the winter, it was more likely the summer had got them. The mosquitoes could be thick around Belmont, and his parents usually spent their summer months at their home in Natchez. But it was sold to pay for what the crops had not, and, thus, his parents had spent two summers in Belmont.

The carriage slowed to a stop, pulling him from his dark thoughts. Yes, best he be rid of this place and the burdens it would give him. He noticed the scene out the window once more and his chest constricted. Burned homes, toppled buildings, and ragged-looking people lined the streets of Greenville. He'd been told things had been bad here, but seeing it with his own eyes stirred him.

Westley opened the door and slowly climbed out. After paying the driver for his services, he turned down the main street in town. He'd elected to come here before going on to Belmont to see if he could locate his father's solicitor. The carriage rolled away just as he was about to tell the driver he'd changed his mind, as it seemed too little remained of this place to be considered functional. As the hackney left him, he leaned upon his cane and started forward. Father had always said God gave a man but one direction. One could not go back, so he must move forward as best he could.

Dust billowed up around Westley's feet. The few people going about their business on the street passed him without so much as a glance. Dressed in plain black trousers, a gray vest, and broadcloth jacket he'd purchased for the journey, he did not draw the attention his uniform would have stirred. He recognized one or two of those who passed by him but did not call a greeting. Would his former Greenville neighbors recognize him? And, if so, how would he be received? Not with joy, he felt certain. And if he happened upon any of his boyhood friends, they would likely greet him with a pistol. Ducking his head, Westley continued to the solicitor's office, only to find that it had been reduced to a pile of blackened bricks.

The livery, then? The jingle of tack made him look up as a carriage came down the street at a quick pace. Surprised, Westley took a step back, lest he risk being trampled. As the carriage rolled past, a young woman inside stared at him through the window. He frowned. *Was that...?*

The carriage carried on and then pulled to an abrupt stop about fifty paces past him. The Negro driver hurried down and opened the door, and two ladies in hooped dresses emerged into the dust their carriage had roused. They stepped into a ramshackle building that seemed to be the center of activity.

Deciding it probably passed for a general store, Westley headed that way. He would likely find what he sought in one of two places and, as he didn't care for the idea of a tavern just yet, he would first find what he sought at the mercantile.

Ignoring the ache that had now become a throb, he hobbled down the road and through the front door. Nodding at a proprietor he didn't recognize, he looked to the sparse shelves several patrons mulled over.

"Mr. Remington!"

A woman's gasp made Westley cringe. So, it didn't take long for him to be recognized. Steeling himself for the scorn he would face, he turned to the female's voice and discovered a lovely woman in a yellow dress.

"It *is* you!" She began fluttering her fan. "Oh, Mama!"

An older woman appeared behind the younger and recognition slammed into him. The dour Mrs. Martin narrowed her gaze at her daughter, then it flew wide as she looked to Westley.

"It can't be!"

"I know!" The younger woman's cheeks bloomed a soft pink.

Westley studied her. Could this be the same little Miss Martin he remembered? The one with the rounded face and form who had twittered about at neighborly gatherings? It seemed so, though this young woman hardly resembled the girl from years past.

He opened his mouth to offer greeting, especially as the young lady did not presently shower him with scorn, but her next words caused his own to lodge in his throat.

"Won't she just be faint with joy?"

She?

Mrs. Martin fingered the buttons on the collar of her navy blue dress. "Indeed. Seems she won't be needing those widow's gowns after all."

Widow's...?

Westley cleared his throat. "Excuse me, ma'am, but I—"

Miss Martin clasped her hands. "Can you imagine it? Oh, I would so love to see the surprise on her face when you get home."

"Home?" This question managed to make it through the constriction in his throat.

Mrs. Martin lifted her brows. "Why, of course. Did you not know your young bride and child are at Belmont?"

Westley filled his lungs and slowly released. What game did this woman play? Had some imposter set sights upon his family home? Perhaps he should fish out further information. "I was injured and have been under the care of the doctor for several weeks."

"Oh, yes, yes," Miss Martin said, her fan fluttering. "Your missus said that they received word you were missing and assumed dead. But the poor dear held out hope you would return."

Westley felt his blood quicken.

"It was rather odd, you see, as none of us saw her arrive. It seems she traveled to the house alone to have your son."

"My son?" Westley croaked. Impossible. He had abstained from knowing a woman, even one from the abundance of those who hung around the camps for men to make use of to relieve their baser hungers. Therefore, there were none who could claim he had sired their child.

At least, not with any thread of truth.

His anger began to seethe. What trollop had decided to use the news of him missing from his unit as an excuse to try to steal his name rather than admit her sin?

"Oh, look at him, Mama." Miss Martin's pink lips turned up. "She told true. Looks like they did marry in a flurry of emotion."

Westley forced a smile. When he got to Belmont, that tart would soon regret making him her target. For now, though, he might play the game.

"You've met her?"

"We were over for tea last week. I must say, Mr. Remington," Mrs. Martin said, eschewing his military title, "I would have never expected you to wed a Confederate girl." She smirked. "Perhaps there will be some redemption for you in this town after all."

Westley frowned. Not a Federal camp follower then. Who was this woman who had stolen his name?

"We are leaving just as soon as Mama gets some thread to patch my dress again. We could drive him out there, couldn't we, Mama?"

Westley slid his gaze from the sunny young woman to her dowager mother. The elder Martin woman's mouth hitched, and something sparked in her eyes. Suspicion?

"Why, of course, Opal, dear. I would be glad to see the happy couple reunited." She offered a smile that held little humor. "I'll be only a moment."

Westley followed Miss Martin outside, her incessant words slipping across his ears without taking hold. He'd expected to find any manner of things at Belmont, but not this.

"Mr. Remington?"

Westley focused back on the young woman, who tied a large bow under her chin to secure her bonnet. Her gown frayed a bit, and the ribbons and flowers on the bonnet were worse for wear.

"I asked what became of your speech. You sound as though you didn't grow up a stone's throw from here."

As intended. Westley tried to give an apologetic smile. "I have been away many years."

Her forehead creased, and he decided to turn the subject off him.

"I see Greenville did not fare well. How are things at Riverbend?"

"Oh." She lowered her gaze and much of the delight slipped from her countenance. "We still have a roof to ward off the rain and walls to stay the wind. The rest we can make do without." She turned warm brown eyes toward the street. "Many here did not fare as well."

Westley inwardly groaned. He was such a cad! What was he thinking to ask such a thing?

"Though none fared as well as Belmont." Mrs. Martin's

clipped words intruded on the conversation as the door clicked behind them. "But I'm sure you know that."

He did, and he could not fault the woman her bitterness. "My father's letters said as much, but I have heard naught of Belmont since his passing."

Some of the steam went out of Mrs. Martin's scowl as she waved for her driver to untie the horses. "He was a good man. We were all sad to see him go. The only good of it is that your mother went soon after."

Good? How could losing both of his parents at once be a good thing?

She blinked, tears pricking her otherwise cold eyes. "It is hard on a woman living her remaining years as a widow. Be glad your mother didn't have to suffer it during these hard times."

Her soft words bore so much pain, all he could do was incline his head. "Perhaps you are right."

"All the more reason to have joy this day, Mama," Miss Martin said as the driver opened the carriage door. "Mrs. Remington will receive the great blessing of not having to face what she feared she would."

Westley nearly corrected the young woman who he thought had misunderstood that his mother also died, but then realized she referred to the imposter.

He offered a tight smile. Something must have happened to Sibby. She would have been a force for any actress to deal with, and, colored or not, she would have never handed over Belmont. There were two women in this world Westley esteemed. One was dead and the other must be gone. It seemed there would be no stragglers to see off Belmont after all.

Westley assisted the ladies inside the carriage and then seethed in his humiliation of struggling inside behind them. Though the leg throbbed as he sat, he refused to let his fingers seek the comfort of massaging it.

"Does your leg hurt you much, Mr. Remington?" Miss Martin asked.

He nearly lied, but that would be both dishonorable and ridiculous. "It does."

The carriage lurched forward, and another spasm of pain shot from his thigh to his toes.

"I wonder," Mrs. Martin said, her reedy voice filling the carriage. "Why you did not send word to your wife that you were alive."

"I did not know she was here." The truth.

"Hmm. Where else would she have been?"

Westley tugged at the collar of his shirt, which seemed to grow tighter the more he was in this woman's presence and contemplated telling her he did not have a wife. But he had become intrigued with this imposter who was bold enough to make such claims, so he wanted to see what she would do when confronted.

"It took weeks after my injury to awake. Only then could I convey my name and rank. I am told the army sent word thereafter." Again, the truth.

"I see." The older woman sat back in her seat and studied him, the questions behind her dark eyes thankfully not springing to her thin lips.

"Well, we have had difficulty with correspondence, Mr. Remington. Things being what they are, if letters are not delivered by messenger..." She let her words trail off.

They rode in silence for a time, until it seemed Miss Martin could no longer contain herself.

"She is quite lovely," she said with a mischievous grin. "I can see why you would be so taken with her that you married in a rush." A smile holding notions of romance Westley doubted he was capable of turned up her mouth.

"I am sure she would be glad you thought so." Most likely

true. Women forever hunted for compliments.

Miss Martin pressed her fingers to her lips and looked out the window. "Ah, the joyous reunion awaits."

Mrs. Martin chuckled. "I dare say, it should be most interesting to see."

Westley declined a response. Interesting, indeed. The carriage made the turn from the river road to the drive up to Belmont, and he ran a hand over his freshly shaven face. *Now, little imposter, we shall see what game you play.*

Chapter Thirteen

Ella rubbed her temples. "Sibby. The Yank gave us two weeks, and already one of them is past. We *must* discuss this."

Sibby's nostrils flared. "Now, you look here. I done told you I is workin' on it."

Ella nearly groaned. Why did this woman make all things difficult? Patting Lee where she kept him tied to her chest, she began to pace around the library. "What is it that makes you so against listening to reason?"

"What?"

She'd thus far played along, but the more she did so, the more Sibby seemed to mistake her gratitude for weakness. She pointed a finger at the other woman. "There are things you are not telling me."

Sibby narrowed her eyes. "You don't know nothin'."

Obviously. "Only because you will not tell me. How am I to help?"

Sibby let out a long sigh and then suddenly her shoulders drooped, as though a burden kept hidden weighed them down. In that moment she seemed much older than her years.

Ella sank into one of the armchairs in the library and motioned for Sibby to take the other. "How are we to keep your home if you sit by and allow the army to take it?"

Sibby perched on the edge of the chair and picked at her fingernails. "I never did wanna be like the white ladies, you know."

Ella frowned, wondering what that had to do with their conversation, but held her tongue.

"Mrs. Remington, she was always worryin' over folks. Makin' sure they was cared for and all."

Not a bad thing. Ella may have liked this lady who, from what she'd heard told, was vastly different from most others.

"My ma, she was thataway, too. Was her that told all us what to do, and her that all the Negroes under the Remingtons looked to. Then she died."

Ella started to offer condolences, but Sibby kept talking.

"I weren't but eighteen summers, but with Mrs. Remington so sick with worry over the war and her boy, it went to me to run things for her like my ma did."

Ella watched Sibby closely, some of the woman's desperation to keep a tight hold on things making more sense.

Sibby met her eyes. "Then Mr. Remington died, and the missus…well, she weren't right in the head after that."

"Oh."

"I was right glad Mr. Westley and Mr. Remington weren't here to see her like that. Scared folks the way she had dem fits…"

Ella plucked at the hem of her sleeve. "I'm sorry."

Sibby took on a faraway look. "Onlyist thing that made her smile was my Peter."

"Your son?" Ella asked softly.

Sibby nodded. A tear slid down her cheek, but she quickly flicked it away as though it had no place upon her. "Then he took sick, too, and Mrs. Remington, well, she just couldn't bear it."

Ella's throat constricted, and she tightened her grip on Lee.

Sibby's eyes flew to the child and she shook her head. "I tried to tell her it weren't her fault."

Though Ella had guessed that something must have happened to Sibby's child, she had not wanted to pry.

Sibby drew a breath and rose. "He died two days 'fore she did."

Ella stood and placed a hand on the woman's arm. "I'm so sorry, Sibby. Truly I am."

She stepped away, and the softness that had made her speak such things hardened once more. "Weren't nobody left 'round here to take care of folks, so I had to do it. Been doin' it ever since, and I is goin' to do whatever I gots to do to make sure we is safe."

Once more returned to the positions they had thus far held, Ella frowned. What kind of things might Sibby have done to take care of the people? From what she'd seen of the fields, cotton harvesting wasn't one of them. Gardens somewhere, perhaps? The cellar shelves held jars of preserved vegetables that must have come from somewhere.

"I do not understand, Sibby. You wanted me to help." She followed Sibby out of the library.

"No. I just wanted you to keep away them soldiers," she snapped.

What had happened to the woman who had only moments ago shared painful things of the heart? The one who seemed to be open to reason?

"As I am trying to do!" Annoyance flared, and Ella struggled to keep it down. So long as Lee had a place to live and milk to nourish him, well, that was what mattered most. But now Sibby's stubbornness could undo it all. Ella took a deep breath and rubbed the baby's back. She needed some fresh air. "What about the crops?"

"What about 'em?"

Ella hoped the woman would see reason. "If we plant something, then perhaps the army will be satisfied that we are providing living space and work for freedmen, and the Yanks will grant leniency on the taxes until we can produce a harvest."

Sibby fanned herself with her hand. "You know that ain't nothin' but foolish hope."

Ella set her teeth. Why must this woman be so difficult? With the prospect of losing everything, she had no choice but to put aside her efforts at meekness. "Fine. Then I shall begin selling off plots of the land so the taxes can be paid."

Sibby's mouth fell open. "You gonna do no such thing!"

"Why not? It seems a perfect solution."

Sibby continued to stare at her, and Ella moved past her to go up the stairs. It took a moment longer than expected, but the woman soon followed. "You ain't got no right to be sellin' what ain't yourn."

A smug smile Sibby couldn't see tugged Ella's lips. "Don't I? Why, there are carpetbaggers aplenty looking for land to buy, and since everyone knows I am mistress here, who would think twice about my ability to sell it?"

"You-you…" Sibby began to stutter, and Ella could nearly feel the frustration pouring off of her.

Ella walked to the end of the upper hall and opened the door to let in the afternoon breeze. "You think on it. Then ask your people. You will see that I am right."

Sibby pressed her lips and refused to say more.

Satisfied she would win the argument, Ella stepped out onto the upper front balcony to let the mid-May breeze wash over her. Bold words, indeed. Would the state of the country allow for her to sell land that didn't belong to her? It would be worth a try.

Movement drew her attention to the end of the drive, where a carriage made the turn off the river road. A carriage she had seen before. She frowned. "Sibby, did you invite the Martin women over again?"

"Now, listen here. We can talk 'bout you askin' women to

tea later. Right now we gots to…" She slowed as she noticed Ella's pointing finger. "What they doin' here?"

"That's what I just asked you."

Sibby scoffed. "What? You think I invited 'em?"

"You did last time." Ella lifted her shoulders.

"Did not."

"Then how…?" Ella shook her head. She didn't have time for this. Guests were arriving, and she was in her work dress. She began tugging on the strips of cloth around Lee. "Here, hurry up and take him so I can get into another dress."

Sibby took the baby in the crook of her arm, and they scurried into Ella's room. She crossed to the wardrobe. "They is gonna expect you in the black 'un."

Ella had already thought the same. Sibby tossed the simple frock to her, and by the time the carriage wheels drew close enough to hear, Ella had donned the cotton dress and started to tie a ribbon about her waist. "Will it do?"

"I reckon. Get on with you then."

Ella reached for the baby. "I'm taking Lee with me."

Sibby shied back. "What for?"

Ella lifted her chin. "Because he's my child, and I wish it." And if he cried, she might be all the sooner to get rid of her uninvited guests.

They stared at each other for a moment, then Sibby handed over the boy before grumbling something under her breath and stepping out of the room. Sibby hurried down the stairs, and Ella followed her at a slower pace. She had just taken the first two steps when the front door opened.

Ella frowned. Sibby had not had the time to make it to the door, so the Martin women must have opened it on their own. The nerve! What kind of people had the audacity not only to come over uninvited but to let themselves in as well?

Another thought occurred to her, and Ella's heart began to

flutter. Had her ruse been found out? Did the Martin women come bearing accusations that made them bold?

Just then Sibby let out a squeal, and Ella clutched the baby tighter. Had the sound seemed born of fear rather than delight, she would have hurried back to the second floor, but curiosity drew her to the landing.

"Mr. Westley! Oh!"

Ella came to a halt midway down the staircase and stared. It couldn't be. Her heart thudded so furiously in her chest she thought it might burst from her. Lee began to squirm, and just then did she realize she had squeezed him too tightly.

"You is alive! Oh, have mercy. I just..." Sibby's words came to a tumbling halt, and she spun around to look up at Ella, who still stood transfixed on the stairs staring at the scene before her.

Sibby stood beside a man whose presence filled the entry—a man who was supposed to be dead. Mahogany hair topped a stern face that was all the more handsome for the masculine set to his jaw. Wide shoulders and a lean physique, he looked very much the warrior Sibby had described him to be. All except for the cane at his side, which he leaned upon heavily.

So this was the man she had claimed to be her husband? Her heart dropped. No wonder the Martin women had been skeptical. Never would Ella have garnered the attention of one such as he. She stopped herself short. What was she thinking?

The man stared at her, his dark eyes assessing everything from her widow's dress to the baby in her arms. To her surprise, he said nothing about her presence. Oh, but what would he do when...?

"Don't you wish to greet your wife?" Mrs. Martin asked, slipping to the man's side. She raised her eyebrows at Ella, as though she had figured out the game.

Ella glanced past the man to the women who waited in the

still moments that had surely not been as long as they seemed. Miss Martin wore a wide smile that evidenced she expected Ella to come to her senses and throw herself into the arms of the husband she was supposed to dearly love.

Ella opened her mouth to try to stop the humiliation, but the man spoke first.

"Indeed. I am most eager to see you, *wife*."

Ella's mouth unhinged, and she stared.

He looked at the baby. "And is this my son, as well?"

Finding her senses, Ella glanced to Sibby, but the woman seemed just as confused as she. Did this man seek to trap her?

"Mr. Remington, I—"

He held up a hand. "Come now, surely I am Westley to my wife?"

She gulped and took an unsteady step closer. Perhaps he thought to save face in front of his neighbors. But why continue thus? When later he threw her out, he would only have all the more explaining to do.

"Mr. Westley, Ella, she..." Sibby stammered.

Mr. Remington gave a firm shake of his head, sending a lock of hair dancing across his brow, and Sibby seamed her lips.

Ella came forward, descending the stairs and coming to stand before the man a head taller than she. "This is, um, this is Lee," she managed, glancing at the baby.

His eyes lingered long upon her face, and then something that seemed like understanding lit a spark in eyes so dark a brown they neared black. Finally, he glanced at the child. "A handsome boy."

Unable to contain herself, Ella spoke words that burned in her throat. "I thought you were dead."

A smile tilted one side of his mouth. "So I see."

A fire lit in her chest. Did this man toy with her? She had not meant anyone harm, merely needed someone to care for the baby. She stared at him, all the more flustered when amusement shone in those arresting eyes as well as upon his well-formed mouth.

"Come, Mama," Miss Martin interjected. "We should leave them to such private matters, should we not?"

Ella had all but forgotten the Martin women were standing in the room. She darted a glance past Mr. Remington to Miss Martin. The young woman offered Ella a smile even as her mother looked to be near on spouting an accusation.

"I do thank you for the ride, ladies," Mr. Remington said, the deep timbre of his voice smooth with the genteel words of one born to privilege. "But if you would be so kind as to forgive my eagerness, I would now like to speak privately with my wife."

Mrs. Martin sniffed. "Of course. We bid you good afternoon, Mr. Remington." She nodded to Ella. "Mrs. Remington."

Ella knew she should give some sort of farewell, but what did that matter now? She would probably never see these women again. Her eyes darted to Sibby, who stared at the floor, and then back to the handsome man in front of her.

What was this that caused a tremble in her knees? Could it be the way his eyes held her own as though they were some great treasure to behold? She gulped. No. It had to be the fear of losing a home for Lee that caused her legs to be unsteady.

The door clicked behind the departing neighbors, and it seemed her composure left with them. She swayed and thought she might fall until a hand grasped her upper arm and held firm.

"Are you well, *Miss*?"

Ella looked up into his eyes and, when she discovered a measure of concern pooling within their depths, found herself all the more confused. Why did he not pummel her with harsh words? Or at the very least, demand to know why she had labeled herself his wife?

"It was the baby—" she said through lips that seemed too dry to form words.

She stood steadily now, but still he did not release her. He looked down at the child. "You needed Sibby to help with the nursing?"

Ella nodded.

"I should have guessed as much." He swung his gaze to Sibby. "Did you know that the Martin women believe this woman is my wife?"

Sibby's eyes grew large. "But, suh, we done thought you was dead!" Sibby shook her head. "And she done showed up here with that babe right when them soldiers did."

"Soldiers?"

Growing uncomfortable at the nearness of this man and the odd sensation it sent through her, Ella took a step back and he released her arm.

"The blue soldiers. They wanted to make sure we weren't no slaves."

Mr. Remington reached up to stroke a firm chin devoid of whiskers. "I see."

"Please, sir," Ella said, finally finding her voice. She schooled her words back into those of a Southern lady, though it was likely too late. "This is my fault. I needed someone to help with the baby, and when I arrived the soldiers wanted to speak to a Remington. Without thought, I pretended to be one so that Sibby could care for the child and I could get them to leave."

To her utter amazement, the man chuckled. "Did you now?"

"Now, Mr. Westley, we done thought you was dead," Sibby said again.

He cocked an eyebrow. "So you keep telling me."

Sibby wagged her head. "We thought that with no white

folks here they was gonna make us leave."

The man frowned, and Ella wondered if he believed the claim.

"I can't say that I didn't think that myself. How many of you are still here?"

Sibby looked down and away. "A few."

Mr. Remington shifted his weight to rest more heavily on the cane. Sibby noticed the action and pointed to the parlor. "Why don't you go on in there and sit. I is going to get you somethin' to drink. You hungry, too?"

"No. Some tea would be good, though."

Sibby bobbed her head, and Ella watched her go. The woman seemed too eager to serve and far too submissive to be the same one who had lived with Ella these past two weeks.

She returned her gaze to the man before her. His shoulders slacked some and Ella wondered just how tired he must be. Perhaps exhaustion alone kept him from sharp words. She turned to follow Sibby to the kitchen when his voice stopped her.

"I would have you join me. There is much for us to discuss."

Knowing she had no other choice, Ella inclined her head and stepped around him, hurrying into the parlor. Her mind awhirl, she shifted through the various hardships that would soon befall her. How foolish of her not to consider the possibility that this man might return! The letter had said he was missing, not for certain he was dead.

She crossed the patterned carpet and placed Lee down in the cradle, then took a seat beside him on the settee. Once settled, she forced herself to keep a steady gaze on the one who would determine her fate. Mr. Remington slowly made his way across the room as though each step he took pained him.

As he settled into the chair farthest from her, he regarded

her with cool curiosity. "So, Miss, tell me. Who exactly are you?"

Ella placed her trembling hands in her lap. Who was she, indeed?

Chapter Fourteen

Westley watched the arresting creature before him as she fiddled with her black dress. Hair the color of a sunset and green eyes that sparkled like emeralds had caused him to alter his course. He'd had every intention of calling out her deception upon entering, with the added bonus of having neighbors behind him to verify the tale. He almost felt bad for leading the Martin women to believe such a woman belonged here, but that could easily be explained. He'd meant to set a trap.

When Sibby arrived first, his thoughts of a trap were derailed. With Sibby here and a part of the scheme, well, he couldn't help himself. He wanted to see what kind of woman had managed to cow her.

And then he'd set eyes on the imposter...

He clenched his teeth. Intriguing, that's what he would name it. He was intrigued by this woman who had the nerve to claim his name and who even now defied him by taking so long in answering his simple question. Did she dare to cook up another lie?

He cleared his throat and those eyes the color of a faded gem set upon him once more. "I'll ask you again, Miss. Who are you?"

She glanced at her baby and resolve tightened her soft features. Her fidgeting stilled, replaced by a steely calm he'd often seen young soldiers try to effect when faced with something they feared. She lifted the boy from where he slept and held him against her.

She lifted her chin, further showing off the curve of her neck, which Westley instructed his eyes not to linger upon.

"My name is Eleanor Whitaker."

Odd, the way she spoke, as though her voice carried some clue he couldn't quite grasp. He let his eyes carry over her smooth complexion and pert little nose that turned up slightly at the end. He should send her out the door, but curiosity stilled him. A few moments more to understand her purpose would matter little.

He tapped a finger on his leg, turning his gaze from her to the parlor that appeared unchanged since last he sat here. "And what, Miss Whitaker, caused you to claim to be my wife?"

She moistened her lips. "As told, sir, I came here seeking a wet nurse. When I pretended to be a Remington once I heard Sibby say none were here, it was only because she looked distressed and...well, I desperately needed someone to care for the babe."

There it was again—a soft bit of lilt to certain words. Her accent gave her away as Southern, but something else tinged it. Irish, perhaps? Or Scottish? Her eyes caressed the boy in her arms, and something hard in Westley inexplicably softened.

"As I hoped, the soldiers seemed satisfied with the small deception and soon departed. Sibby agreed to care for my son, and I had thought that would be the end of it."

The ache in his leg grew in intensity, and Westley set his jaw against it.

As though misinterpreting his discomfort for anger—which he should feel, yet strangely did not—she shifted in her chair. "I do hope you understand I did not mean to cause you any trouble." She held his gaze, though he suspected it was difficult for her to do so.

He couldn't help the smile that tugged on the corner of his

mouth. "You can imagine my surprise when my neighbors informed me that my *wife and son* waited for my arrival."

"Yes, well…" She toyed with the fabric of the dress again. "They came to tea, and by then we had decided that it would be a good idea to let the ruse stand."

We? Why had Sibby agreed to such an outrageous claim? A question she would very soon have to answer.

Westley regarded the small woman who dared where she should not. "And what, do you suppose, I am to do with you now?"

Her lip quivered slightly, and he was overcome by the irrational urge to smooth it with his thumb.

"I would ask that you let me stay. For a little while, at least, good sir."

Westley leaned forward. Now she would venture to ask him to keep up the pretense of being his wife?

"As a hireling, of course," she continued quickly, as though sensing his unrest. "I would continue helping tend the house as I have done the past couple of weeks, and in return my son and I have a place to live. You may tell all of my deception. I am unconcerned by what others will think of it."

Interesting. He could have allowed it, he supposed, if not that he had come to sell the lands. He frowned at her. Fetching though she may appear, she was naught more than trouble. And something in the flutter of her lashes told him she *did* care what his neighbors would think of her.

"I'm afraid that won't be possible," he said, linking his fingers together.

She blinked at him. "But…"

The baby made a small noise, and she clutched him to her. Then, before Westley could react, she was on her feet and hurrying to the door. "Excuse me, but I need to find Sibby to feed him."

Westley watched her go, perplexed. What had happened that she could not nurse her child as a mother ought?

His thoughts returned to Sibby. His mother's last letter, the one that Sibby had sent along with her own telling of Mother's death, had told that Sibby's own baby had also died from the sickness along with his parents. The child had been born to her seven months after renegade Confederates had found her man, Joe, on the road from buying supplies in Greenville. Mother's letter stated that Joe claimed to be a freeman, and they'd hanged him for it.

Mother told him about everything going on at the plantation, as though she wanted to be certain Westley missed nothing. Mother said she worried over Sibby's bitterness when Joe died. Westley stroked his chin. That bitterness had likely only gotten worse after Sibby lost the infant as well as the man. Was the grief over her own son why she had nursed other children? And where did these babes keep coming from? That had been, what, four months past? And still she had milk to give?

Too many questions, and he was too tired to contemplate them all. Still he waited, but the imposter did not come back once she delivered the child upstairs. Not that he expected differently. She likely fretted over his unannounced return and hesitated to continue their conversation. He rose from his place in the parlor and headed for the stairs. If she would not come to him, then he would go to her.

A knock at the door altered his steps. When he opened it, a young man in blue shadowed the entry.

"Good day, sir. I have come with news for the family."

Intrigued, Westley accepted the folded paper and popped the seal. His eyes skimmed the brief words and he groaned.

> *To the family of Major Westley Remington,*
> *The United States Army is pleased to inform you that*

Major Remington has been found alive.
We join you in your joy.
Lieutenant John Peyton

Westley nearly laughed. This must have been the letter the corporal had said was sent to Belmont. How ironic that he should be the one to receive it. What would Miss Whitaker have done if it had arrived before him? She probably would have scurried off before he arrived and he would have never set eyes on her. A surge of relief over the chance to confront such an interesting woman irritated him. Ridiculous!

"We are exceedingly sorry for ill tidings, sir, and leave you to personal matters," the man said, interrupting Westley's thoughts with words the poor fellow had probably spoken far too many times.

The man began to turn when Westley chuckled. "On the contrary, Sergeant. It seems I am alive and well."

Confusion lined the man's rigid features. "Sir?"

Westley slipped the missive in his shirt pocket and gave it a pat. "As I returned home with the news that I am still alive before this letter did, the news has already been received."

The man nodded, seeming too weary to join in Westley's unexpected bout of good humor. "Very good, sir. Good day to you." Then, as though remembering himself, the sergeant wheeled back around and snapped to attention. "Then you must be Major Remington." He gave a sharp salute. "I meant no disrespect, sir."

Westley gave a half-hearted salute in return. "You could not have known. Carry on."

"Yes, sir. Thank you, sir." The sergeant hastily retreated.

When Westley turned back around, a small Negro girl stared at him with large eyes set in an inquisitive face. She didn't make a move to address him or scurry from his presence, so

Westley grunted. "Hello."

"You 'member me?"

Westley eyed her. How was he supposed to remember all the children who ran about this place? He shook his head.

She leveled clear eyes on him that bespoke of how much the nation had already changed. "I is Basil. I help Sibby with the washin' and the ironin' and the cleanin'."

He moved to go past her to the stairs. He placed a hand on the railing when her next words stilled him.

"You gonna let Miss Ella stay?"

He studied her. "Ella?"

She tilted her head as though he were dull. "You know, that white lady you was talkin' to?"

"Miss Eleanor Whitaker?"

She bobbed her head. "Yeah. Ella."

"Ella." He tried the name and decided he liked the sound of it. It seemed soft and inviting. Somewhat opposite of the stiff yet fiery woman who regarded him with sparking eyes filled with something akin to distrust.

The girl crossed her arms. "You gonna throw her out? She got nowhere to go."

Despite the ire he should feel over one of lower rank speaking to him thus, Westley chuckled—as seemed to be becoming a habit on this rather peculiar day. "You like her, do you?"

She clasped her hands behind her simple pink dress. "Yes, suh. She a real nice lady."

Hmm. A nice lady who lied to the United States Army and convinced Sibby to let her run a house she had no business in. "That so?"

"Yes, suh. And she ain't like other white ladies."

Intrigued, Westley shifted the cane to his other hand and leaned his weight on the rail. "Oh?"

"Yes, suh. She ain't afraid of workin'. She scrubs in the kitchen just as hard as I do, even though Sibby keep tellin' her not to."

Not a woman of any means or family status. That seemed right. He'd briefly considered that she could be a displaced woman who had lost her home and seized upon a standing house without proper owners. But something about that didn't fit. Perhaps this Negro child would tell him things the lady might not.

"Do you know where she comes from?"

The girl shook her head.

"What about the baby? Surely his father would like to know he is here?"

The child shifted her stance. "Don't know his father."

"You mean she didn't tell you anything about her husband?"

"That boy's daddy ain't her husband." The little girl wrinkled her nose. "She ain't got one."

Westley's jaw constricted. As originally suspected, though briefly discarded. A harlot. She'd come here pretending to be a widow to hide her sin, just as Westley first believed when the Martin women said a *wife* waited for him at home.

The little girl's eyes flew wide as she realized she'd said something she ought not. "What you gonna do?"

He growled and turned for the stairs.

The girl's repeated question followed him as he made the turn on the landing, but he ignored her. Of course. It made perfect sense. His first instinct of a camp follower had been correct. And, *of course,* she would come here!

Why had he not thought of it sooner? His mother allowed trollops to find succor here. There had been plenty of talk whispered behind gloved hands, and certainly such gossip openly circulated amongst the unfortunate women.

Miss Whitaker came to find such aid, only to discover his mother dead and no help to be found. So, she had taken advantage of Sibby's softness toward children and plotted to take over his household!

Anger heated with each painful step he took until it nearly bubbled over by the time he reached the top of the stairs. The nursery. She would be in there.

Rather than step out of the upper hall onto the rear porch and enter the nursery by the outer door, he decided to cut through his mother's room instead.

Another thought sprang to mind, and he forced himself to reconsider. What if some renegade soldier had forced himself upon a hapless woman and the child had resulted? He'd heard tales of such from both armies. Perhaps he jumped to accusations too quickly. In either case, however, he could not alter his course! She could not stay any more than he. Admittedly, he was intrigued by her at first. But it was better that he stomp out any reckless feelings and end this farce before it could get any worse!

With sweat on his palm, he clasped the doorknob and flung open the door to the rose-painted room...and nearly lost his composure over the sight before him.

Chapter Fifteen

Ella screamed and dropped to the floor behind the bed, her heart hammering wildly. What in tarnation was that man doing in her bedroom? Holding the widow's dress she'd been changing out of up to her chest, Ella peered over the top of the bed.

Mr. Remington stood frozen in her doorway, his face contorted in an odd mixture of anger, confusion, and embarrassment.

Ella seethed. How dare he fling open her door unannounced? Just because this was his house... She stilled. Owner of Belmont or not, he didn't have the right. Did he?

Mr. Remington appeared to regain some of his senses and narrowed his eyes. Had he not the common decency to avert his eyes? Humiliation pulsed with the flutter of her heart. Worst of all, he did not seem to be inclined to shut the door.

"What are you doing?" Ella screeched.

The muscles in his jaw convulsed. "What are *you* doing in my mother's bedroom?"

Changing! She'd thought to put her work dress back on before going to face the man once more. Perhaps then he would see her less as the woman pretending to be a widow and more as a poor working woman in need of employment. Never did she expect for him to burst into her room!

"This is the room Sibby told me to sleep in," she said, keeping her tone measured as best as she could. "The better to be near my son."

"You do not stay in the nursery with him?"

She clenched her fists. First he would not give her the consideration of allowing her to dress before he continued to question her, but now he thinly veiled his insinuation that she fell short as a mother. "Sibby sleeps in there so she can feed him when he wakes in the night."

The man stood even more rigid, and his forehead creased above the eyes that bore into her.

After a few more heartbeats, Ella could take it no longer. "Sir! If you don't mind, I would like to finish dressing before we continue this most inappropriate conversation."

Surprise startled him from whatever contemplations overtook his mind, and his dark eyes focused on her once more. Then, ridiculously, they lit with an indecorous amusement.

The heat burning in her face intensified. "Be gone!"

The man had the gall to smirk at her before finally stepping back and pulling the door closed. The nerve! And here she thought that plantation gentlemen would surely act more civilized than those that had come upon a woman traveling alone. She ground her teeth. No. She would not think on that.

Miscreant or not, she would have to face him. Still on her knees, Ella pulled the faded tan dress over her head, buttoned the clasps at the base of her throat, then climbed to her feet to shake the skirt down over her petticoat.

"Are you finished yet?"

The deep timbre of his voice permeated the door and Ella startled. He listened at the threshold! Furious, she rounded the bed and flung open the door. He stood there, propped on his cane as though nothing untoward had just occurred.

She tried to steady herself. "Mr. Remington…"

"Major."

She inwardly groaned. "*Major* Remington. I am very sorry you did not expect to find me in your house, and I can understand how you must feel, but bursting in on a woman in private quarters is simply unacceptable."

"As my mother is dead, I did not expect *her* private quarters to be occupied."

Ella crossed her arms. "Yet, once you saw the room was used, you still did not remove yourself."

He shrugged, and Ella's blood pounded. Such arrogance!

He narrowed his dark eyes on her, his gaze unabashedly roaming over her from face to foot. She forced herself to remain still.

"Odd, really. Not at all what I expected."

She blinked at him. Whatever could he mean?

"Regardless, it simply won't do." His brow creased. "I must insist that you find alternative accommodations."

Her heart tripped over itself. "But, please, sir. Surely I can continue to work for my keep?"

He shook his head. "That won't be possible. You see—"

"Mista Westley!" Sibby burst into the room, the bundled child in her arms. She glanced to Ella, who must have looked stricken, because Sibby's frown deepened and she crossed over to her.

As Sibby passed the baby to Ella, she spoke low. "I is right sorry. Once he's had his say, ain't no changin' it. But I'll see what help I mights can find for you."

Speechless, Ella could only nod as she pulled Lee against her. *Oh, my sweet wee one. What shall we do now?*

Mr., ah, *Major* Remington cleared his throat. "Sibby. I have many things I need to discuss with you."

"Yes, suh. I done figured that." She tossed a look at Ella before following him to the stairs.

The major glanced back at Ella. "And you and I will continue this discussion later."

Ella turned away before he could see the moisture that

blurred her vision. She closed the door to the room that would no longer be hers, placed a tearful kiss on the baby's brow, and then began to pray.

Each step sent pain flaring up his leg, regardless of how much of his weight he attempted to place on the cane. By the time Westley reached the bottom of the stairs, beads of sweat formed across his brow and attempted to slide toward his eyes, lines of moisture betraying his weakness. He grunted and used his free hand to smear them away.

"Dat leg hurtin' you much, Mista Westley?"

He regarded the woman as he paused to rest in the foyer. "Why do you call me that?"

A spark glinted in her eye. "We don't call no man Masta no more, suh."

He grunted again and turned toward the back of the stairs to the doorway that would see him to the comfort of the library. "You were free years before Lincoln's proclamation. What does that matter?"

"Just do, suh."

He could understand that, he supposed, but that had not been the reason for his question. "Regardless, that is not the issue. I simply ask why you eschew my military title."

Some of the defiance left her voice. "Oh. Sorry, suh. You wants I should call you Major Remington?"

She followed slowly behind him and waited until he settled his frame into a leather chair near the fireplace. "Yes. That is my preference." How odd she thought anything different.

He resisted the show of frailty rubbing his leg would bring. Already he had revealed far too much of his pain. His men would be ashamed of him. A warrior crumbled by his pitiful intolerance of a little discomfort.

Sibby looked at her feet, twisting her hands.

Westley watched her, wondering how long it would take before she started talking. He waited.

Just when he suspected he might have to voice questions they both knew he wanted answers to, she launched an assault on words that sent them spraying from her mouth like shrapnel.

"I had no idea that girl was gonna show up on the porch. But she came right on up with that baby, and he was just a squallin'. I knew he need somebody to feed him, so I took him and left her out there with them soldiers. Truth told, I thought she'd be gone soon as they were. But, no, suh, she came right on in the house and asked me if she could stay here."

Westley ran a hand through his hair. "I would have thought the same. Usually the women Mother had here did not stay long, especially once they got what they wanted from us."

Her face contorted in confusion, but she merely nodded.

She said no more, so Westley prompted, "So she told you that she claimed to be my wife…?"

Sibby twisted her hands in front of her again. "Yes, suh. And, well, it seemed like a good idea. Seeing as we done thought you was dead and all."

In other circumstances, Westley might have laughed. "I see."

"What you going to do with her now? She ain't going to leave that baby."

Hmm. A harlot who loved her child and refused to abandon him in order to return to her profession. Had she by chance been forced into it to survive? Become a camp follower who intended to do laundry and ended up taking payment for men to come to her tent instead? He'd seen it happen too many times.

Westley settled deeper into the comfort of the chair, every muscle in him aching for a bed. Ironic, seeing how he had been so desperate to escape one not too long ago. He regarded Sibby. If he told her now of his plans to sell the place, then she would only fly into a fit he didn't feel like dealing with at the moment.

"I'll think on it and decide tomorrow."

She pressed her lips into a line and stared at him, something flickering in her eyes.

"What?"

She shifted her weight. "Well, there's somethin' else you needs to know."

He propped his elbow on the armrest and rubbed his temple. "What?"

"Well, Miss Ella told them soldiers that we was going to share the crops between the colored folks. I thought that there was a good idea at first, 'til I discovered we ain't got no good seed to plant."

None of that mattered. If the soldiers came back to check on the situation, Westley would take it in hand.

"Then another soldier came and we thought he was goin' to come see if we did like she said we was goin' to do. But that weren't what he came for."

Interest piqued, Westley leaned forward. "Then what did he come for?"

"He said we gots two weeks to pay all the taxes else they is takin' the place."

Not unexpected, but inconvenient all the same. "When was this?"

She counted on her fingers. "Week ago, I think."

Westley groaned. One week to find a buyer, or else he would have to pay the taxes from his personal accounts. He had the funds—his father had been wise to move all of his accounts to Northern banks and place them under Westley's care—but he did not want to dip into them if he didn't have to. He preferred to sell, then settle all debts from that.

"What you gonna do, suh?"

"I'll take care of it."

She seemed like she wanted to ask more, but his expression likely told her that would not be wise. "I done sent Basil to get your room ready, suh."

Westley gave his approval, then thought better of it. "No. Prepare my father's room instead."

Sibby's forehead furrowed. "But, suh, that room…"

Connected to Miss Whitaker's, he knew. "I am master here now, am I not?"

Something in her eyes hardened, but she dipped her chin. "Yes, suh. I'll get it done."

She turned and started out the door, her spine stiff.

"And have a bath heated as well. I could use one," he called as she scurried out.

"Yes, suh."

Westley frowned, wondering what had made her fortify her defenses. He lolled his head back. What a lout! He'd meant as the owner of the house, he would lay claim to the man's bedroom in the main section of the house rather than his childhood chamber on the side wing. Not that he meant to be master here in the way that had died with the war. He groaned. He didn't wish to antagonize Sibby over a misunderstanding about Belmont's most comfortable bed.

Or perhaps you seek less a featherbed than an excuse to be nearer the imposter.

He grabbed hold of the thought and flung it aside. Only to keep a closer eye on her. He forced his thoughts back to Sibby and the others who might remain here. Yank or not, master or no, this was still his house, and the people living within it should respect his orders just as the men under his command had—understanding that he did what he thought best for all.

Except these people were not soldiers, and he acted the

cad. The pain pulsing in his leg harmonized with the throb in his temple, swelling to a tormenting symphony.

Westley groaned. Home again to a house he didn't want, to aid servants who bucked under his care, and deal with a wife he didn't marry. He dropped his chin to his chest. Perhaps he should have started reading from that Bible after all.

But then, how could things possibly get any worse?

Chapter Sixteen

The soft glow of early morning had breached the drawn curtains, marched across the floor, and roused Westley from fitful slumber some time ago. How long, exactly, he couldn't say. But long enough that the thoughts vying for attention in his head now gave way to the study of the movements and voices on the other side of the door.

The singing captivated him first. A tender hymn of grace that resurfaced memories of his mother humming the same tune. He listened to the young mother on the other side of the door as she sang to her child and wrestled with the decision he had to make. Then those sweet sounds turned to low whispers that pulled him from the comfort of the quilts.

Westley palmed the loathsome cane and pushed to his feet, slowly making his way closer to the portal that separated him from the odd woman on the other side. Bare soles hardly making a sound, he pressed his ear to the door.

"Miss Ella, there ain't nothin' I can do."

"I can't leave him, Sibby."

"If you take him, who gonna feed him? You sure 'nough can't do it."

A small sob broke through the panels of the door and lanced him. The muscle in his jaw convulsed. How could he, in good conscience, separate mother and child? Or worse, toss them out so that both might starve? What had happened that she could not nurse her child?

"Come with me then, Sibby."

Westley tried to shield himself against the desperate words, but they only sank farther into his resolve.

"Can't do that neither. Got too many people here that needs me."

"I cannot…"

The words dissolved and Westley pressed his ear closer.

"I cannot lose the only one I have."

The pain in the woman's voice rallied a long-forgotten desire to protect, and Westley groaned. The whispers on the other side of the door carried a frantic tone, then moved away. He set his teeth against the ache in his leg and moved across the room to endure the tribulation of dressing.

He'd donned his trousers and linen shirt when the expected knock came at the door to the upper hall. "Suh?" Sibby said loudly enough to be heard through the closed door.

Westley fastened the top button. "Yes, Sibby?"

"You be needin' any help?"

"No."

A prolonged silence. "I got food made, if you wants any."

He ran his fingers through his hair, noting that it now curled above his ears, and called, "Thank you. I shall be down shortly."

A thought gripped him, and he hobbled to the door. When he opened it, Sibby still stood on the other side, as though she had no intention of moving on while he finished his morning ablutions. He studied her a moment. "I'd like Miss Whitaker to join me for breakfast. We have things to discuss."

Sibby shot a glance to his mother's bedchamber. "I'll asks her, suh, but…"

"But what?"

Sibby lifted her shoulders. "I think she already knows what you is goin' to say."

Westley arched his eyebrows. "Oh? And who read my

thoughts and conveyed them to her?"

Sibby crossed her arms. "Ain't like it's hard to see that you don't want her here. And 'sides, she done said you told her she can't stay."

That he had. He shifted the cane. "I have a few more questions for her. Then I will make my decision."

Sibby pressed her lips tight and studied him for a moment. Finally, she shrugged. "All right." She started to turn back toward the rose room.

"Sibby?"

"Yeah?"

"Last evening. When I said I was master, I didn't intend it to be taken as you thought."

She eyed him cautiously. "What'd you mean?"

He rubbed the back of his neck. There was a time he would have reprimanded a servant for speaking to him in such a disrespectful manner. But such trivialities mattered little in light of all she had endured. "I wanted the comfort my father's bed provided. And as I am now the owner of this house, I thought it my due to sleep in the master's chamber. My meaning did not extend beyond that."

Her shoulders lowered. "Oh. I, uh, thank you, suh."

"I consider all those that reside at Belmont under my protection." He allowed meaning to weigh his words.

"What 'bout Miss Ella?"

He ignored the question and asked one of his own. "Who has been taking care of you since my father died?"

Sibby's gaze fell to Westley's boots. "We been takin' care of ourselves."

"We?"

She shifted her weight. "Me, Basil, Nat, and…a few others."

He narrowed his gaze. Did the woman avoid a direct answer on purpose? He opened his mouth to prod her to speak further, but the protest of hinges drew his attention to the right.

Miss Whitaker poked her head out of the door, caught sight of him, and darted back within.

"Miss Whitaker!"

She looked out once more, red-rimmed emerald eyes wide. "Yes?"

"I would like for you to accompany me to breakfast."

Her delicate eyebrows joined ranks. "Why?"

He suppressed a smile that seemed to want to surface whenever this contradictory woman was near. "So that we may both be nourished."

She tilted her head and her sunset hair—with its red, copper, and gold tones shimmering—caressed her cheek. "I mean, why do you wish to eat with me?"

He grunted. "I should think that obvious. I desire your company."

Pink tinged her cheeks. "Oh."

Westley narrowed his gaze. Something did not fit about this woman. She'd known men, and yet blushed at simple statements and hid her partially clothed form. He gestured toward the stairs. "Shall we?"

She looked to Sibby as though she required permission from the servant woman. Westley cut his eyes to see Sibby give Miss Whitaker a nod of approval before she spun around and hurried down the stairs.

Miss Whitaker stepped from the room in a dingy cream and tan dress, the child wrapped in a shawl and tied to her bosom.

One corner of his mouth pulled up. "An interesting way to tote a child."

She glanced down at the baby and shrugged. "Keeps both hands free. And, besides, he seems to like it."

Westley gestured toward the stairs, and she hurried on in

front of him, her feet fluttering about like a windswept sparrow. By the time he won the battle of the staircase, she had already disappeared into the dining room.

The cane an ever-present demotion of his pride, Westley crossed into the dining space and found Miss Whitaker looking out the window, her forehead creased.

He paused. "See something of interest?"

"Oh!" She dropped the curtain entangled around her slim fingers and spun around. "Um, no. Just a pretty bird."

Why should he be surprised that lies came so easily to an imposter? Worse, why should he be taken aback at his own disappointment to hear them slither from such beautiful lips? And there, again, that hint of lilt in her words that seemed more pronounced with her nervousness. Keeping his thoughts to himself, he rounded the long table and pulled one of the carved chairs from its place. She looked at it for a second, then stiffly settled on the cushion. He bent slightly at the waist.

"If you will excuse me a moment, I'm going to the kitchen to see if Sibby has any honey. I haven't eaten any in months, and I am rather fond of it."

She tugged on a curl hanging down by her ear and glanced at her baby. "All right."

He slipped out of the door at the front of the dining room that led to a small portico on the side of the house. Then he stepped off the brick pavers and onto the soft earth. At least the damp ground muffled the sound of his steps and eliminated the annoying tap of the cane.

As his time as a soldier taught him, Westley measured his movements and eased around the long wing of the house, coming up to the open section near the kitchen. Nothing moved about in the yard. No vagabond Confederate militia lurked about seeking easy prey. The wind whispered over the grass, making it sway in a gentle waltz. A squirrel barked at his companion and a mockingbird trilled.

Perhaps Miss Whitaker had merely watched a bird after all. Westley rolled his shoulders. The military mindset had been ingrained in him for too long. Now he searched about for enemies when only wildlife trespassed on Belmont lands. He almost started to feel foolish creeping around his own home when he heard whispers.

He pressed his back against cool bricks that had been fashioned from the sandy clay of the banks of the Mississippi and slowed his breathing.

"You sure? We might wanna wait."

Westley strained his ears but could not identify the voice of the speaker.

"Can't. We done made a promise."

He narrowed his eyes. Sibby. What was she about?

"Here. Take this with you. Better do it at night, just in case."

A few moments later, the door to the kitchen banged and footsteps moved over the floor. Westley straightened himself, stepped back onto the bricked sidewalk and made no effort to mask his footsteps and thump of the cane. When he stepped into the breezeway and to the kitchen door, Sibby looped the handle of a basket over her arm, her focus on the food she gathered.

"Sibby?"

She yelped, and a covered platter in her hand teetered. She stumbled to right herself and grabbed it with both hands. She turned wide eyes on him. "Suh! You done scared me!"

He watched her carefully. "My apologies." He glanced around. "Is anyone else in here with you?"

She stiffened. "No, suh. Just me."

He tapped his finger on the cane. "That so? Hmm. I thought I heard someone talking as I approached."

Sibby let out a long breath and then a laugh that seemed counterfeit. "Oh, that was just me, Major Westley."

"Oh? Then to whom were you speaking?"

She shifted her stance. "No one, suh. I was just talkin' to myself."

Westley tilted his head. More lies swarmed around Belmont. "Odd habit to keep, Sibby. You best be careful before others begin to think you are going mad."

Her fingers gripped the platter tightly. "Yes, suh. I'll be rememberin' that."

He stared at her and her gaze darted to the space behind him.

"Well, I best be gettin' on to the house afore these here biscuits get cold."

Westley stepped aside and motioned her past. When she slid through the door, she turned guarded eyes on him. "Was there somethin' you needed out in the kitchen?"

"Oh. Yes. I nearly forgot." He tried to smile. "Do we have any honey?"

Something flickered across her eyes but she shook her head. "No, suh. Things like that are right hard to come by in these parts."

And yet, there seemed to be plenty of items stocked in the pantry. How had they kept the Rebs from raiding those supplies? Beyond that, how had they gotten so much to begin with when stores were scarce and wares even more so?

As though reading his thoughts, Sibby's eyes darted to the kitchen. "Mr. Remington hid lots of stuff under the house. We always had sumthin' to eat. Not plenty like before. But sumthin'."

Westley watched her.

She straightened her shoulders and turned toward the main part of the house. "I got Nat to bring all that stuff we had left up outta down there and put it back in my kitchen." She glanced over her shoulder. "Seemed best, seein' as how the war's over and all now."

Over. Perhaps in the papers, but Westley knew better. Men would fight past the time when the governments called it to an end, and then the fires of battle would rage in hearts and minds for a long time to come. He'd studied war. He'd lived war. He *was* a man of war. His very name spelled out W.A.R.

There were many things in this life Westley did not understand—women chiefly among them—but war always thrummed through his veins. He followed Sibby back to the dining room, watching the tightness in her shoulders and the stiffness in her neck.

And as sure as he knew war, Westley knew something more. Whatever Sibby hid from him she would fight for. Whatever made lies shoot from her lips and deceit glow behind her eyes would be protected as surely as soldiers protected their lands.

They came back to the dining room and Miss Whitaker's gaze flickered between him and Sibby. Did she know what secrets had taken up residence in Belmont? Or did she simply guard the ones that waltzed behind those arresting green eyes?

He turned up the corners of his mouth and slid into the chair at the head of the table. And then, as though secrets did not drift like ghosts among them, the three each pretended to be something they were not—he, the genteel Southern gentleman; Miss Whitaker, the refined widow; and Sibby, the loyal housekeeper.

Chapter Seventeen

Ella looked through her lashes at the major as she pried open the biscuit on her plate. What had riled him? He did well hiding it, as far as men went, but she could tell something bubbled beneath that calm exterior. He sat relaxed in his chair, his movements unhurried. But Ella had learned to sense when men boiled within. Her father often fooled many people, and few ever suspected the inferno that raged beneath his smiling features.

But Ella had always known. All too well.

Ever since childhood she'd possessed a way of sensing certain things about people. Perhaps that came from watching her parents for clues about what they hid from her, or perhaps it had been bestowed upon her by the Maker as a form of self-defense. Regardless of the origins, her intuition now told her that whatever transpired when Major Remington went to the kitchen stirred something restless within him. His movements seemed too casual and his manner too at ease to be genuine. In her experience the man who looked the most in control was often the one that erupted.

"You study me, Miss Whitaker."

Ella startled. Had she let her gaze linger too long upon him? She fluttered her lashes and forged a smile. "Surely you are used to women's attentions."

He stiffened, and she realized her mistake. How utterly foolish of her! He already thought her a loose woman. To one such as he, she would always be an undesirable bit of rubbish to be discarded once he tired of her. Why that caused an ache, she didn't know. Ella squared her shoulders. Let him think what he would. "My apologies, Major. I did not mean to be forward."

His gaze roamed her face as though he would discover something there. She forced herself to keep his gaze. He seemed curious about her. She could work with that. Curiosity meant interest, and interest meant this might be her opportunity to sway him.

She placed her hands on both sides of her plate. "I know you are a military man, not merely a volunteer for the war."

He made no response.

"Therefore, I assume you will soon be returning to your duties?"

He dabbed his mouth with a napkin and regarded her evenly. "You assume correctly."

A good start. She plowed ahead. "Then may I also assume that you would do well to have someone care for your home while you are absent for long periods of time?"

His mouth twitched. "That's what I have Sibby for."

She straightened herself and tried to show more confidence than she felt. "Of course. But as she and I discovered, not many accept a Negro woman running a household. Even though you Yanks claim the war was fought to end slavery, I have yet to meet a Federal soldier who did not regard the colored people as incapable of such things."

His nostrils flared and she feared she'd tread across something she should not. But she could not stop now. "Therefore, it would be prudent for you to have someone in place to handle such matters for you in your absence."

He watched her for a moment, and then the dark shadows in his eyes flitted away and something that almost resembled mischief took their place. "And you believe you are qualified for that position?"

She bit back a retort that clawed for freedom on the tip of her tongue. How dare he sound so arrogant! Just because he thought her a harlot did not mean that he could also think her a simpleton. She rubbed Lee's back to remind herself about the child at stake and forced a smile she did not feel. "I believe, sir, that I have already given evidence of such. I am a hard worker and learn quickly. I could serve you well."

He regarded her for so long she began to hope she would move him, but then he shook his head. "I do feel for your plight, Miss Whitaker. And, in honor of my mother, I will do whatever I can to be sure that you and your child receive the charity you came for. But you cannot stay here."

Her stomach constricted, and she feared she might lose the little she'd eaten. "But—"

He held up his hand and swiped it through the air as though such a gesture could silence her. Ella seethed.

Insufferable Yank!

His eyes widened and he looked as though she had struck him, and only then did Ella realize that the words had not been contained in her head but had flown from her mouth! She covered her lips, but the damage had been done.

His eyes clouded. "I should have expected such from one who is so in bed with the Southern cause that she named her child after The Marble Model."

Confusion arrested her next words and cut furrows in her brow. "Who?"

He tapped a finger on the table. "The King of Spades."

Ella clicked her tongue. "You speak madness."

"For a woman so enamored with General Lee, one would think you would be aware of the things men dub him."

Her mouth went dry. General Robert E. Lee? He thought she named her son for a man of war? She detested all things to do with war! She narrowed her eyes. So be it. Let him think she named the boy for the Rebel general. Better he thought that than know her wee sweet baby had been cursed with the cur's own name.

"Better that than be named after a devil," she said through clenched teeth.

His lip twitched. "A devil?"

Ella pulled Lee tighter against her, and he started to squirm. "What else would you call one who so loves the flames that he turns them on defenseless women and children? What other than a devil would wage war not against the enemy army, but instead sets its sights on devastating citizens? Leaving children to starve and women to fend for themselves!"

Anger burned within her and she stood so quickly from the table the chair toppled to the rug. "Aye, the devil, those Yanks."

She no sooner gained her feet than he stood to his. A growl rumbled from within him. "What know you of war, woman?"

"What do I know?" She clenched her hand at her side. "I know plenty. I know that Yankee flames ate my home and my family. I know soldiers are naught but men devoid of morals, men that use war as an excuse to ravage and pillage like pirates. I know that while men are off to defend what is being invaded, they leave behind families ripe for slaughter at the hands of *devils* who would rather demoralize the innocent people than fight in civilized battle." Her chest heaved. "That, sir, is what I know."

He stared at her, the muscles in his jaw jumping under the skin. She knew she had roused this military man to the kind of anger that should have made him act out every atrocity his kind was known for, yet he remained frozen in place, the fury of his deep breathing belied by the questions raging in his eyes.

Knowing she had sealed her own fate, Ella swallowed hard. Oh, why had she let loose such things? While true, it did her no good to voice them! Now the tiny seed of hope that she might be allowed to remain had been ground beneath her inability to keep her thoughts and feelings under guard.

Knowing the recourse that would soon follow, she denied frustrated tears the opportunity to sting her eyes. Then she turned and walked calmly from the room, leaving the fuming Yankee devil to his demons.

Westley measured the pounding beats of his heart and then breathed slower, bringing his pulse down with concentrated effort. Furious, he watched her stalk out of the dining room. He gripped the edges of the table. She had no idea the things that needed to be done to win a war—no concept of the choices men must make to save the lives of many.

Memories of torches and flames seized him, and he squeezed his eyes shut. A tactic, he told himself. A simple method to bring the South to heel and all the sooner end the struggle. There had been times, yes, when the orders made him cringe, but he justified their actions and kept his mind from lingering too long on the effects of what they'd wrought. A harsh thing, perhaps, but necessary. Still, though Westley's own men had burned barns as ordered, they had never set a torch to homes. The distinction would likely mean little to her, however.

The same thing he told himself over and again on the battlefield. The lie he used to scrub away the guilt as he lit fields on fire and watched them burn. But the depth of the anguish and fear in those green eyes clawed at him.

In a way, every word she hurled at him stank of truth. While the army tried to starve out an enemy, they damaged women and children. While men bent to the fever of battle, the innocent who'd had no say in the conflict suffered.

Westley rubbed the back of his neck. Perhaps not entirely innocent. Had he not seen women use their ample skirts and their wiles to smuggle supplies? Seen them spy and deceive? A war must be fought on all fronts. Such things could not be helped. Though a tragedy, some civilians got stuck in the crossfire. That was the way of war.

He dropped back into his chair and massaged his temples. Her words kept slithering back to him, slippery syllables that carried the weight of guilt like a millstone around the neck. And though he longed to deny it, he had to admit that he could not blame her. She had lived that pain, and he possessed no right to deny her the expression of it.

He rubbed a hand over his face and tried to dislodge the image of her that even now remained in front of him—how her eyes sparked when she threw her daggers at him. A dragon, that one. A tiny dragon, to be sure, but one with flames and claws to spare. And her voice…

Westley allowed himself a moment to let his anger fizzle beneath the intoxicating quality of her voice, even if what came from her lips aimed to wound. The more she raged, her Southern sounds shifted into a lilting Scottish as exotic as her sunset hair. Had she been reared among immigrants?

He shook his head. He should not try to unravel the mysterious woman whom he felt certain hid more layers than he had yet seen. That path only led to further trouble.

Curse it! Westley pushed to his feet and plucked the cane from where it rested upon the table and shifted it in his hand. He would do right by her, but only to honor his mother. His curiosity over her continued to make things worse. If he had sent her away yesterday, he wouldn't be contemplating his own morality now.

Her mysteries did not matter. He did not need to know why she'd hidden her Scottish accent behind a Southern one or why she blushed when he said he'd like her company. He didn't need to discover why her sparkling eyes could seem so innocent one moment and hardened the next. And he did not wish to know the story or circumstance that left her with a fatherless child upon his door.

He ground his teeth. He needed none of those answers. He needed only…

"See! It was a good thing I didn't call him Archibald!"

The little dragon's voice bounced around the foyer and smacked into Westley like a volley. *Archibald?* What did she rant about now? He shifted his weight and moved toward the door.

"Now, Miss Ella! You come back here!" Sibby's voice followed the sound of clicking shoes across the floor, and then was nearly lost with the slam of the front door.

He took two steps toward the foyer when Sibby appeared in the doorway, her arms crossed. "What you do to her?"

Westley curled his lip. "Excuse me?"

Her eyes flashed, and he nearly felt a pang for his harsh tone, but he had not the patience for her bayoneted words at the moment.

"What you say to her that made her storm outta this house?"

"She called me a devil, and I dared to disagree."

Sibby's mouth fell open, but she snapped it closed. "She took the boy wit her!"

He rolled his shoulders. "He is her child, and she can go where she pleases."

Sibby gasped. "He ain't! And she got no way to feed him." She whirled around and strode out.

"Where are you going?"

"I's bringin' them back, and there ain't nothin' you gonna do about it!"

The door slammed again, and Westley groaned. Not one, but two fiery women furious with him. And here he'd thought he'd left the war behind. He stood there a moment, maybe two, then he walked to the foyer and plucked his hat from the hook.

He twirled it in his fingers, sat it on his head, and paused. No. He would not chase after that woman. She hated him, and he couldn't say he blamed her. What a fool he'd been to think he could return to the South and not be hit full in the face with the destruction the North had caused here. Had he not set fires to fields and barns? Did he not see men twist railroad lines to send the passengers to their deaths? Yes, he carried that responsibility. He played a part in what war had made of Eleanor Whitaker, and countless others like her.

How often had he dismissed tales of soldiers plundering under the guise of the Confiscation Act? Westley closed his eyes. He'd turned his head when men boasted of finding women alone. Making sport of them.

He placed the hat back on the peg and trudged toward the library. No, it would do no good for either of them for Westley to go after her. Sibby's odd words tickled his ears, but he smothered them under forced indifference. Another mystery about Miss Whitaker he did not need—nor want!—to know the answer to.

He thumped his cane down the foyer, each tap reminding him of his frailty and stirring the pain in his leg. Perhaps he might still find Father's secret bottle of brandy behind *The History of Europe*. Something to dull the ache in his leg. And more, perhaps, to dislodge the images of laughing faces that he'd ignored instead of reprimanded and countless other memories searing in his head. Then, tomorrow he would leave money for Sibby to take care of the girl and her son. Next, he would go to the Federal outpost and pay the taxes for Belmont.

And then what?

He hobbled into the library, plucked the book from the shelf, and smiled at the niche behind it. A decanter still sat there, the amber liquid inside promising to sooth his frayed nerves and relieve some of the pain. He slid his fingers over the smooth crystal and pulled it from its resting place.

He grabbed the beveled glass from behind it and poured it half full, then sat on the armchair. What then, indeed?

He leaned his head back against the cushion and pulled a long draught from the glass. The liquid burned his throat and slid all the way to his stomach, lighting a fire in his gut. With two more gulps, the fire increased. By the time he had drained the glass, the fire had started to burn away the throbbing in his leg.

But the flames did not find the memories, nor did they diminish the guilt. Major Westley Archibald Remington. *W.A.R.*

A man born to war. A man that, if he were to admit it to himself, did not find the glory he sought in battle. Instead, he found only anguish, pain, and darkness. War made men do things they would have never thought to do in pleasant society. It twisted soldiers from men of honor to men who were little more than plunderers, murderers, and thieves.

Men who spilled their devious ways on women. Women like Ella.

He rolled her endearment name around in his mind. Testing it, feeling it. Why hadn't he seen what was so obvious? Her shyness...her fear? Those things did not drape a woman who had taken coin for her services. They cloaked women who had things stolen from them.

Westley sighed and closed his eyes. He would let her stay. Let at least one woman scarred by what men had scourged find safety.

Then, when the accounts were settled, he would go west. And never force her to look upon his devil's face again.

Chapter Eighteen

Ella tucked a restless piece of hair behind her ear. The wind continued to tug bits free, and by the time she reached the river road, wayward locks scurried over her nose and irritated her eyes. She pulled Lee tighter against the cold air that denied the presence of late spring.

He made little gurgling noises that scraped at her heart. How long would it be before those sweet coos turned to hungry wails? She drew a long breath, letting the wind course an icy path down her throat to cool the burning that forewarned tears.

Oh, why hadn't she stilled her tongue? She'd let her temper get the better of her. Try as she might to be nothing like Papa, she carried the same tendencies as he. Mama called it the fire of the Scots. When she was a girl, Papa had been feisty, and a bit hotheaded, but always gentle with her. But after Mama died…

She shook her head. It didn't matter. They were both gone now, and Ella was on her own. Sometimes she wondered what life would have been like if Papa had approved of that sailor. A fine-looking Navy man from the New Orleans port. He'd come to their farm one balmy spring to buy a new stallion for his younger brother and had taken a shine to Ella. A week later he returned and offered for her, though they had only just met. A girl of seventeen, she'd been taken by his handsome face and the thought of traveling the world. But Papa would have none of it. He'd said the man swam the wrong way, and no lass of his would be a notch on that man's schooner.

She'd had no idea what he meant at the time, but she'd

stayed mad at him for a month. No other men had shown any interest in her, and then the war came and made devils out of men that might have had the chance to be decent. At least as decent as someone who saw the fairer sex as goods to be traded or a prize to be lorded over could be anyway.

She looked down at Lee as the cold wind gained strength and began to carry a fine mist. He would be different. She would raise this one to be nothing like her father or the soldiers who had ruined this country. She would rear her little Lee to be a man of character, with a soft heart toward women. And someday a young lady would be worthy of Ella's treasure, and more wee ones would cling to her skirts.

She lifted her hem and started forward again. A strong son and a bushel of grandchildren. She didn't need anything more than that. So she would do what she must to secure the only future that offered any hope at happiness.

Droplets of mist swirled on the wind and landed like tiny diamonds on Lee's head. Ella frowned. She'd let her anger carry her out the door before she thought anything through. Halfway down the drive she told herself she would go to town and ask after another nurse. She'd even heard of women giving goat's milk to babes in need. If she could figure out a way to get a goat, she and Lee wouldn't need to depend on anyone. But now she stood at the edge of the river road in paralyzing indecision. She could neither keep the baby out in this weather nor return to the house.

"Miss Ella!"

Sibby's voice carried on the wind and flitted around Ella's ears. Heat radiated from her chest and chased away the chill that began to gather in her limbs. She cringed. Perhaps she could scuttle away and pretend she didn't hear. Sibby would want to dress her down for certain. She'd said some terrible things to Major Remington, and Ella knew the affection Sibby held for him.

She snuggled the wee one closer and turned. No use further setting flame to any help she might have remaining. She'd take the scolding and beg for mercy. For Lee's sake.

It plucked at her pride, but Ella held her ground and watched Sibby scurry down the drive, a blue scarf draped over her head. When she reached Ella, her breath came out in smoke that mingled with the mist.

"What you thinkin' traipsin' around out in this here nasty weather?"

She hadn't been thinking, but what good would it do to admit it? They already thought her low on wits. "I intended to go to town. I did not know the weather would so quickly turn foul."

Sibby drew her eyebrows low, creating dark curved lines that sat heavy over her eyes. "You ain't talkin' no sense. Now get on back to the house."

"The major will not want me back inside."

Sibby snorted. "I done told him I was acomin' to get you."

Ella hesitated. Would he let her return? At least until the weather passed and she could find a way to care for Lee? "You are sure that is a good idea?"

Sibby grabbed Ella's elbow and started to tug. "Good idea or not, I ain't lettin' you stand out here and get that baby sick."

Fear lashed at her, and Ella drew Lee closer. He looked peaceful, sleeping in his little cocoon. Droplets clung to his lashes, but he didn't seem to mind. His pink cheeks were flushed with warmth from being held so close.

Sibby tugged again. "Don't you go lettin' some stubborn ideas make no fool out of you."

Ella relented. It wouldn't do to keep Lee out here. Might as well face the man's wrath. She'd suffered men's fury before and survived. She could do so again. And this time she wouldn't be held down in the dark shadows. If he were going to beat her, it would have to be in the daylight in front of the people of Belmont. Without a word, she ducked her head and followed Sibby back toward the long lane that led up to Belmont.

Wind whipped her hair and tugged Sibby's mumbled words from Ella's ears before she could comprehend them. The mist turned to drizzle, and by the time they made the bend and could see the house, the drizzle turned into a downpour.

As icy water slid off her hair and down her nape, Ella shivered. The thin cotton dress stood no match against the biting rain, and in moments sodden fabric clung to her limbs and tangled around her feet.

"We need to hurry!" Sibby yelled, her last word lost under the crack of thunder.

Ella lifted her skirts higher, exposing her ankles and most of her calves and broke into a trot. Lee bounced against her, and she thought he would cry out, but he remained silent. Pulling the babe tighter with one hand while trying to keep the fabric from tripping her with the other, Ella ran.

Sibby kept pace, her body not encumbered by an infant. *Boggin* skirts! Always they tangled about the legs. A man's invention to make it harder for women to get away! The wind gusted harder, as though chiding her for using one of Papa's Scottish words that she knew wouldn't be acceptable in polite company. Well, good thing that word had stayed in her head where it belonged.

Not like the others she'd spit out at the Yankee major without the first bit of thought.

Ella clenched her teeth and blinked against the driving rain. A bit farther and they would reach the house—safety from the storm, if not from the man within.

Suddenly Sibby squealed and her hands flew up in the air as her body lurched to the side. Ella stumbled to a halt and whirled around, only to find Sibby lying on the ground and clutching her ankle. Mud splattered across her bodice, and Sibby's shawl took flight like a tornado-swept blue jay.

Ella dropped to her knees, sodden skirts landing hard in the muck that accumulated near the carriage block. She adjusted the baby and reached to grasp Sibby's shoulder. Rain ran in rivers down the woman's dark skin and mingled with the sea of mud beneath her. "Sibby! What happened?"

"Don't know. I tripped on somethin'." She wailed. "It hurts right awful!"

Ella grasped her upper arm and tried to get her to her feet. "We have to get you inside!"

Sibby grabbed her leg and moaned. "I can't! Get Mista Westley!"

Ella set her teeth and struggled to her feet, her shoes sliding and sending her careening sideways. She stumbled through the mud and blinked her eyes against the stinging rain. The stairs made her feet tangle in her skirts and she nearly fell, but she managed to right herself and pull her soggy frame onto the front porch. The wind plastered her dress against her, but at least she no longer stood beneath a waterfall.

She threw the door wide, and it slammed against the wall. "Major!"

No reply. Torn with uncertainty on whether to search for him or try to put Lee down and help Sibby by herself, Ella hesitated for a moment, dripping water on the polished floor. She bit her lip. If Sibby had broken her leg, Ella wouldn't be able to carry her into the house.

With a groan she lifted her soggy skirt once more and carefully traipsed across the floor into the ladies' parlor. She tracked mud across the fine rugs, passed through the pocket doors into the men's parlor, left a trail of leaves and dirt inside the dining room, yet still didn't see the man anywhere.

"Major!" she screamed, frustration and fear pitching her voice to a near wail.

A noise. She scrunched her nose and followed it to the door under the stairs that hung ajar. Ella put her fingertips on the fine wood and shoved, sending the door flying backward and banging against a set of the library shelves.

Major Remington startled in the leather armchair, the glass in his hand rolling to the floor. His dark eyes sprang open, and in one movement he leapt to his feet and threw his fists in the air.

Ella couldn't breathe. Major Remington's pupils were dilated as he tried to focus on her. Her gaze darted to the glass on the floor and then up to the small table where a nearly empty decanter perched precariously on the edge. She forced air into her lungs.

He'd found the devil's drink and would be in its clutches. She backed away slowly, her pulse pounding in her ears. Perhaps she could close the door and find a way to secure him inside.

Clarity pushed away the fog in his eyes and he dropped his hands. "Miss Whitaker! What are you doing?"

Ella stared at him. Was he in the drink's clutches or merely startled from a deep sleep? Her hand tightened on the doorknob.

The confusion—and dare she think worry?—on his face lowered her pulse. Perhaps only the final dregs of sleep.

"Miss Whitaker? Are you all right?"

Ella jerked her chin toward the foyer. "Sibby fell. She can't get up, and she's stuck out in the storm."

Confusion marred his deceptively handsome face, and he plucked his cane from where it rested against the bookshelf. Ella groaned. He wouldn't be able to carry Sibby either! He could barely carry himself.

As though sensing her thoughts, his wide shoulders stiffened. "Best you wrap your son in a warm blanket and come help me."

Ella slipped around him to pluck a folded quilt from the other armchair by the hearth. He waited, and Ella scurried around him and away before he could grab her. He made no move to snatch her, however, and by the time she wrapped Lee tightly and laid him in the cradle in the parlor, he passed through the foyer behind her. The thump of his cane went to the porch and then disappeared beneath the howling wind and rolling thunder.

Ella rubbed her fingers across Lee's brow, but he didn't stir. His skin felt warm beneath her chilled hands. Perhaps the quilt made him too hot. She loosened the edges and draped it over him. He sure slept soundly for one who had been jostled so much.

She leaned nearer to put her lips on his tiny forehead when shouts from outside reminded her of her mission. Ella straightened and, telling herself he would be safe for a few moments without her, hurried out into the rain.

The major had managed to get Sibby off the ground and had one of her arms draped over his shoulder. He supported her under her ribs and leaned hard to the side, letting the cane support the weight of them both. He grunted, and tried to snatch the cane free from the muck it lodged in.

Remembering herself, Ella plunged into the flying current of water and ran down the front steps. She slipped on a slick bit of ground and nearly lost her footing, but managed to regain herself and duck under Sibby's other arm.

A flash of light scored the sky, searing lines in Ella's vision. She tightened her grip and tugged her shoes from the mud that wanted to claim them. On Sibby's other side, the major mumbled words Ella guessed were curses. They slowly moved forward against the current of icy rain, each step a disjointed lurch.

Major Remington struggled against Sibby's weight and his own, the cane in his hand sliding on the ground and seeming to make things all the more difficult. Ella tried her best to hold as much of Sibby's weight as she could, but each time the woman took a hop forward, Ella felt as though they would all tumble to the ground.

A few more steps, each seeming to take hours rather than moments, and they made it to the bottom of the stairs.

Sibby cried out when they almost dropped her trying to get up the front steps. Never had Ella tried to support so much weight, and the steps nearly proved her undoing. By the time they reached the cover of the porch, she and Major Remington were both heaving air.

They pulled Sibby inside the house and deposited her on the settee in the parlor. Ella reached down and slipped her hand under Sibby's knees, shifting her to lie down.

Sibby wailed and turned her head into the cushion. Ella glanced at Major Remington's scowl. "Do you think it is broken?"

The muscles in his jaw worked and he lowered himself to the floor. With gentle fingers, he probed the skin around Sibby's lower leg and ankle. When he tilted her foot up, she screeched.

Ella bit her lip. "Is it broken?" she asked louder.

Major Remington growled. "If only you would give me a moment, Ella, I will try to tell you."

Her breathing stopped. The sound of her name on his lips, even said in annoyance, sent a shiver down her spine. She stood there dumbly until she reminded herself to draw air. As the shiver died, anger brought heat. Who did he think he was, calling her by her Christian name without invitation? Indignation chased away more dangerous feelings and settled on her chest like an anvil.

"Well, Sibby, I think you have sprained it," he said, his tone gentle and not at all like a heartless soldier. "There is some swelling, but I don't think you've broken anything. We'll keep it lifted for tonight and send Nat after the doctor first thing in the morning."

Sibby sniffled. "He ain't here."

A shadow passed over Major Remington's features, but he swept it away before Ella could analyze it. "Oh?" The word, obviously meant to sound unconcerned, fell heavy on the room. "And where could he have gone?"

Tears streamed from Sibby's eyes, and she chewed on her lip.

Major Remington grunted. "Very well. We will send another."

"I will go."

He turned his eyes on Ella. "You?"

She put her hands on her hips. "Why not? I can send the doctor back here whilst I care for other business."

That infuriating amusement that seemed to take residence in his eyes at the strangest times flared. "Oh? And what business, might I ask, could you possibly have in town?"

Ella crossed her arms. Arrogant *bampot*. "I don't see where that is any concern of yours."

His Adam's apple bobbed, and all humor left his eyes, taking them from gold-flecked hickory to mahogany. "Indeed."

Ella grasped the sides of her dress, trying not to shiver. She must look like a drowned kitten. All bones and angles and matted fur. She reached up and smoothed her hair, sending water droplets down her neck.

He studied her, no doubt seeing her as a wretch. He opened his mouth to say something when a tiny cough turned their attention to the cradle. Ella stepped past Major Remington and knelt beside Lee.

She frowned. The wee one's cheeks were cherry red, and he wriggled under the quilt. Ella pulled it from him and placed her fingers on his face. He felt hot to her touch. Alarmed, she scooped him up, and he coughed again, a terrible hack that sounded like wind through reeds.

Major Remington leaned over her shoulder and peered at the babe. "You should change out of those wet clothes before you hold him. A child that small can take to sickness quickly."

Her heart pounded, and she wanted to fling words at him defending her ability to care for her own child, but she bit them back. It would be a lie. She knew nothing of caring for a baby. Her chest constricted. And what if he came down with an illness from her temper-induced walk in the storm? She could not bear it.

He laid a hand on her shoulder, the weight of it bringing an unexpected comfort. "I shall watch him while you change."

"What...wrong with the boy?" Sibby asked, her voice threaded with pain.

"Nothing," Ella lied. "I'm sure he just needs to be cleaned and fed." She slipped out from under the major's touch.

"That's good then."

Ella settled Lee back into the cradle, leaving the quilt off of him. She looked at the major, and the compassion on his face stabbed her. How could he go from arrogant Yank to concerned gentleman in so short a time? She pressed her lips together. It didn't matter. Any man who lingered with the drink could not be trusted. "I'll only be a moment."

He considered her for a few seconds and then, without a word, lowered himself into a chair next to the settee Sibby occupied.

"Miss Ella...?"

She leaned near Sibby. "Yes?"

Sibby squeezed her eyes tight. "I do hurt somethin' fierce."

Ella patted her shoulder. "I am terribly sorry, Sibby. I wish there were something I could do to ease your pain."

"Well..." Sibby drew a shuddering breath and then clenched her teeth.

"Well what?"

"I got some laudanum in a tin in the back of my drawer," she whispered.

Laudanum? Where had Sibby gotten such a thing? Medicine was nigh impossible to find, most of it being used for the soldiers if they were able to get any past the lines. Ella dismissed the thought. Sibby had likely stored away all manner of remedies that belonged to her mistress. Why should she be surprised? It seemed very little of the war had tainted Belmont.

She gave Sibby's shoulder a squeeze. "Very well. I shall bring it to you."

Sibby turned her face back into the cushion. Ella rose and grasped her skirts. As she turned to leave, her eyes slid over the major and the odd expression on his face. Then his focus snapped to her, and their gazes locked.

Something in that moment sent a fire sparking through her middle and flying to every inch of her limbs. She backed away, terrified though somehow unable to force herself free of the intense gaze that watched her. He continued to brazenly stare at her until she whirled around, spraying droplets, and hurried from the room. And even then she could still feel the embers of his eyes following her.

Chapter Nineteen

Westley tapped a finger on his chin and eyed Sibby where she lay on the settee. The conversation he'd overheard near the kitchen returned to him. It seemed likely the hushed tones and Nat's absence were related.

He rolled his shoulders. Or perhaps he merely saw shadows where none existed. It could mean nothing that Sibby had medicines—a rare commodity, especially this far south. She may have just been able to keep some hidden. And as for Nat's absence, they were free people and could move about as they chose. Still, the suspicion niggled.

"Sibby?"

She sniffled. "Yes, suh?"

"Where is Nat?"

The tightening of her neck and shoulder muscles gave Westley a clear indication of her stress over a simple question. He narrowed his eyes.

Sibby fidgeted with the cuff of her sleeve. "He, uh, done went to fetch some flour for me."

Westley sat back in his seat, not wanting to dub her a liar but not believing her either. He intended to question her further, but the babe coughed again. Westley shifted his weight and peered over the edge of the cradle. Nestled in a lovingly prepared nest, a tiny round face with rosy cheeks beneath dark little eyes stared up at him.

Who had fathered this child? And under what circumstance? He looked nothing like his mother, so he must favor his sire. Unless…

Westley leaned closer. Unless he wasn't hers either. Shame seeped into his chest. Could it be possible that Miss Whitaker had somehow rescued the child rather than birthed him? In the heat of their argument, Sibby *had* said that the boy wasn't Ella's. Had he wrongly assumed things about her? It would certainly explain the inconsistencies.

The child wriggled a fist free from the coverings and waved it in the air at Westley. His mouth curved. "A young fighter, are you?"

He felt, rather than saw, Sibby turn eyes upon him. Still, the little human held his attention. So innocent, this babe who had not yet been tainted by a cruel world. A pity that would not last for long. Growing up in a war-torn land with only an unwed mother to care for him would soon force many unpleasant things upon the child.

The boy gurgled, making happy little noises and swinging his fist, and Westley clenched his hands. A right shame, indeed. A sudden cough ripped the happy look from the cherub's face, making his features scrunch. As the cough subsided, the babe began to cry.

Westley frowned and peered closer at him.

"Ain't you gonna pick him up?"

Westley glanced at Sibby, who tilted her head back to regard him.

He scratched his head. "Well, I—"

"I can't be liftin' him myself, so you is gonna have to do it."

Westley regarded her a moment, her face painted in an odd emotion he could not place. She thrust her chin toward the child. Westley clenched and relaxed his fingers. It seemed there would be no other option.

He gained his feet and reached into the cradle, his hands

appearing much too large and cumbersome. How to lift the boy without causing harm? Westley shifted his weight to his good leg and bent closer, trying to get an arm under the baby. The little fellow squirmed, his cries gaining intensity and causing Westley's anxiety to spike as though he were saddling up for a skirmish.

"Just scoop him up, Major Westley. You ain't gonna break him."

Damaging him was precisely what Westley feared. He ground his teeth and put both hands under the child. With the tiny head cupped in his hands, he lifted the baby from the cushion. Then he stood there, paralyzed, with the infant lying on his upturned forearms. He bounced his arms gently, and the boy's cries softened. "Here now, little fellow. There's nothing to fear. Your mother shall return shortly."

The soft, soothing words spoken in a gentle tone Westley didn't know he possessed flowed from his mouth and, to his utter amazement, calmed the crying. The baby looked up at him, blinking dark eyes as though he knew he held Westley under his spell.

"Hmm. Seems like that little man be likin' you, Major Westley."

Westley stilled. "Nonsense. He merely wished to be removed from the cradle."

"Hmm. Well, he needs to be out of dem damp wrappings anyhow." She twisted around farther, trying to get a better look, and shifted her injured ankle. She winced and pain clouded her face.

Westley limped over to the settee, the inability to use his cane making him feel unstable. He took careful steps, lest he drop the child. When he made it alongside Sibby, he extended his arms to her. "Here."

She shook her head. "I ain't going to be able to do it."

His stomach tightened. "Then we shall wait for Miss Whitaker."

"Why? You mean you can't unwrap him and then wrap him up again in another blanket?"

Westley shrugged, the little boy rising and falling with the movement of his shoulders. "Such is women's work. It can wait for her to return."

"Well, then, I reckon that him gettin' the sickness be more important than you doin' *women's work*."

The disdain that dripped from her lips cut him. He clenched his teeth and had to speak through them. "And what of his infant's wrappings? I know nothing of the proper changing of such things."

Her face contorted, then understanding smoothed her features. "Miss Ella can do that part. You just go on and make sure his gown and blanket is dry." Pleading leapt into her eyes, and Westley could not deny her. She'd lost her own son to coughing sickness. It stood to reason she would be overly concerned about such things now.

Westley considered the best way to handle his task. Never had he held such a fragile thing. Finally deciding the floor the safest place for the assignment, he painstakingly lowered to his knees.

Ella pulled the dripping frock over her head and draped it across the back of a chair. She shivered. Soaked all the way through her corset *and* her chemise! She pulled off every stitch of clothing and grabbed the towel by the washbasin. She rubbed her arms and legs until they tingled and then turned her attention to her hair. She wrung out its lengths until the cloth would absorb no more of the moisture and then padded toward the armoire.

She made it three steps when the mirror claimed her attention. Copper and cherry hair fell in wild waves all the way down her back, and her skin looked splotchy. She crossed her arms over her chest and hurried away. She needed to dress quickly, lest the major get some mad idea to barge in on her again. Seeing her in her underpinnings had been mortifying enough.

Ella wrinkled her nose. Her only corset was soaked, and her spare chemise was in the wash. Oh, the shame of it. She hadn't the time to wait for the things to dry, and she couldn't very well put on wet garments underneath the fresh ones. She'd just have to put on a dress without them and pray no one noticed. At least until after Sibby had her medicine and she could return upstairs with Lee. That is, if the major would let her.

She bit her lower lip and tugged a work dress out. She paused. Maybe not. If Major Remington saw her as a lady, perhaps he would treat her with more respect. She pulled down the blue silk gown Sibby had altered. Yes, better she look like a lady in proper attire. Assuming one could be *properly attired* for begging.

Ella plucked a petticoat from the trunk and stepped into it, then let the dress slide over her head. As long as she didn't entirely undo the fasteners, she could get into it without Sibby's aid. She managed to tug on the strings behind her back and get the ribbon tied at the bottom of the bodice.

There. That should suffice. Ella ran her hands down the bodice. The fabric slid against the skin underneath, and she felt naked without proper undergarments. Why, she was worse than a harlot. Dressed in naught but a petticoat and a gown! The scandal of it.

Ella stepped back to the mirror and examined herself. The bodice left her neck and the hollow of her throat exposed, but otherwise appeared modest. She leaned closer. Could anyone tell she didn't have any stays on?

A knock pounded on her door and Ella yelped.

"Miss Whitaker. I must speak with you."

Strain laced the man's voice, and Ella placed a hand to her thudding heart. "I'm not ready."

A growl. "Your son requires you."

Her heart beat faster, and Ella hurried to the door on bare feet, leaving her ruined shoes by the bed. She cracked open the door and peered at him. "What do you mean?"

He shifted his weight off the cane. How had she not heard its thump up the stairs?

"He requires...cleaning." Red splotched the man's neck and spread to his jaw, getting lost beneath a day or two's worth of beard.

Ella's mouth twitched. This hardened soldier was embarrassed by an infant's need for fresh napkins? Thankfully, she contained her odd amusement at his discomfort, lest it anger him. She could not afford to antagonize him further, not if she hoped he wouldn't toss her out into the daunting shadows tonight.

He cleared his throat and she realized she'd been staring. "He is quite restless, and as Sibby is still in pain..."

"Oh! The medicine." She'd forgotten. How selfish of her. Worrying about clothing while poor Sibby lay in agony down below. Ella threw open the door, and the major's eyes widened. He took a small step back, and then his gaze unabashedly roamed all the way down her figure before returning to her eyes.

Determined not to show the mortification that surely already reddened her face, Ella lifted her chin. "I told you I was not yet ready. I haven't had the opportunity to pin my hair."

His eyes darkened. "I like it falling free."

She gathered the locks at her nape and tugged them to the front, her fingers seeking to undo enough of the knots to tame the disarray into a braid. "A man should not see a woman with whom he is not intimately familiar with her hair around her shoulders. It isn't proper."

His brows lifted, and mischief danced in his dark pupils. "Oh, but don't you remember? You *are* my wife."

Her fingers stilled and her pulse quickened. He didn't think to use her ruse to take advantage of her, did he? Her fingers flew faster, and she tried to conceal a tremor that found its way into her voice. "Not in truth."

He watched her, emotions parading across his face. Curiosity, attraction, confusion.

Ella turned her back. "If you will excuse me, I will pin up my hair, fetch Sibby's medicine, and be down shortly."

"I will retrieve the laudanum. You should see to the babe."

She snatched a few pins from the dressing table and hurried back to the door. He still darkened the frame. "Well? Do you not know where it is?"

"I know."

Infuriating rascal! Then why did he still stand there? "It is in her drawer."

"I heard."

"In the nursery."

"Yes."

She twisted the muddled braid at the back of her head and jammed the pins into it, scraping her scalp. Ella stepped up to him, crossing her arms over her chest. "Will you not allow me to pass?"

He stepped back, gave a small bow at the waist, and swept his arm out. "Certainly."

She had to walk by him so closely that her skirts swept over the top of his mud-caked boots. Heart hammering, she fled down the stairs, the wood cold beneath her toes.

By the time she reached the parlor, her pulse thudded in her ears so loudly she couldn't even hear herself think. The nerve of that man! Whether he saw her as a harlot or not did not give him the right to look at her that way!

Her stomach twisted. Though she must admit—even if she did not want to—that the appreciation in his eyes did not turn her blood cold as it should, but rather set it aflame. Nothing about the intensity of his gaze had been like the predatory gleam she'd so often seen from other men. This was something different.

Ella stepped into the parlor and halted. "Sibby! Why is Lee on the floor?"

Sibby lifted her arm from where it had draped over her face. "Major Westley done put him there."

Ella crossed the rug and dropped to her knees, glad she didn't have any crinoline to hinder her. "Why in heaven's name would he do such a thing?"

Lee lay on the outspread quilt, wearing a different gown than the one she'd put him in this morning. He sucked on his tiny fist and looked up at her. "Why…?"

"He made sure the boy be dry, seein' as I can't be doin' it and you was upstairs."

Ella pressed her lips into a line. Major Remington had changed him? She reached down and rubbed his little face.

Sibby chuckled. "But he weren't goin' to change his napkin. Said that was for you to do."

Oh, the napkin. She'd forgotten to fetch a fresh one from the nursery. "But why is he on the floor?"

Sibby lifted a shoulder. "I reckon he thought it be safer that way."

Something within her lurched. Major Remington had done these things? The man who made his living killing had changed her child? Had worried over dropping him so he had made a soft place on the floor? Tears pricked at the back of her throat. "How did he do it?"

Sibby turned her head and regarded Ella. Her eyebrows lifted, and it seemed she understood what Ella really wanted to know. "He plucked that boy from the cradle and soothed his cryin'. He was abouncing him and talkin' to him real sweet-like. Then he fixed him that little place there and changed him into one of the spare gowns I keep down here."

Ella stroked Lee's head. Major Remington, the Yankee devil, had so gently tended her son? Ella opened her mouth, but words would not come.

Sibby regarded her closely. "Yes 'um. I been knowin' him for all of my life, and I ain't never seen him treat anything so gentle. Was like he was afraid he were going to break that babe."

Ella lifted Lee and cradled him in her arms and her heart lurched. That was what Lee should have had...a mother who loved him and a father who gently tended him. Instead, Lee would have an imposter mother and no father at all to teach him how to be a proper man. She snuggled him close and he began to cough, his little body shaking with the effort.

Ella turned worried eyes to Sibby. As the fear she'd struggled to contain within herself manifested on the other woman's features, Ella's heart pounded harder.

Oh, Lord. If he suffers because of my folly I shall never be able to forgive myself.

Chapter Twenty

Tears streamed down Ella's cheeks as she wiped the cool cloth over Lee's heated face. He hadn't eaten in hours and refused each time they had tried to get him to suckle.

Ella made another pass around the nursery, past the bed Sibby watched her from, and back to the wash basin. It had been quite the task, but with help from Basil, she and Major Remington had managed to get Sibby upstairs once the medication had taken its effect and dulled the pain.

"Miss Ella, you gonna have to calm down," Sibby said, interrupting her thoughts. "You bein' like that ain't helpin' nobody." Sibby pushed up on her elbows and adjusted the pillow behind her. Outside, the wind howled and banged against the window as though it demanded entrance to the nursery.

Ella stopped her pacing and dropped the rag back into the basin. "I'm going for the doctor."

Sibby's eyes widened. "What for? So you can die out there in this here storm?"

"I have to do something!" Ella caught back her voice, the screech in it likely to draw the major from his chamber. At least he had not thrown her out. Nothing had been said about her outburst, and when the major finally retired some hours ago, it had been with concern on his features.

"I'm sorry, Miss Ella." Sibby's words were filled with an ache Ella did not wish to hear. "I knows how hard it is."

Ella sniffed and wiped her sleeve across her face, not caring that she smudged the fine silk. She had an idea about what put so much pain into Sibby's voice, and she didn't want to hear more.

"We's gonna make sure someone gets the doctor in the mornin', Miss Ella. We is. But in the middle of the night, and in this storm—" She shook her head. "We just can't go now."

"But what if tomorrow is too late?" Ella whispered.

Sibby's eyes brimmed with tears. "It won't be. God won't let me lose dis one too."

Ella turned her face away, but Sibby kept talking. "I be knowing the terror you feel."

She turned back to Sibby, not wanting to hear what she knew came next.

"I know because my Peter died of a coughing sickness with the masta and missus." Sibby swallowed hard, and when her eyelids fell closed, tears slipped out from underneath her dark lashes.

Ella gripped Lee tighter. She shouldn't ask. "The...the same sickness?"

Sibby's eyes flew open. "Oh, now, we don't know that. Look here. Maybe he just done breathed in too much of that rain."

Oh, this was all her fault! If only she hadn't run outside. Ella shook her head, the tightness in her throat making it difficult to breathe. "You are certain there is still a doctor around?"

Sibby's gaze dropped to the covering across her lap. "He came out here before. I reckon he still be in town."

Ella squeezed her eyes shut for a moment and then resumed her pacing. Lee coughed again, a deep sound that seemed impossible for one so small. "I'm sorry, Sibby. About your baby. I can't..." She drew a shuddering breath. "I can't imagine."

Sibby nodded but didn't say anything more. Ella paced until her head began to swim with exhaustion. She glanced back at the bed. Sibby slept, no doubt aided by the dose of medicine Major Remington had given her. Perhaps she should find some rest as well.

The lamp on the table cast flickering shadows across the walls, like insects scurrying to and fro. Ella adjusted the wick and lifted the light with her free hand, increasing the depth of the shadows pooling around her feet. Her head began to throb. Yes, she would have to rest. She could lie down with Lee next to her for just a few moments.

The door between her room and the nursery stood open and Ella passed through it, holding the lantern high and sending inky shadows scurrying from her path. She set it on the dressing table and considered changing out of the blue gown she still wore. But she was too tired to worry about the wrinkles.

Ella laid Lee in the middle of the bed and then crawled in next to him, curling her body protectively around his. *Oh, my wee one. I am so sorry.*

Tears slipped down her cheeks and onto the quilt, pooling under her face. Papa was right. The more she tried to help, the worse she made things. After Mama died, she attempted to take over her duties, cooking and caring for the household, but she had fallen short in every way. Her burnt or undercooked meals making their scarce supplies nearly intolerable, Papa had turned ever more to spending their funds on whiskey rather than food.

Aye, Lass, you can ruin anything.

Your ma would be ashamed of ya, this place lookin' like it does.

Don't you ever think, girl, before ya open yer mouth?

His words pelted her, dragging up time after time when she had failed. His comments had cut her, but she'd known he'd spoken truth. It was her poor work and sassy tongue that drove him to the devil's juice. And that night when he'd slapped her...aye, she'd deserved that too. She'd called him a good-for-nothing, bottle-toting coward and blamed him when that last colt had died.

Rebel soldiers had taken the colt's dam before he was ready to wean, and Papa hadn't even tried to stop them. The poor thing had starved, and she'd screamed at him for it.

A strangled sob broke free, and on its heels more followed. Fire burned in her throat and at the back of her eyes, and pulsed through the throbbing in her head. She'd failed to save the colt, just as she'd failed to keep Papa happy, or make it safely north, or bring anyone to help Cynthia birth Lee.

And now...now he lay here with her, barking coughs shaking his tiny body. All because she was every bit the ninny Papa had said.

Something warm and heavy settled on her shoulder and Ella jerked, her feet flying out behind her and smacking something solid. The shadows had sprouted demons again, and they had come for her! She flipped to her back, her heart galloping.

A monstrous shadow loomed. She opened her mouth to scream.

"Cease, Ella! It is only me."

The cry died in her throat. Her breath hitched. "Major?"

He grunted. "Who else would it be?"

Confusion flittered in her chest. "Why...why are you in here?"

He leaned closer, his face practically indistinguishable from the shadows. Hadn't she had a lamp? What had happened to the light?

"I heard noises. I came to see if you were all right."

All right? She was anything but. "I am fine."

He reached out and his fingers brushed the edge of her jaw, moving soaked tresses from where they clung to her skin. "I think you speak falsely."

"I..." She wanted to deny it, but the pain in her chest

would not let her. "I am sorely afraid."

His hand cupped her face, and the gentle gesture let forth another heaving sob.

Miss Whitaker shook, her body appearing desperate to hold in a grief that sought just as desperately to free itself. He ran his hand down her hair, gently stroking. "Easy, Ella."

She shuddered, as though the sound of her name affected her as much as it did him. He stroked her hair, uttering words of comfort until his leg began to ache. Still, she strangled sobs in her throat and would not let them free. He shifted his weight and moved to go around the other side of the bed so that he might sit without pressing up against her.

Her hand flew out and grasped his sleeve. "Please...don't go."

So much fear in her voice. He placed his hand over hers, her small fingers cold beneath his own. "I meant only to go to the other side of the bed. I will stay if you wish it."

Could she possibly want him, the one she'd called a devil, to stay with her? Her grief must be deep, indeed, if she would seek comfort from one such as him.

Her hand slipped from beneath his and he wondered if she decided against her request. He used the bed posts as support and walked to the other side. He glanced at the door to his own room, which he'd left open—it had proven to be too much of a temptation. Slipping through it, rather than coming to the door at the hall, had seemed much more intimate. Something done between husband and wife, as the rooms were designed for. But he was no husband, and she no wife. And, thus, he trespassed.

He sat on the bed, his gaze traveling over the babe and to the woman who wrapped herself around the child. Her display of protectiveness sparked the same in him, and he wondered at the fervent urge to wrap himself around her as she did the baby.

"I am sorry." Soft words, so quiet he almost missed them, drifted across the great expanse of the bed. An arm's length only, but it seemed a great ocean separated them. An ocean he had the strangest desire to sail.

"You need not be." He would not have her apologize for the pain that claimed her. Unable to resist, he reached over the babe and allowed his hand to feel her face once more. She turned her cheek into him, and his world shifted. Unnerved by the sensation that burned within him, he removed his hand.

"I should not have called you such things," she whispered in the dark.

Westley tilted his head back and stared at the ceiling he could not see. "You had every right. I sense that this war has done things to you...as it has to me." That last part he had not meant to say, yet it clung to the end of his sentence and would not remain within the privacy of his head.

She made a strangled sound, and despite his better judgment, Westley turned and laid himself out on the bed. On the pillow across from him, she shifted, though to get closer or farther away, he could not tell. "It is all right to let the feelings out sometimes."

She gulped, and then sniffled. "I do not wish to be further marred by weakness." Bitterness tainted the words, and he wondered at the source. "Yet, as much as I try to hold them back, these boggin tears—" she jerked to a stop.

Westley chuckled. "What is that word?"

She turned her face away. "One of my papa's. 'Tis not a nice one, I'm afraid. And not befitting a lady." She gave a bitter laugh. "But then, since I'm not one, I suppose it doesn't matter."

Lee coughed a deep and ragged sound that sliced through

Westley's contemplation of her statement.

"Oh, wee one," Ella cried, pulling the baby closer to her. "This is my fault."

The jagged pain in her voice tore at him, and he reached across to touch her once again. "You must not say such things. You are not at fault for a sickness."

"But I…"

"No," he said firmly. "You went out in the weather, yes. But you were not there for long, and even then only because I provoked you."

Another sob, this one let free. He rolled closer, trying to see her in the dark.

"Hear me, Ella. You cannot blame yourself."

"Say it again."

He rubbed her shoulder. "It is not your fault."

"No, the other."

He frowned, then set his jaw. Of course, she would want to hear again that he was the one to blame. She deserved it, even if only for the sake that his claim would ease her suffering and give her someone other than herself to fling her loathing upon. "I provoked you. If you need one to blame, then I shall shoulder it."

She made a funny noise. "Not that, silly man. My name."

"Ella?"

"Aye, I like the way it sounds coming from you."

Heat swarmed through him, and he wanted nothing more than to pull her into his arms and feel what her lips would be like under his.

Suddenly she yelped and grew stiff. "Oh, I shouldn't have…" She scooted farther away, so near the edge of the bed that she might fall from it. "Daftie fool," she muttered.

"Westley."

She sucked air. "What?"

"I would like it if you called me Westley."

She didn't respond for several moments, and as the child barked out another cough he wondered if she'd fallen asleep.

"Probably best I call you Major, sir. Seeing as I would still like to work for you, if you would allow it."

He tried not to let the steel in her words bother him. Of course, she would first be concerned with her security. How could he expect her to learn to trust him if ever she feared for her safety? The very fact that he longed for her to trust him was something he had better not dwell on.

"You may stay, Ella." He resisted the urge to reach for her once more. "You were correct. I need someone to manage the house in my absence."

Her breath caught. "Truly?"

"I give my word." The word of a Federal soldier, one she would not be likely to accept readily.

"I...thank you."

They lay in silence for a time, and her breathing grew deep and even. He lifted on his elbow and turned to put his feet on the floor.

"Must you go?"

He stilled. "I thought you were asleep."

"I cannot. The shadows...still they haunt me."

He laid back on the bed, the nearness of her and the scent of her rain-washed hair making it difficult for him to keep his thoughts from drifting where they should not. He dared not ask the meaning of her words, afraid it would launch him into a place he would be unable to return from.

Lee coughed again, each heaved breath a labor. If he did not get the child a doctor soon, death might very well soon steal him from his mother.

"As soon as the storm breaks, I will get the doctor for him."

He could feel her relax, a settling that echoed somewhere within him. "Again, I am in your debt."

She did not argue, nor insist she had business to see to in town. Perhaps trust would bloom after all. He contemplated the silence, and then broke a vow to himself that he did not need to know the truth behind her mysteries. "You are not his mother, are you?"

The tension returned, thicker even than before. It settled between them, a great fortification with sharpened pickets turned against him.

"I am his mother, and he is mine."

Westley turned her words over in his head. Without the aid of light by which to study her features, he had to rely on rhythm and tone. "Yours, yes. That I can see."

She let out a breath that drifted across the quilt and stirred the hair on his brow.

"Even still, you did not birth him."

She sniffled. "How did you know?"

Relief, thick as molasses, poured over him. She had not been used and forced to bring a child into the world born of man's wickedness. Neither did she sell herself for men's pleasures. The more he watched her, the more he did not want to believe that it could be true. "It explains much."

Lee coughed again, rough and deep, and she nuzzled against him. "Not of my blood, but of my heart. And now I will lose him."

His fists tightened at his sides. "I will do all in my power to see that you do not."

"Why?" The whispered word hung in the air, tempting him to lay bare depths of him that he dared not explore.

He cleared his throat. "It is the right thing to do."

She edged closer. "Is that all?"

What was it about the dark that tempted people to speak things they would not in the light? And what had happened to the tiny dragon that shot flames at him only hours ago? This sweet nymph had taken the dragon's place. No more scales, the nymph was all smooth edges and an enchanting tongue, laced with a melodic accent that threatened to breach his defenses. He shifted his body and his thoughts—both tight with unanswered longing.

"Where did you get him?"

She sighed, as though knowing they had waded into waters better left unstirred. "His mother died bringing him into the world. I tried to save her but failed in that as well." Her words were weighted, as though there was more to her meaning than what she said. "Cynthia told me about your mother..." Her tone began to slur with exhaustion. "And she said I could find help for him here."

That explained much as well. He tried to see her in the dark. If only he could watch her eyes, see what tricks played behind them. The question plagued him. How had Ella come to be at a harlot's birthing?

Perhaps she had been in a bawdy house after all.

Yet even as the accusation raked over his thoughts, he found he didn't care. Whoever she had been before Belmont...well, it mattered not.

"Ella?"

She didn't respond, her breath whispering softly. She slept, the child resting in the safe curve of her body. They both needed the rest. He turned on his back.

Better that she sleep, ignorant of all the things that swarmed within him. Better that she slumber while he doused the embers of a flame that would do neither of them any good.

He eased from the bed, careful not to wake her. He watched her only a moment longer, then slipped back to the coldness of his own chamber. Yes, sleep had granted him a great mercy. Now he would not be foolish enough to reveal more of himself than would be wise.

Chapter Twenty-One

Color. Color more vivid than any she'd ever seen. Ella ran her hand through the air, expecting the radiant blue to dissipate under her fingers. Light. Light so unnaturally bright she should have had to squint, yet didn't need to. The light pulsed around her, coming from every direction and not leaving any room for the slightest shadow. Not a shade of darkness touched the pristine sky or the ground around her.

Ella turned and brought her gaze down from the dazzling sky and to the earth below. Where was she? She took a step forward and grass rippled beneath her feet, swishing against her gown and tickling her fingertips. So green. More green than any grass she'd ever laid eyes upon, it danced in the gentle breeze as though it knew the answers to all of life's secrets. She cupped it in her hand, marveling at the silky texture.

Warmth enveloped her—the way sunlight felt upon the skin on the most perfect spring day. Ella wrapped her arms around herself and closed her eyes. A sensation draped over her, something she'd not felt in so long. Peace. An overwhelming sense of peace. Wherever this place was, she didn't want to leave. She stood there for several moments, allowing the feeling to slide over and around her, shedding light on places too long cast in shadows.

Finally, Ella opened her eyes and looked down. She wore a startling gown of the purest white. So clean and clear it almost glowed. She turned, admiring the way it fit her perfectly, as though the seamstress had known every contour of her frame.

She ran a hand over it, the smooth fabric glistening under her touch. Such a fine garment, and nothing at all like the dirty or ill-fitting dresses she usually wore.

Her hair, left free, swayed in the breeze. She captured a strand and examined it. Had it always been this color? Such a glorious red woven with bits of gold? Or was it only that way because of the brilliant light? She dropped the strand and looked around. Other than her, only one thing stood in the great expanse of vibrant blue sky and never-ending brilliant green grass.

A tree, wider around than three of her could reach hand in hand, spread majestic branches to the sky. Star-shaped leaves, an effervescent green even brighter than the grass, perched upon the regal branches like the finest birds. Ella ran her fingers through the tall stalks as she walked, letting the grass brush against her palms and send ripples of joy through her tired soul.

She approached the tree and placed a hand upon its trunk, expecting rough bark. Instead, the trunk of deepest brown boasted a velvety covering that even a queen might envy. Ella tilted her head. Odd, indeed.

She turned and looked out over the field, the light around her nearly feeling alive and bringing every sense awake. Something caught her attention. A scent. Nothing at all like anything she'd inhaled before. She could only describe it as something like sweetness, love, and…goodness. It gently caressed her, and she breathed it deeper, allowing her lungs to swell with the pleasure of it.

"Hello, Ella."

She turned, the brilliant white gown flaring out around her. A man stood by the tree, resting his hand on the trunk and regarding her with a smile. Clothed in white even more brilliant than her own, he reached out a hand to her.

Where she should have felt fear, instead Ella felt only acceptance. She slid her fingers into his and allowed him to pull her into the open.

"May I have this dance?"

Ella smiled. "But there is no music."

He lifted his brows, his face glowing with sunlight. "Is there not?"

As the words left his upturned lips, Ella noticed the sound. Pure and clear, yet unlike any instrument she had ever heard before. He bowed, and she giggled and made a curtsy. As the music swelled, he spun her around in the grass, her feet moving and gliding in perfect harmony to a tune she couldn't name. Joy spread through her, and she threw back her head and laughed.

She let go of his hands and twirled, feeling like a small girl again. The grass spun around her, a carousel of green and light. She threw her hands in the air, trying to touch the sparkling sky.

"Ah, so there you are."

She slowed and turned to him, the smile on her face wide enough to make her cheeks ache. "What do you mean? I have been here the entire time."

"Have you?"

Something within her stirred, and her heart shifted. Memories came at her like clouds to ruin a clear day.

Ella placed her hands on her head, but the recollections didn't go away. She saw herself as though she were outside of her body. There she stood after her mother died, dressed in a dirty skirt and torn blouse, a bruise where one of the stallions had nipped her arm. She'd tried to care for the huge, angry creature to please her father but had been terrified.

The vision shifted, and she sat hunched over something in her lap, her fingers pricked as the needle slipped again. She'd strained her hands and eyes learning to make the finest lace like her mother, though she'd never liked it. She'd pretended, because Papa said lace would make money and drawings would not.

Ella closed her eyes and saw the faces of several children—their mocking smiles at her worn clothing, the whispers behind their hands about her odd behavior. Oh, how she had shifted herself to try to make them like her more. Hiding bits here and changing things there.

She'd long ago learned to discover the things about herself that made other children laugh or scorn her and tuck them away so that she would not feel the sting of their rejection again. She learned to bury her love of colors and art under Papa's admonition that such things were foolishness and a waste of a woman's time. She'd taken the joy drawing had given her and boxed it up, sliding it underneath responsibilities that he'd said must come first.

She'd stopped tying colorful scarves in her hair even though she liked them, because the other girls made fun. She learned to cover up the Scottish in her words so that people wouldn't hear them and turn up their noses.

And then she saw herself in the inn once more, scrubbing dishes and telling herself that she was lucky to be there. Determined if she worked hard enough, if she acted the right way, that the owners would find worth in her and praise her efforts.

She breathed deep, letting the visions—clearer than even when she'd lived them—wash through her.

After all that, she'd come to Belmont, desperately wanting to be something more than she truly was. Hoping to play the lady and watching her efforts once more crash down around her. And her sweet little Lee—her only hope to find another person in this world to love her and fill that sprawling void that yearned to love and be loved in return. A tear slid out from under her lashes and coursed down her cheek.

A hand cupped her face and gently swiped the tear away.

"Under all of that is the real you. The beautiful soul you tried to paint over."

She blinked away the tears and stared into the intense eyes before her. "Who are you?"

He smiled. "You know who I am."

"No, I—" She stopped. But she did know. Somewhere deep within her she had known him for a very long time. She just didn't remember.

He clasped her hand, warm fingers that radiated caring enveloped her own. "Come, sit with me."

She let him lead her to the tree and settled down next to him. She plucked a blade of grass and twirled it between her fingers. Questions swirled in her, but she was afraid to voice them. What if she upset him and he made her leave this beautiful place? Could she stay here? Would he bring Lee, too? Oh, and if he came, would he still be sick?

"You should rest, Ella," he said, his tender voice seeping into her thoughts and soothing them away. "Ever you worry about tomorrow before tomorrow comes. Does not each day have enough troubles of its own?"

Ella dropped the grass and leaned back against the tree, comfortable at his side though she didn't know why. "I'd say that each day has troubles aplenty, that's for certain." She drew her bottom lip through her teeth. "But not here. Here it is safe."

He didn't respond, and Ella could sense he wanted her to discover something. Already she knew but didn't want to accept it. Still, the words came from her lips as though of their own accord. "But I cannot stay here."

"The time has not yet come."

She closed her eyes and let her head drop against his shoulder. "I don't know what to do. The troubles seem like they will overwhelm me."

"Yet, how can you add a single hour to your life by worrying?"

Ella wrinkled her nose. "I suppose I cannot."

They sat in peaceful silence for a few moments, until he coaxed revelation from her once more. "Why do you hide?"

She watched the grass sway in the breeze. "I don't know." She didn't really. It just seemed to be the safest thing, the thing that protected her tender heart from pain. By doing so, and pretending to be strong, she had learned to build walls that others dared not breach.

"Perhaps by doing so, you have made it harder."

Had he read her thoughts? "No. When people see me for me, they never like me."

"Hmm. But I do."

She turned to look at him. There was something so familiar about him, yet she couldn't place it. She wanted to say that was because this was a dream and he wasn't real, but the words would not leave her mouth.

He lifted his brows, as though he knew her thoughts anyway. Then he smiled, and everything within her seemed to glow. "But, Ella, do you not know that who you truly are is special?"

Ella shook her head, fear and anger writhing within her and threatening to ruin all that was perfect here. "There is nothing special about me. I am nobody important." She clutched the brilliant white dress and held it firm. "I am no spotless girl deserving a man who adores her and children who love her. I have no great talents, remarkable beauty, or astounding intellect." She bit down her tears and crossed her arms like a petulant child. "What, then, could possibly be special about me?"

He chuckled and wrapped his arm around her. Safety and peace poured through her and unraveled her anger. Ella breathed in the scents of sweetness and beauty and wanted nothing more than to stay in this strange dream place.

He hugged her against him. "I think you know why you are special. You only need to discover it again."

Ella began to feel drowsy and allowed her eyes to close. "Do I? I don't remember what you say I have forgotten."

"Seek it and you will find it." His voice, so sweet yet so majestic, drifted on the languid breeze, tickling her senses and shifting her world.

She yawned. "Find what?"

"The truth." He kissed the top of her head. "The truth that sets you free."

She relaxed and listened to the melody that hung in the air. Then she felt herself change and the scents upon the breeze dissipate. And she knew what it meant. "No!"

Ella bolted upright, only to find herself in the rose room of Belmont Plantation. A startled cry jarred her back to reality, and she looked down at Lee beside her. She plucked him from the bed and rocked back and forth. "Hey, now, wee lad. I didn't mean to frighten you."

Lee settled and blinked up at her, his tiny face reminding her of the strength she would need. Memories of the night before began to plop down upon her like the slow beginning of a downpour.

The storm. Lee's cough. Sibby's leg. And Major Remington....

Ella looked down at the quilt that covered her rumpled dress and tried to shake strange sensations from her. Had he been here in the night? Or had that only been a part of the unnervingly realistic dream she'd had?

The field. The tree. Ella shivered. Never had a dream been so vibrant or clear, so dramatically realistic, the colors so pure and the sounds so clean. And him...

The thought of him brought an ache. She knew him, and yet didn't. She closed her eyes as she rocked Lee and tried to remember his face. All she could recall of it was light and goodness, beauty and love. Somehow his features didn't matter. Not the color of his eyes, nor the shape of his nose, nor the way his hair framed his face mattered. Not a single distinction that usually defined a person clung to him. All that could define him was the way he'd made her feel.

She'd felt almost like a truer version of her own self. Dangerous, that. Such vulnerability would bring only one thing— pain.

Lee coughed and began to wiggle, and Ella pushed aside the dream. No matter how clean and beautiful a place her mind had imagined, it wasn't reality. The real-world colors were dimmer, and problems she could not afford to ignore pressed upon her. The dream provided a nice fantasy, but here stood the truth of her life. A precarious situation and a fragile babe who needed her to be strong. She couldn't afford to frolic in dreamland while little Lee needed her.

Ella swung her feet off the bed and headed to the door that led to the nursery. She paused and looked over her shoulder at the door on the other side, the one that connected to the master's chamber. Did Westley yet sleep?

She chided herself. What would possess her to call the major by his given name, even in her own mind? Perhaps he had invited her during that hazy time when he had trespassed on her privacy and her heart, but if she allowed herself to do that, the name might very well pass through her lips as well. She turned back to the nursery. No, that wouldn't do. No matter what he had said then, if that time even existed, it would not be safe for her to open that door.

Ella straightened her spine and drew the familiar walls back around herself like a heavy cloak. Burdensome they might be, but there was safety in familiarity. She smoothed her features and settled her restless spirit as best she could.

She found Sibby sitting up in bed, her foot propped on a tower of pillows. "Mornin', Miss Ella. Our little man hungry?"

Ella coerced a smile from her lips. "I hope so."

Sibby reached for him, and Ella handed him over, once more thinking about the goat. Would it be wrong of her to wish to feed him on her own? Major Remington said she could stay. She wrinkled her forehead. At least, she thought he did. Time would tell.

Lee coughed and turned his head, but then, thankfully, began to nurse. Ella let out a breath that stirred the hair hanging in disarray around her face. "Oh, thank goodness. I was afraid he wouldn't eat."

"Me, too. This here be a good sign, Miss Ella."

She ran a hand over her hair, relief washing over her. "I still want to go to town and fetch the doctor."

Sibby kept her gaze on the child. "No need."

Ella opened her mouth to protest. Just because he now ate didn't mean that his cough wasn't a reason to still worry.

"Major Westley done gone."

Her mouth felt dry. "He what?"

"He done left with the first light." Sibby's mouth twitched like she knew something Ella didn't.

Ella crossed her arms. "He shouldn't be walking that far."

Sibby shrugged. "I weren't gonna tell him that. He can be right stubborn once he done set his mind to something."

Ella stood there, unsure what to say. She wanted to ask if Sibby knew anything about whether the major had mentioned her employment, but she dared not. She feared that if she said such hopes aloud, they might all the sooner be crushed.

"Why don't you go on and get washed up and put on a fresh dress?" Sibby's words tugged her from scattered thoughts that flitted on a wind of uncertainty.

"Yes, a clean dress would be nice." Ella turned, her hands

clasping and unclasping in front of her.

She put one foot over the threshold when Lee made a strangled sound, coughing up milk and sputtering. Ella spun around. Sibby draped the cloth over herself and patted Lee on the back. "There now. Easy."

Her heart thudded. She should be the one caring for him. Ella set her teeth. She would find a goat, and with it the ability to not rely on another to care for her child.

"You go on now, Miss Ella. I's got him."

Ella stepped into her room and closed the door behind her, reminding herself how grateful she was for Sibby's help.

Ella pulled the widow's silks from the armoire, donned her dry underpinnings, and fastened her hair into a sensible bun. She regarded herself in the mirror, her trembling fingers trailing over the fabric that felt too coarse, her watering eyes sliding over colors that were far too drab.

She clutched the fabric at her chest. *Seek*, he had said, *find the truth*. The truth about what made her special. Ella looked at dark circles that gathered under her eyes. *Special*. She wanted to spit the word. Why had her mind conjured such a thing? What cruel jest did it play upon her, tempting her to look for something beautiful where nothing existed?

Ella pressed her lips into a line. She would have to forget that dream, else she would too deeply ache to return to it. She arranged her features so that the woman returning her stare appeared calm and in control.

Then she gathered her defenses and strode from the room.

Chapter Twenty-Two

Westley rapped the head of his cane on the neighbor's door and stepped back. Dew clung to the grass and made diamonds drip from green spears. To his right, a bird called to its mate in the early moments of a new day. Hopefully, the dowager wouldn't be too furious with him for tapping upon her door at this inappropriate hour.

The Martins' home, Riverbend, sat in the curve of the Mississippi and was, therefore, aptly named. Many men, Westley's father among them, had told Mr. Martin he'd built his mansion much too near to the river, but the man didn't listen to reason. Westley wondered how long it would be before the mighty Mississippi overflowed her banks again and Riverbend washed away.

Westley stepped forward to knock again when the heavy oak door creaked open and a Negro woman with a plump middle and gray hair peered out at him. Her eyes darted behind him as though she expected someone to accompany him.

"I am Major Remington, here to ask an important neighborly favor of Mrs. Martin, if you please."

Her eyes widened with recognition and she bobbed her head. "Come on in whilst I go gets the missus. She just done got up."

Westley entered the house and didn't bother removing his hat. He wouldn't be staying long. The woman scurried away and left him alone in the entry. Westley frowned. It seemed Miss Martin had not been exaggerating. No paintings hung on the walls, no rug donned the floor, and, from where he stood, Westley couldn't see a single stick of furniture.

If he didn't know better, he might assume the house had been abandoned. The click of heels turned his attention to the stairs. Mrs. Martin, wearing what he thought to be the same deep navy blue dress he'd seen her in last time, descended the stairs with a look of surprise.

"Mr. Remington. What brings you to Riverbend? And at this hour?"

He dipped at the waist. "My apologies for arriving unannounced, and so early in the morning."

"Indeed. We haven't even taken our breakfast yet." She offered her hand.

He bowed over it and gave the slightest whisper of his lips over her papery knuckles. "My sincerest apologies." She opened her mouth, but he didn't give her a chance to pepper him with a lesson on manners. "And, I must also apologize for my behavior when last we saw one another. I fear it was rather barbaric of me not to bid you a proper goodbye. I do hope you will forgive my indecency and not let it come between long-standing neighbors."

She regarded him flatly. "Very well. You are forgiven. One can let such things go, I assume, given the circumstances you found yourself in." Mrs. Martin looked behind him. "Has your wife joined you? Opal has been asking after her. We don't have all that much, but I suppose you could join us at the meal."

Westley shook his head. "I'm afraid not, on both accounts."

Something sparked in her eyes and she appeared relieved. Were things so dire at Riverbend that they could not afford to invite neighbors to dine with them? If the furnishings were any indication, it appeared that might very well be the case.

Westley cleared his throat. "And the reason she is not at my side," he said, carefully avoiding both using her true name or calling her his wife, "is the very reason why I have come to call so early."

"Oh?"

"The baby has fallen quite ill, and it is imperative I go to find the doctor. I've come to beg the use of your carriage so that I do not have to walk all the way to town."

Mrs. Martin fingered the fabric at her throat. "Oh, my. That is just terrible." She seemed sincere, the concern in her eyes replacing notes of suspicion. "Of course, you may use our carriage. I'll send for Freddie to ready it for you."

Westley gave a slight bow. "I am in your debt."

A quarter hour later, after a promise that when the baby was healthy Ella would come to call on Miss Martin, Westley snapped the reins and turned the pair of ragged geldings toward town.

The steady plod of the horses' hooves reminded him of the ticking of a clock. Time that slipped away from him—his time at Belmont, his time away from the army, the time the child might have left if he did not find the doctor soon enough.

He tapped the reins and brought the horses to a trot, the rough gait jostling their harnesses and vibrating Westley in the seat. They didn't carry on that way for long, however, until they eased back into a lumbering walk. Poor beasts. They looked as though they'd had a tough winter. If he'd thought himself up to the task, he would have only asked for one to ride into town rather than tiring both with the carriage just for himself. Perhaps he could repay them with a sack of oats for the creatures. He would need to find his own horse. He would not want to lean on the Martins' thin resources again.

After a time, Greenville unfolded before him, every bit as gray as it had been when he'd first arrived. How long had that been? Days? It seemed months. In so short a time one scarlet-haired female had upended his life. A woman whom the Martins, and who knew how many others, still thought to be his wife.

Westley set his jaw as he passed ruined buildings and blackened bricks. Why hadn't he corrected them? While he waited on the carriage and the women asked after Ella, it would have been the perfect time to lay out the truth. And still he'd hesitated.

Westley pulled the carriage to a stop and looped the reins over the wooden hitching post outside of the general store. Everything within him declared the dishonor of withholding the truth about the nature of their relationship, but he'd done it all the same.

Westley slapped the dust off his hat and tucked it under his arm. Not many folks moved around this time of the day. They were likely still taking the morning meal. Good. The fewer people he saw in Greenville, the better. Westley stepped inside, and the proprietor greeted him.

"Good mornin', sir. What can I do for ya?"

Westley let some of his childhood accent slide back into his words, hopeful it would set the other man at ease. He didn't want the man to clam up out of spite. "Mornin', good sir. Do you know where I might find the doctor?"

The man scratched his thinning hair. "I'm sorry to say we haven't had one come through here in some time, mister."

Westley kept his features even. "A nurse then, perhaps? Anyone who might take a look at an ill infant?" He'd have someone look at Sibby, too, but he'd seen enough wrongly turned ankles to know that all she needed was time off of it.

Compassion lit in the man's eyes. "This your first babe to get sick?"

The question startled him. "I, um, yes. It is."

The man waved to another customer that entered. "Then count yourself lucky, fellow. Most of us have lost too many of

our children these last few years. The ones the fires and
starvation didn't take, the sicknesses did. Can't tell you how
many mothers buried little ones this last winter. Cemetery's half
full of 'em."

Westley stared at him.

"Better that you ain't had none till now. Now that there's at
least a little hope they might survive what ruined this country."

The man wagged his head, and Westley's blood felt too
thick to push through his veins. He dared not comment on the
man's declaration. There was nothing he could do for already-
lost children. All he could do was try to save the one he'd held
in his hands. "Is there no one who can help? He is only a few
weeks old."

The old man offered a sad smile. "What kind of sickness?"

Westley lifted his palms. "He's been coughing a lot. Sounds
a bit strangled."

The older man glanced around and waved him closer.
"Might be the whooping cough. Lots of the babes have been
getting it."

Westley leaned across the counter that separated them. "Do
you know how to treat it?"

"I got something stored in the back. But not much of it,
mind."

Westley narrowed his eyes. Something about the way the
man said it grated against him. His suspicions tingled. "Very
well. I can use whatever amount you have."

The man assessed Westley, then disappeared behind a door
in the back. A moment later he returned with a small brown
bottle and slid it across the counter.

Paregoric Elixir.

Westley turned the concoction over in his palm. "And this
will cure it?"

The man rubbed the back of his neck. "Can't say for sure

that it will. But it does help with the coughing fits."

The man gave Westley a price, and he nearly dropped the bottle. "Are you mad, man?"

The proprietor dared to look offended. "Do you not know how rare these medicines are?" He lowered his voice as though the words he spoke were some grave secret. "Have you been living in a cave somewhere?" He narrowed his eyes. "Who are you, anyway?"

Westley set his jaw and fished currency from his pocket. "I can pay you in Federal funds. But only half."

The man's eyes lit with greed. No doubt the Federal funds, even though only half of the price he'd asked for, would be worth twice as much. Confederate bills were useless. Westley handed over the currency and the man snatched the money away as though Westley might change his mind.

"I have some amber oil, too. You rub it on the neck and chest. Not as good as the elixir, mind, but helps a lot, too."

Westley pressed his lips in a line. Did this man seek to take advantage of him? Would the things even work? His mind jumped back to Ella and how desperately she clung to the child in the night.

He glared at the man. "A bag of oats, too."

The proprietor grinned and snatched most of what remained of Westley's funds.

The knock on the door sent Ella hurrying down the stairs. It must be the doctor! A good thing, too, since Lee had started coughing up thickened spittle this morning and had refused to eat again after that first attempt. She dashed off the stairs and scrambled across the foyer.

Ella pulled open the door and her heart lurched. Not the

doctor at all! A man in Yankee blue tipped his cap, his eyes taking in her black widow's weeds. Ella straightened.

Oh, she had forgotten all about him! Of all the days... Ella forced a tight smile. "Good morning."

"Good morning, madam. I have come to collect the taxes for this property."

Her pulse quickened and her mind scrambled for something to say. She'd never gotten Sibby to agree to anything. Ella smoothed her skirts and nearly spoke with the Southern lady ruse, but why bother? With Westley here how she spoke didn't matter. "Yes, of course." She opened the door farther. "Won't you please come in?"

He hesitated.

Ella gestured inside. Perhaps the invitation would ease the skepticism flashing in his eyes. If she didn't seem too eager to be rid of him, then perhaps he would think she had nothing to hide. "My husband has returned home, and he will be able to take care of these issues with you."

"He has?"

Ella widened the door. "Yes, thank the Lord. And if you don't mind waiting, he should be back from town anytime now." She hoped. "As you know, such things really are better left to men to discuss. Now that he is returned to me, don't you think it wise you speak to him instead?"

Not bothering to reply, he strode into the house, his eyes carrying over the decorative plaster and papered walls. What else was she going to do but hand the man over to Major Remington?

Oh, please, don't let him be angry...

Ella gestured to the parlor. "If you will kindly wait here, I shall prepare some refreshments for you."

"Thank you for your hospitality, madam." His eyes lingered on her dress, and questions littered his eyes.

Ella laughed nervously. "It is quite a miracle! We thought he was dead, and here he is returned to us!"

He lifted his eyebrows and spoke slowly, as though to a child. "Your husband, the Federal officer, has returned?"

Ella resented the mocking tone, but kept a false smile plastered on her face. "He has, indeed! He will be glad to speak with you upon his return, I'm certain. He will want to get this unpleasant business settled."

The man regarded her flatly.

Ella gestured toward the furniture. "Won't you take a seat?"

He stiffly lowered to one of the chairs, his eyes never leaving her face. Before he could say anything else, Ella blurted, "I shall return with refreshments in a moment." Then she turned in a spray of black fabric and slipped out from under his gaze.

Ella hurried up the stairs and back to the nursery, partially tripping on her skirts in her haste. She flung open the door, her heart galloping. "Sibby!"

The other woman yelped and put a hand to her mouth. "You done scared me!"

Ella closed the door behind her. "That Yankee soldier is back."

Sibby's face twisted. "What he want?"

Ella put her hands on her hips. "You know exactly what he wants. We were supposed to be planting fields! And the taxes..." She began to pace. "What are we going to do about the taxes?"

Sibby followed Ella with her eyes. "Why you doin' all that frettin'?"

Lee began a coughing spasm, his tiny body quivering in the crib. Ella rushed to him just as he retched up a thick wad of mucus. Oh, a Yank in the house and Lee with this horrible sickness! Could this day get any worse? Her stomach twisted, and she felt as though she might heave up the empty contents of her stomach as well. She cleaned the baby's face with the rag sitting in the crib.

"Miss Ella!"

Ella swung around. "What?"

"You gonna give yourself flutters."

Flutters?

"Why you all in a tizzy over that man down there? Mista Westley...*Major* Westley, he be here now. You lets him worry 'bout that man."

Sibby's words, so confidently spoken, eased some of the tightness in Ella's chest. She'd said such things to the man below, but she didn't actually believe them. She'd only tried to stall him. But, of course, Sibby was right. This wasn't her house to worry over! She didn't need to prove she belonged here, abide by any new Federal laws, or pay any money. None of those responsibilities belonged to her. They belonged to the major.

Ella wrinkled her nose. "He's waiting in the parlor, and the major isn't back with the doctor yet."

"Then you best get him some tea or somethin'. I gots some bread and fig preserves in the kitchen." She eyed Ella. "You know how to make the tea tray?"

"Of course, I do." She'd worked in a kitchen, after all. How different could that be from serving guests in a fine house?

Sibby held out her arms. "Then you best be givin' me that boy and get to it."

Ella clenched her teeth and took the servants' stairs to the kitchen. By the time she had the bread sliced and the preserves in a small bowl, the tea kettle whistled. She carefully arranged it all on the tray and somehow managed to get it through the house without dropping anything.

She found the Federal man standing stiffly at the parlor door. "I began to think you would not return."

"My apologies, sir," she said as she slipped by him and set the tray down. "I'm afraid my maid has injured her ankle, and I had to prepare these things myself."

"Oh." He followed her to the center of the room and regained his seat. "Very well then. How long do you expect your husband to be?" He pulled a watch from his breast pocket and snapped it open.

"My son is sick and Major Remington went to town before dawn to fetch the doctor. I expect them here momentarily." She poured the tea and handed him the cup. "Sugar? I'm afraid we don't have any cream."

"Thank you, no."

Ella dropped a spoonful of sugar into her own cup and stirred, alarmed to see that her hand shook.

"The doctor, you say?"

Ella held the cup in both hands, afraid the liquid might spill. "Yes."

The man frowned. "The only doctor anywhere around here left for Memphis three weeks ago. A new one was due last week, but he hasn't shown up yet."

Ella's heart pounded. No, no, that couldn't be. Then who would look at Lee? Heat flooded her face and blood pulsed in her ears, obscuring the words the man spoke. She didn't care what he had to say anyway.

If there was no doctor...

Ella swayed. No doctor. No hope. No hope for her wee one.

Ella fanned her face. Hot. Much too hot. Her stomach roiled. "Oh, my, I'm not feeling so well." She tried to stand and became dizzy.

The edges of her vision turned black and Ella swayed again, dropping back into her chair. The man's reedy face peered down on her, and then the world faded away.

Chapter Twenty-Three

Walking as briskly as the cane would allow, Westley made the turn from the river road and onto the drive leading to Belmont. The two bottles in his pocket clinked together with each hitched step he took. He hoped the remedies would do until he could present himself at the nearest Federal outpost and ask after a doctor. Even if the town didn't have one, the army would.

His cane crunched the rocks along the road, in harmony with the throb that gained intensity in his leg the longer he walked. Good thing he had to walk only to the Martins' and back instead of all the way into Greenville. He glanced at the sky, wishing he had a watch. How worked up had Miss Whitaker gotten herself in the hours he'd been gone?

Now that a new day had arrived, would she remember the way she'd wanted him to stay at her side? Would she look at him the way he imagined her eyes sought his in the moonlight? The memory of her whispered words and the desperation in her tears quickened his pace.

As Westley neared the house, the sight of a fine horse with a polished leather saddle brought a furrow to his forehead. The horse, Federal no doubt, nickered at him as he passed. Westley hurried to the front porch and into the house, ignoring the increased pain in his thigh.

A man's voice came from the right. Westley left the front door open and strode into the parlor, and the sight within ignited an inferno in his gut.

A soldier in blue leaned over Miss Whitaker, who lay sprawled out over one of the chairs in the parlor. An askew tea tray covered the parlor table. Westley dropped his cane, and in two strides had the man's shoulder in his grasp.

He flung the man around and gathered his lapels in his fists. The other man's brown eyes widened.

"Who are you?" Westley growled.

"Corporal Briggs."

Westley's nose came close to touching the other man's bulbous one. "And just what, Corporal, are you doing with the lady?"

The man frowned and brought up his hands to shove Westley away, but Westley tightened his grip on the fabric near the scoundrel's throat.

"She fainted!" He reached up and grabbed onto Westley's forearms. "I merely tried to rouse her. I assure you, nothing unseemly occurred!"

Westley shoved the man away, the tinges of rage at the edges of his vision clearing. What had caused him to act so rashly? He raked his gaze down the startled man. The fellow stared at him, seeming unsure what he should do. Deciding the man would not soon retaliate against Westley's aggression, he stepped over to Ella and dropped to his knee. He reached up and cupped her pale face. "Ella? Ella, can you hear me?"

She stirred and nestled her face into his hand. The heat pulsing through him shifted, and he leaned closer. "Come now, you must wake."

She gave a soft moan and her eyelids fluttered. "There you are," she whispered. She turned her lips into his hand. Westley froze, the feel of her silky lips pressing a kiss onto his palm doing something to him he could not describe.

She turned her head, rubbing her cheek through his hand. Ella's eyes lazily lifted, and she smiled. His pulse quickened. Was this what she looked like when her guard fell? Warm green eyes that sparkled and lips that yielded to softness rather than hard lines? "Ella…"

Suddenly her eyes flew wide and she lurched. "Oh!"

Westley leaned back but did not rise. "Are you all right?"

She blinked rapidly at him, wariness falling over her eyes like a dirty veil. "What are you doing?"

Despite himself, he smiled. Ah, the dragon once more. "It seems, my dear, that you fainted in the company of this good soldier."

"I…" Her nose wrinkled. "Oh, my." She sat up and ran a hand across her tresses. "I am terribly sorry."

Westley awkwardly rose, the flare of forgotten pain in his leg stealing his breath.

She placed her fingers to her flushed cheeks. "He said that the doctor—" Her eyes flashed and she jumped to her feet. She began to sway, and Westley grabbed her elbow. She blinked at him. "Where is the doctor?"

Westley eased her back into the seat and knelt beside her once more, even though the effort caused perspiration to prick his brow. "I will have to go to a Federal outpost to find one."

Tears flooded her eyes, and Westley hurried on. "But see here," he said, reaching into his pocket. "I have gotten him medicines for the cough until I can fetch a doctor."

The moisture in her eyes increased and spilled over. Blast. He'd hoped that the offering would be enough to keep that anguish that wrenched his gut from appearing in her eyes.

She reached out and laid a hand on his sleeve. "You bought him medicines?"

"Yes. Two kinds. One you feed him and the other to rub on. They are both supposed to ease the coughing."

Before he could react, Ella threw her arms around his neck. "I thank you." Her words, so sweet, tickled his skin. Then, just as quickly as she embraced him, she flung him away. "Oh!" Her eyes widened. "I…I shouldn't have, I'm terribly sorry."

His mouth twitched. "No need for apology. I am glad you are pleased with my effort."

He painstakingly rose and helped her to her feet, making certain she would not wobble again. "Here. Take these on up to him." He pressed the bottles in her hands.

Her eyes settled on his, questions swimming in their emerald depths. Then as though remembering the man they both had forgotten shared the room with them, she cut her eyes to the soldier. "Thank you. If you would kindly see to this gentleman, I will go tend Lee."

"Certainly." Westley watched her go, things inside him feeling set akilter.

The other man cleared his throat. "Well, I must admit I had my doubts about you and this household, sir."

Westley regarded him with lifted eyebrows.

He straightened his jacket. "You must understand that people have come up with all manner of tales to avoid paying their taxes. It would seem, however, that at least part of her story is true."

Westley watched the wiry man run a hand through his blond hair. "Part?"

The corporal's gaze crawled across him. "Obviously, the affection of man and wife is between you, so even though she wears the black, it would seem she belongs to you."

Westley let the words slide over him, trying to ignore the odd feeling they tried to stoke.

The man shifted his weight. "She also stated something else about you. Do you know what it was?"

Westley shrugged. She could have said any manner of things. "As you are being vague, I do not know to what you are referring."

"Hmm."

Aggravation brought by a lack of sleep and the biting pain in his leg slaughtered Westley's patience. "See here, Corporal Briggs. I am Major Remington—Third West Virginia Cavalry Regiment, Third Brigade, Army of the Shenandoah—and I would like to know what business you have in my house."

The man instantly straightened and snapped to attention. "Forgive me, sir, I had to be sure. But I'm certain you can understand our caution with such things."

Westley begrudgingly acknowledged the truth in the man's statement and forced his anger out with a long breath. "I do. Take your ease."

The man relaxed as he looked Westley over. "Medical furlough, sir?"

The reminder sent another wave of searing pain down his leg, but he refused to reach for the cane that still lay on the floor where he'd dropped it. "I was injured at Sayler's Creek. I have been given leave to see to family matters after my father's passing, and I will return north and to duty thereafter."

The man bobbed his head. "Very good, sir. Seeing as you are a Federal officer and therefore a citizen of good standing," he said, plucking papers from inside his blue frock, "then once the taxes are paid and the proper forms signed, all will be in order."

Westley accepted the papers and unfolded them. Line after line of assessments filled the page. "You are sure these are correct?"

The man shrugged. "I delivered what I was given, sir."

Westley glanced up at him and he diverted his gaze. "If you have any questions, though, Major, you can present them to Lieutenant Colonel Larson in town. He has an office in the old bank."

Westley clasped the papers so tightly they crinkled. "Please inform him that I shall call upon him tomorrow to settle the affairs."

"Very good, sir." The man turned and looked over his shoulder. "Thank your wife for her hospitality. I can see my own way out."

He snapped a salute and then left without waiting for a response. Westley watched him through the window until he disappeared around the bend. Then he let out the air that burned in his lungs and sat down to rub the ache.

He dropped his head back and stared at the ceiling. Trepidation thrummed in his chest and pumped its way through his veins. If the numbers on the papers were correct, then all of his money in Washington wouldn't cover his father's debt. Even if he took out every cent, he would still be deficient. Westley rubbed his temples and tried to ease the thought that repeated in his head with each contraction of his heart.

He was going to lose Belmont.

Chapter Twenty-Four

Ella rubbed the downy hair on Lee's head, relieved to see him sucking on the cloth she'd dipped in the medicine. It had taken her an enormous amount of effort yesterday, but she'd accomplished it.

"I still can't believe you done got him to suck on that rag."

Ella swelled with pride at Sibby's words. In this, at least, she had not failed. Lee looked up at her, his little eyes growing heavy. "I just hope it works."

The elixir had seemed to make him rest more peacefully last night. She hoped this morning he would start to eat, but the elixir made him quite sleepy, and he still didn't take much milk because whenever he was awake, the coughs caused him to be unable to nurse. If he got too weak, Ella feared he would not be able to recover.

Sibby mumbled something and swung off the bed to place her feet on the floor.

"What are you doing?"

Sibby looked at her like she was a dullard. "I needs to get up."

Ella shook her head. "You need to wait until I get the major before you get up. You know that."

"Can't."

Ella pursed her lips. "And why not?"

"Cause he ain't here."

She hadn't heard him leave. "Oh? Where has he gone?"

Sibby rose and balanced on one foot, holding on to the bed

for support. "He said he was agoin' to the army post."

The declaration took Ella by surprise, and she looked down at Lee to hide the disappointment that might betray her by appearing on her face. Her wee one had drifted off to sleep.

He looked peaceful as Ella laid him in the crib and draped a crocheted blanket over top of him before turning back to Sibby. "Has the major already returned to duty?" *Without the courtesy of a goodbye?*

Ella chided herself. The man did not owe her that. Or anything else, for that matter. He had been more than generous by even allowing her to remain in his home, seeing as she had both insulted him and lied to him.

Besides, wouldn't his absence be a good thing? It certainly would be easier without him here. The way that man unsettled her…well, she couldn't deal with that on a daily basis, now could she? And they still hadn't discussed the things shared across her quilt.

"No," Sibby said, pulling her from her muddled thoughts.

"I'm sorry," Ella replied, embarrassed that she'd been caught contemplating Major Remington. "What did you say?"

"I said no, Major Westley didn't go back to workin' in the army." She shrugged. "Least, not yet. He done said he was goin' after a doctor."

Of course. How ridiculously foolish of her. After she'd lost her senses in the parlor yesterday, he'd said he hoped to find a doctor at an army post. How could she have so soon forgotten something so incredibly important? Ella swept a loose lock back into her chignon and pinned it, feeling a wave of relief. "I do hope he finds one."

She told herself the *only* reason she was comforted by the news was because the wee one still needed to see a doctor. And not at all because it meant Westley hadn't left for good.

Drat. She'd thought of him with the intimacy of his first

name again. She really must cease doing that.

Sibby tried for a step on her injured ankle and swayed.

"Sibby!" Ella leapt forward and slipped under Sibby's arm. "What's gotten into you? You can't just walk off on your own."

Sibby groaned. "I was feelin' better and the swellin' done gone down some."

"You still can't walk."

Sibby took a moment to answer, as though there was anything she could come up with that would change Ella's mind.

"You reckon Major Westley be mindin' if I use one of his canes?"

Ella almost chuckled, but then realized Sibby was serious. She wagged her head. "I don't think he would like you up and about, risking making that ankle worse and making you stay in bed all the longer."

Sibby considered her a moment. "You's probably right."

Ella started to turn her back to the bed.

"But I still gots somethin' I need to do."

Ella lifted her eyes to the ceiling. "All right. What is it you need to do?"

Sibby's gaze probed at Ella from the corner of one slanted eye and then she straightened her already stiff spine. "I needs to go to the kitchen."

Ella balked. "That's all the way down the stairs! You can't do that."

Sibby hesitated and then, to Ella's surprise, consented. "I reckon you's right."

Finally, some sense. Ella steered Sibby back to the bed. "Good, then. The major wouldn't be happy with me if I let you fall into trouble."

Sibby gave her a funny look as she settled on top of the quilt. "I needs you to send Basil up here."

"Why? If you need something from the kitchen, I can fetch

it for you."

Sibby shook her head adamantly. "Ain't nothin' like that. I need to talk her 'bout sumthin'. She should be in the kitchen."

Pushing aside annoyance she knew she shouldn't feel, Ella tried to remain pleasant. "Fine." She paused in the doorway. "Would you like another draught of the laudanum? You're looking a mite peaked."

Sibby pursed her lips, then let out a huff. "No, I don't need none. It don't hurt near as bad as it did before."

Unconvinced, Ella crossed back over to the bed and peered closer at the swelling still making Sibby's ankle a little puffy. But it did look better than it had when she'd first injured it. Perhaps it was not as bad as they feared. Besides, Sibby would know her own pain level. Ella brushed her hands down her skirt. "Well, if you change your mind, let me know."

"Thank you, Miss Ella." A strange look came into her eyes. "You is right kind."

Ella smiled, peeked into the crib to be certain Lee slept peacefully, and then slipped down the stairs to find Basil. The girl had been scarce these last couple of days, hardly showing up in the kitchen and never underfoot as she had been when Ella had first arrived.

Ella found the kitchen cold and empty, and though she doubted she'd find Basil anywhere in the house, she checked every corner just to be certain. She even poked her head into the smokehouse and cellar but didn't see a soul.

Ella turned back to the rear porch. She'd just have to tell Sibby the girl had not come to the house today. She paused and tapped her chin. Sibby did seem intent on speaking to Basil, and if she wasn't at the house…well, then Ella knew where she might find her.

She looked out toward the field that stretched out behind the yard. This *would* be the perfect time to see what they kept so secretive back there. With the major gone, Sibby in bed, and Lee taking a nap…

Ella turned on her heel and lifted her work dress above the tall grass before she could change her mind. She made it across the yard and to the small line of trees beyond it where she'd heard Basil singing that day she'd discouraged Ella from crossing over the deep rut in the ground. She slipped into the trees and regarded the gouge in the earth, a stream of muddy water languidly carrying leaves and bits of debris from one location to another.

Ella wrinkled her nose. The creek might prove to be a bit of an obstacle. She set her shoulders. Well, if Basil could do it, so could she. Ella glanced around. No one moved in the yard, and only the sound of a chattering squirrel met her ears. If she were to fall, only the twittering birds would laugh at her humiliation. She tugged her skirt and petticoat up to her knees and made a mighty leap.

Her foot caught on the bank on the other side and she slipped. Ella churned her feet, but only succeeded in sliding farther down. Finally, the toes of her already badly worn shoes caught, and she scrambled up the other side. She brushed her palms off on her skirt and examined it. She'd smeared a bit of dirt on the front where she'd hit her knees, but otherwise she was none the worse for wear.

Ella straightened herself and picked her way through the scraggly trees clinging to this side of the bank and stepped out into another open field. This one seemed even less tended than the one closer to the house. Forgotten stalks of picked-clean cotton plants reached for the sky like bony fingers from the grave. No wind stirred them, as though even the breeze didn't wish to wake the dead.

Just ahead, a path emerged through the tangle where the passage of feet had bent the stalks into submission. Ella held her skirts as close to her sides as she could and picked her way through the fingers that tried to snag her fabric.

A thin line of trees waited on the other end of the sea of dead cotton stems. It seemed as though it took her an hour to make her way across, her heart hammering in her chest in slow motion. What would someone do if they saw her out here alone? She knew all too well that lawless men and bushwhackers roamed freely and could appear from anywhere.

If she raised a scream, would Sibby hear her? Even if she did, what would the injured woman be able to do about it? Likely, Ella's cries would only bring more evil men from hiding.

She quickened her pace, ignoring the sounds of snagged and ripping cloth. Did a shadow move over there, out of the corner of her eye?

She set her teeth and lengthened her stride. *It's nothing. There's no one out here after me.* The thought did nothing to ease the quickening of her breath.

By the time she reached the miniscule cover of the trees, her heart felt as though it might leap from underneath her bodice and flop upon the ground like a fish. Ella put her fingers to her cheeks in an effort to cool them.

Safe. All is well. No one but me and the bonny birds.

Ella repeated the words until her breathing returned to normal. She squeezed her eyes shut, only to have them fly open when a strange noise arrested her attention and reminded her that she would do better to remain unseen. Ella ducked behind a twisted cypress and peered out to the next field.

There. The settlement Basil said Ella should never visit. Two lines of cottages stood in neat rows, some of them even with whitewashed walls. Behind each of them on this side, a small fenced garden boasted rows of vibrant plants soon to be teeming with ripe vegetables. Dark-skinned women in bright headscarves worked hoes or stood around talking in the sunshine while little ones ran around their skirts.

Ella tilted her head. How very strange. Every mile of Mississippi she had traveled shared a common theme. Homes were burned, abandoned, or otherwise left in disrepair. Yet here, not only did the mansion itself remain unharmed and fully intact, but apparently the former slave quarters fared far better than any community Ella had seen on her way from home to here near Greenville.

She peered closer at what might have been a pleasant scene if not for the large man standing at the end of the row of homes holding a rifle. Ella narrowed her eyes and tried to make out the distinct features of his face, but he kept turning his head to scan the horizon. He waited on something, the tension in his shoulders evident even from this distance. Whatever he watched for, it had him worried.

Ella worked her lip between her teeth. A thriving community hidden back here with an armed guard? Obviously, this was what Basil and Sibby wanted to keep from her. But why? If the freed people residing at Belmont were working the land and appeared to be living well, then the soldiers wanting to enforce the Freedmen's Bureau's laws should be quite satisfied.

She must be missing something. But what?

She watched the people milling about a few moments longer, finally deciding to ask Sibby the reason behind the secrecy. The major had said she could stay, and if she lived here, then she deserved to know what transpired on these lands. Didn't she?

Of course, she did. She would continue to portray the lady of the house, and, as such, it would not do for her to be unaware of what happened on the lands supposedly left to her tending.

Why, she should just march right on down there and make it known that she knew they lived a prosperous life and that she was glad of it. They need not fear her trying to take anything away from them.

Ella straightened her dress and took one step forward when a shrill whistle stilled her progress. The man on guard lifted his weapon and spread his feet. The women halted their work, and the children gathered close to the adults. Ella froze as restless energy swarmed about the people, so tangible she could nearly see it slithering among them in the form of crossed arms, ducked heads, and perked ears.

Ella pressed closer against the tree, trying for a better look while still attempting to remain hidden. Good thing she hadn't stepped out from the trees. From the way these colored folks acted, coming upon them unannounced could prove dangerous.

The settlement's inhabitants moved toward the man standing guard, gathering behind him with their eyes trained on the horizon. She followed their stares and saw a team of mules appear where the land met the sky. She frowned. They were bringing a wagon through the field?

Mesmerized, Ella watched as the wagon, followed by two more, pulled closer to the cottages, the beasts straining against their load. The progress was slow, what with the wagon wheels lurching and dipping in the rutted ground as they moved across the fallow lands.

As the caravan neared, Ella could distinguish several young black men leading a string of livestock that appeared to be tied behind the farthest wagon. There were two cows, not exactly healthy-looking, but certainly not starved, and was that…?

Ella gasped. A goat!

Could it be a female that might provide her with the milk she needed for Lee? She clutched the fabric at the front of her dress. Even if the major said she could stay, it would be prudent to make other arrangements. Train Lee to take the goat's milk so that if for any reason she needed to leave, they would not be dependent on anyone.

The three wagons rolled to the settlement and came to a stop, their heavy loads covered with great canvases that concealed whatever lay underneath.

Now what could they possibly have?

"Miss Ella!"

Ella yelped and stumbled backward, tripping on a root and landing on her backside. She looked up to find Basil wringing her hands.

"What is you doin' here?" Basil whispered, her eyes darting back to the quarters behind Ella.

"I was looking for you." Ella climbed to her feet and brushed leaves from her skirt.

Basil grabbed her wrist and started to tug. "You gots to go, Miss Ella."

Ella planted her feet. "I will not."

"Miss Ella," Basil's eyes grew round, "did any of 'em see you?"

"Why, no, I was just watching…"

Basil tugged harder. "Then you gots to come wit me. Now!"

Ella relented, but only because the fear in the girl's voice made her wonder if the child would face some kind of punishment if Ella were discovered. She allowed Basil to tug her through the trees and back across the dead cotton field to the creek.

"Basil, are you going to tell me what's going on?"

Basil allowed Ella to pull free from her grasp. She studied the mud on the toe of her shoe.

"Basil?"

The girl sucked air. "Miss Ella, you don't know nothin' about how dangerous it be."

Ella lifted her eyebrows. "I happen to be quite aware of

how society has crumbled and men now run amok as lawless bandits."

Basil watched Ella, her dark eyes seeming far too old to be set in such a young face. "I'm not talkin' about them army deserters."

Ella crossed her arms. "I'll have you know that Major Remington has invited me to stay at Belmont." Though they had not openly discussed it, Ella knew what had transpired in her room the night of the storm had been real. "Now, I want to know what is going on."

Basil fidgeted. "Ain't for me to say."

"Very well." She hoisted her skirts and leapt across the creek much more gracefully than her first attempt. She turned just in time to see Basil's surprise before jutting her chin at the girl and stalking toward the house. As she suspected, Basil was soon on her heels.

"Now don't go gettin' sore at me, Miss Ella. Ain't my fault."

"Of course not. You're only a child."

Basil's face clouded.

Ella knew she'd prodded the girl unfairly but kept her features passive. "But since Sibby has sent for you, then you can explain to her what's going on."

"That don't make no sense," Basil groused. "She already know."

Ella's lips turned up. "Precisely as I thought. And as soon as I take you back into the house, then both of you can tell me what's happening."

Basil quickened her steps and came in front of Ella. "No ma'am. That ain't—"

Ella stepped around her, undeterred. "Then perhaps we shall wait for the major to return."

Basil gulped.

"I'm certain he will wish to know if anything out of sorts is happening on his lands, don't you think?"

Basil made some funny noises and Ella kept going until she reached the back door and wrenched it open.

"Miss Ella!"

She paused and looked back at Basil. "Yes?"

Her shoulders drooped. "All right."

"All right what?"

Basil glared at her, and for a moment Ella wanted to forget the entire thing. But she couldn't do that. If something was going on that could put Lee in danger, she needed to know.

"I's goin' to tell Sibby you was sneakin' around."

Ella shrugged. "She's the one who sent me to find you. That's all I was doing…looking for you."

Basil put her hands on her hips. "Well, go on then. Best we done get this over with."

Ella smiled, though she felt no satisfaction in it, and headed up the stairs with Basil on her heels.

Chapter Twenty-Five

Colonel Larson sat back in his seat and took his time looking over the papers Westley handed him: the tax forms, his commission papers, and the signed medical furlough from General Sheridan.

He squinted close-set eyes at the tax forms, and Westley instructed himself to remain at ease. He'd remained awake most of the night contemplating the taxes that put Belmont at risk while simultaneously forcing himself not to trespass into Ella's room.

The temptation nearly proved too much when, during the night, he'd heard her singing a hymn while the child's coughing fits grew worse. How he'd wanted to console her.

What about the woman tempted his thoughts to stray to such things? Why did she stoke something in him to want to shield her from all manner of pain? Perhaps it was that underneath her dragon's fire he'd glimpsed a tender soul—a playful nymph with sparkling eyes full of life and beauty. In her he saw someone unique, intelligent, and captivating. He was attracted to her—undeniably so. But mere attraction had never caused such stirrings in him before. He'd wanted to pummel that soldier when he'd seen him standing over his Ella.

His Ella?

He clenched his jaw. What would possess him to think such things? It must be the soldier in him wanting to protect the weak and the innocent. Anything more did not bear consideration, as it would only cause more difficulties when his furlough ended.

Westley forcefully snapped his attention back to the matter at hand. Late morning sunlight drifted through lazy dust motes dancing on the warm spring air. They swirled around what had once been a banker's office and made little circles around the colonel's bowed head.

The place smelled of damp ash and rotting wood, and he could guess that the man across from him was less than pleased with the conditions he found himself in. The sentiment to leave the South and return home permeated the disposition of every man in Federal blues whom Westley had spoken to upon his arrival at this post. Occupation was hardly a palatable affair.

The colonel folded the papers and snapped his amber gaze up to Westley. "Well, Major Remington, it seems you have quite the tale. Word is you were supposed to be dead." He gestured toward a chair near the oak desk.

Relieved to be off his leg, Westley took a seat. "I don't know about supposed to be, sir, but I assuredly am not." He rubbed his leg. "Though I've been told I came rather close."

The man leaned forward and laced long fingers together on top of his desk. "A relief, I'm sure, for your family."

"What remains of it," Westley replied carefully.

"My corporal says your wife is a Southern sympathizer, as were your parents."

He gave a nod.

The man arched an eyebrow. "A rather difficult complication for a man in your position, I daresay."

Westley pressed his knuckles into his thigh. "My family and I remained in good standing, even though we differed over the war. I would not go against the vows I'd made upon graduation from West Point, and my father could not go against the state that he so loved. We spoke little, but affection remained."

Colonel Lawson stroked an auburn beard. "Are you aware,

then, that your father ignored all Federal taxes during the course of the Rebellion?"

"Since all Southern states did the same, no sir, it doesn't come as a surprise."

Larson's chair squeaked as he leaned back again. "It seems there is some discord among those in Washington concerning what is to be done with seized lands and accumulated taxes."

"I have heard the same."

The colonel held Westley's gaze for a moment, as though contemplating something. "Tell me, Major. Do you intend to return the plantation back to cotton production?"

He tilted his head. "I am a career military man, sir. I intend to return to duty after my medical furlough." Something flickered on the man's face that gave Westley pause. "But why do you ask?"

"Well, as you know, cotton is in high demand, and there are certain…allowances, I believe, for loyal citizens able to return some stability to the market." He shrugged. "This is not my area of expertise, mind you, but as I am sympathetic to your circumstances, I thought it might be worth mentioning."

Westley kept his features passive, though uneasiness began to squirm in his gut. Something shifted in the colonel's words, as though he hid some kind of agenda. Westley chose his words carefully. "Unfortunately, sir, with as much as my father owes, I am doubtful I can even cover the debt, let alone afford the planting."

"A pity, that."

Indeed. What would he do if he had to sell Belmont? Then where would Ella and Lee go when he returned to duty? And what about Sibby? Were his mother alive, she would be sorely displeased if Westley did not at least secure new employment for her favorite maid.

"I hear some are offering the work to the former slaves,"

Larson continued, interrupting his wandering thoughts. "Promising them a portion of the crops and payments after the harvest."

Westley scratched his head. It didn't seem all that different from what they had always done. "If any remain who have not fled north, that could be a possibility, I suppose."

The other officer snorted. "There are more than enough loitering about. I'm sure you can find plenty of backs willing to bend to the work if you promise them it's worth their sweat."

Perhaps the man had a point. "But first, the taxes."

Colonel Larson came to his feet. "Well now, let me make a few inquiries, and we will see what can be done for a loyal soldier who served his country well, shall we?"

Westley stood, finding the ambitious light in the officer's eyes odd. "I would be most grateful, sir, for anything you could do."

The colonel smiled broadly. "Certainly, Major. I would consider it my pleasure." He motioned toward the door. "I will send word as soon as I find out if anything can be done."

"Again, sir, you have my gratitude."

"If there is anything else you need, let me know."

Westley grabbed his cap and hesitated in the doorway. "Actually, sir, there is one other thing."

"Yes?"

"Do you know where I can locate a doctor?"

Ella swept into the nursery in a flurry of dirty skirts. Basil darted around her, hurrying to where Sibby lay on the bed.

"Sibby!" Basil spouted. "She done saw them bringin' in the wagons, and—"

Sibby darted upright, her eyes so large in her face they

looked like white marbles. "Shush girl! Watch what you is sayin'!"

Ella crossed her arms and stood in the doorway, watching the exchange.

"Didn't you hear what I done said? She *saw,* Sibby!"

Sibby's eyes darted to Ella, and a mask of indifference lowered over Sibby's face. "Saw what?"

Ella lifted her brows. "Come now, Sibby. We aren't going to play this game, are we?"

"Don't know what you is talkin' about. I don't know what you done think you saw."

Ella stared at her.

Sibby sputtered. "They was…they was a new family supposed to be acomin'. You probably saw them movin' they stuff."

Basil studied her shoes and shifted her weight from foot to foot. Silence settled on the room, thick and heavy like a sodden cloak.

Ella waited a moment to see just how uncomfortable the two might become, then cocked her head. "That so?" She *tsked.* "Well, my, my, they sure had a lot of possessions." She tapped her chin. "And quite a few livestock."

Sibby shrugged too-stiff shoulders. "I reckon. Don't know nothin' much about them."

"Yet they are coming to live at Belmont." She flicked her gaze to Basil, but the girl remained as still as stone. Ella looked back at Sibby, who stared at her with her chin lifted. "Hmm. Odd, really, seeing as how you seem to know everything about *everything* that goes on around here."

Sibby pressed her lips into a line.

Ella shrugged. "Very well. Since no one seems inclined to talk to me about it, I will simply bring up the matter when the major returns."

Sibby's mouth fell open. "No, ma'am. That ain't a good idea."

"Oh?" Ella crossed her arms. "And why not?"

Sibby rubbed the muscles at the nape of her neck. "He don't need to be worryin' with none of that. It be the concern of our people."

"People who live on his land."

Sibby's gaze narrowed, but for some reason Ella simply could not control the words that slipped from her mouth. "Well, I suppose I will tell him what I saw, and let him decide if he wishes to concern himself with it."

Basil groaned. "Miss Ella, what done got into you?"

Lee began a coughing fit and interrupted her reply. Ella hurried to the crib and scooped him up, bouncing him and trying to ease the spasms. Behind her, the other two shared harsh whispers.

Lee began to choke, and Ella turned him to the side so he could cough up a thick wad of phlegm. "Oh, heavens, wee one." Ella groaned and stroked his back. Why were the medicines not making the sickness go away, leaving her desperate prayers unanswered? Had she not suffered enough already?

The whispers stopped and Basil came closer, peering at the baby as he finally caught his breath and began to cry. "Is he gonna be all right, Miss Ella?"

Tears sprang to her eyes. "I hope so, Basil." Ella rocked him until he settled some and his cries turned to pitiful whimpers.

"You wanna give him some more of that elixir?" Sibby asked, her animosity seemingly forgotten.

Lee sniffled, his dark eyes blinking up at Ella. She shook her head. "I don't think he should have more so soon." She laid him in the crib and lifted his gown. "But I can rub on the amber oil and see if that gives him some relief."

Lee shivered as she rubbed his tiny chest and prayed that the treatments would work and that Westley would return soon. If only he could find a doctor, then Lee would be safe. Surely the doctor could give him something to ease these spasms.

Please, let him return quickly.

No sooner had Ella flung the prayer heavenward than she heard noises from downstairs. Basil and Sibby shared a concerned look, but Ella ignored them as she gathered Lee to her chest and scrambled toward the stairs.

She made the turn on the landing and came to a halt halfway down to the lower floor. Major Remington placed his hat on a hook and turned to look at her with a weary expression.

He was alone.

Ella craned her neck to look at the door behind him and took two more steps down. "Where is the army doctor you went to fetch?"

The major's eyes softened, and he reached out a hand to her. Ella remained rooted in place, dreading the words that would come next.

"Ella…"

"You couldn't find one, could you?"

He scratched his head. "No. I found one."

Ella hurried down the remaining steps and tried to skirt around him to open the door. He reached out and caught her arm. "He isn't here."

Ella had to lift her chin to meet his eyes, her short stature feeling all the more diminutive so near his height and breadth. "What do you mean?"

Westley lifted his hand, and when she remained frozen, he ran his thumb along the edge of her jaw. "I'm so sorry, Ella. He said he could not come. He had men to see to, and then his orders were to go to one of the hospitals in Memphis."

Ella stepped away from his disconcerting touch and turned

a watery gaze on Lee as she began to pace the foyer. "But, then, who will see to him?"

"I did explain the symptoms to the doctor, and he concurs with the shopkeeper's assessment. It is most likely the whooping cough."

"And?"

Despite her bristled tone, he continued to look at her with compassion. "And he said that we already have the treatments the doctor would give. There would be nothing more that he could do."

Ella jerked to a halt by the parlor door and clutched the baby tighter. "But…I'm not sure the medicines will work!" Her voice hitched, and she hated the frustrated tears that gathered in her eyes.

His cane thumped over the floor and then his hand rested on her shoulder, and the comfort it brought ushered more tears to the surface. She should not enjoy his touch so. Nor should she wish to move closer to him or yearn to breathe in more of his scent—a mix of something like fresh rain and leather.

Curse her weakness. She needed to worry about Lee. The tears spilled over onto her cheeks, and despite her self-admonition to do otherwise, she did not resist when Westley pulled her closer, tucking the baby safely between them. Something in her lurched, and she foolishly wished that they were a family and that he were Lee's father and she his mother in truth.

Westley stroked her back, and she felt some of the tension drain from her. He would not touch her so if he did not care, would he?

"Easy, Ella. It will be all right. We have the medicine. Your baby will be fine."

A sob bubbled in her throat. "I'm a terrible mother."

Westley stepped back and cupped her chin, forcing her to

look into his deep brown eyes that brimmed with concern. "Do not say such a thing. Anyone can see that you love your son."

Ella shook her head. "Oh, Westley. Love or not, I shouldn't have tried to keep him. What do I know of properly caring for a child? I should have done what was best for him and not just what I selfishly wanted."

His eyes sparked, and she wasn't sure if the reaction came from her confession or the fact that she had let his given name slide from her lips.

His knuckles caressed her cheek and then he let his hand rest on her shoulder as he looked down at Lee. "Come now, you know that isn't true."

Ella sniffled. Such kind words, meant to soothe her guilt. But such things were hollow. "I was so foolish," she continued as though he'd never spoken. "And look, now he is sick because I didn't take him to the orphanage as his mother, his real mother, asked me to do."

"Ella." Her name snapped from his lips, as though to revive her senses. He put his finger beneath her chin. "Look at me."

She reluctantly lifted her gaze, like she was a soldier under the influence of his commanding voice.

"The doctor said the whooping cough takes days to show signs. It starts as a sniffle and grows from there. Lee likely had it before I even arrived home."

That still didn't mean she hadn't made matters worse. She always seemed to make things worse.

He dropped his hand. "Have you been giving him the treatments I brought for him?"

Ella nodded. "They have helped him sleep more, and they seem to ease the coughs a little but…"

As though to disprove her claim, Lee began another coughing spasm, his little body wracking with coughs so violently that

Ella had to tilt him and pat his back to help him spit up the mucus.

Westley reached out to take him from Ella, and much to her surprise, she allowed it. Westley cradled the baby in one arm while Ella cleaned his face.

"This is what the doctor warned would happen," Westley said as Ella tugged the soiled blanket off him, leaving him in just his gown. "He's going to cough up the thick spittle until he clears it from his lungs. After that, if he doesn't choke and he hasn't grown too weak, he should begin to recover. With the treatments—and as my mother would insist, prayer—he should be just fine."

Ella stared at the man she'd not too long ago called a devil. The gentle way he held the child and the soothing words he tried to speak to her stirred a longing in her she would do better to squelch. She straightened her shoulders. "Then I will be diligent in making sure he keeps taking the treatments, and I will try to be sure he eats as much as we can get him to take."

Westley handed the baby back to her. "Ella, you are a good mother to this child. You took it upon yourself to care for him when I doubt anyone else would have." He lifted his brows. "And I don't know that I have ever seen a woman quite so protective. You are like a bear with her cubs."

The unexpected thought made Ella chuckle, despite the gravity of the moment. "You think so?"

He smiled, making him even more handsome. "I do. Or perhaps still a dragon. I haven't quite decided."

Lee coughed again and Ella bounced him, but at least this time he didn't spit anything up. After the fit eased, his eyes drifted closed. Ella followed Westley into the parlor where he propped his cane against the settee and settled his large frame.

"A dragon?" she asked as she laid Lee down into the cradle.

He chuckled. "Indeed. A tiny dragon with flaming hair and

sharp claws."

She knew he jested, but she frowned anyway. She did not mean to have sharp claws.

He must have sensed her thoughts, even though she kept her back to him.

"I did not mean to offend. I meant it as an endearment."

How did he do that? Read the private things that swam in her head as though she'd spoken them aloud? It was disconcerting, to say the least.

Ella sat on the edge of the chair near the cradle and studied the man across from her. A dragon as a term of endearment? What a strange man. She wrinkled her nose, and he chuckled again.

She turned her gaze to the window and, though she could feel his gaze heavy upon her, refused to meet his eyes.

He shifted, and she could feel him leaning closer. "Would you mind telling me something?"

Given their earlier conversations, she could hazard a guess as to what he wanted to know. She turned her gaze from the safety of the window and let it settle back on him. "You wish to know about how I came to be with Lee?"

Conflict shifted in his eyes as his gaze roamed her face. "I do."

"Very well." Ella told him of how she happened to be at Lee's birthing, and the things that Cynthia told her about the Remingtons and their kindness. Westley nodded at several intervals, but let her finish her tale before he sat back and considered her.

"So that is how you came to show up at the house with him." He ran a hand through his hair. "Of all the things I speculated, that wasn't one of them."

Her brow furrowed. No, he'd seen her as a harlot. "Yes, and you already know what happened then. I claimed to be your..." Why did the word stick to the roof of her mouth?

"My wife," he supplied.

Something about the way he said it made it seem like the title felt heavy on his tongue as well.

Ella cleared her throat. "Aye. That's the truth of it. So now you know the whole of my pitiful tale."

Westley cocked his head. "I doubt that. I would like to know how you came to be employed at that inn in the first place."

Her mind scrambled. To begin that story would lead to the revelation of more secrets, and those she was not yet ready to share. She forced a laugh. "Nothing to tell there. I was trying to get to the North and ran out of money."

He stroked his chin and watched her in that odd way he had that made her feel like he tried to see her soul. Try as she might, she couldn't contain the shiver that the look sent down her spine.

"Are you cold?"

Mortified, she forced a nervous laugh. "No, sir. I'm fine." She cleared her throat again. Why did it feel so clogged? She glanced at him, only to find the expression in his eyes even more potent. Perhaps a diversion would avert his ardent study of her face. "Major..."

"Westley."

She inclined her head. "Major Westley—"

He laughed. "No, Ella. Just Westley, if you please. I believe I've already given you leave to call me by my given name, have I not?"

Her mouth went dry. Oh, no. This was not at all where she wanted to steer the conversation. Did he wish to discuss those private moments they never should have shared? "I, uh..."

He chuckled again. "Why, Mrs. Remington, your face has turned an alarming shade of red."

Ella's eyes widened, and she lurched to her feet. His laughter died and alarm replaced the mischief in his eyes. Her throat constricted. He shouldn't tease her so. Not when hearing him call her such a thing made her ache somewhere deep in the forgotten places of her heart.

"Ella, I—"

She held up her hand. "Please, just don't." She gently lifted Lee from his place and held him close.

Westley rose and made a move toward her, but she shook her head. "I need to go."

He set his jaw, the little muscle on the side of his face twitching. He gave a single nod as she gathered up what little dignity she could and hurried from the room.

She couldn't do this. She couldn't stay here, dependent on Sibby with her secrets and lies and Major Remington with the way he stirred feelings in her that made her senses go awry. No doubt a man like him was used to charming the fine ladies with such words and gestures. They were probably all accustomed to such things, and the flattery did not unseat the elite the way it did Ella. But she was a simple girl, and she did not like the way her defenses had begun to crack around him.

She'd only known him a matter of days! What kind of blubbering mess would she become a month from now, or however long it took for him to return to the army? No. That simply would not do. She would have to make her own plans and devise a way to make sure she had options.

Ella stomped up the stairs, her resolve growing with each step. Yes. What she needed most were options.

And she knew just how she was going to get them.

Chapter Twenty-Six

"What you mean you want a goat?" Sibby furrowed her forehead, creating wrinkles that resembled a freshly plowed field.

Ella tried to get Lee to suck the rag dipped in the elixir, but he kept turning his head to the side. "Just what I said. If you want me to keep quiet and stop asking questions about whatever it is you have going on back in that field, then I want my goat."

Basil tugged at her hair. "But what you want with a goat?"

Sibby snorted. "She want to try to make that baby drink goat milk. But it ain't good for him."

Ella rubbed the rag over Lee's lips, trying to get him to open his mouth. "Plenty of people do it, and their children are just fine."

Sibby came off the bed and tested her weight on the crutch Westley had fashioned for her. She leaned heavily on it but managed to hobble closer to where Ella swayed, as Lee began to cry from her efforts.

"Now, Miss Ella, this don't make no sense." She frowned down at Ella's increasingly desperate efforts but had the good sense not to comment on it. "Major Westley said you could be stayin' here, and I ain't goin' nowhere. There ain't no reason to make that boy drink no goat milk when I can nurse him."

Lee opened his mouth to scream and Ella squeezed the rag to make a few drops of the elixir drip into his mouth. "Please, wee one, drink," she whispered fervently. She bounced him, and he began to quiet some. Hopefully, he would ingest the drops, and they would help the coughs.

Basil stepped over to the oil lamp and lit the wick, dispelling some of the gloom that had gathered in the room. Evening had come early, ushered in by the heavy clouds that hung low over Belmont and smothered the final rays of day. "Miss Ella, you wants for me to bring you up something to eat?"

Lee started another coughing spasm, and Ella squeezed a few more drops into his mouth.

"Now don't you go chokin' him. He's spittin' stuff up, not swallowing it down." Sibby made a move to reach for Lee, but Ella swung him away.

She resumed her trek around the nursery, stepping past Basil, who stood with her hand on the doorknob and watched Ella warily as though she feared Ella might take leave of her senses soon if she hadn't already.

Ella narrowed her eyes at Sibby. "And what if something happens to you? Or Westley changes his mind. Then what?"

Sibby's eyes flew wide, and Ella realized her mistake. She drew air deep into her lungs, held it, and let it out slowly. Then she cleared her throat and resumed her pacing. "Major Remington will soon enough return to duty and cannot be counted on for any aid."

"But, Miss Ella…" Sibby started talking, but Ella refused to let her interrupt.

"Therefore, I require a secondary means of caring for Lee should anything happen to you or I once again find myself alone with a hungry infant."

Sibby grumbled and inched her way back to the bed and sat. Basil, whom Ella had nearly forgotten, still stood by the door. She elevated her voice. "Miss Ella, you didn't eat no supper. You wants for me to bring you sumthin' up?"

"No, thank you."

"But we got some mighty fine ham in the kitchen."

Ella smirked. "Oh? Shared by the new family that came with three wagons and a procession of livestock?"

Basil scowled. "You want it or not?"

"I'm not hungry."

Sibby grunted. "You is gonna end up fainting clean away again. Then what gonna happen to that boy iffin you drop him on the floor?"

Sibby's words ground Ella's feet to a halt. The woman had a point. She gathered up Lee's medicines from the table by the crib and stalked toward her room. "You are correct. I shall lie down with him."

"But, Miss Ella," Sibby sputtered. "Don't you wants—"

"If I need you, Sibby, I will call." She forced some of the tension from her shoulders. "And I would greatly appreciate you securing a goat for me. A healthy one. We can keep her in a pen up here by the cistern."

Sibby pressed her lips into a firm line, but finally bobbed her head. Ella pushed through to her room and closed the door behind her. After doing so, however, she realized she had forgotten to bring a lamp. Shadows clung to the walls and swathed her room in darkness. Even the moon remained hidden, refusing to give Ella any aid in making her way over to the bed.

Her eyes drifted to the ribbon of light that seeped from under the door that separated her chamber from the confounding man on the other side. As though without her consent, Ella's feet drifted toward the sliver of light like two moths drawn to the flame.

What did he do in there? She shook her head. What did it matter?

Lee coughed and she moved away from the door, lest Westley discover she stood so near. Feeling with her foot, Ella located her dressing table in the gloom. She held both medicine bottles in one hand and had to tip the larger one sideways to place it down.

It slipped on the marble and tilted precariously. Fumbling to set down the amber oil, Ella tried to quickly grasp the elixir again, but it began to roll. "No!"

Ella lunged, startling Lee who began to wail. Her fingers darted toward the bottle, sliding over the smooth glass as it rolled toward the edge of the marble top. It hit the floor with a sickening crack. "No, no, no!"

She dropped to her knees, her fingers clawing through the shadows to find Lee's only hope at survival. They plunged into something sticky and her heart sank. Yards of fabric pooled around her and she laid Lee in her lap so that she could use both hands to cradle the leaking bottle.

The rag. Where had she put…?

Light flooded the room, and the clomp of boots sounded over the floor. "Ella?"

The murky darkness scattered from the lamp's path, and the light caught on the cracked surface of the brown bottle in her hands. The crack ran along the full length of the glass, and the thick liquid seeped onto her hands. "Please, a rag…something!"

Westley moved away, taking the light with him. Lee started to cry, a pitiful sound that dissolved into yet another horrendous hacking fit.

Please, God! Why do you never answer my pleas?

"Here, give it to me."

Ella's fingers tightened on the bottle, and Westley had to pry it from her grasp. He lifted Lee's life away from her along with the bottle! She began to weep. No doctor, no treatments, and no more hope.

Lee wailed, and Ella plunged her elixir-soaked finger into his mouth, rubbing it against the insides of his cheeks. He would get this much, at least!

When she got what she could into his mouth, she pulled him against her chest, her tears cascading down her face and landing on his head as she rocked herself back and forth.

Anguish bubbled in her, a fountain that had filled with each tribulation until finally the loss of hope sent it spilling over. Why? Why must she gain someone to love only to lose him in such a cruel way?

"Ella…" Westley bent beside her and cupped her elbow. "Come now, get up."

She shook her head and hugged the coughing infant tighter.

"Ella." The major's voice became more urgent, poking at her like a needle. "Ella! You're holding him too tight!"

Fear burst through her and she gasped, loosening her grip on Lee.

"Hand me the child and get up."

That voice again. The stern one that held no room for argument. Like a good soldier, Ella relinquished her child and climbed to her feet. Did he seek to take the baby from her? She wouldn't have really done him harm…she didn't mean…

The sobs broke free and then his arm was around her shoulders, pulling her close. "Be calm, Ella. You must be calm."

She gulped air and willed the sobs to stop, straining against them like a cracked dam against an entire ocean. Finally, with great effort, the hitching sobs subsided, only to be replaced by ragged breathing and silent streams of tears.

A knock came at the door to the nursery. "Miss Ella?"

Basil.

"You needs help, Miss Ella?"

She opened her mouth to respond, surprised when the major spoke instead. "I have her, Basil. You may return to your rest."

If the girl was surprised by Westley's presence in Ella's

room, she gave no indication and the house fell silent. Too silent.

Ella peered at the baby tucked in the major's other arm. As though sensing her gaze in the darkness, Westley gave her a squeeze. "There, see? He sleeps."

"But...the medicine..."

"He's had some, and I've wrapped the bottle to try to stem the leak. As soon as you are safely settled in bed, I will find another bottle to put it in."

"Oh...I... Thank you, Westley."

He pulled her against his side, and to her astonishment, placed a kiss on the top of her head before turning her to the bed and gently coaxing her to sit. He leaned down to peer into her face. "Can you hold him for a moment? I am going to get the crib."

She reached out her arms. "The crib?"

He handed Lee over, who did indeed sleep. Had the elixir so soon taken effect?

"Yes. I am going to put it against your bed so that he may sleep close to you, and you will have no fear of him falling from the bed."

She'd never thought of doing that, but it certainly made sense. She didn't reply, and he moved off. In the shadowed light offered from the lamp sitting on her dressing table, Ella watched him walk toward the nursery with an uneven gait. Would he always walk with that limp? She suspected that if he did, it would somehow wound his pride.

But did he not know that he would be no less formidable even if he spent his days in an invalid's chair? The man exuded a strength that surpassed that of his sturdy frame and thick build. It went far deeper, and therefore could not be taken from him by a mere injury.

Westley tapped on the door to the nursery and waited until

Basil opened the door. "Um…yes, suh?"

"Step aside, Basil. I am moving the baby's crib."

Basil moved back out of sight and the major strode through the door without the aid of his cane. Basil said something low that Ella couldn't make out, but Westley's words were clear.

"I can get it on my own. I don't need a child to help me with lifting."

Ella rose to help him, but then thought better of it. He would probably take even less kindly to her offer. Besides, he'd told her to sit here with the baby.

Marveling that she didn't chafe at doing as he asked, Ella remained still, watching as Westley maneuvered the piece of furniture through the door and pushed it up against the side of her bed. He straightened, and the sight of him made Ella's pulse flutter. Never had a man had such an effect on her. Gentle as a lamb one moment and a bull the next.

He turned and closed the door to the nursery, and Ella rose and walked around to the crib. She laid Lee down gently and rubbed the top of his head. Westley came to stand behind her, his smell of rain and leather tickling her senses as he peered over her shoulder at the child.

"Lee will be better."

Oh, how she wished such assurances could be made true simply by speaking them. "He's not named for a general, Westley." The words slipped free of her lips. Foolish, perhaps, but she couldn't help the need to let him know the true name of the child he had taken such pains to care for.

A grunt. "Oh?"

She wiped drying tears from her cheeks. "He's named Westley Archibald Remington, just as you are."

He shifted behind her, searing her heart with his sharp intake of breath. She brought a hand to her mouth. *Bampot lass!*

Why had she thought he would be touched by the declaration? The right to name a firstborn son of his blood with his generational name had been tainted by her stealing it for another. Why had she not thought of that sooner? "I'm sorry. We thought you were dead and to keep the ruse…"

His hand fell to her shoulder. "I understand." His words were thick…heavy. As though weighted by something more.

Ella swallowed, not trusting herself to words. They stood there for several moments, watching Lee sleep.

"The medicine!" Westley dropped his hand and turned away. "I must see to it."

Ella startled, surprised she had let herself wash away in those moments and neglect something of such importance. "Oh, yes! The medicine. Where did you put it? I think I can dump out one of the jars of preserves, and…"

Westley made a low noise somewhere between a growl and a groan and ground Ella's words to a halt. "I told you I would take care of it. Why, woman, do you have such a difficult time letting me care for you?"

Ella's breathing arrested in her lungs. "I, uh…" She swallowed hard. "Thank you."

He scooped the bottle from where he'd left it on the table by her bed. "You should ready yourself to retire."

She nodded.

He stared at her, as though he expected more.

"Would you…I mean, if you don't mind…" The words died on her tongue, unable to breech the defenses of her lips.

"Yes. I will return the medicine to you before I go to my bed."

She clutched the fabric around her throat, but before she could respond, he slipped out of the room, leaving her with the swaying shadows. Ella quickly stripped down to her chemise and then wrapped herself in a dressing gown. Leaving her hair in its pins, she climbed into the bed and sat on top of the coverings. Then, feeling awkward, rose and began to pace.

Roughly twenty or so trips around the room later, a small knock came at the door. She slipped past Lee and tugged it open. She stepped back without a word and gestured for the major to enter. She knew he shouldn't be here, not in the intimacy of night with her in a dressing gown.

But she didn't care. Her heart ached and his nearness did something to sooth it…and made it ache in a different way.

He walked into the room, tension in every hard line of his face. Had she offended him by giving Lee's true name? Or because she had a difficult time letting him help her? Likely both, along with every other difficulty she had speared him with. She closed the door behind him and traced his movements across the room. Why did he remain so patient with her?

A Yankee devil no more. She had given him every reason to lash out at her, every right to pepper her with hateful words or even the back of his hand, yet all he did was worry over her and Lee. He took pains to care for them. She pushed the sentiment aside. He was merely being kind, not showing any special affection. She would do well to remember that.

Westley set a tall crystal object on the dressing table and Ella came closer to look upon it. She recognized it from the day of the storm. She stepped back. "For what have you brought the devil's juice?"

He tilted his head. "Beg your pardon?"

Ella pointed at the decanter. "I'll not have you with the whiskey in here. Best you take it and go."

He rocked back on his heels and regarded her. "Why?" The word hung between them, laden with more questions than that small utterance should carry. He leaned closer to her, his disheveled hair falling across his brow. "Do you fear a man's drink?"

She crossed her arms. "'Tis the devil's drink, and it turns even decent men to scallywags."

His lips curved in amusement, his cloying nonchalance pricking at her like her mother's sewing needle. "A sip or two at the end of a long day does not a devil make. Most men enjoy brandy with their cigars. There is no harm in it."

She hugged herself tighter. "Aye, but one drink leads to another and then more after. And before long, the man is lost and only the drink remains."

The ease left his features and the planes of his face tightened. "Did someone hurt you?"

Her breath caught. "What do you mean?"

He leaned closer in the flickering light of the lamp, his dark eyes catching the light and making bits of gold shimmer in their mahogany depths. "I mean what I said. I'd like to know if a man indulged too much in his drink and it brought you to harm."

Ella turned away, but his hand rested on her shoulder, not allowing her the chance to flee his words. "I would like for you to trust me, Ella."

Had his voice deepened? Tears gathered and slipped down her cheeks.

His fingers tightened. "Please, I would like to know."

Ella drew a ragged breath, and words that would do better to remain locked away sprang free. She hung her head. "Aye. My papa became too fond of the whiskey after Mama died. It turned him into a man he was not. A heartless man."

She pulled from his grip, and he let her go. She went to the bed and sat. "But you are right. That means nothing for you and your choice to take the drink. I ask only that you don't do so in here."

He rubbed the back of his neck, the light behind him casting a glow around the edges of his hair but shrouding his face in darkness. "It was the only bottle I had."

Her brow furrowed.

"I poured out what remained of my father's good brandy. I rinsed it with water out in the cistern, and I poured the rest of Lee's medicine in here."

"I...oh." Her shoulders slumped.

He took a step closer and then hesitated. "I am sorry for your father."

She looked up at him, wishing she could better see his face.

"But I give my word I would never harm you."

Such a word wasn't wise. People often didn't mean to hurt others, but they always did.

He took another step. "Do you believe me?"

"Aye, I do." The declaration sprang forth against her better judgment, but she realized that despite all experience telling her she only left herself open to pain, it was true.

He chuckled. "Do you know your voice takes on a different sound when you are tired or angry?"

She pressed her lips together. Would he now pry into her heritage as well? Why did this man seek to peel back layers of her, searching for things she preferred stay safely tucked away?

"I find it enchanting, that lilt in your words."

Ella blinked. He didn't mean to degrade her for it? "You do?"

He stepped closer, and she had to crane her neck to look up at him. He made a sound deep in his throat that churned something inside her.

"I don't think you know what you do to me, woman."

In another step he towered over her. She tilted her face up to him. Would he try to kiss her?

Her heart hammered. She should get up. Move. But she remained planted where she was, her gaze darting from the intensity in his eyes to the fullness of his mouth, and she realized that if he did try to kiss her, she would allow it.

Welcome it, even.

He groaned and cupped her cheek. "Indeed, I don't think you have a clue." He leaned down and pressed his lips to her forehead, and fire erupted in her chest.

He stepped away, and before she could gather her wits, he stood in the doorway to his room. "If you have any need of help, I will come at your call." He drew a deep breath. "Good night, my little dragon."

Then he closed the door and left her awash in churning emotions and a longing she feared she might never again be free of.

Chapter Twenty-Seven

The light washed over her, drifting upon a languid breeze into every hidden place within her. Ella kept her eyes closed and breathed in the clean air. Fresh, without the taint of either ash or sickness. Pure, as when she'd been...

Her eyes popped open. Color exploded in her vision, as vibrant and flawless as the last time she'd visited this perfect dream world. Ella breathed deep and ran her hands down the brilliant white gown that once again clothed her. It was so beautiful here, but not complete. Not without...

She turned her head, and there he was again. He smiled at her, and nothing else seemed to matter. She returned his smile. "I came back."

He gestured for her to rest against the velvety tree. "We have more to discuss. Are you ready for it?"

She hesitated, knowing that whatever he wanted to talk about would likely open up places in her better left alone, places she had covered over with careful attention and locked safely away. What good could it possibly do to open those doors again? She'd worked so hard to forget the shadows and the pain. She'd made of herself a great fortress, a warden with the key.

The key to her own prison.

"Do you know how a physician cares for a wound?" he asked, forcing her to abandon her contemplation and focus her attention.

Ella wrinkled her nose. "I suppose."

He rubbed at something in the bend of his wrist, and Ella

leaned closer to look at it. A scar? "For him to care for the wound properly," he said, smiling at her as she studied his hand, "he must first open it up, then clean out the infection before he can close it once more."

Ella looked away and drew her knees to her chest. She did not want her wounds open and exposed. It was simply too painful.

"Through the pain comes healing."

Had she spoken her thoughts aloud? She looked at him from the corner of her eye and nodded, though only because she didn't wish to speak on it further.

"Do you want to be healed, Ella?"

She stared at him. What an odd question. Who wouldn't want to be healed? But even as she thought it, she knew the answer. If she fought the healing because she did not want to endure the pain, then the healing would be all the more difficult. She sighed. "Aye. I do."

"That is good then." He leaned back against the tree and stared out into the field, seeming not to be in any hurry to do more.

Ella frowned, then decided merely to do as he did. She leaned back and took a deep breath, watching the way the grass swayed like millions of tiny dancers.

"Who are you?"

Ella blinked, startled by the words. "You don't know?"

He chuckled. "I know every hair on your head and have numbered them all. In my hand, I hold every tear that has fallen from your eyes."

Ella plucked a blade of grass and rolled it between her fingers. "Yet, still you ask."

He looked out over the field again. "Who are you, Ella?"

She drew a shuddering breath. "I don't know."

"You know, but you have forgotten."

The memories she'd seen the last time she came here flashed before her eyes but didn't seem to fit. "I am..." Ella plucked another blade of silky grass and tossed it away. "Well, I am not my mother. I was never good enough to replace her. I'm not the boy my father wanted or even the girl he tried to get me to be. I'm not a lady, or really a mother..." Her voice hitched.

"So you are not the things you do or the titles you strive to achieve?"

She considered for a moment. "No. But then, if I am not what I do or say, then who am I?"

"Who, indeed?" He smiled. "Let's try another way. Who am I?"

Ella froze. Something wiggled in the back of her mind and she narrowed her eyes.

"Do you remember?"

She let her lids drift closed and found herself in another memory. There, somewhere in the far corner was some-thing...something she'd tried to store away. A memory she did not wish to look upon, hidden behind a locked door. Ella walked toward it and paused.

"To heal a wound, you must first open it."

She clenched her teeth and wrenched open the door. She was in her old farmhouse again. The night her mother died.

Ella backed away. The door faded and she blinked at the field again. "No. I can't."

He grasped her hand and squeezed, giving her the courage she did not have on her own. She drew a deep breath and, upon her exhale, came to stand in her mother's room once more. Ella clutched her white gown and stared at a much younger version of herself crouched by Mama's bed. Hair wild and dirty face streaked with tears, the child version of herself continued living out the memory as though the current Ella had not walked into the room. The girl cried out, pleading that the wasting disease would not take Mama from her. Ella's heart constricted as she watched herself cry out for someone to help her.

Mama's eyes opened, clearer than they had been in days. "Darling, I will not be here much longer."

Ella whimpered. "No, Mama. You can't go." The fire in the hearth had long since died, and the chill seeped deep into her bones. She tried to tuck the frayed quilt around Mama's thin frame.

Mama took a great effort and pulled her hand from the covers so that Ella could grasp the thin bones that were all that remained of the strong hands that had tended her and loved her. Mama rubbed her thumb across the backs of Ella's fingers. "It is time, my love. He is calling me home."

She pressed closer. "Who is, Mama?"

"Jesus, baby. I am his and he is mine, and it is time for me to go home to him."

Ella grabbed the quilt, grasping it so tightly her fingers hurt. "But, Mama..."

"Shhh." Mama's eyes fluttered closed, and it took her a moment before she reopened them. "Remember what I taught you?"

Mama had tried to teach her many things. How to care for the house, how to bake pies. She'd taught her to make delicate lace and speak like the fine ladies from the life she'd left behind to marry Papa. Mama had taught her many things, but too much remained that she didn't know. Who would show her how to be a woman?

"The most important thing, darling."

She knew what Mama meant...the thing she'd pointed out as she read the Bible and said prayers over Ella each night before kissing her cheek and telling her good night.

Mama weakly squeezed her hand. "Tell me."

Ella's words quivered. "You told me that Jesus saves us.

That his sacrifice on the cross makes it so that we shed the robes of our transgressions. He allows us to wear the robes of his righteousness, and by him we are saved for eternal life."

Mama sighed softly. "Good girl. You must never forget that. If you put your heart in his hands, repent of your sins, and let him be the Lord of your life, sweet Ella, then you will never be alone." She drew a breath that rattled in her chest. "You'll never be alone, and when the time comes, you will get to be with him for always. Then you will see me again."

Mama tried to give Ella a weak smile. Ella trembled. "I don't want to be alone, Mama."

"Then you have to call on him, sweet girl." Her chest heaved. "You have...to..." Her body strained forward and Mama gasped for air that would not come.

"Mama!" Ella shook her, but her body sagged against the threadbare pillow.

The child Ella clutched her limp hand. "No, Mama!"

Ella stood by the door and watched herself, reliving the terror she'd felt in that moment. Tears streamed down her face as her younger self fell to her knees beside the bed.

"Please! Mr. Jesus, if you hear me, I'm sorry I'm not a good girl. I'm sorry that I make mischief and I talk too much and I do things I shouldn't. But, please, I don't want to be alone. I believe what Mama said was true. I believe you made it so that she could be with you and that you can take all those sins away. Don't forget me, Mr. Jesus. Please. I believe, too."

Light filled the room and Ella watched herself crumple to the floor. She remembered calling out, and she remembered feeling something warm wash over her. But she knew what would come next. Papa would burst into the room and yank her up from the floor and fling her out, cursing at her for not helping Mama, for not coming to get him.

She took a step back, wanting to see that part even less

than she'd wanted to see this. But time froze, and the light grew brighter. Ella turned, and there he was. He smiled at her, then walked to the younger Ella still on the floor. He put a hand on her head.

Ella gasped, and returned to the field. She blinked. "You...you were there."

"And I have been there for everything else." He stared deep into her eyes. "For everything."

Her heart lurched, everything suddenly clear. He had been there, too, that night of terror in the shadows...had been there when men separated from the gloom and came for her...had saved her from what might have been worse than all her other pain combined.

"Nothing can snatch you from my hand."

Tears streamed down her face.

"Not even you forgetting me can separate you from me."

Ella put a hand to her heart. She *had* forgotten him. She'd talked to him some in the beginning, but as she'd asked him to make Papa stop his drinking, and for the war to end, and for things to get better at the farm, and he had not answered her, her disappointment with him had grown. He did not fix the problems or make her pain go away. And so she had grown angry. She'd tried to push him away and forget him. The girl who had cried out was locked away, and a hard woman had replaced her. A woman whose prayers were more wishes than conversations.

"I will never leave you nor forsake you." His gentle words tugged at her, breaking through each stone she had carefully placed and tended.

She looked at him and saw only love in his eyes. How could he love her when she had turned away from him? When she had been so angry at him that she tried to lock him away and forget him or only fling half-hearted requests his way when she never actually expected a reply?

"Now, I ask you again. Who are you?"

He grew brighter, so bright that she could barely see his form. Ella looked down at her dress, the pure white gown. "I am yours," she whispered. "That is who I am."

The light wrapped around her, sweet and beautiful. It pulsed with each throb of her heart, giving her strength and courage that was not her own.

"That is who you are, Ella. You are mine. Mine because I made you, and mine because I bought you at a price."

Ella breathed deep, feeling the light of truth touch places buried in her heart and vanquish lingering shadows in her dark corners.

"You are loved."

The light swarmed around her, the sounds of peace and warmth blending into a melody of acceptance. The notes vibrated in her chest and blended in harmony with the light filling her soul.

"Washed through my sacrifice and held to the end of time for my glory."

Ella lifted her hands to the light. "Yes, Lord. I am yours. I am beautiful because you are beautiful, and I am accepted and loved because I belong to you. You are what is special in me."

"Never will I leave you." His voice filled the air and every part of her senses. "When you walk through the valley of shadows, I am with you. When you pass through the storm, I will be there."

The light filled her, then seemed to stream through every pore.

"Love me first. Seek me first. And all other things will be added to you."

Ella drifted on the words until she settled into something soft. She snuggled into the warmth of her bed. Next to her, she could hear Lee breathing.

Pain gathered like a dark fog and pooled around her, tugging at her grasp on the light. "But what about him?" she whispered to the darkness of her room. "Did you not hear my pleas? Will you let him die?"

He spoke again, his voice all around her. "If I take him, then what?"

Ella clutched her heart. "Then I will be..."

"Alone?"

She shook her head, loosening her grip a little. "Not alone, for you are with me."

"If I choose not to heal him, what will you do?"

Ella opened her arms wide. "Then I will hurt to the depths of my soul, but I will love you still."

The light burning behind her closed eyes faded, but along with it the deep fog of fear receded. Ella blinked and rolled to her side, watching the infant take ragged breaths in the dark of her room at Belmont. Tears burned in the back of her throat. "I will love you still," she whispered. "But, please, Lord, don't take him from me."

Chapter Twenty-Eight

Westley tugged the hat down on his head and hesitated at the door. He'd stayed up all night contemplating a decision that would affect the remainder of his life. He glanced back at the stairs. No, he would debate it no longer. He set his jaw and tugged open the door.

Late May had grown pleasantly warm, even at this early hour when the dew still clung to the grass and birds twittered their morning symphony. His cane thumped down the stairs and to the drive of Belmont where the mud had not fully dried from all the rains.

He would have to beg a nag from the Martins, but perchance he could purchase a horse in town. Likely, however, all the decent mounts had been confiscated by one army or the other. Perhaps the Martins would be willing to rent one of their geldings to him. His leg should be well enough for riding. Though it still ached, it grew steadily less troublesome.

After a rather pleasant quarter hour or so stroll, Riverbend came into view. The stately home offered Greek revival columns and a wide porch that Westley had played on when he was a boy—back when life had seemed so easy and he hadn't any more cares than facing his mother's wrath for ruining another good set of breeches.

He lifted the head of his cane and rapped on the door, then stepped back to check his pocket watch. A quarter to nine. A more respectable hour than his last visit, to be sure. A moment or so later, the door swung open and the house servant offered a perfunctory smile.

"Mornin', Mr. Remington. You wantin' to see the missus again?"

"Yes, please, if she is available."

The woman widened the door and gestured for him to enter. "You can wait in the parlor whilst I goes and gets her."

Westley removed his hat and tucked it under the arm of his russet broadcloth jacket before moving into the room she indicated. In here, a set of furniture gathered closely around the hearth, and a pianoforte rested in the corner. At least they hadn't been divested of all their furnishings as he had first thought.

"Mr. Remington, how pleasant to see you again." The tinkling of a feminine voice interrupted his contemplations of the state of affairs at Riverbend.

"Miss Martin." Westley bowed. "The pleasure is mine."

She lifted her fingers. "When I heard you came to call, I hurried down in hopes of seeing your wife and son, but it seems they have not accompanied you."

Westley accepted her outstretched hand and touched his lips to her knuckles before indicating she should sit. "I am afraid the baby is still quite ill, and Ella has hardly left her room."

Miss Martin perched on a frayed cushion and shook her head, sending her tight brown curls swinging. "Oh, I am so sorry to hear of the troubles, Mr. Remington. That is such a hard thing for a parent to bear."

Westley nodded, not sure what else to say on the matter. Thankfully, Mrs. Martin chose that moment to make an entrance. Westley rose and bowed.

"Good morning, Mr. Remington. May I assume you have come to ask for the use of my carriage again?"

Westley straightened. "I would not wish to take advantage of your kindness again, ma'am."

Something about her seemed to relax even as she waved her hand airily. "Of course not, dear sir. It is hardly an inconvenience."

"I was hoping, perhaps, that I might purchase one of the horses instead?"

Mrs. Martin clasped and unclasped her hands in front of her plain black gown. "Well, I'm afraid then we won't be able to use the carriage without the pair."

The Negro woman poked her head in. "You wants any refreshments, Mrs. Martin?"

Mrs. Martin turned, but before she could answer, Westley spoke up. "Thank you for the kindness, but I am afraid I am once again going to be boorish and take my leave quickly. I do hope you will forgive me."

Mrs. Martin waved the woman away. "Certainly, Mr. Remington. You are surely a busy man." She regarded him a moment, then seemed to arrive at a decision. "I am sorry we will not be able to sell you the horse. They were rather difficult to hang on to during the war, what with us having to hide them in the woods and all, and I am afraid I simply cannot part with one now."

Miss Martin rose from her place and moved to stand by her mother. "Mama, do you think it would be all right if I were to call on Mrs. Remington? Her baby is still ill, and I'm sure she would delight in some female company."

"I'm afraid Ella has been much too distraught for company, Miss Martin," Westley said.

The young woman bit her lip, and suspicion flooded Mrs. Martin's eyes. "How very strange that she has hardly been out of that house since she first arrived."

Westley flexed his fingers. "As I said, the child is gravely ill, and she will not be removed from his side."

Miss Martin took her mother's arm and offered a charming

smile. "Of course, we understand, sir."

"I thank you." He shifted his gaze to the dowager. "Perhaps I may rent the use of one of your horses instead?"

Mrs. Martin lifted her nose. "Don't be absurd. I do not run a livery. The neighborly thing to do would be to allow the use of one's provisions if one's neighbor is lacking."

The words stung. Westley glanced around the room, painfully aware of how much more Riverbend had suffered than Belmont. He forced a polite smile. "On the contrary, ma'am, it seems only fair that I make a trade of some kind…?"

Mrs. Martin pressed her lips together, but Miss Martin gave her mother's arm an obvious squeeze. She beamed up at Westley. "Well, Mama and I could use a few staples."

Westley bowed. "A list, Miss Martin, if you will, and I shall see that it is fulfilled when I return the horse. I will need to go to town today and will return the animal to you on the morrow."

Mrs. Martin seemed about to object, but her daughter stepped forward. "Thank you, sir. This will be mutually beneficial for us both." She looked over her shoulder at her scowling mother. "Don't you agree, Mama?"

The older woman stretched her lips into what could be called a smile. "Of course, dear."

After receiving a short list of flour, sugar, rice and other such necessary items from Miss Martin, Westley received the horse from a young stable boy and swung into the saddle, grateful he could mount it.

He tipped his hat to the women watching from the porch. "Good day, ladies. I shall return tomorrow."

Miss Martin lifted her hand, but her mother remained stoic. Westley turned the nag and urged it into a reluctant canter, feeling their eyes on him until he made it to the river road and out of sight.

Once free of their stares, he allowed the poor beast to slow to a walk. The ride gave Westley time to sort through his thoughts, but not through the strange emotions that warred within him. He could not deny that he felt an urge to protect the little dragon living in his home, and though he was somewhat unnerved by the lengths he was willing to go to see her safe, he wasn't entirely surprised by it either.

Westley reined in at the old bank and tied the horse to a hitching post. Inside, Lieutenant Colonel Larson agreed to see him.

"Major Remington!" Colonel Larson said, waving Westley inside his small office that still smelled of wet ash.

Westley stepped inside, snapping his feet together and standing at attention.

"At ease, Major."

Westley relaxed and placed his hands behind his back.

"I was going to send a man out to your residence this very day. How convenient that you thought to save me the trouble."

Westley shifted his stance. "You have news for me, I take it, sir?"

The man gestured to a chair by his desk. "Indeed. It seems that the majority of the overdue taxes are to be waived, given your dedicated service to your country."

Westley accepted the chair and kept his face passive though relief swirled through him. "That is welcome news, sir."

"In fact..." He leaned closer, as though his words shouldn't be overheard. "I have received word that implies loyalists who are intent on helping reestablish the cotton industry may even receive some aid for their efforts."

Westley lifted his brows.

"Hearsay, mind you," the colonel said, leaning back, "but pleasant tidings nonetheless, I'm certain."

Westley nodded, though he wasn't so sure. He needed to

return to duty. Who would prepare fields and produce the crops? Perhaps he could hire some men...

"So, you see, Major," the officer said, interrupting Westley's contemplations, "it is quite favorable news." He fished a file from his desk and offered it to Westley. "Only a quarter of the original amount is required. Aid for the war effort, you know."

Westley wanted to argue the legality of the taxes as a whole, but he did not wish to antagonize the man. Besides, the amount was within his means, and it would keep things simple. And keep him from seeming insubordinate. Westley placed the folded document inside his breast pocket and rose from his chair. "This is most welcome, sir. I thank you."

The officer rose with him, seeming pleased, and stepped toward the door.

"Sir, I am afraid," Westley said with a grimace, "that the funds I brought with me on furlough are dwindling. I will need to secure this balance from my bank in Washington."

Colonel Larson waved his hand, his manner a bit too friendly. "Understandable. Have it within a few weeks, and all should be well."

"Yes, sir. Thank you, sir." He turned toward the door and then stopped. "Pardon me, sir, but do you happen to have a telegraph nearby?"

The colonel followed him from the office and out into the warm day. "We have one we use for official correspondence. Why do you ask?"

Westley rubbed the back of his neck, then set his shoulders. "I have an important message I must get off to General Sheridan."

The colonel's lips turned up into a sly grin. "So long as it's official army correspondence then." He turned on his heel. "Corporal!"

A young man jogged out from around the side of the building. Westley held back a chuckle as the young man he had discovered in his house widened his eyes. He came to a halt, gave Westley a nervous glance, and threw up a salute. "Yes, sir?"

"Take Major Remington to the telegraph."

"Yes, sir." He turned to Westley with an expressionless face. "Right this way, sir."

After bidding Colonel Larson a good day and following the fidgety corporal to the telegraph, Westley sent one message to the general and another to his banker, rationalizing that securing funds to cover the taxes the army had presented him with would have to count as *official business* as well.

On his way out of town he was able to procure some of the Martin women's supplies from the quartermaster general's tent. What he couldn't get from the army, he determined he would have to search out later. The three bags of rice, four bags of dried peas, and a few pounds of salt pork would have to do for now.

As he turned the bony horse toward Belmont, Westley tried not to let the fact that he had only a few coins remaining in his pocket bother him. Once the funds arrived from his bank, the matter of the plantation would be settled.

The town buildings passed from view, and he was glad to see the bright trees again as opposed to the grays of Greenville. He looked up at the sky, noting how pristine blue it seemed today. He turned his focus back to the road, but after only a moment or two his mind once again wandered.

By the time he arrived at Belmont, the day had grown to be one of vibrant sunshine and air washed clean by the rains. He drew a lungful of it and let it out slowly. It was peaceful here. And peace had not been something Westley had longed for in quite some time. He'd dashed off to war with hopes of great honor and glory. Instead, he was tired, war weary, and lame— likely for the rest of his life.

Westley pushed the bitterness aside before it could take root and ruin the peace that nature had granted. He would not let his lameness define him. To do so would only make of him an even weaker man. And he had too many responsibilities to succumb to that.

Westley reached the barn, which could certainly use a fresh coat of whitewash. He kicked open the doors from where they hung up on the untrimmed grass and led the horse inside the dank interior. He frowned. It seemed no one had been in here in quite some time. Westley turned the animal around in the dusty aisle.

He patted the horse's neck. "Too pretty of a day to keep you in that dark barn. How about I hobble you here in the yard and you can help me tame some of this wild grass?"

The horse's nostrils quivered, and the gelding tugged on the bridle, plunging his muzzle toward the ground. Westley laughed and, after a brief survey of the barn for a bit of rope, secured the horse's legs so that the gelding could wander about the yard without running off. Then he gave the beast another pat and turned toward the house.

His hand had barely rested on the doorknob when an agonizing scream cut through the house and sliced into him. Startled, Westley wrenched open the door, dropped his cane at the bottom of the stairs, and took the steps two at a time.

Ella's wails came from behind her door and his heart lurched. The boy. Fear gouged him, making mincemeat of his insides. He stood frozen in the upper hall, unsure he wanted to see what waited on the other side of the door.

Please, God, I beg of you. Don't take the boy from her.

The words leapt forth, seeming of their own accord. But God would not listen to the likes of him. Whatever they faced, they would face it on their own. With a fortifying breath, Westley jerked open the door, taking in the scene in a single glance. Ella clutched the child to her chest and sobbed, her shoulders heaving. Basil stood in the corner wringing her hands with tears streaming down her dark face, and Sibby stared at the child, her features stricken.

He must be dead.

Westley hardened his jaw and walked to Ella with a hitched gait. She looked up at him, her eyes vacant and red-rimmed. The haunted look twisted his gut.

No! Had the woman not suffered enough? He clenched his teeth so hard he thought they would break.

"Oh, Ella. If only there were something I could do." He reached out to touch the babe's head, then let his arm drop to his side and closed his eyes.

Where are you, God? You are not who my mother claimed. You do not care about us suffering souls banished to your creation.

He opened his eyes to find Ella staring at him.

"He…he's barely breathing, Westley," she said, blinking up at him with desperation as though he could do anything in the world to stop what would come next. "I…I tried to pray, but…" her voice disintegrated as she stared at him.

Westley knew, from somewhere deep within him that he could not explain, that if this child died, the woman before him would never again be the same. The little dragon who had set her claws so deeply into him that he would never again be the same would shrivel into a mere shadow of the fiery woman he had come to know. And he could not abide by that.

God, I need to know. If you exist, let me see it. Show me. Please, I beg of you, sinner that I am, hear me!

Westley reached out his hand and placed it on the baby's head. For her. This he could do for her. "God of creation, the one my mother called the One True King, Maker of heaven and earth, I beg of you to hear my plea."

Ella stilled, her eyes growing wide. Westley's pulse quickened. He had not prayed since he was a child. Who was he to call on God now when he had never submitted to any of the Creator's ways? He bowed his head anyway. If there was any hope at all, even as unlikely as it might be, it would be in prayer.

He cleared his throat. "Lord, forgive me, a worthless sinner who has done much evil in your sight, for coming to you. But Lord, this child needs you. I beg of you, show us that we are not completely forgotten, and that somewhere up in the heavens you still hear the desperate cries of men."

The baby stirred under his hand and began to cough weakly. A tingle ran through him, starting at his core and shooting like lightning to his fingers. He drew a quick breath. "God, I beg of you to heal this child as you did people when you walked the earth. I..." He hesitated, and his voice grew raspy. "I believe in you, and that you are able. Please, Jesus, be willing to heal this boy."

Lee gulped a mighty breath and began hacking. Ella squealed and turned him to the side, and the baby coughed up thick lumps of mucus. Westley stepped back, amazed. Had his prayer been heard?

Ella patted the baby and Sibby wiped away everything the child spit up, time and time again. He kept coughing, his tiny chest heaving violently. Westley's fists tightened as doubt set in. Would the child end up dying of the spasms instead of peacefully in his mother's arms?

Finally, when Westley thought he could endure it no longer, the coughing subsided. Ella bounced the baby and smeared the tears off her face. Then she looked up at him with wonder in her sparkling green eyes and he shifted uncomfortably.

"Your prayer has been answered."

His Adam's apple bobbed. "We don't know that yet."

"Ha!" Sibby pointed a finger at him. "This here be a miracle, plain and simple."

Westley rubbed the tight muscles on the nape of his neck and took a tentative step closer. "Perhaps."

Ella beamed up at him and held out the boy who carried his name. "Come and see." She dipped her delicate chin toward the babe. "He heard you, Westley, and he answered."

Westley stepped closer and cupped his hand under the child's head, drawing the baby up to his chest. The tiny face tilted toward him, blinking clear dark eyes. Westley stared. His prayer had been answered, and God had unequivocally shredded all of Westley's doubts about whether the Creator heard their cries. Perhaps he did not answer all of their pleas, but he *had* answered this one.

His chest constricted as the baby wriggled a fist from the wrapping and waved it around. Despite the tumultuous emotions battling within him, Westley smiled. "Ah, little fighter, there you are. You gave your mother and me quite a scare."

He heard Ella's quick intake of breath and realized that he had spoken as though they were a family. This protectiveness he felt, would it be enough? He held her in affection, of that he could admit.

He caught Ella regarding him. As he held her gaze for an instant before she glanced away, her eyes revealed something her words never could. Something that stirred things deep within him.

She stepped closer and laid a hand on his arm as she smiled down at the baby, and he knew she held him in an affectionate regard as well. Suddenly the decision that had weighed on him all night and had plucked at his mind all day came to rest.

He would ask Ella to shed the ruse and take his name in truth.

Chapter Twenty-Nine

Ella watched as Westley spread out a large patchwork quilt next to one of the magnolia trees in Belmont's front yard. Light caressed the tree's shiny leaves and dropped to the green grass as birds sang softly overhead. As though to place a finishing bow on such a fine scene, a butterfly glided down and drifted around Westley's head.

Three days had passed since he had prayed over Lee, and her wee one had gained strength with each passing hour thereafter. A miracle, indeed. She swayed, rocking Lee gently as he cooed in the dappled light under the tree. Looking at him now, she would never guess he'd been very close to the grave. He'd regained his appetite, and his little cheeks were rosy.

Ella sighed with contentment and let her gaze drift back over to the man who set down a picnic basket on the corner of the quilt. Dressed in dark trousers and bracers, he'd taken off his jacket and had rolled up his shirt sleeves, leaving muscular forearms exposed. He must have been a rather large man, indeed, to be this strong after so long a battle with injury. His shoulders stretched the fabric as he bent to straighten a corner of the quilt, and the way he'd left the collar of his white shirt open exposed the hollow of his throat.

He looked up and caught her eye, and she felt her cheeks warm. But she smiled anyway, enjoying the way the gentle breeze teased his hair. "You were right. This is a perfect day for a picnic."

He grinned, then shoved his hands into his pockets and

stared at her somewhat sheepishly. He had been acting rather odd these last days. He'd been kind and attentive, but…also a bit nervous. The intensity of the other night seemed to have affected him greatly. She'd tried a few times to engage him in conversation on the matter, but he seemed reluctant so she'd let it go. Whatever spiritual issues he faced, he was not yet ready to discuss them.

She offered a reassuring smile and then lowered to her knees to nestle Lee in the blanket Westley had arranged into a little nest for him. Lee swung his tiny fists around, then took to sucking on one of them. Ella rubbed the top of his head and then sat, arranging her voluminous skirts around her.

"I'm making a dress for you."

Ella blinked. "I'm sorry, what did you say?" The corners of her lips twitched. The very idea of this stoic soldier contemplating fripperies amused her.

Westley ran his fingers through his hair. "Well, I'm not making it, of course. Sibby had your measurements." He lifted his broad shoulders. "So I gave them to the seamstress."

Ella smiled. He seemed almost boyish. "That was most kind of you, but rather unnecessary."

Westley shook his head. "No, it is quite necessary. I don't want you wearing those widow's gowns anymore."

She inclined her head. "Very well. I have others."

He tugged on the collar of his shirt, seeming restless, as though the topic of dresses caused him some kind of angst. "Not the ragged work dresses, either." He held up a finger before she could respond. "Or anything that came from that har—" He glanced at Lee and cleared his throat. "Any of the items you procured from the lady of the night."

"Oh." She wrinkled her nose. "Has my wardrobe become an area of concern for you?"

His jaw twitched. "I merely think that as the lady of this

house you should be attired appropriately."

An uneasy feeling slid through her. There could be only one reason he worried over such things now. He was preparing to leave. She'd known such a time would eventually arrive, yet she had grown lax in her efforts to guard herself against it. Despite her determination to feel otherwise, the thought of him departing tugged at her heart. "I see. May I assume, then, that you are getting ready to return to duty, and you will honor your agreement to hire me as an overseer for the house?"

Instead of answering right away, Westley turned to the picnic basket and plucked two plates out, handing one to Ella. "You are partially correct. I sent a telegram to my superior officer, and it has been decided that I will take a position in the western territories."

Ella accepted the plate and set it in front of her. "The western territories? I have heard that is dangerous." She lowered her voice and leaned closer. "There have been tales that redskins will cut the scalp from your head." She shuddered.

Westley chuckled. "Precisely why there is a need for men to go, and when I volunteered, they were all too happy to accommodate me."

Ella's mouth went dry. "You volunteered for that?"

He regarded her closely. "I did. Three days ago, when I went to see Colonel Larson to settle Belmont's debts."

Ella clasped her hands in her lap. It was no business of hers where he chose to go. "I see. Well, Major Remington, I will pray that you remain safe in all your endeavors."

The little muscle in the side of his jaw twitched, which Ella had come to learn meant that something she'd said upset him.

"I leave in three days."

"Three?" she squeaked, horrified that her emotions could so easily be read. She turned her gaze away. "I thought you stated your furlough lasted for months, and it has hardly been that long."

"I know. Furlough has been cut short."

By orders, or his own request? Ella tried not to let the idea that he would rather return to the army than stay here with her hurt, but her heart disregarded her wishes. As though to soothe it, Ella reached up and fumbled with the lapels on her gown.

Westley's features tightened as he pulled thick slices of fresh bread, slabs of ham, and a jar of pear preserves from the basket. He set about fixing the plates, and Ella watched him somberly. She had no reason at all to be upset. He had agreed to hire her, and she would have more luxury here than she'd ever known. And the position of lady of the house would offer her some manner of security.

"Ella, I have been meaning to ask you something."

An odd tone to his voice had her setting down the fork she'd been fidgeting with and looking up into his eyes. He stared at her, flashes of emotions she could not place sparking in his intense gaze. Ella's breath caught.

"Why is there a goat by the cistern?"

Her breath left her in a whoosh. "Pardon?"

His shoulders slumped. "I...wondered why there was a goat in a makeshift pen by the cistern."

She blinked at him.

He cleared his throat. "I asked Sibby about it, and she said I should take that up with you." He cocked his head. "Where did you get a goat?"

"Sibby gave it to me."

"Where..." He shook his head, his eyes suddenly brimming with amusement. "What is the goat for, Ella?"

She glanced at Lee. "Milk. In case for any reason something were to happen, I would still be able to care for Lee."

Concern chased all traces of humor from his eyes. "You worry that you might be in a desperate position?"

Ella bit her lip. "Well, I have learned that one never knows what tomorrow may hold. I find it prudent to prepare as much as possible."

Westley plucked a slice of fluffy bread from the plate and tore off a chunk, rolling it in his fingers. "As much as I am able to do so, I have determined that I will protect you and be sure that you are comfortable and secure."

Warmth spread through her, and she quickly doused it. "I'm afraid I don't understand. Did you not just say that you would be leaving in three days?"

"I did."

"And you shall offer me all of these things while you are all the way out in the western territories?" The bite in her tone surprised her, and Ella had to tamp down her emotions before they found their way farther out of her mouth.

Westley watched her, his intense gaze searing into her. "Ella, I—"

Ella held up a hand. "Forgive me, Major. That was entirely inappropriate of me. I do not know what possessed me to say such a thing." She conjured a smile and forced it to take up residence upon her lips, though they seemed to balk at the effort. "I am deeply grateful that you have allowed me employment and a place of residence at Belmont. Of course, those things have given me a great measure of security."

He leaned back on his hands, his plate now as forgotten as her own. A breeze lifted bits of his sun-kissed mahogany hair and sent locks dancing across his forehead, and Ella found herself wishing that he were not so handsome. She crossed her arms and looked away. Though she must admit that even if he were not such a physically appealing man, she would still be attracted to him. Something deeper than his refined looks and muscular build called to her.

"I am not hiring you as a housekeeper," Westley said, jarring her from her thoughts.

Alarm swept through her.

"And I do not wish for you to continue with the ruse. I—"

Ella threw up her hands, arresting the remainder of whatever he was about to say. "You lied!" She lurched to her feet, too filled with energy to remain docile on the ground. She whirled around to glare at him. "You said I could work here! Now that you are leaving, you are going to send me away?"

Her breathing increased, and Ella clenched her hands at her sides. A good thing she had secured that goat. Lee had not seemed interested in any way of eating other than nursing, but she would simply have to teach him. She'd been wise to take her options in hand. How could she have so easily forgotten that underneath their charm men could not be trusted?

Westley rose and stepped over the uneaten food, reaching for her. "Now, Ella, calm down. You didn't let me finish."

She stepped back away from his grip, her pulse pounding. "There is no need for further explanation." She made a move toward Lee. "Since it is your intention for me to leave the premises, I see no reason why I should stay here a moment longer."

She reached to pick up Lee, but Westley caught her by the arm and used his bulk to turn her to face him. He chuckled. "And here I worried that perhaps you didn't hold true affection for me."

She stopped breathing. She blinked up at him. Did he think to mock her? She sucked in a gulp of air and opened her mouth, but no words came out.

"I'm not hiring you and I want you to drop the ruse because I have something different in mind."

Ella snapped her mouth closed and narrowed her eyes. She would be no man's leman.

Westley dropped her arm, rubbing at the back of his neck.

In His Eyes

"This is not at all how I planned this to go," he mumbled.

Ella's brow furrowed. The man made no sense.

Westley straightened, and he looked the stern officer once more. "Miss Whitaker, I intended to ask you to take my name in truth, as my legal wife."

Her jaw unhinged and she shook her head to clear the pulsing in her ears, certain she had heard him incorrectly.

"Now, don't say no just yet before you have even heard my proposition," he said with a growl.

Ella stilled. Proposition? Had he not just asked her to marry him? Her heart fluttered. Had Westley Remington become fidgety because of her? Did he…love her? She tried to swallow and found her throat too thick to do so.

"It would be in name only, of course."

Her heart shuddered in its ascent and crashed on shattered rocks below. "Name only?"

Something flickered in his eyes. "As my wife you will have access to my accounts and a manner of protection. And if anything happens to me out West, I can rest in the assurance that you will be provided for and secure for the remainder of your years. Lee will inherit Belmont, and you will both be able to live a comfortable life."

She clutched the fabric at her throat, unsure how to feel. He offered her safety and protection. With his name in truth, she would be able to have both freedom and respectability. Ella blinked back sudden tears. It solved all of her problems. Why then did she ache?

She swallowed back the burn in her throat. "You are sure you would sacrifice all of that for me? What if you meet a lady with whom you would want to share your home and life in the manner a marriage is supposed to be?"

"That will never happen."

Hope began to blossom.

"I have dedicated my life to the military. I never intended to wed. This way, you are protected, and my family lands have someone to inherit them upon my death."

Ella glanced away, trying to bring her emotions to heel. A life as an unloved wife with a mansion and plenty to eat was far better than an unwed mother facing scorn and a life filled with scarcity. She drew herself up and squared her shoulders. "And you would make Lee your heir?" Why did this feel like a business arrangement instead of a marriage proposal?

"I would. He already carries my name. No one ever need know he was not born of a union between us."

Ella rubbed her arms, though the day was rather warm. Westley stepped over to her and placed his hands on her shoulders. She breathed in the earthy scents of him.

"It's..." His words trailed off and she looked up at him, seeing as many emotions swirling in his eyes as she guessed flickered in her own. "It's the best I can do."

Because he was an honorable man, a friend who would give much to take care of her. He did not care for her in the way she must acknowledge she cared for him. Perhaps had even begun to feel something deeper... She set her jaw. She should be grateful. She forced her lips to turn up. "I appreciate your concern for me, Major Remington."

Something akin to hurt erupted in his eyes, but he blinked and it was gone.

"You are sacrificing much for my son and me. I am grateful for your offer and agree to your terms."

He reached up and ran the rough pad of his thumb across her jaw, a motion that seemed far too intimate for a man who wanted to wed in name only. Confounding man! He should not toy with her so.

She took a step back from him. "How do you suppose we will have a wedding, when it is already presumed I am your wife? I imagine that shall be rather awkward."

He lifted his shoulders. "Perhaps only the Martin women believe that you are already my wife."

"No, Sibby referred to me as Mrs. Remington when she went to town, and several people seemed rather curious about me. I wouldn't doubt that many tongues were wagging over it."

They stood there in silence for several moments, the beauty of the day seeming to have dimmed.

Westley shifted his weight, and Ella just then noticed he'd been moving around without the aid of his cane.

"I have an army chaplain coming by two days hence."

She bobbed her head, not surprised he had known her answer before she gave it. Of course, she would accept the offer of security. "So we shall wed the day before you leave for duty."

"Yes."

Ella pushed aside girlhood fantasies of a fabulous gown and a ceremony with family and friends. Those were things for couples to celebrate love. And such were the imaginings of children not yet seasoned with the ways of the world. In reality, women had very few choices. They could marry well and be provided for, or they could eke out a living from the very few professions available to them. She most certainly would not be the first woman wed to a man who did not love her in order to procure a stable future. "Very well. That should suffice for the vows. I believe, however, we must still have witnesses."

"I shall invite the Martins."

Panic leapt in her chest. "But then they will know I lied to them."

"Perhaps not. We can say that we wished to make our field wedding more official before I returned to duty."

Ella inwardly cringed. More lies. She rather liked Opal and would relish the idea of a neighborly friendship. That would best be done without the untruths. Besides, better the lady shunned her from the truth than befriended her under a shroud of lies. She hoped. "If you are not opposed, I believe it would actually be better if I told them the truth."

"As you wish."

"That settles it then." She stepped around him and scooped Lee up from the ground. "If we are agreed, I shall go pen Miss Martin a note requesting a visit with her tomorrow."

Westley gestured to the disarray on the ground. "But what of our picnic?"

"Forgive me, but I find I am without appetite. Would it be too troublesome to ask you to return everything to Sibby for me?"

Confusion furrowed his forehead, but his words remained infuriatingly conciliatory. "Certainly. I will see you at dinner tonight."

Ella situated Lee in the crook of her arm and tried to offer him her most pleasant smile. "Yes, of course."

She turned toward the house and blinked away tears that stung her eyes, reminding herself that what had just happened was truly a blessing.

The next afternoon Ella stood in the doorway to the parlor and twisted her hands as Basil opened the front door. Mrs. and Miss Martin bustled in, the hems of their wide hoop skirts sweeping over the floor. Opal removed her bonnet and gave it to Basil before clasping her gloved hands.

"Ella! How lovely to see you again!"

Ella smiled and moved closer as the women removed their gloves. She took a deep breath. No more lies. "Indeed. I am pleased you agreed to come to call on such late notice."

Mrs. Martin arched a thin eyebrow. "We were rather curious, I'm afraid."

Opal grasped Ella's hands. Either Opal didn't notice Ella's different way of speaking or she didn't care. "I am overjoyed at the wonderful news that the baby is well."

Ella nodded, bobbing the intricate curls Sibby had worked through her hair. "It was a miracle. He almost died, but then Major Remington prayed over him and..." She lifted her shoulders. "The Lord answered."

Opal put her fingers to her lips. "Oh! What a beautiful story." She looked over the shoulder of her pink gown. "Isn't it, Mama?"

"Quite," the woman said, though she seemed to share none of her daughter's enthusiasm.

"If you will join me in the parlor, ladies, tea will be served soon." Ella gestured toward the room and allowed her guests to pass in front of her.

Opal made a beeline for the cradle. "There you are sweet one!" She cooed, peering down at Lee. "May I hold him?"

"Certainly, you may."

Opal gently lifted the baby and held him against her, speaking in a sugary tone. "Aren't you just the most handsome little fellow?"

Mrs. Martin helped herself to a seat, and Ella settled on the settee nearest the cradle. Opal took a chair just as Basil stepped into the room carrying a tea tray. Sibby had been able to get up and hobble around some, but she still needed to take it easy on her ankle.

Basil plopped down the tea tray and rattled the china, and Mrs. Martin scowled. Ella, however, offered the child a smile. "Thank you, Basil."

She grinned. "You's welcome, Miss Ella. You be needin' anythin' else, you just holler for me."

Ella waved a hand and the girl hurried off. She served Mrs.

Martin, but Opal declined, content to play with Lee instead. Ella smiled. "He seems to like you, Opal."

She beamed up at Ella, her pretty features growing pink. "I adore children."

"So, Mrs. Remington," Mrs. Martin interjected, "Did your husband happen to mention anything about supplies?"

Ella cocked her head. "I beg your pardon? What supplies?"

Opal groaned, but her mother ignored her. "He promised us several things in exchange for the use of our horse but was only able to deliver part of the list."

"Oh?" Ella smoothed her skirt. "Perhaps I may be able to assist. Major Remington has been called to return to duty, and I am afraid he has been rather busy these last days in preparation. Unfortunately, it may have slipped his mind."

Mrs. Martin's nose twitched. "Oh, well. It is no bother, really."

"Please, I wouldn't mind helping."

The older woman lowered the teacup that was partially lifted to her lips, looking resigned. "Well, we just needed a couple of bags of flour and sugar." She waved her free hand. "You know, things that have been harder and harder to come by."

The poor woman obviously didn't want to admit to her need. "I will see that it is done. I know Major Remington would not wish for his promise to go unfulfilled. That would hardly be appropriate as you have already upheld your side of the exchange."

Mrs. Martin seemed to relax and began to sip her tea again.

Ella smiled. "I am certain Sibby still has some of her stores remaining, so I shall have it for you today."

Mrs. Martin's eyes flashed. "Am I to understand you're suggesting that your slave…"

"Freedwoman," Ella corrected.

Mrs. Martin narrowed her eyes. "That your *freedwoman* has stores of supplies on hand?"

Ella plucked at her cuticles. "It would seem that Sibby had a way of hiding away all of Belmont's supplies, and she has managed to keep everyone fed."

"Hmm." Mrs. Martin tapped her chin. "Odd that those supplies wouldn't have run out by now."

"Now, Mama, you've been reading too many novels," Opal gently chided, lightening the suddenly heavy mood that gathered in the room. She glanced at Ella. "Thank you for your generosity."

They settled into the mundane and polite conversation expected of ladies of stature until Ella could no longer stand the tension in her nerves. She set down her now tepid teacup. "Ladies, I fear there is a matter of importance I must discuss with you."

"Oh?"

"Oh?"

The Martin women spoke in unison, both of them leaning forward in their seats. Whereas Opal looked concerned, her mother practically dripped suspicion. Ella withheld a groan. This wouldn't be easy.

"First, I must ask your forgiveness." Ella took a steadying breath. "My dear ladies, I fear I have lied to you."

"Ha!" Mrs. Martin set down her teacup with a clink. "I knew it."

"Mama!" Opal scolded. "You are being churlish!"

Mrs. Martin ignored her. "Mr. Remington conceived a child out of wedlock with his immigrant mistress and then sent you here to hide your shame."

Ella gaped at her. Good to know what they thought of her. Ella stiffened her spine. "No, Mrs. Martin, that is most assuredly not the case."

"Mama!" Opal admonished, her face growing pale.

The older woman lifted her shoulders, seeming far from apologetic. "What, then?"

Ella drew a deep breath. No matter how she went about this, any esteem she'd had in their eyes would be gone. How foolish of her to think that she would be able to let them see the real her and she not be scorned. Her temper flared, and she struggled to keep it in check.

"I am not a harlot, ma'am, nor am I someone's leman. Certainly not Major Remington's. Lee's mother died during his birthing, and I brought him here because I had heard the late Mrs. Remington was known for helping children find orphanages. Of course, at the time, I had no idea that Mr. and Mrs. Remington had passed on."

Mrs. Martin scowled, and Opal pressed her lips together. Nothing for it but to move forward.

"When I arrived, there were Federal soldiers demanding that Sibby get the master and lady of the house." She lifted her palms. "Forgive me, but Sibby seemed so distraught that I pretended to be the lady of Belmont. Everything else…sort of happened after that."

"Oh, my!" Opal exclaimed, her eyes bright. "What a tale of intrigue."

Mrs. Martin stared at her, but thankfully kept her lips sealed.

"So you see, we kept up the ruse so that the Federal soldiers wouldn't confiscate Belmont and Sibby could be a wet nurse for Lee."

Silence. Well, except for the sound of her pounding heart and the blood pulsing in her ears. The Martin women stared at her, and Ella could feel her cheeks flaming.

Then surprisingly, Mrs. Martin chuckled. "Well, that certainly explains why Mr. Remington seemed somewhat confused when we saw him in town and we asked after his wife and son."

Ella wrinkled her nose. "I'm sure it came as a shock."

Opal leaned forward. "Why do you suppose he didn't say anything?"

Ella shrugged. "I think it was because he wanted to see what was happening at Belmont first." She looked at the patterned rug, a pang of something unwelcome piercing her heart. "But then, after I told him my plight, he let the ruse slide."

Mrs. Martin steepled her fingers. "In the times we saw him after that, he never once mentioned you were not really his wife. Why is that, do you suppose?"

Ella tried to smile. "He was protecting me. Which is what brings me to the next issue." She clasped her hands in her lap. "Major Remington and I are to speak vows in front of an army chaplain tomorrow, and we would like to ask for the two of you to stand witness."

Mrs. Martin clucked her tongue. "My, what an intriguing mess."

"Oh, hush, Mama." Opal beamed at Ella while she rocked Lee. "Isn't it romantic? He comes home, surprised to find a beautiful woman in his house, they fall in love, and this poor orphan child has a family to call his own." She sighed wistfully, and Ella's stomach clenched.

"Nonsense." Mrs. Martin gave an unladylike snort. "Now who has been reading too many novels? You sound like you are spouting the tale from one of those silly romances you like."

Opal's lip poked out. "Say what you will. I still think it's beautiful."

Mrs. Martin rolled her eyes. "They probably agreed to wed so that Mr. Remington could have someone tend Belmont while he is away and care for him in wifely ways when he's home, and so that she will have the only security afforded to a woman of her situation."

Ella's heart constricted. Mrs. Martin had managed to pluck exactly the right chord. The part about wifely duties struck her. She hadn't even considered such a thing! Though Westley had said in name only.

"That is simply terrible, Mama," Opal stated, seeming a bit miffed.

Mrs. Martin cocked her head and looked at Ella expectantly.

Ella grimaced. "I'm afraid your mother is a bit closer to the truth."

Opal groaned.

"Major Remington and I will wed so that I will have a home and so he will have someone to pass his lands on to, should something happen to him in the western territories."

"The western territories?" Opal fanned herself with her free hand. "Oh, the horror of it."

Lee began to fuss, likely because the lady held him too tightly. Ella reached for him, and Opal handed him over, still looking a bit dazed.

Mrs. Martin plucked her teacup from where she'd left it on the tray and poured herself a fresh cup. "I say that you are very lucky. Why, I dare say that the odds this would turn out so well for you were mighty slim indeed."

Ella nodded, unable to deny the truth of the statement.

Opal's lips turned down. "Well, there is still a wedding to consider." She brightened. "Do you have a gown?"

Mrs. Martin scoffed. "What a silly question, child."

Opal's cheeks flamed, and Ella offered her a smile. "Major Remington was kind enough to have a new dress fashioned for me. It won't be a wedding gown, of course, because that would hardly be practical, but Sibby said they ordered a functional dress that would complement me. Major Remington is to pick it up from a seamstress today."

Opal smiled, but her eyes seemed sad. Ella tried not to dwell on that and turned back to the dowager. "I am terribly sorry for deceiving you. It was not my intention to become an imposter. It sort of happened."

To her surprise, Mrs. Martin grinned. "Think nothing of it, dear. It was right clever of you outwitting those Yanks. And I am glad you have been able to find a means of security for you and the child. Opal and I will be happy to provide witness so that you may legalize your vows."

It all seemed rather impersonal, these wedding guests agreeing to perform a function at a wedding service that was more the signing of a business agreement. Throughout the remainder of the visit, Ella had to force herself to keep up polite conversation, and when Opal swept her into a tight hug on her way out the door some time later, tears stung her eyes.

"Don't you worry. I'll come by, and you and I will have a lovely time to pass some of the days after he leaves."

Ella squeezed her new friend and stepped back. "That would be exceedingly kind of you." She would delight in a bit of diversion from the emotions that would be certain to plague her.

Basil loaded up two sacks each of flour and sugar, plus a few jars of preserves and a loaf of Sibby's bread into the ladies' carriage. Then the women took their leave and Ella closed the door behind them, somehow feeling much emptier than when the day began.

Chapter Thirty

Ella stared at herself in the mirror, wondering just exactly where this woman had come from. Gone was the ragged-looking waif that scrubbed dishes in the Buckhorn Inn, and in her place stood what appeared to be a refined lady.

She turned, letting the hem of the wide skirt twist around her slippered feet. Westley had managed to order a fine gown, and Sibby's measurements meant that it fit her every curve perfectly.

She eyed her reflection, admiring the dress's green hoop skirt with ruffled black trim and the fitted jacket with silk edging and delicate stitching. The blouse underneath clasped at the base of her throat, and as Ella reached up to feel the edges of her lapel, she smiled. She appeared modest yet stylish, elegant yet practical. It would seem the man did well in choosing attire fitting for the mistress of Belmont.

Even the garment's colors complemented her complexion, and the deep green accentuated the fiery tints of her hair. Yes, it would seem her future husband had thought of everything. Ella turned away from the mirror, taking her place in her dressing chair just as Sibby opened the door from the nursery.

"Oh, good. You is ready for me to get to that hair." Sibby hobbled into the room, looking like a flustered hen by flapping her walking stick around like a broken wing.

Ella nearly giggled at the show Sibby made of it. It seemed they now had *two* people in this house that begrudgingly moved about on a cane. The thought snatched the gathering grin from her lips. What a terrible thing to think! Neither of them wanted to depend on a cane, and for her to find amusement in it was just cruel.

Sibby propped the cane she'd borrowed from Westley against the dressing table and began pulling a boar's hair brush through Ella's tangle of curls. "We gonna have you looking right fine today, ma'am. We sure is."

Ella wrinkled her nose. "What's gotten into you?"

Sibby's hands stilled. "What you mean?"

Ella twisted so she could see the woman over her shoulder. "You have been acting strangely the last couple of days. You talk to me differently, too."

Sibby lifted her eyebrows and gave Ella a look that seemed to say she ought to know better. "Well, you ain't no pretender no more. You is going to be Major Westley's lady for real now." She yanked on a tangle and Ella yelped. Perhaps it served her right for thinking such a callous thought about Westley's and Sibby's use of canes. "Now Miss Ella, you knows that being the real lady of Belmont makes things different."

Ella mused over the words as Sibby twisted and styled her hair, leaving a mass of coppery curls piled on the back of her head and falling past her collar. Would Ella, rather than Sibby, really be seen as the one in charge here once she wed Westley in truth? She wasn't entirely sure how she felt about that. However, it might give her a bit of power to dig up a few answers.

"All right then," Sibby said, plucking her from her thoughts. "You is ready." She took the cane and moved back, eyeing her handiwork. "Yes'um, that looks right nice."

Ella rose and smoothed her hands down the skirt. "Sibby, I hope you don't mind that—"

"Now you hush that," Sibby groused, cutting off Ella's words.

Ella lifted her eyebrows.

Sibby placed her hands on her hips, the docile tone she'd been using suddenly gone. "I know what you is about to say, and don't you even bother doin' it. Belmont needs a lady, and the major done chose you. Best you be rememberin' that."

Ella declined to answer, knowing that if the circumstances hadn't been what they were, then Westley would have never chosen her in a thousand lifetimes. She reminded herself that being an unloved wife with a life of means and security was a much better option for Lee than her trying to work and never really having enough to feed them.

Ella squared her shoulders and assumed the look she'd seen Mrs. Martin use.

Sibby grunted. "See there? You look like one of dem already."

Before Ella could reply, a knock at the door drew their attention. Sibby hobbled over to it and opened it, gesturing for Westley to enter. She moved past him and out into the hall, yelling orders to Basil as she started down the stairs.

Their gazes met and Westley's eyes darkened as he ran a hand through his hair, messing up the tidy way he had combed it away from his face.

"Ella, you look…" He cleared his throat and blinked, and then suddenly she was once again faced with the stoic soldier. He straightened, and his eyes became unreadable. "You are quite lovely. The seamstress did well."

She held his gaze. "You are rather dashing today, too, sir."

Dressed in a dark gray broadcloth suit with a green cravat—that matched her dress, she noted—knotted around his neck, Westley was so handsome it caused a fluttering feeling in her middle. Was she really to be the wife of such a man? A man who would always gain cloying looks and fluttering lashes from every woman he met and cause unwanted jealousy to sour her heart?

Her pulse quickened. Did he mean to marry her in name only so that he would be free to enjoy the company of women out West without truly breaking any marriage vows? Something hot stirred in her stomach. She really was a *doaty* lass. How very dense of her not to see that sooner. That was the very nature of the arrangement.

Somewhere deep inside she'd actually hoped to marry for love as her mother had. Despite her family's disdain, Mama had married Ella's father because she'd loved him. And her father had loved Mama deeply in return. Her loss had been more than Papa could bear. But she ought to bury such sentiments now, lest they corrupt her thoughts further.

Ella lifted her chin and strode past him. "Let us not keep the guests waiting."

Westley mumbled something behind her, but she kept walking. He didn't want her. He wanted someone to tend his house. That much she knew and had agreed to.

Why, then, did she feel this burning anger where she should not? He had no real obligation to her other than providing her with a home and funds to care for Lee. Of course, Westley would take his comforts in whatever beautiful woman opened her arms to him.

Ella shoved aside her irrational jealousy, more angered at herself for being hurt over it than anything. She caught herself before she stomped all the way down the stairs—and slowed her pace to a more respectable descent.

The man was sacrificing much to marry her. She would do well to remember his kindness and generosity and be sure to treat him with more care. Without him, she would be out on her own again.

Ella forced her breathing to slow as she approached the ladies' parlor where the chaplain and the Martin women waited. As soon as Ella crossed the threshold, Opal rushed over to grab her hands.

"Oh! You look beautiful, Ella. That gown complements you perfectly." She looked at Ella's throat and frowned. "Though you really do need a pin for your collar."

"As I was about to tell her when she fled the room," Westley said, coming to stand by her.

Ella glanced at him, noticing he didn't carry the cane. "I did not *flee*." She inwardly groaned at the petulance in her tone.

The corners of his mouth twitched, and she had the suspicion he tried to suppress a smile. Really, what did he find so amusing each time she got angry?

Westley reached into his pocket. "I was going to offer you this, but you did not give me the chance."

He uncurled his fingers and Ella stepped closer. "It's a brooch."

"It was my mother's," he said softly, his words almost reverent.

Ella leaned closer. Made of gold, the brooch had one large emerald in the center with several smaller ones dangling underneath. The piece probably cost as much as one of Papa's good stallions.

Opal clasped her hands. "Oh! How beautiful!"

Ella stepped back. "I cannot accept that. It's far too priceless."

Westley frowned. "You are my bride, so I'm afraid I must insist."

"But..." *His bride.* If only that were true.

He stared at her, the intensity of his gaze making her insides quiver. "Besides, once we say the vows, will not all of what is mine also be yours as well?"

Ella bit her lip. She could not refute such a claim. "Thank you. It is a beautiful and most thoughtful gift, and I shall wear it proudly."

Westley stepped close and pinned it at her throat, his scent of rain and leather battering her already frayed nerves. Why did this man have to affect her so? Wouldn't this be much easier if she felt nothing for him—the way he felt nothing for her?

He stepped back and smiled, his white teeth stark against his sun-kissed skin. "There. You look wonderful."

Ella tried to return the gesture but found that her lips refused. Westley's jaw tightened, and he turned toward the man in a Federal uniform that Ella had forgotten. He and Mrs. Martin had both ceased their conversation and were watching Ella and Westley.

Westley swept his arm out toward Ella. "Lieutenant Hays, may I introduce my bride, Miss Eleanor Whitaker."

Ella slid her gaze to the stout man with a friendly face and warm eyes.

He bowed politely. "A pleasure to meet you, miss."

Ella inclined her head. "Thank you for agreeing to come out today, sir."

The man smiled, creating dimples in his cheeks. "It is my pleasure. If you are ready, then we shall proceed with the service."

The Martin women took seats, and Ella noticed Sibby and Basil slip just inside the door and press themselves up against the wall. Westley noticed them, too, and smiled even as Mrs. Martin scowled.

Ella felt as though she were outside of herself as she came to stand in front of the chaplain. As a child, this had not been what she'd dreamed of. She glanced up at Westley. Though she must admit, never had she envisioned a better looking groom. Ella shoved the thought aside and focused on the minister as he opened a worn Bible and began to read a portion of one of Paul's epistles to the Corinthians.

As he intoned on about the virtues of love, Ella couldn't

help the bitterness that began to take root. Would they have patience and kindness without love? Would they believe all things and endure all things without the binding moorings love provided? Tears burned in her eyes, and she had to force her lids to stay open so that they would dry up and not betray her by sliding down her face.

"Do you, Major Remington, take this woman to be your wedded wife? Do you promise to honor her, cherish her, and keep her under your protection for all the days of your life?"

Westley pulled something from the interior pocket of his jacket. Questions danced in his eyes. She glanced down at the ring in his hand and watched as he slid it onto her finger. "I do."

The chaplain turned his attention to Ella. "And do you, Miss Eleanor Whitaker, take Major Remington to be your husband, to honor him, respect him, and have none other beside him?"

Ella tightened her hand to keep the ring that was too big from slipping from her finger. Why did Westley's vows not include a mention of faithfulness as hers did? Perhaps because he had no intentions of making such a promise.

For Lee. "I do."

Something that she could not understand flickered in Westley's eyes.

"Then by the power vested in me by the Father, Son, and Holy Spirit, and by the Army of the United States of America, I now pronounce you Major and Mrs. Remington."

Westley grinned, and Ella bit her lip.

"You may kiss your bride now, sir."

Ella's heart lurched. He wouldn't do that, would he? They were to wed in name only.

But even as the thought flittered in her mind, he stepped closer. One heartbeat, and his hand cupped her cheek. Another, and his face hovered over hers. Ella tried to swallow, but her mouth was too dry. She ran her tongue over her lips to moisten them, and saw his gaze follow her movements.

His pupils got larger, and then before she could move, his lips gently brushed hers. Soft, like a delicate whisper, and chaste, as it should be for a sham of a marriage. Ella felt herself relax, and her eyelids flutter closed.

Then he pressed closer, and Ella sensed something she had not known before. Something wild and beautiful. Wanting to grasp what caused this feeling of flight, she pressed her lips back against his and he groaned, slipping his other hand to the small of her back and pulling her up against him.

She fell into him, and for a few seconds she felt safe, warm, and...loved. Remembering herself, she snatched her head back. Westley's eyes flew wide, and he stepped away as well. The chaplain chuckled as they stared at one another.

"It is one of my favorite duties, joining a man and woman so in love into the holy bonds of matrimony."

Ella dropped her gaze, opting for studying the polish on the man's boots rather than risk him reading anything more in her eyes.

Someone started giggling, and Ella looked up in time to see Opal throw her mother a smug look. Mrs. Martin watched Ella and frowned, and Ella looked away again.

"I know the ring is too big," Westley whispered. "I will have to get it adjusted to fit."

Ella nodded, not paying much mind to his words. A moment later she scrawled her name on a document and in less than a quarter hour, the event that forever altered her life was finished. The chaplain offered them his hopes for their joyous life together, declining the refreshments that Basil set out in the dining room, and bemoaning the need to return to town.

The Martin women stayed for a time, and Ella did her best to remember to smile and make polite conversation but found herself often enough distracted. She kept glancing at the man who was now her husband. A more legal lie than her last one, but a lie all the same. He would not be her husband as God intended, and as Ella watched him laugh and share old stories with Mrs. Martin, Ella realized that she would be bound for life to a man that would daily break her heart. She would love and not be loved in return. She would ever wait for him to come home, while he would always ache for his freedoms.

"You didn't hear what I said, did you?"

Ella blinked, and Opal came back into focus. "Oh! I'm sorry. What did you say?"

A sly smile tilted the lady's lips, and she shot a covert glance at Westley. "It seems your thoughts have gone astray, Mrs. Remington."

Ella wrinkled her nose. "Opal! I merely…" Her words died when she could not think of any excuse that would not be an outright lie.

Opal giggled. "See? I told Mama I was right."

Ella shook her head. "No, you are forgetting we did not marry for love. There is nothing romantic to it. Better that you get that silly notion out of your head."

"Hmmm. Out of mine, or out of yours?"

Ella crossed her arms, watching the two at the other end of the table. *Both of ours, I suppose.* Westley had made it abundantly clear that he had no romantic notions about this marriage. "Opal, I have come to believe your mother may be correct. I suspect you have had your nose in far too many romance novels."

Opal flicked her gaze to Westley and then back to Ella. "I dare say that kiss says otherwise. That was no perfunctory display."

Ella ran her tongue over her lips, remembering the stirring he had caused, but pushed the notion away. "He is a man, Opal.

Of course, he's going to enjoy kissing a lady who will let him."

Opal frowned and opened her mouth, but her mother spoke before she could say what was on her mind.

"Come, Opal dear, it is time we take our leave."

Opal rose from her chair and grasped Ella's hand. "I shall come to call on you two days hence, and we shall have a long talk, yes?"

Ella returned the squeeze. "I would like that."

Westley took her arm, and as a counterfeit couple, they walked their guests out. Mrs. Martin gave Ella an unexpected embrace, her eyes showing concern.

"If you need anything, dear, do not hesitate to call on us."

"I thank you."

Westley wished the ladies a good afternoon and they stood on the porch until the last of the dust from the carriage settled. Westley shifted his weight off his injured leg.

Ella turned to him, saying the first thing that came to mind to break the tense silence. "I see you did not use the cane today. May I assume your leg is feeling better?"

"Some." He rubbed the back of his neck. "I find that I can walk on it without assistance, though I fear there will always be a hitch in my gait."

Ella turned to look at him, the vulnerability on his face slicing through her. She reached up and patted his jaw. "Do not let such a small thing worry you. It is but another warrior's scar. A mere reminder of your bravery and strength of survival."

Relief flooded his eyes and he smiled, looking less the soldier and more the generous yet protective man she had come to love.

Aye, she loved him, foolish lass that she was. There was no denying that she did. She stared at him a moment, and then turned her face away before he saw things in her eyes he ought not.

He took her hand and she let him, knowing it would hurt all the more when he let go. And together they stared out over the front yard of Belmont as the wind whispered promises through the trees and the birds sang a melancholy hymn.

Westley held the doorknob until all the coolness of the metal disappeared into the heat of his palm. He should not open the door. He should not. It turned easily under his hand, unlocked. He would not open the door, and open something he might not be able to close again.

The door swung open on silent hinges, revealing the rose room bathed in warm light. Ella looked up from where she sat at her dressing table, running a brush through her hair. She paused, letting the strands fall in cascades of fire down her back. She set the brush down and turned to look at him, neither of them speaking.

He remained frozen in the doorway, unable to look away from the woman that today's vows had made his wife. The little dragon who was now his to have and to hold. Fire lit in his gut, and he tried to tamp it down but found he could not. Ella put her brush on the table and stood, a floral dressing gown that he recognized had once belonged to his mother falling lightly about her legs. She looked small without all those petticoats around her.

She watched him, yet she did not chastise him for being here. He crossed the threshold.

She was beautiful. He'd noticed it the first day he saw her, but it had intensified with every bout of verbal battling and every time her voice took on that lilt when she baited him with a quip.

Westley took another step into the room, further trespassing where he was entitled to be and yet…wasn't. He knew that this time he came to this room as a husband came to a wife's chamber, and that changed things. The other times he had come, it was to comfort.

Ella's eyes flashed, and he saw that she knew it too. She moved a few paces away, staring up at him with wide emerald green eyes. What did she expect of him on this night—the night that was supposed to bind man and woman as one flesh?

Questions danced in her eyes, and he wanted to answer them all. He lifted his hand, and after a slight hesitation she placed her small fingers in his. He urged her a bit closer and picked up a lock of hair that fell down over her shoulder.

"It's soft, just as I imagined it would be," he said, his voice husky.

"You thought about what my hair would feel like?"

He rubbed the tress between his fingers. "That and more."

Her eyes widened and she stared at him. "What have you come for?"

A simple question that did not possess an equally simple answer. "I came to see you. I will ride out tomorrow."

He dropped her hair and took a step closer, the distance between them but a handbreadth. She turned her face up to him, and he remembered the feel of her in his arms earlier today. He had kissed ladies before, and while he had always found a thrill in it, none of them had ever stirred him the way she had. No woman had made him want to give up anything for her. And that terrified him, yet sent a thrill that coursed through his blood like lightning and made him ache to feel the softness of her skin beneath his fingers.

If only for this night, could he forget what he'd said about them being wed in name only and make of her his wife in truth? Ella blinked up at him, desire and fear conflicting in her eyes.

He ran a finger over her lips. "Do you want me, Ella, as I

want you?"

She swallowed hard, her green eyes alight. "I know not of what you speak."

He chuckled. "Do you not? Surely you are aware of the ways of men and women."

A dark cloud doused the fire in her eyes, and she stepped back. "Aye, I've seen the ways of men."

The muscles in his jaw tightened, and the bite in her tone clipped his desire. He frowned. "Did someone hurt you?"

She shook her head and stepped away, wrapping her arms around her middle.

"Ella...?"

She lifted her shoulders. "Three men tried once, but they didn't make it...all the way."

Every muscle in his body tensed and he growled. "What do you mean?"

"It's nothing. I was fine. Bushwhackers." She barked a humorless laugh that made Westley's teeth grind. "Lucky for me that cowboy came down the alley shooting at them and they scattered."

Westley stepped closer and gripped her shoulders. "Did he kill them?"

She shook her head, soft tendrils of hair sweeping against her cheeks. "No, but he scared them away for me."

Some miscreants had attacked her and had tried to take from her what she would never give them. If he had been there, he would have likely gunned them down and watched them bleed. He never allowed his soldiers to abuse women, enemy or no, and most bushwhackers were the devil's own spawn.

"Westley!" Ella gasped. "You're hurting my arms."

He blinked and dropped his hands, unaware that he had started to squeeze her. "I'm sorry. I did not mean to hurt you. My anger seems to have gotten the better of me."

Her eyes softened, and he ran a hand through his hair. "The very thought of someone hurting you—"

She laid a hand on his shirtsleeve. "Thank you. It's been ages since I have known such protection."

He reached up and cupped her face. "Know that I would never take anything from you that you were not willing to give."

"Of course," she said, even as relief flooded her eyes. Did she think that he would ever do such a thing?

He stepped back. He had come to her room when she wore nothing but a dressing gown, his mind filled with things that were not at all in alignment with the agreement that their vows were spoken in name only.

She took a step toward him, and then another. Her eyes burned with questions, but she slipped her hands up his shoulders and back behind his neck. "Westley."

His name came out more breath than word, and his lips came to hers. She yielded to him, and passion erupted within him. His hands explored the back of her head and tangled in the glory of her hair.

Her fingers slid up the nape of his neck and grabbed at his short tresses, further stoking the passion straining for release. He wrapped his arms around her and lifted her from the floor. She sucked in a breath but did not remove her lips from his even as he turned her and laid her on the bed.

He kissed her cheeks, then let his lips leave trails down her jaw and onto her neck, and when she shivered, he lay next to her. He wanted to know her in every way a man could know a woman. Not just in her body, though he desperately wanted that now, but in her heart and mind. He wanted to explore every part of her, teaching her to trust him.

"Westley...?"

He tested the softness of the place where her neck met her shoulder. "Yes?"

"Do you love me?" Her voice trembled. "As…as I do you?"

He paused, the words slamming into him. "You are my wife."

She chewed her lower lip, and he could feel what had just been soft and yielded to him start to harden. "Aye, but you did not answer my question."

"I feel a great stirring for you, Ella. You have…captivated me."

She released the breath held captive in her lungs, and he lowered his head to find that tender place once more, but her fingers slipped into his hair and gently eased him back.

"I do not want to ask you to stop." She drew a long breath and eased away from him. "But I am afraid I must."

Westley slowly rubbed her shoulder. "Do not say that you don't want me as I do you. I will know it to be a lie."

The lamplight danced across her skin, flickering against it and tempting him to see more of her.

She ran her hand down his jaw. "That I will not do. But I cannot perform an act of love without love." She shook her head. "Vows or not."

"Ella, I…"

She placed her fingers on his lips. "Don't. Please don't speak any words to me that do not so fill your heart and mind that they have no choice but to spring from your lips. If you hold any affection for me, do not say words that we will both regret come dawn."

Westley swung off the bed and heard her gasp. What a callous cad! He clenched his fists. He had nearly let his desire run away with him under the excuse that this woman was legally his wife. But he had asked her to wed in name only. Now he had come to try to take something intimate from her without the decency of providing her the real relationship that must come first.

"I'm sorry. I shouldn't have come."

Even in the dim light, he could see the pain that filled her eyes. Pain he had caused by his own selfish desires. He turned his head away. "You were right. I am naught but a devil. I must beg your forgiveness for attempting to violate the agreement we set forth."

"Westley, I…"

He looked over his shoulder. "Better that neither of us say words we would regret in the morning."

She snapped her jaw closed, and as moisture glazed her eyes, he turned away. He could not stand to see the pain replace the warmth in her eyes, knowing he was the cause. "Goodnight, Ella."

She didn't respond, and he moved toward his own room. He paused and turned to look at her. "You have stirred something within me, little dragon. With you near, I am a better man. A man quick to humor and teasing such as I have not been since I was a boy." He flexed his fingers, tension so tight in his body he felt like a spring coiled too tightly. "I long to know everything about you."

She rose and came closer, searching out his face in the lamplight. "As I wish to know you. Is that not what draws two people together?"

He chuckled. "I am most surely drawn to you. The very thought of being separated from you on the morrow has so driven me to madness that I flung aside all of my better judgment just to seek the warmth of you."

Ella came closer and slid her hand over his arm. "So then you do feel for me as I do you, and this bond between us can be more." She turned her eyes up at him, further tempting him to take what she offered. It was what he so desired yet knew he should not gain without first securing her trust.

She'd wanted to know if he loved her, but he didn't know if he truly understood what that meant. He put his hand on her shoulder. "I do not know if I can say the words you wish from me. I want to protect you, provide for you, and do everything in my power to see that you live a happy life."

Her emerald eyes swam with emotions that threatened to unmoor them both. He must hold fast. "My beautiful, precious Ella. Know that I long for you, and that I will do everything in my power to care for you."

She bit her lip and turned her eyes away. "But you do not love me."

Did he? The chaplain had said that love was patient, kind, longsuffering, not puffed up, or envious. And Westley was none of the good things and all of the bad. He was prideful, arrogant, and rather impatient.

How then could he love as she wanted him to love when he could provide her with none of those things?

Pain flooded her eyes, pain he had caused. A good thing he returned to duty on the morrow. The less he was here to hurt her, the better. "I require but a bit of time."

She straightened her shoulders, and a determined look came into her eyes. "It is enough, husband. Come, make of me your wife in truth."

Westley clenched his hands, wanting nothing more in that moment than to give in. "You said you wished only to do so with a man who loves you."

"You are my husband."

Westley took a lock of her hair and twisted it in his fingers. "And as your husband, I wish to gain your trust by honoring your wish." He leaned down and kissed the top of her head. "Goodnight, Ella."

She drew a deep breath and leaned into him. "Goodnight."

He turned from her and closed the door before he risked

sweeping her into his arms and making himself a liar. Back in the coldness of the master's chamber, he lay down on his bed and stared at the ceiling. He could give her a home and a safe life for the child. He would hold her in the greatest regard and treat her with gentleness.

But as something clawed deep within him seeking to break free, he wondered, would that be enough?

Chapter Thirty-One

Ella turned over on her back and watched the dawn chase away her sleepless night. Today would be trying, and she had spent several hours attempting to pray away the hurt that stuck to her soul like tar. He didn't love her.

He'd said some beautiful things. But the more she'd contemplated the conversation, the more she was sure he was trying to be gentle and kind. He'd only felt desire for her. While she could not deny she'd felt the same, she wanted something more. She wanted him to love away the empty places inside her and to return this feeling that seared her heart.

Is it too much to ask for the man I am bound to for life to love me?

Ella closed her eyes and drew a deep breath. On the other side of the door, she could hear Lee waking and Sibby singing softly to him. He would nurse, then sleep again for a few hours. And while he slept, the man for whom he'd been named would leave them.

She swung her feet off the bed. She had survived this far on her own. She would do so now. Ella pulled on her simple tan day dress and tamed her long hair into a tight braid before twisting it into a sensible bun and securing it to the back of her head.

She didn't want to remember the way his fingers had felt against her scalp, but the memory pushed through. She washed her face in the basin. Her eyes were red, but there was nothing she could do about it. She straightened her collar and then turned to the dresser. She'd found something there she knew that Westley would need on his journey.

She could hear him rise in the next room and listened to his footsteps move around for a few moments before fortifying herself for what lay ahead. She slipped out of her room and down the stairs, where she would wait for him in the foyer. She would not allow him to slip away unnoticed.

She didn't have to wait long.

Westley clomped down the stairs in his Yankee uniform without the aid of his cane. She watched him as he descended, from his polished boots to the shoulder boards on his shell jacket, until his eyes locked onto hers.

His expression was hard. Stone erased the gentle curve of his lips, and steel glinted in his eyes, replacing all the things she had glimpsed in their depths last night. He paused on the steps.

"Miss…" He cleared his throat. "Forgive me, Mrs. Remington."

Her heart lurched. "Westley."

He came down the last remaining steps and hefted a haversack over his shoulder. "I have borrowed a horse from the Martins to take to the depot. Someone will return it to them. If for any reason something happens to the horse, please make sure that a replacement is found for them."

"I will."

He shifted his weight. "And do not let Sibby take advantage of you. She has a good heart, but you must take care not to let her attempt to browbeat you."

"I shall do my best."

"On the dressing table in my room I left you a list of names and account information. Should you need funds, contact those men and give them the information." He reached up and squeezed her shoulder. "If anything happens and you need me, send for Colonel Larson. He has promised that any letter you write will be posted to me, and that if you are ever in dire need, a telegraph will be delivered to my outpost."

Ella pulled her lower lip through her teeth. "Will you write to me?"

His eyes softened. "Would you like me to?"

"Aye, Westley, you know I would." Even if he would never feel for her as she did him, she would need to know how he fared. "I want to know that you are safe."

He dropped his hand. "It is time I go."

Ella lifted the small object she'd brought down with her. "I found this in your mother's dresser. I think you should take it with you."

He took the little book from her and ran his fingers over the cover. "My mother used to read this to me when I was a child, telling me all the rules God had for us."

Ella tilted her head. "It's more than just rules, Westley."

He turned his lips up in that way she knew meant he was amused with her words. She clutched his arm and stepped closer, peering up into his face. "You know that, right? He is the way of salvation and healing."

Westley's eyes grew wary. "I am glad you believe as strongly as my mother did. But I—"

"*You* were the one whose prayers were answered. You saw the miracle that happened, yet you still doubt?"

His eyes became troubled. "I do not doubt. I know that he is real, and that sometimes he answers when he wants to." He cupped her cheek. "And I am so glad he decided to see your pain and, for once, do something about it."

She turned her face into his hand. "Promise me you will read it."

He stepped back. "Why?"

"Because I want you to see him as I do. He is warmth and light and goodness. Only he can take what is dark in us and begin to wash it away."

Westley's jaw twitched.

"Please? For me?"

He inhaled slowly. "For you. Though I make no other promise."

She slipped her arms around his waist and laid her head on his chest. She knew she shouldn't do such things, but she needed to hold him this once before he took his leave. His arms tightened around her, and he kissed the top of her head.

Then he stiffened and pulled away. "I must go."

"Please, be safe."

He pushed his kepi on his head and opened the door. "I will endeavor to do my best. Try not to get yourself into any trouble."

Ella wrinkled her nose. "What trouble could I possibly get into?"

He chuckled, though there was little humor in it. "I will send word when I reach Kansas."

She followed him out onto the porch, the cheery sunshine and twittering birds in stark contrast to the shadows in her heart. He swung up in the saddle, then turned the horse and galloped down the drive.

And in a matter of moments, he disappeared from her life just as quickly as he had first dropped into it.

St. Joseph, Missouri

Westley ran his sleeve over his forehead, his blue uniform already damp with sweat, and the day had not even reached noon. He smiled to himself as he tapped his kepi against his leg to free it from some of the dust before placing it back on his head. Good thing Ella couldn't smell him now. After miles of rail and horse travel and nearly a week without a chance to bathe, his uniform had taken on a rather unpleasant smell. She would surely wrinkle her nose in that adorable way she had and...

He clenched his jaw. Here he was thinking about her again. He shouldered his haversack and stepped into the booming town at the westernmost point of the rail line. He would stay here for a few days until he met up with the company heading out to Fort Aubrey, Kansas.

Westley maneuvered his way into the busy flow of people, horses, and wagons clamoring in the streets. The army was sending him to an outpost to protect western travelers from Indian attack. From what he had been told, he could look forward to a small wooden fortification and a collection of tents positioned around protecting a bit of water and marking the line for the Santa Fe Trail.

And that's what he had given up Ella for? A post in the wilderness to fend Indians off of wagon trains? He was a fool. One thing that his time alone had done for him was give him time to think. And read. And, oddly enough, pray.

It was the thinking part he had tried his best to avoid. Thinking had only caused a chafing that he could not get rid of, no matter how he tried to distract his thoughts. Ever they returned to Ella. This feeling he had, this inability to put her from his mind, both scared and thrilled him.

He stepped around a wagon loaded with supplies and up onto a wooden walkway. This inability to control one's own thoughts must be what caused men to take leave of their senses and act a fool for a woman. This deep devotion he felt for her could not be erased by her absence. If anything, the last days had taught him that separation from her only made it worse.

And that being the case, he had only one choice. He'd promised himself he would decide once he arrived at this port to the western world, but truth be told he'd decided days ago. He would send a telegram back to Colonel Larson in Greenville and ask that the man send Ella a message.

Dust drifted in the air and settled on him, the sounds of braying mules, shouting men, and rumbling wagons creating a clamor of noise and a disjointed atmosphere of hope, fervor, and competition. He had to duck beneath two men carrying some kind of beam and leap back out of the way before an elderly man with a handcart ran him over.

Westley rolled his eyes and straightened his jacket. When this assignment ended, he would muster out and return to Belmont, where he would seek to be her husband in truth. It would take time to win her, but it was a battle he was willing to fight. He would not only have to earn her trust, but her forgiveness as well for the heartless way he had left her. But perhaps, during his western duty, if he penned his thoughts and sent them to her, then in time she might come to forgive him, and when he returned, they could start over.

Westley weaved between countless people gearing up for a harrowing western-bound wagon train and wondered how many of these hopeful faces would survive the journey. The war had only increased the western movement as desperate Southerners tried to start their lives anew in a wild and untamed wilderness. He'd heard enough tales as he made his way to St. Joseph to know that many would find their deaths long before they reached their new homelands, and then those who made it would face relentless hardships.

Westley checked in with his contact officer and was told to report back in four days to join up with a company K heading to Kansas. He hadn't listened to many of the specifics. None of it really mattered. He would serve his six months, and then he would return to Ella.

After securing a room at one of the many bustling inns that

seemed more like saloons, Westley searched out a telegraph office, finding one just two streets over. He stepped inside and waited his turn in line, and after a few moments, the man at the window waved him up.

"What city, sir?"

Westley pushed a few coins across the counter. "Greenville, Mississippi. Addressed to Colonel Larson from Major Remington."

The man dipped his pen in a well of ink and scribbled on a notepad. "Very good. Message?"

"Please send word to my wife. Upon completion of current assignment, I will muster out and return home."

The man bobbed his head and snatched up the piece of paper. "Will you return for a response, sir?"

Would she send word back? Likely not. And he doubted Colonel Larson would waste his time in sending a response down the wire. "No."

The man lifted his brows but didn't reply. Westley turned for the door, but then stopped. "I am leaving four days hence, but if by chance word does return, I am staying at the inn two streets over."

"The Blue Moon?"

"That's the one."

"I'll send my boy if word comes back."

Westley thanked the man and stepped back out into the sunshine, feeling as though he had taken the first step in claiming his wife. And for that, the world outside seemed all the brighter.

He visited a bathing house and then a barber before returning to the inn for the evening meal. He found a table in the back where he could eat alone and pulled out the little book he had promised Ella he would read. So far, he had made it through the gospels and had continued reading on to first John.

As he read over the fourth chapter in the dim light, a verse seemed to grab hold of him and wrench his heart from his chest. Westley ran his finger over it. *Beloved, let us love one another: for love is of God; and every one that loveth is born of God, and knoweth God. He that loveth not knoweth not God; for God is love.*

That was the answer. He did not know how to love Ella as she should be loved, with patience, kindness, and longsuffering, because he had not submitted to the one who *was* love.

Westley leaned back and tapped his fingers, staring at the open book. The reading had begun as an obligation, but to his surprise he continued out of fascination. He had heard the stories, but he'd never noticed something about the Savior. Always the church portrayed him as kindly and meek, but he wasn't weak. Jesus defied leaders, drove out greedy men in the temple, and volunteered for an excruciating death so that he could complete his purpose.

This was someone that a man could look up to. One whom he could learn from. And the more Westley read of him, the more he wanted to be like him.

Lord, forgive me. I called on you as a boy, but I never really knew you. Teach me to live my life according to your ways. Show me your love that I might show that love to others. Especially my Ella.

"Here's your dinner, mister," a wispy girl said, interrupting his prayer.

He laid down the Bible and smiled at her as she plopped the plate of pork down in front of him. "Thank you, miss."

She smiled and moved away to the next table, and Westley put the book back into his breast pocket. He would have to tell Ella what he had been reading, and the discoveries he had made. Perhaps he would pen her a letter tomorrow and send it out before he left St. Joseph.

He cut into his slab of pork, spearing a cube of the white meat and chewing it slowly. No telling what kind of pitiful supplies he would get out on the Santa Fe Trail. Best he eat well while he still had the chance.

A boy sidled up to his table and leaned close. "You the Yankee soldier that sent a telegram to Mississippi?"

Westley frowned. "I am."

The boy reached in his pocket and pulled out a slip of paper. "My Da said I should bring this to you."

Westley accepted the paper. How had a response from Ella come back so soon? He glanced up and saw the boy still lingering and remembered what the little fellow waited for. He fished a nickel out of his pocket and tossed it to the boy. "Thank you, young master."

The boy grinned and shoved the coin in his trouser pocket. "You need anything else, mister, you let me know."

Westley chuckled as the youngster ducked into the gathering dinner crowd and slipped out the door. Westley leaned back and opened the folded paper.

Colonel Larson for Major Remington. Westley's eyes widened as he read the lines, and then he crumpled the paper in his hand and threw it down on the table.

Chapter Thirty-Two

Ella dressed Lee in a cotton gown and placed him in a light shawl she then tied around behind her back. Today would be a good day for a walk to check her garden, and then after that, perhaps she would try again with the goat's milk.

She closed the door to her bedroom and made her way down the stairs. It was still cool enough this morning to take Lee out to see the late garden she had attempted to plant—with a lot of help from Basil—before the day grew too warm for Lee to be out in the sun. Then they would go to Riverbend this afternoon for tea and a visit with the Martin ladies. Such had become her life since she'd wed. She still helped with some of the cooking, but Sibby wouldn't have her doing much of anything else anymore. Her days were spent gardening, tending Lee, visiting with the neighbors…and aching over Westley.

She pushed the longing aside and donned a practical straw bonnet, tying the bow under her chin and wondering how he fared at Fort Aubrey. He should be settled in Kansas by now, protecting brave travelers from losing their lives to Indian threats.

Keep him safe, Father. And, please, help me not to love him.

Such was her prayer throughout each day, one she whispered each time he took hold in her thoughts. And the man never strayed far from those thoughts.

She shook her head as though that could dislodge the pain he had caused. He didn't love her, and she would have to accept that and ignore this dark feeling that hung over her shoulders like a death shroud.

Lee cooed, and she looked down at him. "Ah, wee one, but you are worth it."

He smiled up at her and then sucked on his fist. A shame she couldn't get the goat's milk into that fist, else she might have a chance at getting him to take it. "You are a stubborn lad, you know it?"

Ella opened the front door and stepped outside, only to come stumbling to a halt. At least a dozen men dressed in Federal uniforms dismounted and tied their horses in her front lawn. How had she not heard them approach? Ella clutched Lee against her chest, her heart beginning to hammer.

She remained frozen as she watched them speak to one another, and then a man separated himself from the group and stalked toward her, his gait determined and his face stoic.

The gleam of the sun caused dappled shadows to fall across his stern face as he passed under the magnolia, and his polished boots clicked smartly down the cobbled front walk as they drew nearer upon her. The breeze pulled bits of her hair and sent them scurrying across her nose, but she could not seem to think to brush them away. All she could do was stare at the man as he climbed the front steps and bowed to her.

"Are you Mrs. Remington?"

She glanced behind him at the men who were spreading out over the yard and dispersing around the house. "I am."

"I am Colonel Larson. I am afraid that I am going to have to ask you to come with me, madam."

Ella stepped back. "My husband has paid all the taxes on the lands. He said that the government was satisfied with the state of affairs at Belmont before he left to return to duty."

The officer watched her closely. "This has nothing to do with the taxes, madam."

Another soldier came up on the porch, and the officer

pointed toward the house. He stepped around Ella and threw the front door open.

She drew a sharp intake of air. "What are you doing?" Ella reached to grab the man's arm, but he shrugged her off and stalked into the house, leaving the door open. Ella pointed her finger at the colonel. "You cannot enter my house without an invitation."

He merely lifted his eyebrows and said nothing. She continued to glare at him, even though he did not seem to be affected by the poisonous look in the least.

Finally, he relented. "Mrs. Remington, we have come to arrest a Negro woman reportedly staying within the main house, and I have the proper documents with which to do so regardless of whether you grant permission or not."

"You mean Sibby?" Ella frowned. "Whatever for? She is a freedwoman. I have not been keeping any slaves."

He narrowed his eyes. "We will speak further on it when you come in with me."

"I have an infant. I cannot do that."

The man glanced down, as though noticing the child for the first time, and shifted uncomfortably. "Are you aware of a group of Negroes living on your lands?"

Ella cocked her head. "Are you from the Freedman's Bureau?"

"I am not."

Ella frowned. "I am aware that there is a settlement of some kind. I believe the former slaves gathered there to homestead, but I have never set foot inside of it. My husband mentioned starting to work the lands again but—"

"But you have seen it?" he interrupted.

Ella's pulse quickened. "From a distance. They said I shouldn't go back there."

The man leaned closer. "And tell me, Mrs. Remington, you

didn't find that at all suspicious?"

"I...well, I suppose I did a little, but—"

"I need you to come with me." He began tugging on her arm.

"Why?" Ella stumbled down the steps after him. "I haven't done anything wrong."

"That is yet to be determined."

A scream sliced through the air, and Ella ripped her arm away from the officer. She turned around just as the soldier that had entered the house without permission stalked out, dragging poor Basil by the hair.

Basil flailed her feet, and the man had to hold her at arm's length to keep her from kicking him. He wrenched hard on her head, making her stumble and fall to her knees.

Furious, Ella snatched up her skirts and stomped toward the devilish Yank. "I demand that you unhand her this instant!"

The man glanced behind her at his commanding officer but held Basil in place. Basil saw Ella, and her wails turned to sobs.

Ella whirled around and screamed at the colonel. "Release her at once! She's just a girl!"

The officer had the decency to appear slightly apologetic, but still shook his head. "I'm afraid I can't do that, Mrs. Remington. She is to be taken in."

"By the hair of her head?"

He shrugged. "It seems she may have put up a fuss about it."

Ella opened her mouth, but no words could make it past the constriction in her throat. Insufferable Yank! Did he not see that the poor child was scared out of her wits?

Movement caught her eye, and Ella shifted to see another soldier come from the side of the house and step up to Colonel Larson. He leaned close and whispered something into his commanding officer's ear. The man grunted and then turned his attention back to Ella.

"I must insist you come with me, please."

Ella set her feet and squared her shoulders. "I'll not do a single thing until you release that child."

The colonel's nostrils flared, but he waved his hand at the soldier on the porch. The other man released Basil's hair and snatched her by the arm. Ella watched in horror as he hauled her to her feet and dragged her down the steps.

"Miss Ella! I's so sorry, Miss Ella," Basil cried as he hauled her toward the horses.

Ella scrambled to step in front of them in an effort to stop the soldier from hauling Basil away. "Please, tell me, why are you taking this child?" The man stared down at her, clearly uncomfortable.

"Orders, ma'am."

Tears drained down Basil's face. "I's sorry, Miss Ella. I's so sorry."

Ella's voice began to strain. "I demand to know what is happening!"

"Orders, ma'am," he repeated.

The soldier tugged on Basil again and attempted to step around Ella.

"I's sorry," Basil wailed. "I's so sorry we done got you into trouble, Miss Ella."

Ella's chest tightened. "What did you do, Basil?"

The soldier grunted and pushed Basil out in front of him, making Ella step out of the way.

"What did you do?" Ella called as the soldier pulled Basil away, but she didn't attempt to answer.

Basil sobbed as the man lifted her onto a horse and bound her hands to the pommel. Ella spun around to find Larson again. His back was to her, his head bent low as he conversed with another soldier.

Suddenly, he lifted his head and stalked back toward the porch. Ella lifted her gaze to see Sibby step out the front door, her headscarf askew and her eyes wild. She took a small step forward, still favoring her ankle a bit.

Heat bubbled in Ella's gut and she clenched her teeth. This was Sibby's doing. Whatever she had been keeping secret had landed them in some kind of predicament. She tightened her arm on Lee and jogged back to the porch.

"Sibby! Why are these men here?"

Sibby seamed her lips and looked at her feet.

"Sibby!"

Larson came to stand beside her, clasping his hands behind his back. The other soldier took Sibby's arm and gently helped her down the stairs, leading her toward where they held Basil.

"Sibby! You tell me what you did this instant!"

The other woman looked at her with remorse in her eyes, but only lowered her head as the soldier led her away.

"What will you do with her?" Ella asked the colonel.

The officer frowned. "They will all be questioned."

Ella's mouth went dry. *All?*

"And then justice will be rendered thereafter."

Ella toyed with the brooch at her throat, her mind scrambling for footing on a slippery slope of rapidly worsening events. "Sir, that woman is a wet nurse for my son. I cannot be separated from her or else my child will starve."

The muscles in his jaw hardened, and he looked at her through narrowed eyes.

Her heartbeat quickened. "Please, sir. I don't know what she could have possibly gotten tangled in, but regardless of what she has done, my son will not take the goat's milk."

He blinked at her. "Pardon? Goat's milk?"

"I have tried to get him to take goat's milk so that I may have another means of feeding him, but he refuses. That woman, Sibby, whom you are taking, she is my only way of feeding my son. Please, I beg of you to leave her with me."

The officer took her elbow. "I'm afraid that is not possible. You're just going to have to come with me."

"You cannot expect me to mount a horse with my infant son." Ella scoffed. "It isn't possible."

"We won't be going far."

Regardless of her protests, Ella was hoisted up on a tall roan horse, and the colonel swung into the saddle behind her.

"I hope this animal is well tempered, sir, because if it should spook and any injury befalls my son, I promise you that you will meet with personal harm."

The man had the audacity to chuckle. "I assure you, Mrs. Remington, this animal will obey my commands. As long as you do not make a fool of yourself, there will be no need for you to worry."

Ella huffed and smoothed the shawl around Lee, uncomfortably aware of how close the officer sat behind her. She stiffened her back to keep as much distance as possible between them.

The group of soldiers and their female captives heeded Larson's command, and they followed the drive from Belmont out onto the river road. Would he parade them through town like some kind of criminals?

They'd not gone far on the road when Larson suddenly turned the horse's head to the left and they stepped out into one of the fields. Ella twisted and spoke over her shoulder.

"What are you doing?"

"I am taking you to the Negro camp."

Ella wrinkled her nose. "Whatever for?"

"To see what you know."

Ella turned back forward, speaking loud enough for not only him but the men riding just behind them to hear her as well. "I know nothing of that place. They were determined that I never go there, and I left them to their privacy."

The officer declined to reply to her statement, and they clopped through the abandoned fields, skirting around the scraggly line of trees and avoiding the need to jump the creek by keeping near the river road.

After a time, the settlement came into view. Ella bit her lip. What could a group of recently freed slaves have possibly done to garner the attention of the army?

Everything looked quiet. No one milled about in the gardens, and the place seemed deserted. The people must have heard them coming and fled. She wouldn't be surprised in the least if the soldiers didn't find a soul.

A loud pop cracked in the air and Ella jumped, startling Lee. He began to cry, and the man behind her cursed. He slipped one arm around her waist and dug his heels into the horse. The animal dropped its rear and lurched forward.

Ella screamed.

The man leaned forward in the saddle, pushing her up against the pommel and forcing her to try to lift Lee to keep him from being squished. The soldier ignored her cries, driving the animal forward at a rapidly increasing pace. The thundering sound behind her alerted Ella that the other soldiers kept up.

The horse galloped into the settlement. Larson pulled on the reins and brought the animal to a shuddering stop in the middle of the street between the two rows of neat cabins.

Ella's chest heaved, and she twisted around in the saddle. She lifted her arm and swatted at the man, attempting to slap him but not being able to get the proper angle to do so.

Larson grabbed her wrist and growled. "I wouldn't do that if I were you."

"Do you know—"

Shouts came from the house to her left, and he swung out

of the saddle. His feet barely hit the ground before he started running toward the house. Ella bounced Lee to settle him and gathered the horse's reins, hoping that the animal wouldn't spook. She didn't think she could dismount by herself.

There was another pop of gunfire and Ella strangled a scream. The door to the house flew open and a man stumbled outside clutching his chest.

Behind her, someone shrieked. Ella twisted and saw Sibby's eyes grow wide. She watched as her mouth opened and agony poured out.

"Nat!" Sibby screamed. "No!" She threw her leg over the horse and dropped to the ground, hitting hard on her back because her bound hands could not stop her fall. She rolled to her side as the soldiers shouted and jumped from their horses.

Blood seeped through Nat's fingers and spread across his shirt, turning the white to a hideous shade of crimson. The air stilled as the blood pulsed in Ella's ears, and then chaos erupted around her. Men yelled, and Sibby screamed as she tried to reach Nat.

"Get them back!" Larson bellowed, waving his hands.

Ella pulled on the reins. She couldn't stay here and risk Lee. Clutching her child tightly against her, Ella kicked the horse's sides. He tossed his head and snorted, then danced to the side.

"Come on, you daft creature!" Ella screeched.

She slapped the reins down hard on the animal's neck and it pinned its ears to its head.

Then it lurched and Ella had to hold tight to the reins as it bolted down the road and into the field beyond, leaving men hollering behind her.

For all of her effort, however, Ella made it only a few hundred feet before a soldier galloped to her and expertly snatched the reins from her hand, bringing the heaving horse to a halt and nearly unseating her.

Breathing hard, Ella stared at the soldier, a young man who seemed to be several years younger than she. He frowned at her, and Ella batted her eyes.

"Oh, thank goodness. This dreadful creature is going to be the death of me!"

"But…" The man clamped his jaw and turned the animal back to the settlement.

Ella held her chin high as he paraded her back between the cottages, then thankfully helped her to the ground. Sibby had made it to the porch where she leaned over Nat. He wasn't moving.

Larson snatched her arm. "What do you think you were doing?"

She glared at him. "Protecting my son."

He snarled, but before he could berate her, a soldier jogged up. "We have them, sir. Captured eight men and a handful of women and children. Found three wagons loaded up, too."

Larson turned back to Ella, narrowing his eyes. "Do you know anything about this?"

She flung her hand at their surroundings. "You can obviously see that I do not." She glanced back at Sibby, who sobbed over Nat's body. "Please, tell me what is happening."

"It has come to our attention," Larson said, "that there is a group of smugglers in Memphis that both trade and steal supplies and bring them back south."

Ella put her hands on her hips. "Smugglers in Memphis? What has that got to do with us?"

"It would seem these people use Negros to steal and deliver their supplies. We assume they can move around without notice because of all the coloreds heading north."

Ella blinked at him.

"These men have been smuggling items south, where they are selling foodstuffs, livestock, and medicines they stole from the hospitals in Memphis."

Ella placed her fingers over her mouth. The wagons. The supplies Sibby always seemed to have.

He narrowed his eyes. "Is there something you wish to tell me, Mrs. Remington?"

Ella turned her gaze on Sibby as they pulled her away from Nat. Sibby looked up and her gaze locked with Ella's.

Then her eyes filled with fear.

Chapter Thirty-Three

Ella shifted her weight against the hard stone wall and tried not to move Lee too much. Her back ached, and her arm grew heavy from hours of holding the baby up. The small room smelled damp and something like ash, and Ella shivered against the cold.

Sibby groaned on the other side of the cell. "You needs to go home."

"I can't, and you know it," she bit back, no longer concerned with making her tone more civil. The woman could use a bit of grace, especially since she had lost someone dear to her today, but Ella just couldn't seem to muster the strength to offer it.

The cold stone seeped through her petticoat and skirt, making her feel damp. "He will need to eat again soon."

Sibby sighed in the dark, the sound drifting on the dismal air and settling on Ella like an anchor. "I is sorry, Miss Ella. Ain't never meant for you to end up with me in here."

Ella grunted. "And yet you wondered why I wanted that goat."

"Lot a good it did, seein' as how he won't drink none of that goat milk."

Ella turned her face against the stone wall. "Try to sleep, Sibby."

Silence crept over them, a shadow in its own right. Ella closed her eyes against the darkness, the inky canvas behind her eyes favorable to the thick black maw around her. She should try to take her own advice and get some rest, but it seemed impossible.

A tear broke from the confines of her lids and slid down her cheek.

Westley, how I wish you were here with me so that I might not feel so alone.

Ella choked back a sob. This day had brought her to the end of her frayed nerves and then demanded more. She had been questioned relentlessly, her home raided and searched, the people of the settlement rounded up like cattle, Nat killed, and Sibby imprisoned. Now she was forced to seek rest in a makeshift jail cell because they would not release Sibby, and Ella could not return home without her.

Ella sniffled in the dark, something blacker than the night settling on her heart. Too much. It had all been too much.

I need you.

She breathed in and out slowly until she finally began to drift into a shallow sleep. Then the darkness shifted and began to peel away. The air around her sweetened and suddenly colors burst to life around her. She'd come back! Ella clutched the fabric of her radiant white gown and ran through the field of vibrant grass toward the majestic tree at the center of the field.

It was a great distance, but when she arrived, she was no less winded than when she began. Ella circled the tree, searching. She lifted her hand against the nearly blinding light and surveyed the field around her, but she remained alone.

"Where are you?"

The wind shifted, lifting her hair and teasing it, but no reply answered her call. Ella sat and leaned against the tree, bowing her head. "Even when I cannot see you or when I cannot feel you, I know that you are always with me, because you promised you would never leave me."

"And I never have."

Ella's eyes flew open and she turned to look at him, her beautiful Savior dressed in light. Peace washed over her, and she smiled. "There you are."

"Do you love me, Ella?"

The question surprised her. "You know I do." She leaned her head against his shoulder, grateful for the comfort he brought.

He took her hand and gave it a gentle squeeze. "Tell me what troubles you."

Tears welled in her eyes and she tried to blink them away. "You already know."

He stroked her hair. "Of course, I do. But it is good for you to tell me anyway."

"I...I love him." She meant to say that she was tired, or that she worried about Lee or the people who had been taken. She meant to say that she feared for Sibby and the others and that she wanted Westley to be safe. Instead, the words she didn't want to say were the first from her mouth.

"And you believe he doesn't feel for you what you do for him."

Ella nodded and drew her knees up against her.

"You want from him what he cannot give."

Ella sniffled and clutched the fabric at her chest. Of course, that was true. Westley could not love her. She was too far beneath him. Not pretty enough or refined enough for him truly to love her. Want her, maybe, but nothing more.

"That is not what I said. You are letting the shadows make you forget again."

Ella wiped her eyes and looked at him. "Forget?"

"Who are you?"

She let her fingers uncurl. She was not worthless. No matter what she was in the eyes of anyone else, even the man she loved, in His eyes, she was priceless. She was beautiful, special, and deeply loved. She straightened and wiped the tears from her eyes. "Help me to remember. I forget it easily."

"You will have to depend on me daily. I know that is hard for you, because you think strength is in independence. But my strength is perfected in your weakness. By depending on me, you have strength that far exceeds what you have on your own."

Ella leaned back against him, a small laugh bubbling from her chest. "I'll need you to help me with that, too."

He squeezed her hand. "You want Westley to fill all of the empty places inside of you. You want him to provide for your needs, to be attentive to your every mood, and to understand you at your very core, anticipating your every hurt and desire."

Ella opened her mouth to refute the claim as ridiculous but realized that it was true. "But—" She chewed her lip. "Is that not what love is?"

"I am love."

Ella frowned. "I don't know what you mean."

"You want him to give you the things that only I can. Remember he is only human, as you are. He has weaknesses and flaws, just as you do. You seek to put him in a place that he doesn't belong. I alone can completely fill those needs for you. It is my will that man and woman should become one while on earth, but that relationship is never meant to replace the one you first have with me."

Ella turned her face into him and sobbed. "I'm sorry. It's just so hard when he is the one I can see and touch every day."

"Love me first, Ella."

She clung to him. "I'm sorry."

He stroked her hair. "I love you, and I am with you always."

"Help me to love you first—and from that love have the ability to love others as you love me."

He put his fingers under her chin and lifted her face, wiping the tears from her cheeks. "What will you do if he never loves you?"

"I will hurt," she whispered, "but I will love you, and you will be enough."

He kissed her forehead and drew her close. "Love me first, and never forget that my love is perfect. It casts out all fear."

Ella snuggled closer, drifting into a peaceful slumber that allowed her soul to find rest. How long she stayed there with him, she did not know.

She awoke with a start when Lee cried. Her eyes flew open, met with the dismal jail cell once again. Murky gray light crept over the darkness, giving her just enough illumination to see that Sibby rose from her place on the other side of the room and moved to take Lee.

Without a word, Ella handed him over and stretched her arms over her head and then arched her back. Her muscles protested every move. How many more nights would she be able to sleep this way?

Lord, I really could use some help with this.

She stepped over to the bars, grasping the cold metal in her hands. "Where do you suppose they are keeping the others?"

Sibby grunted. "How would I be knowin' that? You think they gonna tell me?"

Ella drew breath through her nose and let it out of her mouth. Patience. A harsh word would only stir up anger. "I think this used to be a vault of some kind for the bank."

Sibby didn't respond.

Ella turned and tried to study her in the dark. "Is it true?"

"How you think I know that? I ain't never been in no bank."

"That's not what I meant, Sibby. You know what I'm talking about."

"What?"

Ella unwound the tension in her jaw and tried to keep her voice even. "Is what he said about the smuggling true?"

It was quiet so long that Ella didn't think Sibby was going to answer. A noise came from the other side of the door just outside a small vestibule beyond the bars. Ella frowned and turned her ear toward it.

"Miss Ella, you is just not goin' to understand—"

"Shhh!" Ella waved her hand behind her.

"Now look here, you is the one that done asked—"

"Hush, Sibby! I hear something."

Sibby quieted and Ella pushed her face against the bars, straining her ears. A man's voice came from somewhere beyond the heavy oak door that separated the vault area from the rest of the bank.

"What is it?"

"Shhh," Ella hissed. "I can't hear when you keep talking."

Sibby huffed, but didn't say another word. The sounds on the other side of the door grew louder. It sounded like men arguing. Then something hit up against the door. Ella jumped and stepped away from the bars, her hand flying to her heart.

The door swung open, banging against the stone wall and flooding the room with light. Ella blinked as two forms plunged through the doorway and fell to the floor. They rolled, fists swinging. Ella squinted, but could not make out the identity of either man as they tangled together. One of them landed a punch to the other's face. He roared with pain. Then he snatched the one who had punched him to his feet. That man, the larger of the two, swung a fist that landed squarely in the other man's gut. The fellow doubled over as the breath went out of him.

"Enough!" the larger man bellowed, grabbing his opponent by the shoulder and putting him against the wall. "Now where is my wife?"

Westley! She pushed up against the bars and thrust her arm through. "Westley!"

He dropped the other man to the floor and spun around. "Ella!" In two strides he reached her, grabbing her hand and squeezing her fingers. "Are you well?" His gaze roamed over her tear-streaked face, disheveled hair, and dirty dress. His voice deepened and barely controlled rage boiled behind his eyes. "What have they done to you?"

Her heart fluttered at the desperation with which this warrior had come for her. She stared at him, unable to get her foggy mind to garner a response.

"Ella," his voice softened. "How long have they kept you prisoner?"

"She ain't no prisoner," Sibby said with a grunt.

Westley stepped closer. "Then explain to me why she is in a cell."

Sibby sighed. "Here, Miss Ella. He done eatin'."

Ella bent and took Lee from Sibby, turning away as the woman fastened her blouse and came to her feet. Ella wrapped Lee tightly in his blanket and came back to the bars. She looked down at the man who groaned on the floor.

"He lets me out whenever I need it," Ella said, gesturing to the man who must be the soldier they had left on guard.

As her eyes adjusted to the light, Ella could make out Westley's face as he scowled. "I need you to make more sense, Ella."

"They arrested me," Sibby answered, coming to stand by the bars. "They done locked me in here. She in here 'cause of the baby."

Understanding lit in his eyes and he turned back to the man on the floor. "The key, sir. You could have simply told me she was here under her own volition."

The man rolled over and stood, clutching his side. "You will be court-martialed for this."

Westley barked a humorless laugh. "They can add it to the desertion charges."

Ella pressed her lips together. Westley had deserted?

The keys rattled and the door swung open on rusty hinges. Westley stepped inside and pulled her to him, and her knees quivered.

He pressed his lips against the top of her head. "I'm here, my love. I have you."

Love? Did he apply such a word to her? She nuzzled her face into his jacket, letting the warmth of him push some of the chill away. He held her for a moment, then gently eased her back.

"We need to go now. Colonel Larson and I have much to discuss."

"Indeed we do," a voice said from the doorway. "I must say, Major, I am quite surprised to see you here, considering you are supposed to be in Kansas."

Westley grabbed Ella's hand and tugged her behind him. "Did you really think I wouldn't come after I received your telegram?"

"Sergeant," Larson barked. "You are dismissed."

A bit of shuffling feet, and the other man stumbled from the room. Ella frowned and tried to look around Westley's back, but he held her firmly behind him.

"That was merely a friendly courtesy," the colonel continued. "A telegram I sent that had nothing to do with military business, I might add. I did not expect you to defect."

"I will always come for my wife."

Ella warmed and, despite the situation, smiled down at Lee's sweet little face. Westley tugged on her arm, leading her past the sputtering lieutenant colonel.

"Where do you think you are going?"

"She is not under arrest. Therefore, I am taking her home."

Ella planted her feet, making Westley come to a stop just outside the vault room door. "I cannot be separated from Sibby. Lee won't drink the goat's milk."

Westley stiffened and looked down at her. Then he softened. "I will need to arrange for Sibby's immediate release as well," he said, still staring at her even as he spoke to the other man.

"Do you think that is going to happen after you attacked one of my men?"

Westley growled and tugged Ella out into what was once the main part of the bank, where the blessed sunshine devoured the shadows. "If he had answered my questions, it wouldn't have come to that."

Larson followed them farther into the lobby and then stopped and straightened his jacket. "Major, I can understand your position, but I'm afraid we can't release the Negro woman just yet."

Westley's jaw clenched, the little muscles under his skin jumping. "I really must insist."

The colonel spread his feet and clasped his hands behind him. "Tell me what you know of the smuggling operation."

He glared at the man who outranked him, clearly unconcerned that he continued to trample military protocols. "I know nothing of it."

Ella pressed up against Westley's side and watched the other officer narrow his eyes.

"You are certain?"

"Of course, I am certain," Westley snapped. "Do you really think I would allow such a thing to go on if I had any knowledge of it?"

"Your father did."

Westley stiffened, and Ella could feel the tension rolling off of him like thick fog. "What are you saying?"

"Do you really think that a group of Negroes would have concocted and run such an elaborate smuggling operation on their own?"

Ella's heart hammered.

"Of course, they wouldn't," Colonel Larson said, not waiting for a reply. "The operation was organized and run by your father, using the coloreds either to trade or to steal supplies from Memphis and move them back south. Then they would distribute the goods and make a nice profit."

Ella stepped forward. "But why would they agree to such a thing? Wouldn't they be the ones taking all the risks?"

The colonel flicked his gaze over to her. "It was a perfect plan. The men in charge could use expendable people who would mostly go unnoticed in the flood of escaping slaves, and the coloreds took the risk for the benefits it provided. You saw the settlement, Mrs. Remington. You can attest that they lived quite well."

Ella chewed her lip. It explained a lot. The condition of the settlement, the supplies Sibby always had, and even, perhaps, why Belmont had truly maintained its possessions.

"This is all speculation." Westley growled. "Have you any proof my father was involved?"

"It would seem that your father created an alliance with certain officers stationed in Memphis to trade what was left of his cotton. Those men sold it at a premium, and then began trading other things as well."

"And yet you still lack proof," Westley scoffed. "And what officers are you referring to? Federal men, no doubt."

Larson's face darkened. "I assure you, Major, we are looking into that. All the men responsible will receive due justice."

"I will expect to see items of proof rather than mere conjecture."

The two men glared at one another, and Ella began to fear

they might resort to fists. But then Westley seemed to gather himself and gestured to the vault area where Sibby remained, even though they had not locked her back inside. "Regardless of any involvement you claim my father may have had, my parents died months ago. Just because my mother's maid might have known about what they did, she certainly couldn't have had any part of it."

Larson shook his head. "Strange as it may seem, we have concluded that after your father's death, that Negro *maid* sent correspondence pretending to be him and kept the operation going. She was in charge."

"Impossible," Westley said on a long breath.

"I thought the same." He spread his hands, some of his anger appearing to be replaced with confusion. "Who would have ever thought a Negro house slave capable of such things?"

Westley merely stared at Larson. Ella frowned, putting the pieces together. She knew that Westley's mother had made sure Sibby was educated. She could do sums and letters, and Ella could attest to the fact that Sibby could be cunning. And Sibby cared deeply for her people and her home. The men might think that a woman, especially one of color, was incapable of doing such things, but Ella knew otherwise.

Larson cleared his throat. "After searching the house and settlements and questioning the Negress, I have concluded that it is true. We were all as shocked as you are."

Westley looked down at Ella. "What will happen to her?"

Fear stirred in her chest and she looked back at the colonel, letting all her anxieties and pleading show in her eyes.

The man narrowed his gaze and stroked his chin, then a sly smile came over his lips. "Well, seeing as how the operation is shut down, and the war over..." He lifted his shoulders and turned meaningful eyes on Westley. "Perhaps we can work something out?"

Two hours later, Westley signed several documents as Ella and Sibby sat in the lobby of the old bank. Ella wasn't entirely sure what all the documents entailed, only that after a heated argument, Larson agreed for Westley to take responsibility for Sibby and Basil, who would both be released into his watchful care, while all the others would be taken to trial. And somehow a very detailed agreement on cotton production seemed to be at the center of it all. Westley agreed to get the plantation running again using freedmen labor and then the majority of the cotton would be sent to the United States government for five years as a way of repaying the damages done. Ella had no idea what would happen to the Yankee officers at the other end of the smuggling line in Memphis, and, frankly, she didn't care.

Westley finished the paperwork with Larson, and led Sibby and Ella, Lee still sleeping in her arms, out into a bright afternoon. Ella shivered, relieved that she would not have to spend another night in that cell.

She glanced over at Sibby, but the woman kept her focus on the dust underneath her feet. There would be a lot of questions for her in the days to come. But right now, they just wanted to go home. She looked up to see Westley staring at her, the look in his eyes sending sparks of lightning down to her toes.

"How did you know?"

"When I arrived in St. Joseph, I sent a telegram to the colonel asking him to send you a message. He promptly sent word back to me that an operation had been discovered at Belmont and that they were gathering information to make arrests. He said he would send word to me in Fort Aubrey once they had everything figured out a few days from then, but I came straight home. It is a good thing I did, or you may have been in that cell a lot longer."

Ella blinked up at him. "But isn't that against your orders?

Won't you be in trouble for doing something like that?"

He reached up and tucked a lock of hair behind her ear. "I will gladly serve my time for it. Leaving my post was worth it to know that you are safe."

Ella stepped closer, not caring that they were in the middle of the street. "You didn't have to do that."

"Oh, heavens," Sibby grumbled. "Give me that child before the two of you done squeeze the life outta him."

Ella blinked and remembered that she held the baby between her and Westley. She passed Lee to her. Sibby smiled down at the boy. "Best you and me goes and finds us a spot in the shade while you mama and daddy finish they talk."

Ella's eyes widened. Sibby shouldn't have said...

Westley chuckled. "She's right. They should sit in the shade."

He stared at her, something intense in his eyes that made her feel a bit unsteady. Westley grabbed her hand and drew her into the narrow strip between two partially crumbling buildings. He glanced around and, seeing they were alone, pulled her up against him.

Ella tilted her head back and stared up at him, her mouth too dry and her throat too tight for anything more.

"Ella, I must beg your forgiveness for the way I left you. I was afraid I could not love you in the way you deserved. I thought I would never be enough."

She reached up and touched his cheek. "I love you for who you are." She gave him a sly smile. "Flaws, temper, and all. Even if you are an insufferable Yank."

He laughed and pulled her closer, leaving not even a hair's breadth between them. "My little dragon. Will we ever tame the fire on your tongue?"

Ella giggled. "Probably not."

He grew serious and looked deeply into her eyes, his face

only inches from hers. "Good. Because I love you just as you are. Fiery tongue and all."

Her heart pounded. He loved her. And though his love would never be meant to fill every place in her, it sent currents of joy through her. She would have someone to love and be loved in return for the remaining days of their lives.

"The message I sent in St. Joseph was to let you know that after my time out West, I was going to muster out and then come home to Belmont, where I wanted to learn to be your husband in truth."

"You were?"

"Yes." He ran his thumb down the curve of her jaw. "Now it seems I will have to face a court-martial and the consequences of taking absence without leave, but when that is finished, I would like to come home to you." He ran the pad of his thumb over her lips. "That is, if you would let me."

"Oh, Westley," Ella said on a sigh. "I've never wanted anything more."

The warm air swirled around them, and he lowered his lips to hers. Ella fell into him, breathless. She slid her hands up his back, caught up in the expression of love that so filled two hearts that it had no choice but to flow through their lips.

Westley held her tightly, and her heart soared. He would be her husband in truth, and she would be his wife. Ella pushed up on her toes and deepened the kiss, allowing her fingers to splay through his hair. He breathed hard and pulled away from her.

"I love you, Mrs. Remington."

"And I you."

Then he pulled her into his arms once more. And as he led her away toward home, Ella thought that somewhere in the place beyond them, she could hear a sweet symphony of beauty and light playing the song of love.

Epilogue

Ella dipped her paintbrush and made the final stroke. She'd spent months trying to capture everything just right. The birds sang their delight over a perfect day, and Ella set down her paints and leaned back to examine her work. Not exact, but it would do.

A happy little squeal added to the bird's choir. Ella smiled and leaned over to look into the cradle. "Well, hello, little lass. Awake from our nap, are we?"

Her seven-month-old daughter cooed, her toothless grin infectious. Ella laughed and pulled off her painting apron before lifting the child from the cradle and setting her on her hip. The front door banged open and Basil scurried out.

"Now where did he go?"

Ella cocked her eyebrow. "Don't tell me you've lost Lee again."

Basil put her hands on her hips. "You know he think it funny to slip out of them lessons and run off."

Sibby came outside, hauling Lee by one ear. "Here he be. I done found him in my kitchen trying to sneak off with one of my turnovers."

The little boy poked out his lip, his dark eyes part mischief, part pleading. "But, Mama, I was hungry, and I already finished my lessons."

Sibby let go of his ear and crossed her arms. "Then why didn't you just ask me for one of dem tarts, little man?" She ruffled his dark hair. "You knows I woulda give you one."

His lips turned up. "I know. But I wanted to see if I could get it without you seeing me. I'm going to be a soldier like my daddy, and a good soldier has to be able to sneak up on folks without them seeing."

Westley stepped up onto the front porch, the hitch in his gait still evident after all these years, but it did not pain him anymore. He pulled his hat from his head and tucked it under the arm of his cream-colored linen suit. My, but the man was handsome. His gaze slid up to her, and he smiled. Even after six years of blissful union, that smile still sent shivers all the way down to her toes.

Westley turned his attention on their son. "What's this I hear about sneaking up on people?"

Lee bounded over to Westley and grinned. "I was telling Sibby that I was sneaking like a soldier is supposed to do."

"Oh?" Westley tapped his chin in thought. "What happened to being a banker?"

He lifted his little shoulders. "That was last week. This week I want to be a soldier like you."

Westley smiled. "I'm not a soldier anymore." He looked up at Ella and winked. "I like being home with your mama too much."

Lee furrowed his brow. "Why you looking at each other so funny?"

Westley chuckled. "Go on and get yourself a treat, boy, and then go up to your room and do an extra lesson for giving poor Basil so much trouble."

Lee pouted and shoved his hands in his pockets. "Yes, sir." He trudged back inside, but a moment later poked his head back out. "But when I finish, can we go fishing?"

Westley laughed. "Only if you do all of your letters correctly."

Lee gave his father a serious look and made a salute. "Yes, sir!" Then he dashed back into the house, leaving Sibby and Basil to scramble after him.

Westley wrapped his arm around Ella's shoulder and looked down at the baby. "I think Ailsa's hair gets to be more like yours every day."

Ella smiled. "She still has your eyes, though."

Westley chuckled. "They might be shaped like mine, but where she got that stormy blue, God only knows."

Ella smiled and pressed into Westley's side. "Come, I have finished my painting."

Westley followed her to the canvas. "You are finally going to let me see it?"

She laughed. "It is finally finished."

Together they stood in front of the painting that would soon hang in their parlor, always to remind them of who they were and *whose* they were. The colors were not bright enough, but no paint on earth could emulate such beauty. She'd captured the way the grass swayed in the wind and a majestic tree pointed its spires to the sky. Star-like leaves shone in the bright light, tinged with tiny bits of gold.

"It is beautiful, Ella."

She smiled and snuggled against him. It *was* beautiful. Peace flowed through her. Someday she would see that place again. Someday the tiny glimpses she'd been blessed with would be permanent.

And when that time came, she would dance with him again.

*D*ear Reader,

I hope you enjoyed Ella and Westley's story. I'd love for you to take a few moments and leave a review online. It means the world to an author to get feedback from readers, and having readers share about my books helps me keep putting stories out.

For more stories with Ella, Westly, and Belmont, don't miss the Belmont Christmas story The Hope of Christmas Past or Opal Martin's story in The Heart of Home.

If you would like to really step into the story, be sure to visit Belmont Plantation in Greenville, Mississippi. It's a beautiful place to step back in time and relax. And if you stop by, be sure to send me a picture! I'd love to see you in "Ella's" home.

Happy Reading!
Stephenia

Join my newsletter to get updates on writing, book sales, exclusive giveaways, and more! As my thank you for joining, I'll also send you a FREE novella.
dl.bookfunnel.com/u9qdt7amwv

Discussion Questions

1. Ella feels like she doesn't have many options in life and her society, and therefore she often tries to make her own solutions. Do you think that women today have the same issues? How do you think things have changed?

2. Westley struggles with his physical wounds as well as the ones in his soul. Have you or a loved one had a physical injury that affected personal perception? Westley feels his limp makes him less of a man. Do you think people with physical conditions feel the same? Why or why not?

3. Ella struggles with feeling worthless. Why do you think that is? Have you ever had circumstances or something in your past that made you feel that way? How do you think we can overcome or correct this feeling?

4. Ella learns that she has forgotten who she really is. Do you think that Christians can sometimes forget who they are in Christ? Do you think that aligning our identity with Him changes the way we see ourselves?

5. Ella has dreams where she goes to a special place of beauty and light. Do you think that God still speaks to His children in similar ways? Have you ever had an experience or dream that made you feel closer to Him?

6. Westley and Ella learn that they cannot love each other the way they want to until they understand Who to love first. Do you think that as people grow closer to God they grow closer to one another? How does putting God first affect our relationships with those around us?

7. It's your turn. Where do you see Ella and Westley's story going from here? What challenges do you think they will face in the future, and what joys might they discover together?

Historical Note

The Hillman farm was used as a hospital after the battle at Sayler's (sometimes written as Sailor's) creek, and Union officers were kept in the bedrooms. It stands to reason that General Sheridan's men would have been kept there, and perhaps someone would have taken pity on Major Remington. The character of Mrs. Preston is not based on any actual people associated with the Hillman farm.

The town of Parsonville and the Inn where Ella works are fictional. However, Greenville, Mississippi is located just out from Belmont Plantation and did suffer destruction during the war. The use of a bank as a makeshift offices and jail cell are elements of my own imagination.

According to my research, there were Union officers in Memphis that traded cotton and other items with smugglers who then took those items down into Mississippi. I found no evidence of a smuggling ring similar to the one I used in the book, but something similar could have been a possibility.

The real Belmont Plantation was built in 1857 by the Worthington family. It was purchased in 1853 by Samuel Worthington and two years later he sold it to his brother, Dr. William W. Worthington. Belmont has been restored and now functions as a bed and breakfast and is one of the few antebellum homes remaining on the Mississippi River. If you ever get the opportunity to visit the Mississippi Delta, you simply must stop by Belmont for a heaping dose of Southern hospitality.

Acknowledgements

First, to my Heavenly Father. This book was a journey we took together, and a story that He helped me with each step of the way.

A huge thank you to Joshua Cain, Camille Collins, and Sandra Stillman at Belmont Plantation. I was so thrilled to get to set my story in this beautiful mansion. We were treated with the utmost Southern hospitality on each of our visits, and I loved learning all I could about "Ella's" home. I couldn't have found a better location for the setting of the story. Thank you all.

I'd like to say a special thank you to Andrea Boeshaar for reading the rough draft of this novel. You helped me strengthen the writing, checked my historical facts, and pointed out areas that needed work. Your input was critical to the outcome of the story.

Doc Hensley, my writing has only grown stronger under your guidance. Thank you for your suggestions and edits on my work. Anything I missed is entirely my fault. I'm grateful for your encouragement and look forward to our next project.

Rich Stevens, Kevin Robichaux, and Larry McCluney, I greatly appreciate your help on the historical and military aspects of the story. If I missed anything or stretched history a bit too far, the fault lies with me.

The cover art is one of my favorite aspects of the process. It is so much fun. Taylor, you were such a great sport on our long day of cover shots and video production. My heart skipped a beat when you stepped out in that dress. You truly brought Ella off the page, and you made a stunning model! It was a joy to work with you. And Ravven, you always do such great work on my covers. I love seeing how you make the images in my head come to life. Thank you for another beauty!

As always, a huge thank you to my family. Momma and Jason, you are always my first eyes. Thank you for catching things I miss and giving me encouragement and critiques on my manuscript.

This was also a very proud time for me, since during the writing of this book, my oldest son published his first story "just like Momma". It might be a shameless plug, but this proud Mom would love for you to go check out his children's book *The Adventures of Captain A and Lambme Boy.*

And finally, to my readers. Wow. Where would I be without you? It means the world to me when you send me letters and connect with me online. You have been such an encouragement to me and have given me the courage to keep writing even when things get difficult. My Faithful Readers Team—you are all awesome. Thank you for letting me bounce ideas off you and for giving me your input along the journey.

Thank you all for everything. I'm blessed to have so many great people alongside me.

Ironwood Plantation Family Saga

A series of generational, stand-alone novels

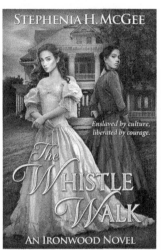

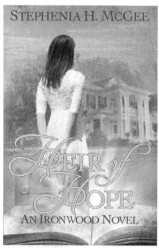

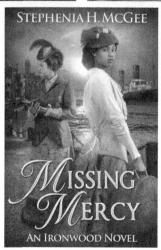

The Accidental Spy Series

A Trilogy

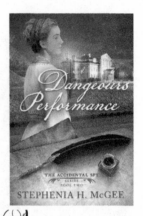

A nation at war....
A plot that could change
the tides....
A Southern Belle and a
Confederate Captain caught
in the crossfires as
America's first presidential
assassination unfolds

About the Author

Stephenia H. McGee has a fascination with hoop skirts and ball gowns, Greek revival homes and horse-drawn carriages, quirky Southern sayings, and home-grown recipes. She lives in Mississippi where she sips her sweet tea on the front porch with her husband and two boys, accompanied by their two spoiled dogs and mischievous cat.

Visit her website at www.StepheniaMcGee.com and be sure to sign up for the newsletter to get sneak peeks, behind the scenes fun, the occasional recipe, and special offers.

FaceBook: Stephenia H. McGee, Christian Fiction Author

Twitter: @StepheniaHMcGee

Pinterest: Stephenia H. McGee